TWELVE DAYS

TWELVE DAYS

STEVEN BARNES

TOR

**A TOM DOHERTY
ASSOCIATES BOOK**

NEW YORK

TWELVE DAYS

Copyright © 2017 by Steven Barnes

A Tor Book
Published by Tom Doherty Associates
175 Fifth Avenue
New York, NY 10010

www.tor-forge.com

Tor® is a registered trademark of Macmillan Publishing Group, LLC.

The Library of Congress Cataloging-in-Publication Data is available upon request.

ISBN 978-0-7653-7597-1 (hardcover)
ISBN 978-1-4668-4908-2 (ebook)

Our books may be purchased in bulk for promotional, educational, or business use. Please contact your local bookseller or the Macmillan Corporate and Premium Sales Department at 1-800-221-7945, extension 5442, or by email at MacmillanSpecialMarkets@macmillan.com.

First Edition: June 2017

Printed in the United States of America

0 9 8 7 6 5 4 3 2 1

For the Old Soldier:
We are "Charlie Mike."
You can rotate home and rest easy.

"Spooky action at a distance" is how Albert Einstein famously derided the concept of quantum entanglement—where objects can become linked and instantaneously influence one another regardless of distance.

—Charles Q. Choi, *Scientific American*

Fundamental biology tells us that survival is the name of the game. So potent is this dictate that in 1973 the psychologist Ernest Becker won a Pulitzer Prize for *The Denial of Death,* arguing that everything we think of as civilization, from cities we build to the religions we believe in, is nothing beyond an elaborate symbolic defense mechanism against the awful knowledge of our own mortality.

—Steven Kotler, *The Rise of the Superman:*
Decoding the Science of Ultimate Human Performance

Shakti asks: "Oh Shiva, what is your reality? What is this wonder-filled universe? What constitutes seed? Who centers the universal wheel? What is this life beyond form pervading forms? How may we enter it fully, above space and time, names and descriptions? Let my doubts be cleared."

—*The Vigyan Bhairav Tantra*

Kali asks: "Oh Yama, what is your reality? What is this terrible universe? What constitutes the cessation of breath? Who stills the universal wheel? What is this ending of life, the dissolution of form? How may we depart it fully, ending space and time, names and descriptions? Let my fears be cleared."

—*The Yama Sutra*

TWELVE DAYS

The document, which came to be known as the Dead List, first appeared on December 12, on Web sites hosted by servers in London, New York, Hong Kong, and Johannesburg, paid for with untraceable debit cards registered to false names. Some indications exist that the orders may have originated in Jakarta, but little else of consequence can be determined:

TO THE PEOPLE OF THE WORLD:

For too long you have ignored the teachings of the one true God. He has tired of your ignorance and blasphemy. And as has occurred thrice before, there shall be a mighty Reaping.

So that you might have time to repent your sins, the Reaping will occur in stages, slowly at first, then more rapidly, a righteous tsunami carrying all corruption before it. Only the Elite will be spared, to continue life in a sterilized world.

In accordance with prophesy, it will happen in this fashion: on December 13, our high holy day, one sinner will die. On the second day, two will perish. Then four, then eight, and then sixteen, doubling every day until the world is cleansed.

Some of these first men and women will be known to the world. Most will not. As all have sinned, none but the Elite will be spared. It is too late to join us. If you are Elite, you know already who you are.

So that the world may know and tremble, the first to die are published below. Some of these names were extracted from the excellent list "The One Hundred Worst Unindicted Criminals," published in the July edition of the American *Rolling Stone* magazine. Others are upon a list to follow. And others, for reasons that will be known in due time, are secrets known only to the Elite.

The wicked will be punished. It is so that all may understand and tremble at the terrible justice to come that the despoilers upon this list will be numbered among the first.

One the first day. Two the second. Four the third. Then eight, sixteen, thirty-two, and so on. Until our Christmas gift to the world, delivered on December 25—Freedom. You will enjoy the end of days without domination by governments or false religions. On that day, among other sinners, the following will die:

> The bishop of Rome
> The prime minister of England
> The prime minister of Israel
> The president of the Executive Yuan of the People's Republic
>   of China
> The chairman of the Federal Reserve
> The president of the United States

All other world leaders will follow in turn. All mortal men and women, save the Elite, will follow. There is nothing any of you can do to prevent this. No medications, countermeasures, or fortresses can protect you. There is nothing any of you can do to save yourselves, or change the inevitable. This warning is only given so that those who are capable might save their souls with prayer.

Merry Christmas

CHAPTER 1

The offices of television station XTRB were located in a two-story brick building nestled between a sleepy residential district and a commercial section of Mexico City known as El Corredor. The building had once been a *carniceria,* rebuilt in the 1990s during an uptick in the Mexican economy, responding to the needs of a society driven more by communication than consumption of albondigas.

The tide of XTRB technicians, artists, and office folk ebbed and flowed at all hours. At first this had seemed a remarkable thing, but in time the formerly sleepy neighborhood had grown to take its renaissance in stride.

Not today. Today the neighborhood was already abuzz, aware that something very special was about to occur.

Former governor of Chihuahua Ramone Quinones, a man not seen in public since his indictment for drug trafficking and murder, was on his way.

Death followed closely behind him.

◆ ◆ ◆

Carlos Garcia had been a producer since the day he had learned it paid more than managing a publisher's warehouse, or more specifically since his sister had married the owner of XTRB. As his mother had often told him, "*Fortuna favorece a los que se casan de riqueza*": *Fortune favors those who marry well.*

And of course, their brothers.

Generally, Garcia considered his new position a decided improvement over the old, but today he realized that his ordinarily focused but intense mood could best be described as "flustered," and that some other emotion lurked just beneath the surface. To his surprise, that emotion seemed to be fear.

As had become his habit in recent months, he vented his anxiety upon Sonia Torres, the tall, slender lovely who anchored the morning talk show. During the seven months of their volcanic affair, it had often seemed to Garcia that her body was a husk filled with live coals. In many ways they were two of a kind. Sonia shared his own fierce ambition, as well as his amorality and political agnosticism, a general disinterest about anything except rungs on the ladder of success. There were times when there seemed nothing of softness or femininity about her at all. In comparison with Teresa, the slack, unresponsive wife who awaited him at home, Sonia was indeed firm. Sinewy. Possessed of that sort of feral strength a man needed to feel, a web of passion drawing him into her fire. At times, the memory was almost more visceral and immediate than he could bear.

But while at work, they could never acknowledge or suggest anything of the passion they had shared. That had been the arrangement when their affair began, and neither of them had ever violated it, regardless of how much he might have yearned to.

So instead of confessing that he wished he had been able to awaken next to her, even once, he barked complaint. "Get that damned shine off your cheeks, Sonia! Damn it! *Makeup!*" She arched one sculpted eyebrow at him, perhaps believing imperfection impossible for such a golden creature as she. Sonia nodded at the makeup girl who hovered at the side of her chair as she tested her mic, and pored over her prepared statements.

Their director, Manny Vasquez, was a short, skinny guy whose major claim to fame was that, as a boy, he had brought coffee to the great Cantinflas on the set of his last movie, *El Barrendero*. How many times had they had to listen to that mess! *Cabron!*

Now, the little man was all nerves. "Have you heard from Quinones?" he asked. "Is this still happening?"

Garcia nodded. "They called me fifteen minutes ago. He's on the way from Juárez International."

Vasquez sighed hugely. "I don't see how we're going live if—"

Before he could finish, the studio's double doors opened, and an intern whose name Garcia could never remember popped her head in. "Thirty seconds to convoy!" she said.

Despite his staff's veneer of professionalism, the excitement was infectious. He sighed. Even the glacial Sonia seemed to ovulate at the very thought of meeting the drug lord. It was true: *"El que no transa, no avanza"*— loosely: *You're not going anywhere if you don't cheat.* His mother had said that as well, bless her mercenary heart.

Reluctantly, he sidled over to the street-side windows in time to see the black motorcycle procession pulling into the spaces marked off with red cones. A black limousine half the length of the block itself miraculously navigated the turn and slid into the underground garage.

He huffed and ran his fingers through his hair. With one last angry glance at Sonia, Carlos Garcia sprinted for the elevator.

◆   ◆   ◆

Twenty-five seconds later the elevator opened on the underground level. Even before the steel slabs parted, Garcia felt the energy wash through the door. Despite his anxiety and thwarted lust for Sonia, he had to admit that XTRB had scored a tremendous coup. Quinones was scheduled to appear in court in just four hours, at ten o'clock. The morning news show created buzz, and Garcia reckoned that Quinones was doing everything in his power to poison the jury pool, tainting and confusing the narrative that he had abused the privileges of office to enrich himself in the business of *narcotraficante*. In a moment, the parking garage boiled with bodyguards and assistants. Steel- and Kevlar-reinforced Mercedes-Benz SUVs with deeply tinted windows and police cars driven by off-duty officers crammed the garage. Bulky men with eyes like chips of black ice were positioned like a line of concrete slabs as the limo pulled along the wall, blocking ten parking spaces that had been set aside with red traffic cones.

The engine died. The door of the limo opened and a tall, elegantly handsome man exited.

With all his heart, Garcia yearned to despise Quinones. There were so many reasons to do so. From the crimes he had been accused of, to his hand-tailored Bijan Pakzad suits (identical to one worn by American actor Tom Cruise and Mexican president Enrique Peña Nieto), to his perfect physical condition (said to be the result of three miles of daily ocean swimming under the view of snipers recruited from the *Grupo Aeromóvil de Fuerzas Especiales,* Mexican Special Forces soldiers. Perfectly competent to deal with rival narco traffickers but Garcia wondered how they were with sharks).

Quinones was perfectly dressed and coiffed, as if he had hosted a dinner party immediately before heading to the studio. The only concession to morning rust was the slight stretch he gave, a twist, almost a preparatory dance motion, as he stepped out of the limousine. His smile bristled with blindingly white teeth, except for one tooth on the left side, which was ever so slightly discolored.

And damned if that didn't somehow increase his charm.

"Just in time," Quinones said. The narco lord's voice was higher, lighter than Carlos Garcia had expected. He took an absurd and childish pleasure in noticing that. He himself possessed a deep, manly voice. One of Quinones' bodyguards interposed himself between the former governor and the producer, then stepped back when Quinones shook his head and extended his hand. "Mr. Garcia. Good to meet you again."

"Again . . . ?" Garcia was taken aback. He had never met the governor.

"Yes." A secret, perfect smile. "Some years ago. You delivered cartons of books to a signing. This was shortly after I became a councilman."

Delivered books? A tiny memory wormed its way to conscious awareness. Perhaps fifteen years ago, when Garcia was managing the warehouse. An emergency call, extra cartons of first editions needed for an autographing by a councilman who had been married to a film star who had recently lost a battle with cancer. The story of their May-December romance, Quinones nursing the faded beauty through her heroic but ultimately futile struggle. The memoir had sold only moderately well, but had shaped public perception, and represented the beginning of Quinones' rise. He had inherited her wealth . . . and that wealth had quite possibly funded his first major heroin purchase. Those profits had funded his expansion into cultivation and refinement.

Or so the rumors declared.

Was the man a gigolo? Garcia had totally forgotten the meeting. Had not read the book. Now he wished he had. The fact that Quinones remembered him, when they could only have possibly met for seconds, was intimidating. He began to reinterpret what he thought he knew about the governor.

In a phalanx, they headed toward the elevator.

◆ ◆ ◆

XTRB would have Quinones for twenty minutes only, and ninety seconds of that was already evaporated. Sonia Torres punched the intercom button and announced: "All right! He's on his way! Everybody get ready. Don't fuck me up!"

The elevator doors opened, and two men the size of double-door refrigerators stepped out, followed by Quinones, strutting like a lord. As if he was ever on the verge of flipping a peso to the peasants. Carlos Garcia, an adequate lover and the toughest producer with whom she had ever worked, was following Quinones like a duckling waddling behind its mother. What in the hell had happened that could transform him from bull to steer in ninety seconds? *Madre Dios.* The interview had not yet begun, and already she was off balance.

"Ramone Quinones," he said, extending a cool, flat hand.

"Governor Quinones, I'm so happy you could make it."

"My pleasure," he said. His smile was so intimate, so open, as if the two of them had just tumbled out of bed together. "Where would you have me?"

The sexual implication was obvious, and she hated the voice in her head that answered: *here. There. Wherever you want. Whenever you want.* Oh my God.

What she said was, "We're set up in studio three. Follow me, please." As they walked, she contrived to brush the back of his hand with hers. The resulting spark was more than static electricity, she was quite certain.

She smiled up at him. He was tall enough that she had to look up to meet his eyes, even in heels. She liked that. "You have a flair for the dramatic, sir."

"Essential in my line of work," he said. Was he about to confess? Where was the damned camera? She fumbled out a question. "As . . . ?"

"A politician, of course."

A trap. A joke. He was toying with her. She suspected that much of life was a game to him. The room was filled with assistants, and assistants to assistants.

"Everyone in their places! One minute!"

Quinones was not the sexiest man Torres had ever met, but he came disturbingly close. She protected her sense of attraction with emotional ice, a tactic that had worked in the past, and one with which he was probably very familiar indeed.

"So glad you could join us, Governor."

"How could I stay away? I wished to see if you were as charming in person as you are on the television."

Very nice. Standard flirtation response. "And?"

"I am seriously considering hiring you to read me the news every morning." She wanted to ignore that, but when a man reputed to be worth over twelve billion pesos mentions employment, it was wise to pay attention. She felt the skin beneath her collar heating up, and in case her face was flushing, engaged in enough paper-shuffling to conceal it.

"Thirty seconds!" her assistant said.

Torres settled into the canvas chair emblazoned with her name. "I've been told to confine myself to the approved questions." For a moment the query, which might have seemed utterly innocent, or even conciliatory, triggered something else in Quinones. Anger perhaps. Or fear?

"And," she continued carefully, "just before I came on, I was informed of a death threat against you. Do you mind if we discuss that?"

"I heard of this list." Annoyance tightened his voice. "The pope is also to be found upon it. Ordinarily I would be amused to be mentioned in such august company, but this is a bad joke, and the height of poor taste. We may speak of this after we conclude our interview."

"But not on the air?"

He smiled. "That might be best."

The makeup girl hovered around him, a hummingbird seeking nectar. He touched her arm. "Making me less hideous?"

She flushed at the contact and giggled.

Torres had to admire Quinones' skill. He used his sex appeal as she did, and she had met few men who were as facile at that as the average woman. Such confidence stirred curiosity within her, triggering a warm, soft sensation between her thighs. Despite her control, she began to imagine the two of them together in bed. Wondering about the touches, tastes, rhythms, and scents.

Damnation.

"Ten, nine, eight, seven—stand by. And . . . we are *live.*" The monitors buzzed, and the titles scrolled.

Their announcer spoke, a ghostly voice booming from the corners of the studio. "Welcome to *This Week,* coming to you live tonight from Mexico City. And now our host, Angelina 'Sonia' Torres!"

The monitors cut to Torres. She flipped the switch in her head, conjuring a brilliant smile. "Welcome to *This Week.* On this morning's live broadcast, we have a very special guest, former governor Ramone Quinones of Chihuahua. Governor, the first question I have is: you've been notoriously private since you left office. Why, after so long, have you finally agreed to be interviewed?"

Whatever momentary discomfort he had experienced had flown. "Ms. Torres, as you know, certain legal matters will soon commence. I thought that it would be best to give my side of the story."

Something within her blossomed, warming. This was one of the greatest moments of her career. Torres barely noticed as the cameramen jockeyed about to find the right angles. "You won't be tried in the court of public opinion, sir."

"True. But I still want to present my story in my way, in my own time."

"Then please," she said. "Tell us your view of the charges."

"Let's have camera two," the director whispered in her earpiece. Instantly, she adjusted her profile.

"As we know," Quinones began, "the narcotics industry has long been a cause of friction between Mexico and the United States. When progress doesn't match whatever is demanded in the editorial sections of their failing newspapers, when inept response to domestic catastrophes or the latest bedroom scandals necessitates a distraction, they need a . . . I believe the term is 'fall guy.'"

She had anticipated that comment. "So you are maintaining total innocence?"

"Oh, no," he said. "I'm guilty." A pause for effect. "Guilty of accepting donations for my children's charity. Guilty of paving roads and building bridges in flood-ravaged sections of rural Chihuahua."

She wanted to laugh, but despite her doubts, he remained seductively sincere. "Governor . . ." she began, but he soldiered on.

"And guilty of having old friends who are rumored, rumored *only* I must insist, to be involved in *narcotraficante*. These three things: money, works, and associations, are all that some *norteamericano* journalists have to accuse me of being a notorious man."

She decided to split hairs. The questions on her sheet were specific to his conflict with the Mexican legal system, but where the district attorney had limited authority to speculate upon things he could not prove, a journalist could go quite a bit further.

"What of the murders?"

He almost smiled. Almost. But the expression was concealed beneath a put-upon air. With irritation, Sonia realized that she was the one who had stepped into a trap.

"Our friends north of the border love their chemical entertainments. And are willing to pay almost any amount to obtain them. That amount of gold attracts greedy men. And where there is greed, violence often follows. It is I, and the citizens who entrusted me with their governance, who feel insulted that so much of this has happened in our state. But these men, these . . ."

He paused, shaking his fingers as if suffering a cramp. "Excuse me," he said. Something different had crept into his voice. Unless she was mistaken, he was being authentic now, the play-games over. Had her question touched something she hadn't anticipated? Excitement percolated. A predatory hunger within her, some relic of a once keen journalistic instinct shook itself to wakefulness and bared its teeth.

"I was saying. These men try to cast me as a villain in a drama they . . . they themselves . . ."

He blinked, flinched as if dealing with a sharp blow to the stomach, and shook his head hard, twice. His eyes were unfocused. Quinones cursed and tore off his microphone, stood up to stretch his left leg. He wasn't looking at her, or at anything at all. Was the man sampling his own supply? Had he come to the studio *high*, for God's sake?

"Governor? Are you—"

"I can't . . . something . . ." His words died in a scream. "My head!" His teeth clamped on his tongue, and in an instant his lips were painted crimson. Fingers tensed into claws and he clapped his palms to his temples, howling pain.

Groaning, Quinones arched backward. The cables in the sides of his neck bunched and crawled, and his cheeks grew gaunt as those Olympic sprinters straining to the finish line, just membranes stretched across a bare skull.

The ex-governor screamed again, then straightened a final time and collapsed. He curled onto one shuddering side like a weeping child.

Torres ignored her director's voice, or the uproar surrounding her and stood, tottering unsteadily. Sound and sight dissolved in her fog.

Quinones' bodyguards rushed to him, rolled him over . . . and then sprang back in horror. His mouth stretched wide in a silent scream. His spine arched violently, a circus contortionist viewed in a fun-house mirror. His fingers splayed and then tensed into tight, clumsy fists. The governor's muscles knotted and strained, producing muffled cracking sounds, like wooden slats splintering under pressure. Blood seeped from the cuffs of his perfectly tailored Bijan Pakzad pants.

Torres' vision swam, then swirled, and she collapsed to the ground beside him.

What is that thing we seek? We walk a line between birth and death, misremembering the one, seeking infinite postponement of the other. Is it any wonder our days are tasteless, our nights filled with restless slumber or furtive grasping? The true aspirant knows both birth and death, fearing neither. Seeks neither pain nor pleasure, clings to neither subject nor object. Seeks not happiness and deigns to avoid grief. It is only in embracing the All that the Nothing appears. And in the Nothing is Everything.

—Savagi, commentary on *The Yama Sutra*

CHAPTER 2

By the time her alarm's insistent burr fluttered the morning air, Olympia Dorsey was already awake.

In fact, she had been awake for almost five minutes. She liked waking up before the hostile alarm clock reminded her that another day was upon them.

She groaned, remembering the days, not so long before, when she had possessed the time and energy for dancing until dawn, or more recently, scaling the Atlanta Rocks! climbing wall three times a week. Olympia wondered if she would ever again have such luxury. Or such a sinewy, toned body. So much had changed in the last three years, including the most obvious. The most painful.

Raoul was gone. For three years now, his absence had been more concrete than most of her waking reality.

Wasn't she supposed to be healing by now? Didn't Dr. Phil say that after a year, such loss began to recede from immediate consciousness, replaced by new concerns?

Instead, the loss was something her mind returned to again and again, like the tip of her tongue searching out the site of a recent extraction. Something precious had been ripped bleeding from her life, and there was no replacing it.

She rolled, yawning, out of bed, and shuffled downstairs. Olympia planned to turn on the coffee, treasuring the last few moments of peace before family became her primary concern.

No . . . not minutes. Because eight-year-old Hannibal stood there in the kitchen already dressed in a favorite red Avengers T-shirt and jeans, waiting for her. He was small for his age, with coppery skin and tightly curled hair.

His body hadn't quite caught up with the size of his head, lending him a babyish aspect that broke her heart anew every god damned day.

Even though he didn't look directly at her, the corners of his mouth turned up in a smile that warmed her darkest moods. His eyes were as darkly chocolate as her own skin, and shone even in dim light. God help her, she loved him more than anything in the world. Mothers weren't supposed to favor children, but that was how she felt, and she prayed that his sister, Nicki, could somehow understand.

Hannibal needed her more.

She hoped he hadn't been standing there all night, counting cracks in the ceiling or leaves on the artificial plants.

He was drawing again, using the dining room table as an easel, and sheets of butcher paper as his canvas. She didn't know why he loved to draw houses, mansions, office buildings, apartments . . . anywhere people lived or worked. Hannibal drew the houses, erased or crossed them out, then drew again as if trying to perfect an image he held in memory, always frustrated, but never stymied. She did not know which was closer to the truth. Hannibal rarely spoke, so she had precious little access to his inner world.

Always the same rough design, although it had grown more refined over the years. By the time he put one of the drawings aside, they sometimes had so many wings and floors that they resembled images from the book *Gormenghast*. He had done this since he was five, with pencils, paint, crayons, and pens, and at this point all she could do was smile.

Her son . . . their son . . . was the center of her life, and God bless Nicki for understanding and not throwing a snit as so many other teenagers might have done. *Why does Hannibal get all the attention? Nobody gives a damn about me, or cares if I live or die . . .*

Not Nicki. Never Nicki, thank God.

Hani shuffled toward her, his eyes cast down toward the ground, as if searching for dropped coins. Usually this didn't cause him to bounce into walls—in fact, she wondered how he avoided that, so oblivious to environments he sometimes seemed. He took small steps, flapping his hands like the wings of a flightless bird. When he finally looked up a tiny smile warmed his face, the expression he almost always wore, unless displaying the pouted frown that so easily tore her heart.

"Hi, baby," she said. "Got words for Mommy?" *Mommy loves to hear anything you have to say. Anything at all.*

She hoped he couldn't hear the pain in her voice. He deserved better than that. Much, much better.

But as always, he did not speak to her—more . . . at her, without meeting her eyes. He rarely looked directly into her face, seemed more comfortable looking at a spot a few degrees to the left or right of whoever he was addressing. "Oatmeal. Want oatmeal. And cartoons."

He moved his gaze to stare up at the wall as he spoke, as if distracted by a ghost. "With nuts."

Cartoons with nuts. That should be easy.

Oh, and oatmeal.

She kissed his cheek, and he wiggled away from her. That stung, but Olympia tried not to see it as a personal rejection. "I love you, too, hon. We have a good life."

Was that wrong? To assume that he was thinking something he had not said? To answer questions he had never asked? Almost as if he understood her yearning, he reached out with one arm and hugged her without looking at her, as if the contact was an obligation, not a comfort.

Once, his hugs had been different. He had clung to her with full body, showering her with small, warm kisses. He had done that for Raoul as well.

Back when Raoul was still alive.

◆　◆　◆

Nicki was awake when Olympia opened the door to her room. The thirteen-year-old knelt on the edge of her bed, staring out through her window, down at the common grass area shared by all the Foothill Village condominiums. A rectangle of manicured green, a basketball court. Behind a gated wall, a swimming pool and spa. So much more than she'd had as a girl, living in the concrete wasteland of Miami's Liberty City.

"Almost time for school," Olympia said. She peered over Nicki's shoulder to share the view. Nicki was five years older than Hani chronologically, a thousand miles from him mentally.

Nicki still wore her hair in braids, still had her baby fat, but Raoul's Seminole cheekbones already lent her face an arrestingly exotic flavor. Even with minimum care, her long dark hair was lustrous, much straighter than Olympia's own tight and wiry curls. Even her wire-rimmed glasses just made her more appealing. Her daughter was going to be a knockout.

"What's going on out there?" Olympia asked, already knowing what had captured Nicki's attention.

Her daughter was focused on the neighbor across the street. If Harry Belafonte and Eartha Kitt had spawned an athletic love child, he might have looked like Terry Nicolas. Fortyish, six feet tall, he seemed to glide as if wearing invisible ice skates.

At the moment, Terry was crouched down on the basketball court, flexing through his morning body-weight exercises. Even before daylight hit the grass he was usually out there, bending and stretching his legs and torso into patterns that resembled nothing so much as a cross between break dancing and a solo game of Twister. On other occasions, he imitated Cirque du Soleil, balancing on his forearms, palms flat on the ground with elbows tucked tightly into his sides, shaven head close to the ground, pushing his legs and trunk off the ground in apparent defiance of gravity, holding that impossible position for sixty seconds or more.

Whatever he was doing, it kept his body looking like an action figure woven of knotted rope. Not an ounce of excess fat dappled his frame. Scars, yes, a fascinating variety of puckered ridges and pale valleys . . . but no flab, as she remembered . . . viscerally.

Viscerally. That was the word, and she fought a blush as the memory swept her in dizzying waves.

She had first encountered Terry fifteen months ago, at a Foothill Village barbecue mixer. Hannibal had run breakneck into him, almost bouncing off into the empty swimming pool. With reflexes that would have shamed a tennis pro, Terry had scooped Hani out of the air and deposited the boy lightly on his feet.

Hannibal had just giggled, unfazed by his brush with disaster. Terry had patted Hani's curling hair, and smiled dazzlingly at her. The impact of that smile was like Yo-Yo Ma strumming a cello string in her tummy.

He had asked her to coffee, and then wrangled her to Mongolian barbecue, speaking of life (Olympia's adventures growing up in Miami, her father an impoverished civil rights lawyer. Terry's on army bases around the world with his constantly reassigned father), dead siblings (Olympia's preemie older sister, dead weeks after birth. Terry's younger brother, victim of a hit-and-run at the age of thirteen), and shared love of cinema (they both loved Poitier's *In the Heat of the Night* and *Lady Sings the Blues,* Leone's *The Good, the Bad and the Ugly,* as well as Kim Jee-woon's *The Good, the Bad, the Weird.* Go figure), all the time carefully ignoring their growing mutual awareness of each other's bodies. One October night he had kissed her, so sweetly she thought she was dreaming. She had surprised herself by kissing him back and then leading him, hand in warm hand, to her bed. Their lovemaking had been exquisite, a revelation of sensual hungers she'd feared she'd buried with Raoul. Banked but not extinguished, when fanned those fires had burned so very, very brightly . . .

She didn't know where things between them might have gone. How far.

But within days of their first date, she had begun to feel an odd panic, a fluttering in her gut almost like mild food poisoning. *He's lying about something. I can feel it. See it when his eyes shift away when he talks about that "consultant" job of his. About his relationship with his room-mate, Mark. Bisexual? Drug dealer? There's a secret here. Be wary. Keep your mind on your family, not this foolishness.*

She recognized that voice instantly: her mother's. Gone but hardly for-gotten. Terry had lost both his parents as well, one of the bonds they had shared.

That is, if stories of his childhood had been true. If *any* of it had been true.

If Hani hadn't responded to Terry with such an evident, naked hunger for male attention, the entire misadventure might have been less devastat-ing. No. There was nothing that could have diminished the pain. Terry had been a wonderfully visceral reminder that life flowed on. And then he was gone, and that was just the way it was.

"Come on. We have to get moving."

Nicki nodded and rolled off her bed. "Need to feed Pax." Olympia smiled at that thought. They shared a backyard with the houses on either side, and their right-hand neighbors, the Haleys, had once again gone on an extended Christmas Royal Carribean cruise and left their lovable doo-fus of a dalmatian-spotted Great Dane in the Dorseys' care. This was the third year they'd pulled that disappearing act, and Olympia was getting irritated.

Nicki, on the other hand, loved walking, grooming, and feeding Pax, and Paxie loved her, so Olympia tended to keep her irritation to herself.

In her nightgown, Nicki's strong, slender body reminded Olympia of her own early teenage years. Ample hips, slightly thick waist, and only a promise of the spectacular figure that had exploded by seventeen.

Olympia had yet to have *that talk* with her daughter, but suspected Nicki knew enough to figure out what had happened between her mother and the handsome neighbor, and accepted it with a wisdom informed by the Internet generation's infinite access to imagery.

"Down in five, Mom," she said, and Olympia knew that her daughter's word was good.

Unlike Raoul, who had promised to stay with them forever.

CHAPTER 3

Shilo Middle School was generally only eight minutes away from Olympia's Foothill Village driveway, but this morning she spent another minute dawdling before pulling out. Terry was heading back to 906 Market, across the street from her own three-bedroom, and Olympia hoped that he would saunter past them without comment or notice. If she pulled out he'd be forced to acknowledge her and . . .

But no, damn it. He waved and smiled, and Hani waved back, although Nicki sat like a stone.

" 'Erry!" Hani yelled. Olympia gave up and backed out, so that their Kia pulled up parallel to Terry. It was cold, but perspiration glistened on his arms, and his cutoff sweatshirt was dappled with wet spots. He made pistols of his fingers and fired shots through the back window. Hani giggled as if he'd never seen anything so funny in all his young life.

Then Terry's eyes met hers, and his hands relaxed. Although nothing save kindness lived in his dark brown eyes, she could barely meet them.

Correction—while she could *see* nothing but kindness in his eyes. But . . . she *felt* something more, as if he was somehow focused beyond her. Saw through her, or this place, and this time, to something else. *You don't want to see what I've seen,* those eyes seemed to say. *What I see.*

I saw it . . . so that civilians like you don't have to.

"Olympia," he said.

His voice was friendly-neutral, but she sensed that it required enormous effort to keep it in check.

Holding back what? Or was that just more wishful thinking?

"Terry," she replied. A game. Tit for tat. Childish, fun, sad in an odd way. She received an answering nod in return. Olympia accelerated away before she could embarrass herself.

♦ ♦ ♦

In the backseat, Nicki tickled and teased Hannibal, who was lashed into his safety restraint. Georgia law did not require an eight-year-old to use a booster seat, but Hani was small for his age and she had no wish to give any Smyrna cop an excuse to pull her over.

As she waited in Shiloh's drop-off queue, Olympia watched through the rearview mirror, disliking the flash of jealousy she felt when Hannibal whispered in his sister's ear.

Some of the time she was sure that the whispers were nonsense, perhaps a favorite poem like "Jabberwocky" or "Eletelephony" or G. Nolste Trinité's classic "The Chaos":

> Dearest creature in creation
> Study English pronunciation.
> I will teach you in my verse
> Sounds like corpse, corps, horse and worse . . .

Hani loved the tongue-twisting rhymes. They calmed and thrilled him. Nicki wouldn't give a clue as to which of their favorites she was engaged in, claiming secrecy was part of a deal she'd made with her brother. But at times she was certain that they actually talked to each other, in a way that he never did with her, or so far as she knew, anyone else in the entire world.

Nicki adored her brother, smothered him in a cocoon of hugs and kisses. He seemed to be more receptive to Nicki's affections than her own. His hand slipped reluctantly out of his sister's as she opened the rear passenger door, blew Mom a kiss, and sprinted off.

Jealousy is a thing of small parts and intimate imaginings. Instantly, Olympia was ashamed of herself and grateful to her daughter for providing a bit of the stability they might have enjoyed in another, better life. Her daughter ran lightly along the line of cars, long dark braids bouncing on her shoulders, graceful as a gazelle. As she vanished into the school, Olympia felt her heart surge with love so powerful it was like being tumbled by a wave. Her vision wavered, and she wiped the back of her hand across her eyes before continuing on.

The Golden Dream community center was another five minutes away through commuter traffic, tucked in the back of a shopping complex dominated by a Best Buy electronics superstore and a Wells Fargo bank. She passed two ethnic eateries, a sports uniform shop, a dry cleaner, and a storefront called Caskets 'n' More. On numerous occasions her reporter's instinct had prodded her to investigate, but she had never quite managed to do so.

She pulled her three-year-old silver Kia Soul into a space between a brown station wagon and a white Mercedes SUV plastered with a faded OBAMA bumper sticker glued down over an even more faded HILLARY FOR PRESIDENT banner. Hani didn't need to be coaxed from the car, thank God. He loved this place. Somehow it lured him "out of himself" more than any other school ever had.

Crackling techno-pop music bounced across the parking lot as they approached, hand in hand. The center hosted classes on dance, yoga, and martial arts, as well as—miracle of miracles—a licensed K through sixth grade private school with a sliding payment scale. She knew that the center was one of many Golden Dream centers in a dozen countries, and one of . . . nine, she thought. Yes, nine. Nine in the continental United States. Olympia knew that they believed in a "common thread" of spiritual truth running through all world religions. And also, thank God, in something called neurodiversity. They accepted everyone.

She'd fallen in love with the center the moment she'd walked through the door. Maria Cortez, a blogger who worked with her at CNS, had first mentioned the Golden Dream centers, in connection with a story about fringe spiritual groups in the Bible Belt.

Whatever their beliefs, they didn't try to proselytize, and despite their robes and blissful smiles seemed pretty harmless.

It sounded too good to be true—an affordable, state-accredited private school that didn't stigmatize kids like Hannibal. When she'd first walked through the door Olympia had been joyously bombarded with the sights and sounds of happy children bounding and kicking and tumbling and twisting like little circus acrobats. From the first moment, Hannibal had been transfixed. And that was all she'd needed to see.

After talking to the director she went to the back room and saw kids hooked to LCD video screens by sensor bands attached to foreheads and fingertips.

Her first question of course, had been: what *is* all of this? The reply had been like a double espresso on a cold morning: the Golden Dream was testing children, and they reassured her that unlike the world in general, or even her own family, they hadn't the slightest inclination to hold her responsible for Hani's condition.

The number of children diagnosed with autism and ADD was skyrocketing, but Olympia was assured this was primarily due to improved diagnostic procedures, not an increase in the number of such children per thousand. Attention deficit disorder was a mental issue, and could be likened to conflicting computer programs causing crashes and slowdowns of a CPU. But the autism spectrum was a matter of external communication. A problem in social interaction. More like a breakdown between the CPU and the monitor or speakers or camera. Perhaps Hani's internal world was simply more interesting to him, with outsiders reduced to no more than unwelcome intrusions.

Thank God the Golden Dream center had welcomed her son, and had immediately done everything possible to provide him with a happy, healthy space. The space was cavernous, large enough to hold two RadioShacks and a Tastee-Freez. She wondered if the recession had had at least one blessing associated with it: making a resource like this affordable on a single mother's budget. The front room was jigsaw-matted front to back, with a narrow walkway around the edges leading back to a door in a pastel-blue wall. The walls were arrayed with weapons and odd pointy tools, as well as framed photos, posters, and drawings, many obviously by the students themselves.

One of the instructors, a slender man with broad shoulders and a flat stomach, was totally engaged with a chunky kid whaling on a heavy bag with clumsy, enthusiastically swivel-hipped tae kwon do kicks.

"That's it," the instructor said. "Fade back, get your distance. There's a sweet spot in every technique. Have to figure your timing and . . ." He suddenly noticed her, snapping his head around. "Ms. Dorsey!"

"Yes?" Olympia asked.

"Your group is meeting in room B." His high, pale forehead glistened with perspiration, as if he had been demonstrating a moment before she walked in. He pointed toward a door at the room's far end.

Unable to remember his name, she nodded a generic thanks. Pass through the door and you entered a maze of cubicle classrooms, each aswirl with its own joyous frenzy, some teaching language arts, some math on computer-linked Smart Boards, and others practicing various gymnastics or dance drills.

Hand clasping hand, mother and son entered a tiled hall, and continued on past three more doors. Through the door's window, Olympia could spy on adults chanting and stretching as instructors in gold-fringed uniforms paced between their rows. The third door opened to a smaller martial arts room, where six children were tying themselves into pretzels.

Releasing her hand, Hani giggled, then howled with laughter and scrambled into a series of rolls and leaps over and around a carefully designed obstacle course constructed of blue matting. All of this was observed and guided by the head instructor, a shaven-headed, smooth-skinned Asian named Mr. Ling.

"I still have a hard time understanding why you provide so much service to your students." Ling could have been anywhere between thirty and sixty. She smiled to herself: the "black don't crack" axiom was nothing compared to some of the Chinese or Vietnamese she had known. "Only six of them . . . you can't be making much money."

Ling smiled. "Not everything is about money, ma'am."

"No," Olympia said. "Not everything. Nice to hear someone say that."

"It is good to find mutual needs satisfied, ma'am." Ling's voice, fractional bow, and patient expression possessed a pleasant combination of Asian formality and Southern gentility. "We have ancient methods for healing and strengthening mind and body, but westerners are quite pragmatic. We believe what we can see. Our task is to demonstrate the value of our methods."

"Well, Hannibal loves it here."

"I assure you, the feeling is mutual." Ling sighed with what seemed deep satisfaction. "For most of these children, we're using rhythmic entrainment, bilateral motion to stimulate cognitive development, teaching them to focus . . . everything we've spoken of . . ."

"But?"

Ling consider for a moment. "But we may be moving Hannibal from this group."

Her stomach clinched. She realized she was bracing for *the talk* that would shake her from her denial that Hannibal could thrive anywhere. Ever. "Why?"

"We've completed his tests, ma'am."

She froze. Then whispered: "I think that he's had enough tests, thank you." A firestorm erupted in her gut. *I thought you people were less judgmental . . .*

Ling touched her arm gently. "No, you don't understand. We're not criticizing Hannibal. Just the opposite. We think he is . . . extraordinary."

Despite his soothing tones, something inside her bared its teeth. "He's been called 'special' before."

"Have you ever heard the term 'indigo child'?"

She gnawed at her lower lip. "No . . ."

Ling smiled again. "The world is a living thing, ma'am. And it responds to challenges, just as nature evolves new species when the environment changes. We believe that children like Hannibal are part of that response. They are . . . special. And we will eventually learn how to nurture their new abilities."

Despite her initial chill, she found her interest piqued. "How?"

"We have a center north of here," he said, "in the mountains. Very lovely." He clapped his hands, as if delighted by a sudden thought. "You should go! I've spoken with our head instructor about it."

"About this class?" Olympia asked.

"About your son. Some children need to focus—that seems to be the issue with ADD. But we believe autistic children are focusing just fine." He grinned. "But not upon the things we wish they'd focus on. Much of the theory suggests that they are unresponsive. We believe that, to the contrary, they are too responsive, too sensitive, and in essence learn to trip a mental 'circuit breaker' to disengage with that intensity. They retreat to a safe place where the input can be managed. Hannibal has tested highly on some special measurements we have devised. Madame has already heard of these results, and is very interested."

"Who?" she asked. "Madame?"

"Madame Gupta." His eyes widened with evangelical fervor. "Our guru and inspiration. You'll be able to speak with her yourself. She's coming here for a demonstration."

"Martial arts? A woman?" Her memory scanned back over the poster-heavy walls, recalling a framed photo of a bronze-skinned, fierce, smiling Amazon in overlapping meditative and martial poses. Very, very feminine features, her fierceness unlike some of the macho MMA women she'd seen, virtually men with breasts. This was different, someone who looked as deadly as a leopard, but still every inch a woman. Her African blood was clear but there was something else, something more exotic. South Asian? Sri Lankan? At first Olympia had found the apparent contrast between femininity and warrior aspect puzzling, but in time it had simply faded into the background.

Could that be the "Madame" he referred to?

Ling smiled. "It is either a new world, or a very old one. Some of the greatest masters were women. But the martial arts are the merest splinter of her skills." A sudden thought brightened him. "You are encouraged to invite a friend, if you know someone interested in such things. The demonstration is rare, and not open to the public . . . but each member, or parent, can bring one guest. Hannibal's father, perhaps?"

"I'm a widow," she said, too quickly.

"I'm sorry," Ling said, chagrined by his faux pas.

She paused. She did know someone interested in such things, didn't she? Wouldn't it be a neighborly gesture to . . .

Damn, who was she kidding? "There may be . . . someone else," she blurted out. "A friend."

"Well." Ling's smile returned. "Why not bring him. Her?"

"Him."

Ling gave a shallow, apologetic bow. "Political correctness in the twenty-first century. Whichever it is. You would both be welcome." Ling seemed to read her mood. "And Hannibal, of course. By all means, please bring him."

He looked over at her son, who was already playing with a set of blocks. And . . . constructing another building, perhaps thinking of the two-dimensional one at home.

Was that a better world he was assembling, one saw-edged block at a time? A happier, healthier world? She wished she knew, and simultaneously dreaded the answer, whatever it might be.

CHAPTER 4

Hannibal dreamed, awake . . .

A thousand rooms, a hundred halls. It was his, all his, and everything within it was the result of his daily efforts. He couldn't remember when he had begun the Game. There may not have been a beginning. It might have always been under construction. And that meant it might never end, and that was good, because it was the safe place, the happy place.

Hannibal was alone, as he had always been alone in here, which was good. That was safe. Alone, there was no one to leave you. No one to tell you what to do (which he often just ignored, anyway).

In the Game, there was nothing but learning and playing and remembering.

Every room had exactly ten objects in it: here, a yellow Pikachu statue, a Michael Jackson poster, a miniature blue electric guitar, a stuffed piranha fish, an Ultimate Spider-Man graphic novel, a DVD of a movie about a Saint Bernard, a bottle of dried watermelon seeds, a blank slate, a pink wig, and a Christmas card from an imaginary friend. Every object bristled with ten hooks. Every corridor had ten rooms. Every wing had ten floors. Every floor had ten corridors.

Every day things happened, opportunities to learn, and he remembered everything, everything, and stored them all in their places. Nicki's morning kiss on a branch of a Christmas tree, next to a gymnastics cartwheel learned yesterday. A SpongeBob joke about pancakes reflected in an ornament next to a crazy slide Pax did across a waxed floor. Funny! If there was something unusually interesting, or something that he needed to know, he could return to it later, find the wing and floor and corridor and room and object on which he had placed the memory, and experience it once again.

He could not share this with Mommy. Wished he could share it with Nicki. Nicki, a warm and loving shape, a happy smile and adoring eyes, strong arms holding him close. His very first memory, the foundation on which all others rested.

Her smile was so strong, like looking into the sun, that he could not long withstand its focus, had to look away.

Touch had grown almost as bad. It felt as if he had no flesh, no bones, only raw bundles of nerves. He heard the way the doctors talked about him. They used phrases like "theory of mind," which seemed to mean that he saw other people as costumes, as bags of skin with nothing inside them. They said it right in front of him, as if he weren't there, talked about how he didn't understand people, couldn't understand how they felt.

It made him want to laugh and cry, but he was afraid that if he started, he would be unable to stop. They thought he understood and felt too little. The opposite was true. Everything threatened to overwhelm him, and he needed a place to be safe.

That was the Game.

Always he had been alone there, but lately, he had begun to wonder if that was still true. There were signs, small signs, that something in the Game was changing. It was most obvious in certain dreams. When he slept most deeply, so deeply that he had trouble awakening in the morning. In those times, he walked the Game and fell into memories of curling on the couch watching *Phineas and Ferb* and *Power Rangers,* or splashing in the pool with Nicki, or riding their neighbors' Great Dane, Pax. He was almost too big to do that now. Pax chuffed and labored but still put up with him, so it was all good.

A few times, potted plants had appeared in the halls, plants he could not remember placing. And through the windows (he almost never peered out the windows. He didn't care what was out there) odd trees had become visible. Palm trees, things that might grow in Florida.

Or Africa.

The last time Hannibal played, he had seen his daddy standing at the end of a corridor. Handsome Daddy, still wearing his paramedic's uniform, still waving and smiling at the son he loved. That was normal, and had happened many times.

But this was different. In the eighth room on the seventh floor of the third wing, a teddy bear sat on a white wooden chair. And on the third of ten hooks on that bear's belt, there was a memory of the time he and Nicki and Mom and Dad had seen *Finding Nemo.* He could go *into* the bear, and inside it were rooms, and floors, and hooks, and in the totality lived every image, every word of every moment of that movie. He could play them forward and backward, take them to the big television room and watch them, surrounded by his toys, and all the friends he had never had.

But the last time he was there, a leafy green shrub of some kind was growing through the floor, like a sprig of grass pushing up through a concrete sidewalk. That wasn't the only strangeness: a little girl had slipped in as well. He did not recognize her. Had never seen her before. She was darker than he, but a little strange, her face thin. Pretty. She sat watching the movie. Something about her posture made him think she was very sad, but she turned and smiled at him.

He was surprised to see her in his special place, but sat away from her, eating popcorn one kernel at a time and watching out of the corner of his eye.

Once, she turned and smiled at him. He liked her smile.

He told her that his name was Hannibal. She said her name was Indra, and that she was something called a *Siddhi*. He had no idea what the word "*Siddhi*" meant.

When he awakened, he knew that somehow she was still there in his mind. Sometimes when he went back he could not find her, but sometimes footprints indented the rugs, or some of his toys had been moved.

He would find her. Would find Indra, the *Siddhi* girl who played with his things. And then . . .

And then . . .

Odd. He wasn't sure what he'd do.

And in its own way, that was fun as well.

CHAPTER 5

Olympia picked up a sausage croissant and a too-sweet mango smoothie at Burger King, then hit Atlanta's freeway network, a concrete web layered over ancient trade routes from a time of plantations and rolling farms. She'd once heard that the entire system was based on a maze of ancient deer trails, and she could believe it. Even more probable to her was the possibility that Native Americans had simply lied to the encroaching white men, and laughed their asses off at the prospect of settlers circling in endless loops, wondering how the hell they got so lost.

The major consolation to the twisty paths is that they did, eventually, get you there.

The Central News Service's production offices were housed in a seven-story building located on Marietta Street and Centennial Olympic Park in downtown Atlanta. Its parking lot was accessed through a key-card gate, and although Olympia Dorsey didn't rate an assigned space, it was usually pretty easy to find one on the second level of the covered parking garage.

It was the best, most promising job she had ever had, a world away from the concrete playgrounds and fragile hopes of her childhood.

Mom and Dad would be proud, she thought. Well, Dad might have been disappointed that she hadn't followed him into civil rights law . . . but under the scowl would be joy, she was sure.

And Mom would have been ecstatic.

She locked her car, walked to the elevator, and rode up to the fourth floor, where for the last two years she had been a floating personal assistant, moving between health and financial sections, not at all what she had hoped for when she had migrated north from *The Miami Herald.*

Still, it was a long way from Liberty City.

By the time Olympia entered the staff meeting room her stomach was growling that the sandwich she'd wolfed down simply wasn't going to cut it, and the gleaming silver tray on a side table contained the answer to her stomach's increasingly rude demands. "Anyone get the last bear claw?"

The white-paneled room was dominated by a long, low table, around which almost twenty reporters and assistants and on-air personalities clustered. Christy Flavor, one of the younger researchers and a friend and failed diet buddy, grinned. "Saved it for you. Mmm. Fried sugar."

"Breakfast of champions." Olympia grabbed the bear claw and took a seat at the staff table's black rectangle. She'd be as lumpy as Christy if not for the fact that her body apparently had a long and forgiving memory concerning her Atlanta Rocks! gym regimen.

Chief editor Grant Sloan glared at her from beneath his bushy shelf of Groucho-level eyebrows. His expression suggested that this was not genuine anger, more a matter of annoyance that he hadn't snagged that bear claw for himself. "Thank you, Ms. Dorsey, for gracing us with your presence. Finally, we can proceed."

She graciously inclined her head. Some of the other reporters laughed. Joyce Chow, CNS's financial face, even smiled.

"When your pixilated visage appears on the six o'clock news buying crack at a barbershop across the street from a grammar school, you, too, will earn a free pass," he said to the others. The Smyrna PD corruption story had been her greatest coup at CNS. Terrifying, surprising herself with just how far she'd been willing to go, Olympia had dressed down and hung around the shop until they trusted her, and then convinced them to sell her enough cocaine to lead her to their source. From there, CNS researchers had been able to observe and record until the police exposed themselves as freelance protection services for the largest drug ring in the Atlanta area.

Devastating, intoxicating, and one of those precious moments when she really felt like a reporter. They'd needed a black woman who could plausibly play the ghetto queen and had never been on air. Liberty City to the rescue. It had taken two weeks to wear Sloan down to the notion, but it had been worth it all around.

"Until then, quiet down," Sloan said, interrupting her thoughts. He warmed up a PowerPoint screen. "All right. Metro, we have the street-lights article. Needs attribution. And there's a tie-in with the sports page and financial. Looks like there may be a connection between the Lakers sale and the NBA stock fraud . . ."

"The McMillian case?" Christy asked.

"That's the one. Athletes dumping their money into pyramid schemes is sexy. Jump on it."

"Will do."

Sloan thumped his fist on the desk, and Olympia jumped. He almost seemed to regret the next item on his agenda. "Now we have something interesting, and I'm not sure where to put it. Exhibit A."

"This"—an image of a Web site appeared on a wall screen. A document of some kind—"popped up on an Indonesian server three days ago. Manifesto from a group calling themselves the Children of Light. They reprinted this article from *Rolling Stone* magazine, listing the hundred worst unindicted criminals. You remember that?"

"Good ink," Christy said.

"Good electrons," Olympia said. That list was exactly the kind of thing she hoped someone would consult *her* on one day. She had a few names that would fit perfectly.

"Well spoke." That was Joyce Chow. As a floating researcher, Olympia rotated between department heads. Joyce was one of her most frequent and enjoyable assignments. "It was on their blog, not in print."

Sloan continued, "They said that 'from this point forward the wicked will be punished, and so that all will understand, we begin with the monsters on this list.' You'll recall that said monsters included the president of Russia, the prime minister of Israel, and the president of the United States."

"Our previous vice president, too." Christy angled for a honey-glazed donut. Joyce smoothly hip-checked her out of position. Good. Let them get distracted, while she concentrated on the potential of this new story. "Let's not leave him out of it."

"Heaven forbid," Joyce said. "That got the Secret Service interested, but the Web site was a dead end. Traced it as far as Nigeria."

"Where," Olympia said, "they are also holding millions of dollars for me, as soon as I get around to sending them my bank routing number and password."

"Let us know how that works out," Sloan said. "Anyway, someone bounced the order around until the trail looked like a plate of spaghetti."

"Well," Christy said. "Nobody's dead, right?"

Sloan shook his head. "That's not exactly true. The former governor of Chihuahua died yesterday morning. Some kind of convulsion."

Now Olympia remembered hearing a radio news item during drive time. "He was on the list?"

"Number seventy-eight. Now, the Elite, whoever the hell they are, promised that one person would die the first day, then two the second, and four the third, and so on . . . until Christmas Day, when, among four thousand others, the twelve worst criminals will die."

Leaning against the wall, Joyce clucked her tongue. "Twelve Days of Christmas. In reverse. Someone has a sick sense of humor."

"We want something on this for the six o'clock segment . . . and on the blog by seven."

Olympia's mind was whirring with possibilities. She shot her hand up. "Put me in, Coach. I can pull a rabbit out of this hat."

"You have an angle?" Sloan asked.

"I see dead people," she replied.

♦ ♦ ♦

Olympia's cubicle was just another nook in the maze, indistinguishable from the others except for a few Christmas cards, the framed picture of Nicki and Hannibal taped on the right side of her computer, and an endearingly clumsy drawing of a hilltop castle on the left.

She sat on her Hello Kitty chair pad and began reading her top handout aloud:

"'Then . . . the power will be handed over to the people. The towers of government and finance will fall. This is just the beginning: all "leaders" must die. And then the rest of the world follows . . .'"

Suddenly realizing she wasn't alone, Olympia turned to find Christy Flavor reading the printout over her shoulder. The backs of Christy's arms were noticeably slacker than in her wall-climbing days. "Pretty fruity stuff," Christy said. "But they got lucky with the convulsion." She paused. "Poison, maybe? Doesn't strychnine cause convulsions?"

"I guess," Olympia said. "Does seem like a story."

"What kind of story?"

She shrugged. "Just general weirdness, but I think we can make it sing."

"How did *Rolling Stone* put that list together?"

Olympia beetled her brows, pretending to search her memory. At times, it was useful to conceal just how "on top" of things she tried to stay. "They surveyed a couple hundred reporters and bloggers around the world. Asked for candidates, and chose the ones mentioned most often."

"Hmm. Know any of the sources?"

"Nope. Think I should find someone who does?"

Christy reread the handout. "End of the world stuff, huh? Counting up that way it would take a couple of centuries to thin us out."

Olympia laughed. "Give that woman a D in math. Doubling the number every day would lead to . . . five million or so in a month, and billions soon after. I would say the world would be empty in about . . . fifty days."

"Guess I can forget that diet," Christy said. "Just in time for the holidays!"

"The end times diet." Olympia sighed. "You don't lose weight, but there's nobody left alive to call you Blimpy."

CHAPTER 6

The Atlanta Racing Federation's open track east of Smyrna hosted go-kart and motocross on weekends, and rented out their facilities during the week. When Terry Nicolas pulled his green Subaru up next to the van with the ATLANTA STUNT TEAM sticker, he could already hear the roar of the engines above his radio's *Morning Zoo* chatter.

By the time he parked and walked up through the tunnel to the stands, his blood was racing faster than the vehicles below. Down in the dust, a truck was looping around the track, pursued by a black-and-white sedan. Rows of orange cones cutting across the curves forced both vehicles into tight swerves and turns.

Perched high in the stands, a skinny man in a wheelchair watched a computer screen divided into sections. That was Ernie Sevugian, their computer god, and Terry knew the computer displayed the scene below from different remote camera angles. One of the screens showed the vehicles moving over computer-generated terrain different than the racetrack below.

Beside the man in the wheelchair was Terry's roommate, Mark Shavers. Somewhat Georgian, his Stalinesque facial features hovered, intense, deeply tanned. Late thirties, massively built, the muscle was not as bouncy as it had been when Terry first met him in Iraq, doing dirty and dangerous things with remarkable flair. He had lost a step or two compared to then, but so had they all. It had been Mark's first combat tour when they met. Those dark-ringed eyes had seen three lifetimes of carnage since then.

"Quite a show," Terry said.

Mark chuckled. "Just a kid who used to like blowing shit up."

"Slice yourself sideways and count the rings," Terry said. "That kid is still in there." Terry had never told any of the others, but his private name for his companions was the Pirates, less in reference to their current enterprise than in honor of an old Milton Caniff newspaper cartoon his father had collected in a series of scrapbooks and shared with his son, one of Terry's fondest early memories.

Terry and the Pirates.

And Dad.

The trail vehicle expertly "pitted" the lead vehicle, ramming its left front bumper to the targeted right rear, spinning it. As the lead vehicle began to spin the trail vehicle braked, kissing the passenger side with its front and pinning the doors shut as they both stopped. On the computer-generated screen the lead vehicle was pinned against a guardrail instead of a row of cones.

"All right!" Mark barked into his handheld radio. "Twelve seconds and controlled the vic. Good. He is almost as good as you, Terry."

The man in the wheelchair grinned. Terry sometimes thought he looked like Rorschach from *The Watchmen.* Ernie Sevugian was his former warrant officer. He was affectionately known as Father Geek. Geek was pale and prematurely bald, his head dotted with perspiration. "You're still assuming they'll take the firebreak." He spoke with an Afrikaans twinge, a bit of confusion about his *f*'s and *s*'s that suggested his Cape Town childhood had never completely faded away.

Mark nodded. "I know Colonel O'Shay, and I know his crew. We have been fine-tuning this, Terry. We just got the latest intel." O'Shay and his crew. Thieving bastards who were going to suffer a very nasty surprise in less than two weeks. Payback was going to be quite the bitch.

Mark began to brief them as if they were in a J-Bad team house instead of a Georgia racetrack. He pulled up a PowerPoint slide with Google Earth imagery and graphic overlays.

"They'll come in at Dobbins Air Reserve Base, get right onto Route 78, and head east to Carolina. Single vic, just O'Shay, Huddleston, and two or three security. Father Geek confirmed a rental for a large SUV. Assume one Secfor will be ready as a tail gunner. Assume all are armed with at least handguns. Automatic weapons are possible but unlikely—they are trying to keep a low profile and can't afford extra attention. O'Shay is always the smartest guy in the room—just ask him." This got several chuckles. O'Shay was pretty damned smart . . . but he had totally underestimated how long Mark Shavers and the Pirates could hold a grudge. A serious, possibly fatal error.

"He will be assuming no one has a clue about him, otherwise he wouldn't risk smuggling in the first place. The heaviest weapon is likely semiauto M4s or similar carbines or shotguns, things that could have been purchased in the last thirty days and not get them hooked up if stopped. My guess is they'll drop a security man outside the base with a few gym bags of gear so they won't have any issues on base, then pick him back up as they leave. Security is tight and random antiterrorism measures could blow it for him if they have weapons on base."

He traced the route with his fingers. "They will be traveling to Charleston. If we crimp Route 78 just east of Aiken . . . they'll see the pyro in front and Geek running the blocking vehicle. Father Geek's big fat Expedition will look just like what they expect to be a threat. Our American Steel there will aggress on their blind side. They'll take the first bypass to avoid what looks like a kill zone, which will be the fire road. They'll attempt to break contact as well as avoid police involvement. They won't be expecting us, but once we engage they'll be spun up and looking for help. Can you handle that, Geek?"

"I can shut down their communications. No one will be able to call out on cell or radio for at least a three hundred meter radius."

Mark nodded his massive head. "Let me take the lead car."

"Be my guest," Father Geek replied.

Mark hopped down onto the track. The driver, a blond, whip-lean former master sergeant named Pat Ronnell, jumped out of the car and fist-bumped him.

"Excuses, excuses."

"Let's do this." He waved up to Father Geek and Terry. "Terry, get down here and get to work! Full rehearsal—make a good single take! You know the director is a dick!" He winked as he said it, making reference to the cover story of being a movie stunt team, working second-unit choreography for a Vin Diesel flick. The track still had some staff mousing around.

Father Geek worked the monitor panel on the right arm of his wheelchair, and the truck backed away from the transport mock-up.

Terry's heart raced. This . . . was the good stuff. He was behind the wheel of a Ford F-350 pickup. Unlike Geek's Expedition, this would blend in on a Georgia highway but would still have the mass to kick ass. One vehicle pits and pins, the other assaults. Terry was the best driver and had the mission to pin O'Shay. This wasn't one of the up-armored pickups they had overseas, but it was big enough to feel like home. The front end had been reinforced and it wore a rectangular, two-meter-square and twenty-centimeter-thick impact shield of Geek's design and Lee's construction, capable of absorbing multiple collisions before deteriorating. On the day of the actual event, there would be no shield. But on that day, they'd be wealthy enough to leave the wreckage behind without a tear.

Terry slid in behind the wheel, belted into the shock harness, and grinned as the engine's vibration tickled him through the seat. At home in an instant. Pat took shotgun, literally. His assault pump was between his legs, muzzle down. Both wore plate carriers—chopped-down versions of conventional military body armor. Holsters rode their hips, bright red training pistols instead of live sidearms.

♦ ♦ ♦

He took it for a lap around the track just to peel off his skin and get the feel in his bones, and by the time he swung back around they were ready for him.

The remotely operated truck spit exhaust and dust.

Terry handled the mass of the pickup expertly, although it was entirely possible that he wouldn't have this position on the critical day. The operation had redundancy built into it top to bottom. His primary job was to stop the target vehicle and keep it pinned. Terry was ready to provide covering fire and extract his teammates. He was also the designated medic and would have his civilian EMT gear in the truck. Each of them were cross-trained and ready for multiple contingencies in case something went south.

Because something *always* went south.

His hands were dry and cool as he took the wheel and swept his truck in. Father Geek tried to evade, but Terry gunned his behemoth, snugged up on the right rear bumper, and turned into the target's center of gravity. The remote-controlled SUV spun as Terry expertly maintained contact, controlling it with his mass and traction. Not for the first time Terry mused that it was a kung fu "sticky hands" drill with trucks.

Even as the two vehicles lurched to a stop Pat was out of the truck, firing round after round into the cab. The first two rounds were "breachers," shotgun shells filled with lead dust. Normally they were used to blow locks or hinges off of doors. He was using them to take out the windshield.

The next rounds were "beanbags," nonlethal rounds. First the passenger seat, which is normally a security member's but is also the "vehicle commander's" seat. Geek and Pat were hoping O'Shay would be sitting there. The next two were for the driver, then one back into the passenger.

Lee and Mark had skidded to a stop behind the target just two heartbeats behind Terry. Both had exited their vehicle. Mark zipped up the driver's side and similarly shotgunned the left rear passenger side as Lee did the same to the back window. Mark reached through the blown-out safety glass, unlocked and opened the door, grabbed the weighted bag on the floorboards, and sprinted back to his vehicle as Lee covered the target with the red training pistol. As soon as Lee turned to get into Mark's vehicle, Pat was sprinting backward the few steps he needed to Terry's truck, the red plastic pistol staying level and controlled as he said, "bang, bang, bang, bang," and mimed putting two rounds in each front tire. Both vehicles backed up a few feet, then bolted out. In less than twelve seconds after Terry made contact with the target's bumper, it was over.

Theoretically, the beanbags kept it nonlethal. The security team was not likely to know O'Shay and Huddleston were smuggling forty pounds of diamonds. It's not their fault two scumbags had hired them. Well, probably. Just like the beanbag rounds would probably not kill them.

Probably.

He knew he should care, but the truth was, he didn't. It would play the way it played.

"Cut!" Father Geek yelled. "No, no, no! This isn't dramatic enough. Vin didn't sign on for this crap! We need to rework the scene, give it more style. Get up here, damn it."

Grinning, Terry, Mark, Pat, and Lee met Father Geek in their ersatz control room. He already had the recorded scene in playback with the terrain overlay. Terry had put O'Shay's virtual SUV into a ditch. Unfortunately, they couldn't rehearse all of the factors in play. They were relying on Terry to smack O'Shay at the right place to make sure the vehicle couldn't simply recover from the PIT, the Precision Immobilization Technique spin, and blow through the ambush. Terry had memorized multiple roads, "driving" them with both POV and overhead views as well as doing his own recons. Once Terry got the stop, the rest of the team would do their thing.

Father Geek nodded approvingly.

"Not bad. I tried to shake you but Terry pinned me, right and proper."

"Hey, old timer, I've heard football players game on Xbox to learn all the plays. With all of our game time, we're naturals!" Lee said.

Terry grinned and raised his voice's pitch, trying to sound like a teen. "Should I join the army? I am really good at 'Call of Duty' and can play it for hours. I think I'd make a really good soldier."

Lee waved his hands back and forth, laughing. "No, man. No soldiers here. 'Grand Theft Auto,' sucker! We're straight-up gangstas, not some dumb-ass soldier boys!"

Straight-up gangsta. Terry felt his lips twist bitterly. *Long way from Iraq, asshole.*

Even as the words left his lips, Lee seemed to realize his humor had fallen flat. Everyone was quiet for a moment until Pat bent over to the cooler next to Father Geek, fished out an iced-down beer, and said, "Yeah, I'm good with that." He then cracked the beer and took a long pull.

"That's the shit right there," Mark said. "That's what I wanted to hear."

Terry felt a mixture of relief, tension, and anticipation. O'Shay and his crew were in for a very bad day, and the idea of snatching away their victory, trapping and plucking them just when they thought they were home free felt like a big wet kiss. Considering the betrayals involved, what they had once been to each other in Fallujah and other points east, revenge was almost worth more than the damned diamonds.

"New Year's Day!" Pat Ronnell said.

"New Year's!" the others replied, and clinked beer bottles. On that day, they were going to risk their lives to steal what had been stolen from them almost ten years ago in Iraq. It had taken one Colonel O'Shay all that time to make the arrangements necessary to smuggle his loot into the U.S.

And if all went right, it was going to take just four minutes to steal it back. Terry didn't feel like a thief: the diamonds had once been Hussein's, then were the Pirates' and then they were O'Shay's, and in a few days the sparkles would be right where they belonged.

Hell, you couldn't steal what was rightfully yours.

Father Geek spun his wheelchair in a circle, chugged the last of his beer, and slammed the bottle down on a table. "Play with me!" he yelled at Terry, and Nicolas grinned in reply.

Terry charged Sevugian, who made a David Copperfield gesture and produced a slender ivory-handled fighting knife in his right hand, holding it in an ice-pick grip. Terry's left foot jabbed knife-edged at Father Geek's face, and Geek replied with a razor-edged parry. Terry's jab was a feint, turning into a hook kick, and then a round kick, to opposite cheeks.

With dazzling speed, the two "played" with each other, mongoose and cobra, fists and feet against blades. Father Geek juggled the slender knife from hand to hand, so swift and precise he actually brushed Terry's pant legs with the point without puncturing his skin, whirling to face every angle. The South African art called "Piper," a twentieth-century concoction extracted from Capetown streetfighters and Zulu knife techniques, as lethal as human motion could be. For two minutes the old and favored game continued, a deadly ballet. Despite his skill, Terry was touched a half-dozen times.

On the other hand, Terry managed to penetrate Geek's defense exactly . . . once. Feinting a heel-hook to the temple and switching it to a side-kick to the gut, just a touch.

Afterward, there was deep breathing, and applause all around.

Terry grinned. That felt good. He and Ernie had a touch of magic together, always had.

Pat took a sip, grinning over the bottle at him. "Quite a show." He gestured at Terry more pointedly. "But back to business. Boy, you'd better not be late on the first, or my first resolution is going to involve kicking your karate ass to the moon."

"Talk, talk, talk."

Another sip. "You better remember. You are good at many, many things. Me, just one."

"And what would that be?" Mark asked. "We've never ever heard."

Pat smiled at the lie. "The only thing I was ever best at was ending people."

Their mechanical wizard/utility driver Lee Baylor was ex–Special Forces, currently unemployed. An SFC, like Terry, a tall Okie with straw hair and a perpetual smile. He'd put on thirty pounds since his best days, but still moved with explosive confidence. "Long way from Fallujah," he said.

Laughter. Not all of it pleasant. That had been a time of blood and fire, a mission embedded within a larger mission, on orders from the POTUS himself.

Pat took a drink and looked at Terry. "Sort of a shame Jayce isn't here to see this."

A pause. Terry wasn't going to let himself be baited. Not now, not by Pat. Sergeant Remmy Jayce had saved Pat's life in Fallujah.

And then later died on Terry's watch.

Terry didn't like to think about it, and forced his mind to slide past Jayce's dying screams without letting himself be dragged down into them.

The man who had saved them. Dying in the jungle, screaming Terry's name.

"At ease with that shit," Mark said. "Fortunes of war. You hear me? Stow it."

"Sure, Mark," Pat said. His eyes glittered at Terry.

"Anyway," Mark continued. "We'll be a lot farther away by January third." A day to ship the loot. A day to travel together to the foreign city where they would sell and divide the spoils. A possible week to do business.

Then . . . a celebratory glass of champagne, perhaps . . . and then they would never see each other again.

"Father Geek," Mark said. "We'll have close to eighty million dollars in Iraqi ice. Current exchange expectations?"

"I've got fences bidding against each other," Geek said. "Two Belgians, a guy in Singapore, and one in Tel Aviv. Anonymous, unknown to each other, and communicating through a little blind board I set up. We're up to fifty-five percent, Cayman accounts. I think I can get sixty."

Jesus Hopping Christ on a plastic crutch. He'd heard those numbers again and again, but still couldn't wrap his head around them. Terry had grown up on army bases, a world where most needs were supplied at a basic level. No real poverty, but no luxuries, either. The idea of such wealth . . . dizzied him. Who would he even *be*? And what did it mean to suddenly become a different, new person when you'd never figured out who you were in the first place?

Mark nodded along to Geek's mini-lecture, grinning like a piranha in bloody water. "We want it closed out before we act."

"These guys do serious business. Four deliveries in twenty-five percent increments. The money will be there, if we deliver."

"Fuck," Pat said. "Almost fifty million dollars."

"Yeah, well—about eight million to you, *mon frere*."

Terry took a long pull. "What are you doing with yours, Mark?"

"Who," Father Geek said, "as XO was technically due a larger share, and chose not, so as to increase the fraternal atmosphere of this noble enterprise."

"Hear, hear." Lee raised his bottle and took another pull.

"But what are you going to do?" Geek asked.

Mark's eyes softened. "There's a little place near South Padre Island I've had my eyes on. I'm thinking if everything goes right I can stay in-country."

"And if not?" Terry asked.

"Ireland," Mark said. "I'm thinking Ireland. Maybe Italy. Or Istanbul. Someplace that starts with an *I*. Or not. Hell, be best for me if you assholes don't have the slightest idea. So that when they catch you—and knowing how sloppy you bastards are, they most certainly will—and attach the jumper cables to various protruding evidences of your alleged manhoods, you may sing soprano with zero impact upon my peace of mind." He grinned at Terry.

Terry thought about the collection of medicine bottles on Mark's dresser, and managed to hold a smile in return. "You, Lee?"

Lee seemed to be chewing on an imaginary straw. "Yeah, well, I'll be able to shit on the job reference."

Terry cocked his head. "The purchasing agent thing?"

Lee nodded. "That's the gig. Fuck, man, everyone was taking money. *Looong* before I got that job."

"The problem wasn't taking money," Mark said, the very soul of reason. "The problem was asking for the damned bribe."

"The problem," Terry said, "was getting caught." No, Mark was right. The stupid thing was asking a supplier for a kickback, just because the supplier's previous agent had been free with the gifts. That had been criminal stupidity, but Terry wasn't in a mood to pile on.

Lee shrugged. "Just how business was done."

"Well, somebody didn't think so," Mark said. "So here we are."

"Father Geek?" Mark asked.

The man in the wheelchair needed no further prompting. "I've got some mates in Cape Town looking into an IP start-up. I could buy in as silent partner, geek out behind the scenes . . . have a good time and still be . . . vapor. Cyber-ghost. Pat?"

"All I want to say is that there is a girl," Ronnell replied.

Terry almost spit out his beer. Ronnell had never had anything remotely like a real relationship in the time Terry had known him. Would wonders never cease? "Whoa! An actual, living female who has the bad taste to lock loins without cash changing hands?"

"One without assembly required?" Geek asked.

"An actual, living female who relishes Mr. Happy. Yes. She runs a secondhand store that hires the handicapped."

Terry laughed. "No one could make that shit up."

"Well," Mark said, hoisting his bottle. "To us."

They lifted their beers in toast, but after the next bubbly draw, quiet reigned again.

Terry waited, hoping someone else would say what he was thinking. No one did, so after a silent curse, he broke the silence. "Mark?"

"What?"

Terry took another slow pull. "What happens if O'Shay's boys don't give up?"

"If the teargas and the shock aren't enough?"

"Yeah," Terry said. "There we are, all auto'd up. We've closed the 78 and shunted them to a side road. Blown out their engine block, and flash-banged the hell out of them. They're pinned, gassed, shit out of luck. But say we do all that . . . and some poor fool starts shooting anyway. What then?"

"Worse," Lee said. "What if the distraction doesn't work, and we get some highway piggies on that stretch?"

"It'll work," Mark said.

"But what if it doesn't?" Geek asked.

"Then?"

"Then."

"We've got *you,* Pat," Mark said, and raised his glass. The others followed in silent toast. Terry's felt as if it weighed a ton. "We've got you."

CHAPTER 7

The Foothill Village condominium complex was probably the nicest place that Terry Nicolas had ever lived. Certainly since a childhood spent moving from army base to army base following his widower father, Captain James Nicolas. Foothill Village wasn't just a place to sleep and eat. It was a neighborhood, with grass and lawns and birthday parties with bouncy houses and yapping dogs and babies and retirees and people living real lives who actually shared their greetings and concerns with one another.

And Olympia, of course.

And that was its own special hell, because he knew he would soon be leaving. And the chances of finding something like this again, someone like *her* again, eight million dollars or no, was smaller than the fine print on his last car loan.

He had just completed his afternoon workout and was on his way back to his apartment when Olympia pulled into her driveway and little Hannibal bounced out of the car in his sparkling blue *karate gi*. Terry felt a twinge. He remembered something that a friend of his had said . . . or was it that he had seen in a movie? Don't mess with single mothers. They don't play.

He had played. Certainly never planned any wrong, but that didn't mean he had done right.

They had "dated." That was what people called it these days when you took someone to bed, shared that most profound, and most trivial intimacy. Dating. Shared personal pleasures and pains. His father's battle with cancer, the massive heart attack that had claimed hers—and the life insurance policy that had lifted Olympia and her mother to a middle-class neighborhood and better schools.

Neither of their surviving parents had lasted a decade after the death of their spouse. Both O and Terry orphaned before thirty, alone in the world.

It had been as if the universe conspired to push them together.

And she had lowered her guard, sharing her cinnamon grace and intimate warmth with him . . . and then slammed the walls back up. Or maybe she'd sensed there was something wrong with him and started clawing, seeking his soft spots, and then simply disengaged. Damn it. With no referee to stop it, once the fight started the low blows had been mutual, and then like two battered club fighters they had limped to their neutral corners, each declaring victory.

It was his own damned fault. She'd smelled "bastard" coming a long way off.

Good for her. You go, girl. As far away as possible.

"Hey, champ!" he said to the boy. Hannibal smiled shyly, but didn't look at Terry, and didn't speak. A beautiful smile.

"Hi, Terry," Olympia said.

"Hi." What a woefully inadequate greeting, considering all they had shared. "How's the little guy?"

Nicki glared at him. The thirteen-year-old had never warmed to him, had liked him even less after Olympia had dumped him, dealing with it with a kind of unmistakable *I knew you were an asshole* energy that made him want to bounce her into the swimming pool.

Was it the dead father that made her so protective? Maybe that business with the police department—he'd seen the patrol cars cruising outside the Dorsey household. Had heard about the harassment, midnight phone calls, and being pulled over by the Smyrna PD for invisible infractions.

Good reasons for mistrust.

Terry made little punching movements, and was rewarded by a matching flurry from Hannibal. Such a terrific little mime. It was as if Michael Jackson was imitating Wesley Snipes: no real structure or grounding or brisant "pop" but it looked great. He fought to keep from gathering the boy into a hug that Hannibal would squirm away from, anyway. Damn it, why was it harder to break up with the kid than with the mother?

"He's fine. Doing well." An awkward moment.

Olympia paused. "His school teaches karate for physical education, and they're having a demonstration tomorrow. Their head instructor, someone named Madame Gupta, is supposed to be there. In person."

"Indra Gupta?" That name made a dinging sound in the back of his mind. He couldn't exactly remember why, but it most certainly did.

"Maybe. I'm not sure I've ever heard her first name. But maybe. You know her?"

"Heard of her, I think." *Ding, ding, ding.* "Really? A personal appearance?"

"Yes. You know her?"

"One of my teachers worshipped her. I think I may have a book she wrote. Critique of a mystic named . . ." He waved his hand, unable to summon the rest of the information. "A long time ago. She must be getting up there."

She ventured a smile. "I can bring a guest. Was wondering if . . ." He got it, and was reminded of why he liked her.

"I appreciate that. Really. O, I . . ." He could feel that something soft and shy was trying to wiggle its way out of him, and wanted no part of it. Damn it, this was no time to be vulnerable. Or to be calling Olympia "O." That felt a little too chummy, considering what they had been to each other, and where they were today.

"It's all right, Terry," she said, cutting off his thought.

He was sure she was telling the truth. Damn it, she didn't have to make it so easy. She didn't have to make him feel that he wasn't the bastard he damned well knew himself to be. "Yeah, well . . . thanks for the invite. What time?"

"Seven. See you there?"

Hannibal performed a few more enthusiastic kicks and punches, giving a crackling good Junior Bruce Lee impression as he did. The display was followed by a shy moment of side-eye contact.

"Hey," Terry said. "That's pretty good."

"You still do karate, don't you?" Olympia asked.

He laughed. "You don't 'do karate,' " he said. "If anything, karate 'does' you." He realized they'd been gazing into each other's eyes a little too long. She looked away. "I'm kind of a dojo bum," he said, trying to lower the tension.

"What does that even mean?"

He shook his head ruefully. "I've bopped around through every style and system you can name."

"Which one is best? Karate? Kung fu? This mixed martial arts stuff?"

He laughed. No, actually he didn't. He wanted to laugh, wished he'd laughed. In actuality, he was warmed that she was interested. And that warmth was uncomfortably localized. "No such thing as 'best.' Depends on who you are, what you want, why you want it, how long you've got . . . too many different variables. The best art is the one you enjoy. If you dig it, you'll stick with it. And . . . probably figure out how to get what you need."

"That makes sense," she said, followed by another uncomfortable silence.

Peripheral vision caught a massive human shape moving toward them. Mark Shavers had shambled out of their condo, noted the conversation, and wandered over. Olympia seemed to see him for the first time, her eyes widening with some private, happy thought.

"Terry," Mark yelled. "Phone." The big man grinned amiably then headed back across the street in that sleepy, bearlike, harmless ambling way he typically affected. And it was most assuredly mere affectation. Terry had seen Mark in close-quarters action, and there were few human beings more aggressively coordinated than his XO.

She laughed shyly. Hannibal grinned at him. There was something too familial about the scene. Terry knew this was not his place in the world.

"Well," Olympia said, "I have to . . ."

"Yeah," Terry said. "Me, too." He turned away.

"Terry?"

"Yeah?"

"I just wanted to say thank you for being so nice to Hannibal."

"He's a world-class kid."

"Yeah, well . . . usually it goes the other way. Most guys want me, and ignore Hannibal. You're different."

Shit. This wasn't the time for this discussion. Maybe there *was* no good time for a discussion like this. "Maybe one day we'll talk about it."

"Maybe one day. Yeah." She paused again, and dug into her purse, extracting a slip of paper. "Here's the invite. Seven o'clock tomorrow night."

"I'll be there."

She backed away, smiling shyly. "Okay." Then she stopped. "Oh. There's one other thing before you go . . ." She glanced at Mark's retreating back, and told him.

♦ ♦ ♦

Terry hummed happily as he closed the door behind himself. Mark was leaning against the wall, smoking one of his thin cigars, a snake of blue smoke curling up to the ceiling. He exhaled a series of rings and gave Terry the fish eye. "Are we forgetting we're here on business?"

"All work and no play . . ."

"Keeps Jack out of Guantanamo. One wrong word and it's shut the fuck up, Carl."

Shut up, Carl. Military humor for a clusterfuck. Something they sure as hell couldn't afford in this case.

Clunk. The sound of ugly reality slapping him upside the head, yet again.

"Oh, and one other thing," Terry said, happy to throw a tomato at Mark's Voice of Doom act. "She said that their usual Santa dropped out of the Foothill Village Christmas party. She wants to know if you'd be willing to play Saint Nick."

That, finally, widened Mark's eyes. "Me? Why me?"

"She says you're jolly. And about the right size."

"Fuck you." He thumped his gut. "This is muscle."

"Increasingly well marbled."

Mark wagged his head, more amused than insulted. "I've missed every Christmas for twenty years. What the hell do I know about Santa Claus?"

Mark's door was open, and through it Terry could see his bed and dresser. The dresser top held at least a dozen prescription bottles, medications Mark took by the fistful, to stave off the injuries and diseases and stresses from a lifetime of hard service in exotic lands. The number of Christmases ahead for his XO was far smaller than the number behind. Single digit, in all probability.

Come on, Mark. Come in out of the cold. Join the rest of us . . . for just a little while.

Terry kept his voice as light as he could. "He knows when you're sleeping. He knows when you're awake. He gets into everybody's house without a hitch . . . guy's SpecOps."

◆   ◆   ◆

Terry had been thinking mischief as he crossed the street. Too busy ruminating to notice the van parked on the street feeding into Foothill Village from Meadow Lane. Or to determine that it contained two men. Its interior walls were crowded with television monitors, currently displaying angles of the exterior of Olympia's house. On the screen, Olympia was ushering her children through the door, and then closing it behind her.

One of the men wrote a notation in his book. He noted the time, and wrote something else in the margins, and then folded the book and slid it into a cubbyhole, and went back to watching.

CHAPTER 8

Terry sat at the edge of his bed. It might have been queen sized with a soft, comfortable mattress, but when he sat on it, leaning with his feet on the ground and elbows resting his torso's weight on his knees, it no longer existed. He had returned to a special mental place, a place in which he had often found refuge over the last twenty years of service, when often the only furniture he had was a cot or crappy locally purchased bed.

Hard decisions were nothing new. Even when given orders, Terry took the time to go over them, before and afterward. There is no such defense as "I was following orders" for an officer. An enlisted man could avoid court-martial simply by proving he'd been given a direct order. But even then, they were expected to use their heads and hearts. He had taught that over and over to the younger soldiers who entered Special Forces after 9–11 when the Special Operations world expanded and needed more and more troops to operate away from journalists and social media, cloaked behind top-secret classifications.

The hairier the operation, the more time he took to make sure he and his Pirates (even from basic, he had always thought of his guys, whoever they were, as his Pirates) were on the "right path," obeyed the rules of engagement. Now he was looking at armed robbery and possible murder. Every one of them knew what they would do if ambushed, so they expected nothing less of those they were targeting.

And that opened an entire world of questions that had first been raised, for him, by his first group commander, Colonel Drinkwater.

There were colonels like O'Shay, assholes who merely wore the rank. Men like O'Shay made careers out of being on all the right missions and getting the right spotlight. The ones who avoided the daily grind of "bug hunts," seeking terrorists the old-fashioned way of lots of walking and talking to locals. All posture and politics.

Col. Drinkwater was the other kind. His first group commander when he finished the Q-course and made it to his first A-team. Drinkwater had been enlisted SF before commissioning through ROTC. He did a lot of mentoring over beers and cigars at the fire pit behind his headquarter building at Fort Bragg. Drinkwater had earned three Purple Hearts, a Silver Star, and a raft of other awards before he pinned on his bars so that all the young troops listened to him. This night had been mandatory fun for everyone who hadn't been in combat yet as well as all the team commanders. Many of the older soldiers were there, too.

And that was where he'd schooled Terry.

"The Geneva Conventions were not made for lawyers, they were made for grunts," the colonel said one night. They were getting ready to go to the Balkans and some of the younger soldiers were eager to "pop their cherries."

"In a regular war, gentlemen, the military are just the fashion police. We kill you for wearing the wrong clothes. You may have volunteered, you may be drafted, you may have been forced into the military at gunpoint—we don't care. We will shoot you, bomb you, set you on fire, nuke you until you glow, and shoot you in the dark—and it is legal all because you are wearing the wrong uniform."

Everyone laughed, some making the barking and grunting sounds that troops everywhere made among their own. Drinkwater wasn't laughing. He was staring off in the distance, not noticing the ash growing on his stogie.

"Special Forces, though, are on the edges. Some days we are training others. Other days we are doing unto others. We don't operate in the open. We do what needs to be done, but we still need to do it right."

Someone sounded off with "Kill them all, sir! No prisoners, no mercy!" The younger troops were raising beers.

The older troops looked to Drinkwater. Somehow, without saying anything, the commander brought everyone to an expectant silence. He looked up from the fire pit and scanned his troops. Terry still remembered it vividly, feeling like those fire-reflected eyes were locked onto him and him alone. Finally, he broke the silence.

"You are operators. You made it through regular training, made sergeant, then made it through the Q-course. The selection process to be an operator is not about pulling triggers, but about being able to adapt and overcome and still be soldiers. You won't have a chain of command out where you work, and what you do won't fit into easy boxes. You have to stay professional.

"We are not going against conventional forces or even insurgents," he said. "We are hunting terrorists." And now, despite the calmness of his words, a lupine quality, a predator energy had shone in his eyes. He was the alpha wolf, running at the head of the pack. "As long as you stay within the lines, you can kill as many legitimate targets as you want and can't be called a murderer, at least not legally. Uniform Code of Military Justice exists because what we do is not civilized and does not fit in with civilian law. The North Vietnamese would put our prisoners on trial for doing their job and then sentence them as criminals. It's why the conventions state only the military can try military, and military tribunals are used to determine whether or not you're a legal combatant.

"I'm telling you this because we're going to a place that has not seen law in a long time. It doesn't change the standards for you. Any of you."

He stared back into the fire. "And if you're in it long enough, you'll fail. You'll cut corners. You'll break the rules. You'll convince yourself it was necessary, or they deserved it, or it saved lives of whoever we are calling the 'good guys' that day."

"In Escape and Evasion training you heard, 'If you ain't cheatin', you ain't tryin'.' " A wave of laughter in response. "Gentlemen, that was training, and it was training to teach you to not get caught and to be capable of outthinking an opponent on his home turf. At no point, however, did we say it was okay to slit civilian throats, to rape, to torture. That is what terrorists do . . . and sometimes, it's what soldiers do."

No one spoke. Under other circumstances, there may have been jokes. Troops can joke about anything. There was nothing joking in their commander's eyes.

"Given enough time, you will fail. You will fail yourself, whether you are caught or not. You will fail your teammates by making them deal with your stupidity, or you will fail them by not acting when you should have. You will have every justification in the world. Everyone does. Saying 'the other guy did it first' is the first one you'll hear, and it is as wrong now as it was back in kindergarten.

"The trick, gentlemen, is to know where the line is. You need to know where the line is both on paper and inside yourself. Sometimes you do break the rules to do what is right. Sometimes you're given bad orders. You were selected because you are professionals and can think for yourself. At some point, if you are doing this long enough, you will cross the line. If you pull yourself back, that's one thing. If you move the line to convince yourself you're okay, that's another.

"Some of you will find you have no problems killing people. By 'people,' I mean legitimate targets. That does not make you a monster. Everyone dies.

Sometimes they need to die sooner." More laughter, deep, like smoke wafting out of a bed of coals. "Since we first organized as clans and tribes, someone had to protect the rest. That meant killing. Just don't forget there are bastards like you out there with the same opinion about making you die sooner. That's being a soldier.

"Some of you will have a problem killing people. That doesn't make you weak. I know you don't think you have a problem right now. It's another thing when you hear them screaming, smell the blood and shit, and realize at the gut level that is a person just like you. Not a 'gook,' 'jap,' 'chink,' 'raghead,' 'nigger,' 'kike,' 'cracker,' 'peckerwood,' or any other bullshit label you may have used when shooting paper targets. Make no mistake, they are people. You may have to kill women, since a woman with an AK can kill you just as dead.

"Most of you will be able to find a balance with this and the mission. My job as your commander is to make sure you have a legitimate target and a legitimate mission. I promise you, you will find few things as satisfying as going into the valley of death, being that meanest, baddest son of a bitch, and carrying out a righteous mission that few on the planet would be able to pull off."

All around the pit, men nodded, sipped. Spines straightened.

"That is fighting with honor. That is my promise to you, as your leader, that I will not only give you those righteous missions, no matter how messy it looks from the sidelines, I will give you and your commanders the information you need to not only do your job, but know why you are doing it and why it was given to you instead of regular military or some jet jock dropping bombs while sipping his coffee."

Drinkwater raised his beer with the rest of the group raising theirs as troops sounded off with "*De Opproso Liber,*" "*Sic Semper Tyrannis,*" and other cheers. After a long pull on the can, he tapped the ash off his stogie and stared back into the fire.

After the noise died down, he said, "Some of you won't be coming home."

The smiles slid off their faces. Many of the newer troops still believed dying was for "that other guy." The older soldiers knew it could be them. Death was joked about a lot. This was no joke.

"Some of you won't be coming home because you died in combat," Drinkwater said. "That is the job. No matter how much you train, how much I plan, no matter what high-tech gear we give you, some farmer with an AK can fill you full of holes. Then you'll be the guy on the ground, screaming for his momma even as your buddies grease that sumbitch and your blood drains out into some godawful shit-filled patch of worthless fucking dirt. Doc will tie off the bleeders, pump you full of drugs, squeeze bags into you, and you'll still die. Then your buddies will split up your gear, arrange for your body to be picked up, then Charlie Mike and finish the job."

Drinkwater was looking through them at this point, perhaps reliving a past event. He puffed his cigar and shrugged. "I can live with that. As your commander, as your comrade, I can live with that. I won't blow sunshine up your ass and tell you that this will never happen, and that anyone who lets a soldier die on their watch is a failure. This is the large print of the job. I hope this doesn't happen, but if it does, we will deal with it with honor.

"Some of you, though, won't come back because you died inside. You lost your way. You forgot how to be a soldier and became just another asshole with a weapon. When I got back into group I looked up my buddies from when I was enlisted. Some were still in. A few of them are with us tonight." A few senior NCOs tipped their beers toward their commander. "Don't believe half the stories they tell, and I won't tell you which half that is." A few laughs, but they didn't break the somber mood.

"Some got out and are upstanding citizens back home. We have given you the tools to succeed at anything you try. Never forget it."

He looked back at the fire. "Some went to Rhodesia. Some went to the Congo. Some went other places. Some were still professionals, just looking for work. They still did it right. Many, though, were just assholes with weapons. The worst ones have files in intel. If you can imagine it, it's in those files. All of that and worse.

"The fucked-up thing—I wasn't surprised who was who. They were slipping when we were out in the bush. And I didn't stop them. We justified . . . no, I justified it, by saying we were not as bad as the bastards we faced, or that is the only thing the enemy understood. Even if I didn't slip, I let those others around me do it.

"I'm not talking some nitnoid rule some pogue in the rear thought would sound good. As you sweep through the kill zone I expect you to tap every swinging dick that had carried a weapon. It's a kill zone, not a play-nice-with-others zone. Be fast, lethal, and be professional. Sometimes people are in the wrong place and get dead. It sucks. Own up to it.

"I'm talking about those lines you know are supposed to be there, like gut shooting someone just to watch them die instead of killing them clean.

Like beating up some old man who was acting too proud. Like looting valuables because 'they don't need it anymore.' It wasn't murdering someone's grandma or raping some ten-year-old, it wasn't so over the line we couldn't ignore it, but it was still over the line. They didn't pull themselves back, and the rest of us let them.

"By the time we pulled out of Vietnam, they were already gone. They couldn't ever come home, not really. Even if they were back in their hometown around people who loved them, they couldn't see those around them as real people or be able to work in the real world. That guy at the end of *Deer Hunter,* playing Russian roulette—I know that guy. All of us old operators know that guy. Whether it was a needle, a gun to their own head, or something else shooting at them, it was about the same."

The fire crackled. Drinkwater finished his beer and flicked the stub into the fire. "Commanders, by the end of the week I want a one-block hour of instruction on the Law of Warfare given to your teams. You will give the legal portion of the class and your command guidance. First Sergeants, you will participate by amplifying and supporting your team commanders by giving war stories of the do's and don'ts. You will make sure not only that your soldiers have the law fresh in their minds, but that it is not just something buried in the back with the rest of the schoolhouse crap. That they understand your no-shit guidance. I suggest you distribute copies of the Geneva Conventions to everyone prior to the class and make it required reading. Once we have the rules of engagement, we'll tune our operations to whatever the JAG says are the hoops we have to clear, but I want everyone to know what right looks like regardless of the ROE. Some rules need to be followed and some need to be nodded at, and you need to make sure you and your troops understand which is what.

"Make no mistake . . ."

He paused, turning to look at the assembled soldiers, some of the best-trained lethal professionals in the world, under his personal care and responsibility.

"Make no mistake, if I come across any one of you so far outside the lines that you are gone, I will personally shoot you in the head, right then and there."

He let that sink in. Then more softly, looking into the fire, "Because that is what I wish I had done for a few guys I once called 'my friend.' Because that is what my younger self would have wanted if I went that far."

Looking back up to Terry, he said, "We look out for each other. We pull each other back. If one fails, it is because we all failed, and I am responsible for each of you just as we are responsible for each other. That is serving with honor. That is knowing where the line is. I'm not worried about crossing the line, I'm worried about how far. I'm worried about whether you pulled yourself back, others pulled you back, or you just kept going until you got caught.

"At the end of the day, I want us all to come home, whether it's in a box or on our feet. We all deserve to come home."

He paused, and then added: "And bring your souls with you."

♦ ♦ ♦

We are across the line. Terry knew that. Was it too far? Some of the guys used to say that as long as you were asking yourself that question, you weren't too far. Terry never bought that. You could swim too far from shore and know you couldn't make it back. The question becomes: do you try to turn around or do you keep going?

He tried to say it didn't matter. He didn't have a home. His marriages to Pam and Angie had both smashed into the proverbial wall, so like the other troop divorces he didn't even feel the right to think the pain was that special. Mom had died so long ago he barely remembered her face. Dad had died when he was nineteen, shriveled by the Big C until he looked more like the Crypt Keeper than the immortal soldier who had carried Terry on his back from base to base around the world.

He had no home but the army, and he was losing that.

The Pirates are my family, and this is what we have decided to do together. It is right for us. This isn't about civilian law. Colonel O'Shay did wrong by us. When he didn't get his star something just twisted in his head, and the shit rolled downhill. We're just making it right by paying him back. Just one time, do this one thing, and we go back across the line as good citizens. We can take care of our own, settle down, and make it right that way.

That's what Father Geek has said, over and over. I've seen rat bastards live fat on foreign aid and covert payoffs. It's only fair we clear the books with O'Shay and come out ahead, just this once. Then we'll pull ourselves back across the line.

Just this once.

Right.

CHAPTER 9

Moscow, West Biryulyovo warehouse district

December brought what Fiodor Nabokov's grandfather Piotr had called *ushaka* weather, the kind of cold suffered during the Great Patriotic War, when they had surrounded and slaughtered the Nazis at Stalingrad. Fiodor had never been able to decide which tales of that horrid, frozen, glorious time were truth and which militaristic fantasy, knew only that whatever had happened in those days had mutated his grandfather from a human being into an emotionless glacier, one who had done his best to transform his son Mikhael into an identically implacable force.

Mikhael had not been quite the golem Fiodor considered his grandfather, but he was still a man with a commitment to survival at all costs. A man who no longer believed in country, but had discovered nationalism to be a superlative foundation for power. *First, Fiodor,* Grandfather had said, *never enter battle alone. Always have a tribe to fight beside you. And secondly, never pass an opportunity to enrich yourself.* For all the chaos and slaughter, fortunes were always made as well as lost in wartime, and those with military connections were among the most deeply enriched.

So with his father's blessings Fiodor had joined the People's Army, and through various combinations of capacity and intrigue had swiftly risen to the rank of colonel. But one of the most important parts of that process was learning who could be counted upon to steal, or assist theft, and thereafter evade detection. Or at least capture.

Or if not that, to die with lips sealed.

Fiodor might not believe in anything in the world other than Fiodor Nabokov, and that was fine with him. The three men behind him in the windowless, unheated, concrete-floored warehouse also believed in Fiodor, so long as he paid them, and that was fine as well. They understood each other. There was no love lost between Fiodor Nabokov and his bodyguards. But rubles had been exchanged, as well as dire warnings about the cost of betrayal. As Machiavelli had said, fear was a far more reliable bond than love.

The only illumination shone from three overhead incandescents casting overlapping pools of sterile light. His eyes adjusted to the darkness quickly, as they always had, a gift of survival from his grandfather. The warehouse within was stacked high with wooden boxes and canvas-wrapped bundles, few of them directly related to the business at hand. The objects of the current negotiations were nestled in wooden crates stacked in a cleared area the size of a boxing ring, squarely in the middle of the warehouse. Soviet SA-7s, the handheld Russian equivalent of American Stingers, heavier and less reliable, but more powerful and accurate under a wider range of weather conditions.

His men were waiting for him, as he had known they would be. The SA-7s were just a teaser, of course, representing a fraction of the weapons liberated before an unfortunate fire had destroyed the Minsk arms depot.

Pity.

"Ah!" he said, exhaling a stream of condensation into the frigid air. "Hammad. It is good to see you."

"And you, Fiodor," Hammad said, each word visible as a puff of steam. Hammad looked a little like the film star Omar Sharif, if the actor had groomed himself daily by striking his face with a hammer. One would have thought they were old comrades, and perhaps in a sense they were. "I was not certain that you would be here."

"I would not miss it. Such negotiations are best conducted between friends." "Friend" meaning someone who would not profit by shooting him in the face, and from whom he could expect a measure of extra-legal professionalism. Regardless of trust or friendship or professionalism, it would not do for Hammad to know that this was Fiodor's final deal.

He was closing down the pipeline. The *Ministerstvo Vnutrennikh Del* or MVD, the Russian security forces, had been nibbling around his finances for some time, and this latest affair, he knew, had focused their attention on his small but lucrative operation. Numerous times over the course of his career Fiodor had very carefully deflected guilt from himself onto less precious, or at least less perspicacious necks, but inevitably the day would come when those precautions would not suffice, and the truth would out. And instinct said that that day had arrived.

He had secreted a half-billion rubles in various paper and metal assets in a dozen different banks under a dozen different names, distributed so that no single deposit was large enough to draw unpleasant attention. But . . . there were limits.

And that damned blog post had brought him perilously close to one such limit. It was easy to deflect some of it as simply Internet rantings, but he knew that Nabokov family alliances cultivated since the last czar now teetered at the edge of disaster. He had been warned, sternly but indirectly by allies in high places, to conclude his extracurricular activities.

The next warning would be a knock in the night.

But if Hammad knew that Fiodor was leaving the business, he might value the Russian less highly. Which could lead to him deciding to default on the current payment, or perhaps even put a bullet behind Fiodor's ear. Which would lead swiftly to his own demise, of course. But Hammad might be egotistical enough to believe he could survive the retaliation. Which he wouldn't. But people had miscalculated before. Millions of them, in fact, and Fiodor was in no hurry to join the long, marching line of the dead ones.

None of these thoughts showed on his face. His smile was welcoming. "So. I understand that we have a gap of some twelve million rubles in the deal."

"My people will go to ninety, and no higher."

"Our price is reasonable. Such things cannot be purchased on the Amazon."

"The price is too high, my friend. Seven million euros is the extent of . . ."

Fiodor missed the last words. A flash of light crashed through his head, and the world went white. His calves bunched with sudden violence. Their twitching had nagged him for the last few minutes and he'd hoped to shake it off, finish his business and get to his masseuse. But this was no twitch. It was more like a bite from an angry rottweiler.

"Excuse me. Is something the matter?" Hammad's flat, battered face was solicitous, but between jolts of pain Fiodor detected a bit of the younger man's contempt for age.

"I am fine," Fiodor said. But . . . suddenly, he wasn't fine at all. He felt something like a thousand knives flaying his skin and splitting muscle to expose the anguished nerves. A brief thought: *I am betrayed!* A microwave device, triggering an epileptic fit. He had heard rumors of such things. The MVD had found him out . . . No! Hammad had somehow poisoned him. Fear and hate and surprise all rose up at the same time, and he screamed,

"It's a trap! Kill them—" before his teeth clamped down, severing his tongue and filling his mouth with blood.

The bodyguards on either side hesitated long enough to draw two breaths, and then bullets ripped through the warehouse walls, sending splintered wood and feathers whirring into the air.

"Stop! Stop!" someone screamed, and by some miracle, they did.

Hammad was down, and so was Fiodor. There remained no one to pay them. But there was a difference: Hammad had been shot just above the right ear. Fiodor Nabokov was curled onto his side, twitching, staring. He grunted and drooled blood, arms and torso knotted horribly, like a yogi attempting to commit suicide by contortion.

Incongruously, one of Hammad's bodyguards crossed himself. One of Nabokov's bodyguards put a bullet between his boss's eyes.

"I don't know what happened here," he said. "But it seems we have lost our employers."

"I only kill for money," the other team leader said. They eyed each other warily.

The second man nodded. "Professional courtesy," he said. And the two teams backed out of the warehouse, eyes upon each other, weapons tilted at the ground, the corpses of their former employers sprawled upon the floor.

◆　◆　◆

The bodies were discovered ninety minutes later, after neighbors reported gunfire in the warehouse. Within five hours the news reached ITAR-TASS, the Russian news agency, and had passed to CNS's stringer three hours later. Someone connected the name with that Indonesian blog, leading to the first documented usage of the phrase "the Dead List." Up until this discovery the list had been an uneasy joke, but reporters began combing the world for news of deaths under similar circumstances. None could be found, but the assumption remained that somewhere, another victim was curled onto his side in some dark place, bleeding from mouth and anus, every bone in his body broken.

And the first headline appeared on the *Huffington Post,* and three other blogs: "Death List Terrifies World Leaders."

"United Nations Crisis Summit."

And inevitably . . .

"End of the World?"

CHAPTER 10

♦

The house had been built in 1874, a six-bedroom castle on the estate of a more imposing structure damaged in some forgotten battle. The larger building no longer existed, but the smaller had been converted and refashioned with modern materials, so that by 2014 it was the most expensive dwelling for a hundred kilometers, a hybrid of stone and glass and concrete. It was the property of Thor Swenson, publicly an industrialist with many interests, and privately the largest arms dealer in Sweden.

At the moment, Swenson was finishing an excellent open-faced *smörgås* sandwich with cucumber and *nötkött*. Their cook's special blend of muesli was excellent as always, a delicate combination of flakes, grains, dried fruits, and *filmjölk* soured yogurt, a treat to his palate since childhood.

His beautiful wife, Frieda, and his daughter, Inga, watching him, Thor dabbed his napkin against his lips, kissed Frieda's pink mouth and his daughter's cool forehead, and plucked his briefcase from the chair as he headed out of the house.

He paused on the front steps. His castle perched on the edge of Rivö Fjord, spectacular in the depths of its blue waters glittering in the morning mist. The legendary warrior Beowulf was said to have made his home here, and Swenson could understand why. This was a place for heroes.

"I'll have to work late tonight," he said.

If he had looked carefully, or at all, he might have seen a thin sheen of ice in Frieda's eyes, swiftly thawed. "I know, Thor. But try to make it to the recital. Inga sees the empty chair."

"I will do my best."

Little Inga's warm blue eyes gazed up at him. "You'll try, Papa?" The recital, yes, and after, her bedtime reading of *The Return of the King*. A favorite.

"Of course." He ruffled her hair fondly, and picked his way down the steps, the ridged gum soles of his Hasbeens loafers stabilizing him upon the morning ice.

The car waiting for him was not ostentatious. A Volvo S60 Polestar, although he could easily have afforded any production automobile in the world. But a Lamborghini Veneno Roadster or Bugatti Veyron Grand Sport Vitesse would have violated his desire to maintain a low public profile. Something that damned blog listing had violated.

His executive assistant, Greta Olson, moved over into the passenger seat as she always did. She was more spectacular than the car itself, a sun-haired, perfectly coiffed, and aerobicized Valkyrie in a Caracina suit.

He was somewhat surprised to see her. Usually an office chauffeur was assigned to pick him up. "Greta?" he asked. "You are here in person, so I assume there is something important."

She nodded. "Too important for even a scrambled line, yes. I received by courier the acceptance of terms. Even as we speak, our Russian friend is completing the negotiations."

"This is good," Swenson said.

"Thor . . . have we made the usual arrangements?"

Even alone in the car, Greta tended to speak obliquely. "The usual arrangements" generally involved an exchange of keys or codes, a slip of paper detailing the location of a warehouse, and a message to intermediaries to finalize delivery.

"No. I knew that they would come to terms. The weapons have already arrived. All I need do is tell them where they can be retrieved."

Greta's perfectly symmetrical face glowed. "Thor . . . that is brilliant. There are so very many reasons we work well together." Her hand glided up his thigh.

Swenson felt himself respond, then remembered the slippery roads. He had traveled them since childhood but in driving, as in running a multinational concern, there was no substitute for a strong and mindful hand upon the wheel. "I must keep my eyes on the road."

"Please do," she murmured.

She slid her head down into his lap and unzipped his pants. At first he was nervous, then gave himself over to the sensation as her hands, and then her lips, embraced him. "Greta. I . . . oh, God . . ." He kept his eyes on the road, but his fingers tousled her hair.

Her only reply was a deeply felt "*Mmm.*"

Swenson groaned, fingers tightening upon the wheel, his eyes fighting not to roll up into his pleasure place. Then . . . his hands convulsed so tightly he felt his knuckles crack. The contraction eased. Something was terribly wrong, but . . .

"*Mmm.*"

"Something is wrong, Greta. Please . . ." He managed to get that out, but pain shot up his neck. His spine. His chest felt as if one of Tolkien's *oliphaunts* was squatting upon it.

Perhaps understandably, Greta mistook his fear and pain for rising passion, responding with an eager "*Mmm.*"

"Greta!" he managed to shriek before his throat closed.

Now, finally, she looked up, her lipstick smeared, suddenly terrified as the tires broke traction with the road and slewed from side to side. Swenson fought the desperate urge to clasp both hands to his temples as the car swerved on the ice.

Greta tried to wrest the steering wheel away from him but his fingers were locked on the wheel as if they'd been welded in place. Beneath her hands, his muscles first writhed like snakes, then suddenly set concrete-hard. He juddered in his seat, eyes wide, so wide that under other circumstances it might have seemed comical.

The car swerved left . . . directly into the path of an oncoming truck. The impact was catastrophic, a combined force of thirty thousand kilos moving at a combined speed of over a hundred kilometers an hour.

The engineering marvel that was the "safest car in the world" absorbed enough of the shock to protect the passenger compartment, but traction with the road became as mythic as Beowulf's encounter with the monster Grendel. The car pinwheeled and hit the side barrier, flipping over and plunging a hundred meters into the water below.

Above them, cars pulled to the side of the road, pale frightened faces gazing down into the conflagration as the Volvo, upside down, settled into the freezing waters and sank.

We are ever becoming, until the Seeker suddenly "is not." And then we have become.

—Savagi, *Transformations*

"Explain," said the student, "the beings known as Shiva and Shakti, and the significance of their union."

"Shiva-Shakti," said Savagi, "represent the male and female energies that have created, and sustain, the universe."

"What then of Yama and Kali?"

"Yama-Kali," replied Savagi, "are the reflections of Shiva-Shakti in space time, which manifest in death and destruction, yet at the same time represent liberation."

"But I do not understand," the student said. "I have studied, and the sages say that Shiva is one aspect of Trimurti (Brahma-Vishnu-Shiva; creations, sustenance, and destruction). How can Yama, who is the child of Suriya the sun god, be Shiva?"

And the master said: "While we make myths to explain that which we do not understand, what we perceive as gods are merely impingements of the one reality into the realm of samsara, the earthly realm of reincarnation. In truth, there is only Shiva-Shakti, and the prime reflection of that in this world is Yama-Kali."

—Dialogue from Savagi's *Transformations*

CHAPTER 11

♦

Terry managed to score the last parking space outside the Golden Dream center, and was grateful to do so. He was surprised by the center's size. In fact, he had shopped at the Best Buy electronics store in the same complex a dozen times without the slightest awareness that anything like a Golden Dream was located in the back.

He was greeted at the door by a wispy guy in a gold-fringed karate outfit. The name MR. LING was embroidered on the uniform. Ling looked fit enough, but his hands were soft, and he greeted the attendees with a New Age earnestness that made Terry want to throw up in his own mouth, just a little.

Three rows of folding chairs had been set up around the edge of a forty-by-fifty-foot patchwork of blue and red squares. The room was packed. Olympia and Hannibal were seated in the front row, watching a dozen students perform flowing, acrobatic, aikido-style breakfalls as part of their warm-up routine.

Hannibal waved at him as he entered, and patted the seat next to him, again surprising Terry at his ability to express himself . . . at certain times.

"Hey, champ," he said. Then added: "O."

" 'Erry," Hani said, smiling broadly, rocking and staring out at the mat. Olympia inclined her head, but seemed to be hypnotized by all the leaping about.

"Take positions!" another man in a uniform barked.

The students lined up in neat rows of seated meditation positions. *Seiza,* it was called.

"Sorry I'm late. Did I miss anything?"

"No, they're just getting ready." Was she blushing? Just a little?

"*Ukemi* breakfalls and so forth? That's pretty standard stuff."

She seemed to avoid his question. "What do you think of the school?"

He scanned the collection of varied weapons on the wall. They included the usual Chinese and Japanese replicas, but also included Filipino, Indonesian, and Turkish implements, all accompanied by images of various masters posing and fighting in flowing postures. All so artistically arrayed that the impression was aesthetic rather than strictly martial. "Eclectic," he said. "Japanese katana, Filipino kali fighting sticks, Chinese triple irons . . ."

"Is that bad?"

He shrugged. "Well, usually that means wide but not deep. Kinda like me. We'll see."

Terry hadn't noticed, but the New Age type in the gold-edged uniform had been hovering close behind him, and now strode toward the front of the school.

"Welcome," the uniformed, smooth-shaven man said to the crowd. "My name is Marshall Ling, head instructor here at Golden Dream. As one of our guests so perceptively commented, we are an eclectic school, drawing from many martial-arts traditions under the leadership of the honorable Madame Gupta. Before we begin, have you any questions?"

A lady with long braided hair and a tie-dyed purple sheath dress raised her hand.

"Yes?" Ling asked.

"I came to see Madame Gupta, but I have to admit that this"—she gestured at the walls—"violence seems contrary to her gospel of peace."

Ling smiled warmly. "I grasp the implied question—"

"*Life respects not weakness. Only strength can protect gentleness.*" The voice seemed to float from all four walls at the same time.

And then . . . an Easter Island statue walked into the room.

At least, that was Terry's peripheral impression. From the corner of his eye, he thought he saw something bizarre: a giant head atop a human body, somehow gliding across the mat.

He turned to look. For a moment his vision blurred, and the illusion persisted. But he blinked, and that impression melted away. The newcomer was merely a slender brown woman entering from the back room. True, she wore a golden robe more ornate than the typical karate uniform, but that was the extent of the oddness.

He shook his head. The visual hallucination had been freakin' weird. He turned to speak to Olympia, was distracted a moment by Hani's grin . . .

And experienced the same peripheral hallucination again. A gigantic block of carved . . . stone, perhaps. An expression humorless, inhuman, disconnected. No feet or legs or even body. Just . . . that head.

But only in his peripheral vision. When he turned again, it was just the slender brown woman. Smiling. Warm.

Wow. He was having a senior moment, about thirty years too soon. Bizarre.

The crowd stirred. All eyes were upon her. Her hair was tied in a bun at the back of her head, but he thought that flowing free, she would prove a woman of extraordinary beauty. How old was she? Her sixties? No, couldn't be. Fifties? At least. But her face was unlined. Her skin was smooth and unblemished. Her body was that of a dancer in her prime. Unbelievable.

Oddly, it seemed to Terry that she moved almost as if she didn't live entirely within her body, as if she were outside it, manipulating herself with strings, a marionette of flesh and blood. Bizarre: he had expected someone who moved like a panther. Just to test, he turned his head sideways and looked at her through his peripheral vision. This time, nothing. Strange.

"Master," Ling said, and bowed. She returned it, her answering gesture smooth but not quite as deep.

"The world," she said, her voice light and strong, "is on the cusp of change. Only the Awakened will make this passage without fear. Without anxiety. Mastering the body opens the door to the heart and mind. Only the ignorant believe these aspects can be tamed separately." The voice was hard to place, melodic but lacking enough inflection to identify a country of origin.

She gestured to the line of kneeling students awaiting her signal. And then . . . the students attacked. They charged in waves, with more determination, variety, and vigor than Terry expected, with no apparent compromise in consideration of her age or gender. Gupta's hands blurred like the blades of a fan as she performed perfect wrist locks and aikido-style deflections and redirections, slamming them to the mat again and again. They bounced up like rubber balls and ran back at her as if she were feeding them energy.

And as she did, amazingly, she continued to speak. Her whirling footwork had no apparent effect on her breathing patterns. He could detect no gasping or straining for breath as she blocked, ducked, or deflected. "In most instances it is not necessary to cause harm, even when one defends. But if harm is necessary, remember the words Lord Krishna spake to Arjuna: '*We must do our duty. If necessary, this may extend to the taking of life, and if so, it must be done with regret, but clarity.*' "

This was followed by another series of student attacks. This time, she punctuated with mimed, whip-quick, and perfectly positioned kicks, chops, and elbows. Awesome focus. She actually seemed to be touching them, but Terry detected no pain reactions at all. Terry felt a grin stretch his cheeks. Madame Gupta's movement was Shaolin-level at the very least. This was extraordinary.

The little woman continued in that fashion, performing astonishing feats of martial precision and acrobatics. Either she was extraordinarily conditioned . . . or something else. Something he had never witnessed, or considered. His heartbeat sped, and he felt a general flush, something that balanced on the edge of sexual excitation. He shifted in his seat, glad that he was wearing loose pants.

"Do not be deceived by the external form of the motion. It is the emotional intent to which I respond." She was speaking without paying any apparent attention to her attackers. Responding instantly, like a mass responding to the pull of gravity, no more "technique" than what water uses to flow through a hole in a bucket.

A masterful display. And what was more, every now and then she interjected little flourishes with her shoulders or hips, like a teenaged female gymnast flirting with the judges and audience.

When Terry finally glanced back up at the clock, almost an hour had passed. He was baffled: time had just melted away. For someone to pull him into that sort of deep flow so effortlessly was stunning. He glanced at Olympia: she was engaged, but little Hani was hypnotized, so fascinated Terry was afraid he might forget to breathe.

Madame Gupta's demonstration flowed on, until the students were drenched with sweat. But even as the windows became clouded with steam, the woman herself barely glowed. Now she wielded a wooden sword against two similarly armed men. With little apparent effort but no sign of choreography she disarmed both with wrist-twists and staccato sword-jabs to solar plexus or side of knee, following with spiraling throws that sent them corkscrewing through the air to *woof* into the mats. The students grinned as they rolled and bounced happily to their feet, smiling like children returning from a dessert buffet.

Olympia leaned over and whispered, "Is she good?"

His response was rapid and certain. "I might know of three people who can do what she just did." *And none of them would look that fine doing it.* He kept that last part to himself. There was no denying the truth: he was responding to this woman physically, and had no idea how to interpret that. Wasn't she too old? Or too spiritual? Or something? Was it blasphemous to wonder what she looked like under that *gi*? "Good doesn't begin to cover it."

His eyes had never left the enchantress on the mat.

"There are times when one must stand against many," she said. "Even then, it is possible to preserve life. Please . . . silence while I gather the proper energies." She stood with palms pressed together, eyes closed, back arched a bit. Then finally she opened them again.

A whisper that carried like a shout: "Begin."

All five students attacked simultaneously. She flowed among them like smoke. While blur-fast and focused intensely, their punches and kicks and grabs missed her without the slightest apparent effort on her part at blocking or evasion. She left them sprawled variously on the mat, streaming sweat and huffing for breath, while she remained miraculously unfazed.

Something changed inside Terry, as if he'd passed some internal threshold of acceptance. Or gullibility. It was just too much. He was watching some impossibly well-choreographed demonstration. It simply had to be fake. *Oh, please. This is bullshit,* he could hear the voice in his head whisper.

"Wow," Olympia said.

"Maybe," he whispered, both heartened by and annoyed with his own cynicism. "It's easy to get your own students to lay down for you."

He'd have sworn his words couldn't be heard three paces away, but although Madame Gupta was across the room, she stopped dead. Turned slowly, as if her head were mounted on a pivot, her face divided by a broad, almost reptilian grin. For just a moment, there was something carnivorous and primal about her . . . then that visage changed, and she was once again the friendly, charismatic, disorienting mixture of maternal and what . . . seductive? She gazed around the room, as if looking to see who had said that, even though he had spoken in low tones.

She locked gazes with Terry, and he didn't blink. He noticed something slightly odd, as if the lights in the room were reflecting from her body and face, radiating a low-level luminescence. "Doubters will always be among us. You, sir. Have we met?"

"Ah . . . no?" Damn it, where had that question mark come from? And that cracked voice! It was an adolescent voice, a *caught with his hand in the cookie jar* voice, an *I'll get my first pube any day now* voice. He was totally off balance emotionally.

In the instant he had lost himself in his internal monologue, she had crossed the mat, and stood beside him. "You have trained extensively." She glanced at his hands, his shoulders, his seated posture. "Tae kwon do, kali, kenpo, I believe. The Hawaiian variant."

"Yes . . ." He turned to Olympia. "You tell her about me?"

She shook her head. "No. Never met her. Terry, I didn't know that stuff about you."

"What we are is revealed to those with eyes to see," Madame Gupta said. "When opportunity presents, it is my habit to invite a skilled practitioner from the audience. Would you care to engage in a little wager?"

"A bet? What kind?"

"A hundred dollars, if you can land a kick or punch on me within two minutes."

Confusion threatened to turn to outright disconcertment. "You mean your head or torso?"

"Anywhere at all."

"And what will you do?"

"Touch you, five separate times, with my hand."

That just seemed weird. Was this some kind of hidden camera stunt? No matter how good she was—and she was amazing—that simply didn't make sense. "A hundred bucks. Even-Steven?"

"I don't understand the term." Her brown face crinkled in confusion.

He found that response comforting. Omniscient she was not. "Straight bet. I touch you, I win your money. I don't, I pay you the same amount?"

Her little brown eyes crinkled. "I don't want your money," she said.

"What, then?"

"We talk, you and I. After the others are gone." His heartbeat began to increase. Well, hell, he'd like to talk with her, too. Preferably alone.

Terry tried to find the flaw in her proposition, and crapped out. "And the trick is?"

"No trick," the little woman said. "I find you . . . of interest."

Terry smiled. Was she teasing him? "Land a punch or kick. Will I have to chase you around the mat?"

"No," Madame Gupta said. "I will remain at arm's length."

Tingling all over, Terry peeled off his jacket. "Sounds like fun. Let's do this." He slipped off his loafers.

He glanced back: Hannibal was glowing, bouncing up and down in his seat like a vibrating chipmunk. Olympia stared, seemingly both shocked and thrilled. He liked that. Almost enough to distract him from wondering just how bruised he was going to be in about a hundred and twenty seconds.

Yerch.

Something about Gupta's manner unnerved him more than he cared to admit. But before he could say anything about it, she spoke again.

"And no, you will not be injured." A sweet little girl's smile. A *Hi, my name is Becky Thatcher, wanna swing with me, Tom?* smile.

"I'm not worried," he lied.

Gupta chuckled as if they shared a private joke.

Damn.

Feeling as if he had just stepped off a roller coaster, Terry walked out onto the mat. He stretched briefly, dynamically, long-lever leg raises to the front and side, then threw a couple of crackling kicks to get the dust out . . . and then faced Gupta, whose smile had not wavered. Ordinarily, his display of ready flexibility elicited *oohs* and *ahhs* from a first-time audience. Not this time. They were silent, expectant.

"Shall we begin?" she asked.

"Wouldn't miss this for the world."

He glanced at Olympia and Hannibal, both leaning forward in rapt attention.

Madame Gupta stood quietly, waiting. Terry edged in, faked right, then shifted left and whipped a blur-fast round kick with his left leg, aiming at her right shoulder. No need to hurt her . . .

Gupta leaned out of the way so that the kick missed her by a half-inch. And suddenly she was *behind* Terry, and her cool, soft palm caressed his cheek.

"One," she said.

Terry's eyes narrowed. He dove at Gupta with a series of fast reverse punches, the Asian version of right and left crosses, driving off the rear leg. She moved directly backward, as if she had a third eye concealed by the tightly curled black hair at the nape of her neck. Then she crouched, and Terry stumbled over her, hitting the mat in a rolling breakfall, pivoting—and Gupta's cool, moist palm was touching his forehead.

"Two." Her eyes were not those of a fifty-year-old. Or forty, or even thirty. She was more like a mischievous urchin.

"Shit." Terry dropped into a series of spinning sweeps, low to the floor. Gupta vaulted him, an actual somersault, an acrobatic clown trick, one hand pushing off on his shoulder.

And stuck the landing, perfectly. "Three."

"What the hell . . . ?" He dove into a leaping kick. A lunging punch. A spinning attack, a blur of back knuckles, kicks, sweeps.

A smiling ghost, Gupta appeared to melt away before Terry, as if slithering in and out of his blind spots. She was right there, right in front of him, but Terry couldn't hit her, couldn't touch her. He stomped down on his frustration and increased his pace again and again, until she blurred into some kind of movement his mind couldn't quite make sense of. How the hell do you cartwheel between someone's legs . . . ?

Then she was on his back, riding him like a cowboy. He fell to his knees as Gupta's slender brown fingers sank into the places in his shoulders where muscles met bone, freezing him for a moment with what felt like electric shock. She touched Terry's forehead with her palm.

"Five," she said.

Terry blinked. "What was four?"

"Is this yours?" She handed Terry his brown leather belt. Terry looked down at his sagging pants, chagrined, and retrieved it. He stood, anger swelling . . . and then bursting like a punctured balloon.

"I'll be dipped in shit," he said, and bowed. The audience applauded wildly. And Terry's was loudest of all.

CHAPTER 12

Demo completed, the subsequent Q & A session began. Olympia, still stunned into silence by what she had seen, felt her mind race with a thousand questions: *who are you? Where did you learn to do that? Am I dreaming?* But none of them made it all the way to lips and voice. The audience bubbled with questions, but most of them were either too mundane or too esoteric. All of hers connected in a single desperate query: *can you help my son?*

She knew she could conjure nothing meaningful and specific, and assumed much of the audience was having the same reaction. None of their questions were remarkable, either.

The session's final exchange was the most useful, and honest. A man in farmer overalls asked: "How can you do things like that? This was amazing!"

"To be honest," Gupta replied, her childlike smile radiating warmth, "it's rather amazing to me as well. But in partial answer, I offer you a quote from the *Spanda Karika,* verse thirty-eight:

"'*Through merging with* Spanda, *the universal vibration, the yogi, though apparently weak manifests the power to accomplish what is needed. Even without food, she is nourished.*'"

She giggled. "And that reminds me that it is dinnertime. Go, and be nourished. Blessings." She pressed her palms together, raised them to her forehead, and bowed respectfully. "I'd like to close our session with the Sanskrit expression that means 'the divinity within me salutes and acknowledges the divinity within each and every one of you.' Namaste."

Murmuring "Namaste" in return, but shaking their heads in astonishment and appreciation, the audience filed out. A few of them slapped Terry on the back, part admiration, part consolation. Blood roared in Olympia's head, and all she knew was that a voice hammered at her: *you must meet this woman. You have to find a way to catch her interest. Maybe you could tell her you're from CNS, and think they should do a segment on her. That might work . . .*

To Olympia, Terry seemed thoughtful, confused . . . somehow younger than he had been an hour before. Like he'd had some of what Nicki called his *swagg* knocked out of him.

Was it wrong of her to enjoy that?

"Thank you for inviting me. This has been fascinating," he said.

"Are you staying?" Olympia asked. Gupta wanted to talk to Terry. Could she and Hannibal piggyback on that? She could sure as hell try.

He snorted. "Wouldn't you?"

Madame Gupta approached them. "Please. Come to my office." When Olympia hesitated, Gupta clarified. "Please. All of you."

Problem solved.

The three followed the little woman down a narrow corridor. Olympia had interviewed professional athletes, dancers, and a tai chi master from Taiwan. Gupta didn't move like they did. She wasn't controlled, trained, sculpted. In fact, when first entering the room, she hadn't seemed particularly graceful. This was something else. Something simultaneously animalistic and angelic. Again, Olympia had that momentary impression of a giant compressed into a tiny body.

She'd had that impression before with other short, charismatic people. Hell, she'd stood in line for an hour to have science-fiction titan Harlan Ellison sign an ancient copy of *The Beast That Shouted Love at the Heart of the World* and gotten that impression. But this was far more intense.

Olympia turned right and entered an office with a frosted glass door marked DIRECTOR. There, three leather-upholstered chairs had been set before a simple wooden desk. The walls were covered with plaques and photos of various notables posing with Madame Gupta: governors, sports figures, chamber of commerce types. Dwayne "The Rock" Johnson, hugging her and giving a thumbs-up. Clasping hands with an aged, bent, but unbroken Billy Graham. A picture of her under some kind of enormous barbell in a ceiling harness. Thousands of pounds, and she was clearly lifting it at least an inch off the rig. Amazing.

Terry and Olympia sat, Hannibal sandwiched between them. Hani was rocking back and forth, "stemming" hard.

Madame Gupta's head tilted slightly to the side. "You are not . . . a family."

"No," Olympia said, and hoped she hadn't said it too quickly. Sharply.

"But you have been . . . together."

Olympia felt a flash of heat. "That's personal . . ."

Terry's brows drew together. "How do you know that?"

"I have eyes," the little brown woman said slyly. "Well, Olympia . . . that is your name?"

"Yes."

"You have a very unusual boy," she said. "Have you ever heard the term 'indigo child'?"

Olympia felt a moment's familiar irritation at a label, any label, swiftly calmed. "Mr. Ling used it, yes."

"What it means," Gupta said, "from the perspective of our philosophy, is a child whose energy has been knotted. Trapped. I believe that we can help him."

"What is it you think you can do?" Olympia asked, her throat tight.

"More testing could be required. Would you be willing to come to our center for this purpose?"

"In the Georgia mountains?"

The little woman smiled. "We would provide transportation."

"Why?"

"It is a joy to serve those receptive of service," Gupta said. "Will you allow me to give your son a gift?"

There it was, hanging suspended in the air. Olympia turned to look at Terry.

He shrugged.

"Yes," Olympia finally said. "Can you help him?" It seemed absurd to ask, but she just couldn't help it.

"Yes," Gupta replied. "But to do this, I must speak to both of you."

She waited, and miraculously, Hani raised his face, until he gazed only a little to Gupta's side, almost meeting her eyes.

"When I was a girl," Gupta began, her voice so singsongy that it was almost like a lullaby, "my father had many occupations. Once, he was a fisherman. He used fishing lines, and he used nets. And the whole family helped, and the way I helped was untangling the nets and the lines. You see, sometimes the lines broke, and we had to tie them together with special knots. And sometimes the nets tore, and it was our responsibility to mend them. But what we always knew was that no matter how tangled everything was, we had more line, more net than we actually needed. Enough to be able to throw away anything that was damaged, and still have enough left to weave a new net or make a new line. Snip, untangle, knot, weave . . . and we could do it so well that you couldn't see that there had ever been a break."

Her voice was calm, smooth, loving, healing. She watched Hani relax, almost as if he was asleep sitting up. Swaying very slightly to and fro, to and fro . . .

"And you know how I'd do it, Hani?"

"No," he said. He'd answered her! Olympia couldn't believe it.

Madame Gupta leaned close to Hannibal, close enough to whisper in his ear.

"Feel your heartbeat," she said.

"He may not be able to follow you," Olympia said.

But even as she spoke, she saw that Hani's constant movement had stopped. His "stemming," his constant soothing rocking motion, had ceased, and the swing of his foot slowed to a bare pulse. He was as still as the pause between two heartbeats.

Madame Gupta paid no attention to what Olympia had said. "In your heart lies the path where we will walk together. Can you hear me?"

He nodded his head.

"There is light inside you," she said. "Perhaps like a spray of mist. Squeeze it down into a more solid, brighter ball."

Odd. Olympia closed her own eyes for a moment, and in the darkness danced a glowing sphere.

"I would imagine I was small enough to crawl inside the ball. Surrounded by light. And I could go even deeper, where it is brighter and more beautiful. And I could see all the different parts of myself, and if they are separated and want to be together I can connect them, in any way they want to be connected, and everything is good."

Hani's respiration had slowed. He barely seemed to be breathing at all. Madame Gupta's hands rested on his chest, and on his back, sandwiching him between her palms. "All I had to do was know what a good net looked like. Feels like. Know what an untangled line looked like. Feels like. And I could just find anything that looked like that, and save it until I found another piece, and another. And save them all together. Because we had a lot more net than we needed. And even if there was damaged net, there were other nets that were healthy. That was the way nets are made."

Hani's eyes closed.

"But what we need to do is store up enough water to flow through the lines. And that means damming it. Not like a bad word . . ." She chuckled.

"Like a beaver," Hani murmured.

Oh, God! Her boy had responded again! Two miracles in a single evening.

"Yes!" Gupta said, delighted. "Like a beaver! What a good, good boy!" She rubbed his hair, and instead of flinching away, he beamed.

"Holding the water back," she went on. "And then when you finally let it out it has so much power. So that's what I want. I want you to store up your energy until I tell you to let it go. Every breath. Every motion. Every step, a little of your energy is stored up and away. Until it gets so big, so wonderfully powerful that it breaks through any barrier.

"This is just for you, Hani. Breaking through that wall. There is another thing I want you to see. Imagine a control panel. It is covered with switches and dials. This is your mind, your wonderful, wonderful mind. And up until now, the dials have all been turned up to eleven. Because of that, your only choice was to wear earmuffs, shutting everything out.

"But if we can turn it down, then you can take the muffs off. If it isn't so loud, you don't have to be afraid. It won't hurt. So imagine if nothing hurt. Imagine if all the wiring and netting was untangled. Imagine if you had control, could turn everything up or down . . ."

And she went on, speaking of control. And power building up and being released. And as she did she touched him, at the top of his head, on his chest, making odd rubbing and tapping motions, almost like a doctor checking the pulmonary cavity, or a plumber tapping a pipe seeking leaks or obstructions.

Olympia blinked herself awake. The voice, slow and smooth, had droned on until she lost track. She hadn't even realized she'd closed her eyes, or drifted away. Hani sat quietly, a model of relaxed attention.

Madame Gupta smiled at her. "We're done," she said.

"What now?" Olympia asked.

"Now . . . we wait. You should start seeing some results very soon. But this is just a beginning, enough to gain momentum. There is much more to do."

◆ ◆ ◆

She turned to Terry, and the impact of her attention felt like someone slapping his forehead. "Have we met, you and I?"

"No," he said. "But I attended a school run by one of your devotees, a guy named Marshall Weaver."

"Oh my." She chuckled. "Mr. Weaver. When was this?"

"Over twenty-five years ago," he said, memory flashing back. A white-fronted school sandwiched between a dry cleaner and a sandwich shop. White mats and mirrored walls, photos of stern, unsmiling Asians and a tall, smiling man who promised to teach the secrets of strength. "I was thirteen years old. A tae kwon do school in Dallas."

"Yes." She closed her eyes for a moment. "Weaver. I'm afraid he was not so advanced as he imagined. How long did you train there?"

"Two years," he said. "I saw you once."

"At a graduation ceremony. You were in the black belt program."

"Yes."

She nodded. "I see." Against reason, he was certain she now remembered him.

Gupta stood up, prowled around Terry as languidly as a curious wolf. "What is it?"

"You left that school," she said. "Before your graduation exercises, didn't you?"

Terry nodded again. "We had to move. I was an army brat, and my dad was constantly shuffled from one base to another."

"That . . . is unfortunate."

"Why?"

She ignored the question. "And since that time, you have studied many styles, and worked very hard, and never gotten the results you hoped for."

Was he that transparent? "No. Never. But . . ."

Madame Gupta's eyes fell. "I am afraid that I should apologize to you."

"Apologize? For what?"

"That program was experimental," she said. "We were evaluating an advanced technique taught in Savagi's book *Transformations*."

Terry brightened. For some reason, he had refrained from mentioning the name he remembered so well. "What was it?"

"I think it would be called a 'kundalini trap,' a sort of collection point for techniques in your unconscious mind."

"'Kundalini'?" Olympia asked. "What is that?"

Terry felt a flash of irritation at Olympia's voice. This was *his* time. It felt as if his entire life had been leading to this single moment.

Gupta smiled. "It is a Sanskrit term. The spiritual evolutionary force in human beings, resulting from balancing the male and female aspects of our psyches."

"So a 'kundalini trap' would be . . . ?"

"A meditative technique, implanted by hypnosis, meditation, or psychological domination by a true master. It creates a 'dam' that stores up spiritual force, or emotional energy, like compressing a spring. It compresses until it has grown sufficiently powerful to be turned against a specific personality block, or a 'kink' in the wiring. One finds similar concepts in spiritual and psychological disciplines from Sufism's '*nafs*' to Scientology's 'engrams.' The 'kundalini trap' is a conceptual structure designed to accelerate learning." She paused. "Unfortunately, if not removed, they may turn into what you might term a bottleneck."

The simplicity of the concept stunned him. And made too much damned sense when he thought back over his own life. What was it? Six brown belts, but no black? Two broken marriages? His inability to completely accept the moral responsibilities of his military service?

God, once he started thinking about it, there was no stopping. "That would explain—"

Madame Gupta burst in excitedly, interrupting. "This presents us with a unique opportunity. You are a quite unusual case. To illuminate through analogy, what happened to you was an artificial version of what happened to young Hannibal."

"Hannibal!" the boy said. Olympia hugged him again, dizzy with joy.

"Yes. Of course he knows his name. Some doctors say he is insufficiently aware. But that is incorrect. He is *too* aware. The world is too intense, so he screens it out, all but the fraction he chooses to deal with. He likely has an extreme fantasy life. An electrician might say he's tripped a circuit breaker. But that very hyper-acuity is a blessing, if we can find the right way to help him. It's all in there, waiting to be released. As all your skills, your true potential, lie dormant within you, Terry, awaiting your command."

Her way of speaking was eerily hypnotic. Terry felt himself swaying, then shaking his head to clear it.

"So for you, Terry, a release from the trap. For Hannibal, we build a protective fortress. The 'circuit breaker' analogy is powerful but imprecise. The limitations of language, unfortunately. In a broad sense, we control him in order to set him free."

"Released!" Hannibal said. Olympia looked like she wanted to swoon.

Olympia hugged her boy again. "He rarely talks. Sometimes he sings. It's . . . confusing."

"It won't be. Not for much longer. This is not an accident. It is not coincidence that brought us all together. I wish to give your son a gift. And this man, if he agrees, will be evidence that my intentions are trustworthy, my methods sound."

"Me?"

"Yes. Think of a dam, holding back a massive reservoir. No matter the rain or snowmelt, it seems there is no water, because you cannot see beyond the wall."

"But it's there?" Terry was dismayed by the plea creeping into his voice. Hope could be a terrible thing. And he didn't want Olympia to think he had come to help himself, not Hannibal.

"All there," Madame Gupta said. "Uniquely . . . there. You are a competent martial artist . . ."

Competent. The term "damning with faint praise" came to mind.

". . . but you could be brilliant, if only your years of work could be unleashed. Integrated. Are you willing?"

Brilliant? Well, he liked the sound of *that*. "Willing?" Along with everything else, the woman possessed a serious talent for understatement. "What do you want me to do?"

"Trust me."

Terry checked internally for about a millionth of a second, discovering to no surprise that yes, he yearned to do exactly that. That some part of him hungered for surrender. "I guess that sounds pretty damned good."

"Close your eyes," she said.

Gupta rose from her chair, and walked around behind him. She inhaled. "Listen to your heartbeat."

Terry closed his eyes. As she continued to speak, her voice seemed to retreat, as if the room had expanded into an echo chamber. He touched his right fingers to the pulse point of his left wrist. Found his heartbeat, a steady, comforting *tha-dump tha-dump*.

"Visualize a light in the middle of the darkness, and allow it to beat along with the life within your heart."

"Yes."

"Good," she said. "Now. Allow the light within the darkness to collect."

"Into what?"

"A child. The youngest 'you' with which you can make contact. Create a child of living light."

Child? He thought he would create a teenager, but there wasn't enough light for that. Maybe sixty pounds of light. A preteen, ten-year-old Terry? No . . . less than sixty. A lot less.

There wasn't enough for a ten-year-old.

Nor a six-year-old.

What the hell? He couldn't even make a *baby*. He was on the edge of giving up, when he realized he had constructed an embryo, which now floated in the dark like a proto Star Child from *2001: A Space Odyssey*. "Yes."

"Good. Allow that child to float in the darkness, at the base of your spine. Now. Roll your eyes upward. Above you, hold the image of the greatest martial artists you have ever seen, or imagined."

A rapid succession of images: Bruce Lee, Mas Oyama, Morihei Ueshiba, Danny Inosanto . . . a series of Asians. Then a series of black and white faces: Sugar Ray Robinson. Sijo Steve Muhammad. Muhammad Ali. Bill "Superfoot" Wallace. Cliff Stewart. On and on.

And then . . . Madame Gupta.

"Yes," Terry said.

"Good. Now . . ." Gupta inhaled powerfully, set herself, rolled her eyes up, exhaled, and with flattened palm, patted Terry sharply on the top of the head.

Shockwaves, bursting in the upper darkness, rolling down his spine like a wave of fire . . .

In the darkness within Terry, light exploded in his heart. The martial images began to dissolve. The younger Terry began to ascend. Flashes of every martial arts class and style he'd ever studied, faster and faster, swirling and colliding. The "embryo" became older and older: teenaged, twenties, then the lower and higher lights collided at his heart, and the light exploded outward to fill him.

Terry's back arched, as if wracked by the mother of all orgasms. A quake originated in his feet, traveling up his ankles, through his calves and knees. He felt his buttocks tense and cramp, his pelvis thrusting until he felt like a living parenthesis. The wave transferred to his abdominal muscles and then his back, traveling up his chest and then his neck and head, as if someone had grabbed him by the toes and cracked his entire body like a slow-motion whip, again and again. His body was not his own. His hands gripped the arms of his chair, and his body contracted, stomach muscles convulsed, legs levitating from the ground, heels drumming. His body undulated, like a gymnast's "flag" position, then rippled as if animated by some primal, mindless pulse.

Then he collapsed, exhausted, and it was over.

◆ ◆ ◆

Olympia felt fascinated, terrified, and awed. Simultaneously embarrassed, as if viewing a homemade porn tape. Terry's convulsions were so amazingly, incredibly intimate that she wanted to flee the room. He tensed again and then . . . collapsed panting and gasping, so limp it appeared that someone had stolen his bones.

"This," Madame Gupta smiled, "is a fair beginning." She turned to Olympia and Hannibal, a kindly, maternal, Dr. Ruth figure. This woman was a chameleon par excellence. So many personas . . . which one was the real Madame Gupta? And could she trust someone who she could not begin to understand?

Fear, hope, and wonder warred in her heart.

"Olympia. Hannibal. I hope you will accept my invitation to continue our exploration at our sanctuary. Now . . . I will speak privately with Terry, if you don't mind."

"No. Not at all. It's Hani's bedtime." Olympia fumbled her keys from her purse, aware that she needed something to occupy her hands, to keep them from trembling.

Terry kissed Olympia's cheek, and she smelled his sweat, its scent something she remembered too vividly for comfort. Hannibal glowed up at him.

"See you later?" she asked. She hated the tremor in her voice. She knew something had happened. Just not . . . precisely what.

"If I survive, I'll be around."

Hannibal hugged him, hard. "Bye, 'Erry."

"Bye, champ."

◆   ◆   ◆

Olympia held Hani's hand as they left. The boy kept looking back at them, waving and grinning, with more eye contact than Terry had ever seen the boy make. Ever.

And then he was alone with Madame Gupta. Terry was both relieved and wanted to run out the door after O and Hani. Absurdly, something deep in his gut felt as if he had been left alone in a cage with a silky, purring leopard.

Absurd.

"You have been well trained," Madame Gupta said.

Terry laughed ruefully. "Never know it by the way you handled me."

"No fault of yours," she said.

"It was as if I was standing still."

She giggled. Again, that disorienting girlish quality. "Yes. It seemed that way, didn't it?"

A moment of silence followed. Terry suffered the void until it felt as if his scalp was frying. "What do you want from me?"

She smiled, a warm and welcoming expression. And he thought again that it was amazing that a woman in her late fifties (she had to be that, didn't she? At least?) could have a face so unlined, a body so defiant of both time and gravity. "That is, of course, exactly the wrong question."

Terry's ears buzzed, as if there were a low-level mechanical whine vibrating in the walls. "What's the right one?"

"What do you want from yourself?"

Terry fumbled for words. "What do I . . ."

She leaned forward. "Terry," she said. "Why are you pretending to be someone you are not?"

The buzz grew louder. "I don't . . ."

She raised her hand, summoning silence. "You have studied art after art, like a man consorting with courtesans rather than marrying and raising a family. Never have you gone deep enough to find the limits of your ego. You have much technique, and little wisdom."

His heart raced, and his stomach soured. This was all too much, happening too fast. "Wait just a minute . . ."

"No!" she said sharply. "Waiting is past. Your ego has limited you to those things that came easily. To your detriment, much was easy. You were too talented for your own good. When it became hard, when you were asked to go deep into your own fear and lack of clarity, when you were asked to disassemble your ego structure, tear it down to the foundations and begin anew . . . you failed the test. Your ego cocoon was too strong."

"My . . ." He shook his head, trying to clear it. "What the hell is an 'ego cocoon'?"

"Yes. Imagine a human soul born into the world. In physical form it is helpless. It must plead for everything it receives, curry favor with those who hold all the power. It defines itself in terms of the roles it learns to play, and each role: son, sibling, student, lover, worker, parent . . . is another mask, ultimately obscuring the spirit that began the journey. Any true discipline tears down the ego so that the spirit can be exposed, then the cocoon reforms according to the new needs. You were too strong to tear down, and too willful to surrender. You built one castle upon the twisted ruins of another, and that upon another, and another."

"Where does it end?" he asked. He wanted to shut her out, but couldn't. "What is 'real' about me?"

"There is a story I heard once," she said. "A scientist was giving a lecture about the solar system, and theories of gravitation. After the lecture, an old woman stood patiently in line to speak, and when she faced him, said: 'You talk very pretty, young man, but it's all nonsense, you know. The earth isn't spinning around any ball of fire. The earth rests upon the back of a giant turtle.'

"The scientist controlled his amusement, and asked: 'And what is that turtle standing upon?'

"'Another turtle,' she replied.

"'And that turtle?'

"The old woman narrowed her eyes. 'Oh, no, young man. I know what you're trying to do, and it won't work. It's turtles all the way down.'"

Terry blinked. "I don't understand."

"That's the problem you get into when your ego asks questions about its own reality. It's turtles all the way down for you, too."

Terry felt his breathing hitch, tried to summon calm. "That's not fair . . ."

She clucked. Her face softened. "It is not fair that we have so few years to live our dreams. But neither is it unfair. It just . . . is. It is not fair that you were born strong and fast, but not wise. But here we are. Because of your gifts, you could probably physically defeat men who might have mentored you to greatness, had you been able to suspend that need to be dominated. You only listen to me now because you know I can kill you, and that is a tragedy."

Some other communication was happening here. Terry started focusing on furnishings and books around the room, desperately seeking diversion, struggling like a wolf ready to chew through its own leg to escape a trap.

"And now," she continued, "and now you come here, and find yourself in my hands. You fascinate me, Terry." What in the hell was the implication there? Mother? Teacher? Lover? "You have studied . . . something . . . that stirs a memory. Of all the paths you have walked, what is the strangest? The correct, honest answer gets you everything you have ever sought."

"If . . ." He paused. "And the wrong answer?"

"And you leave here as you came. Ever . . . becoming. Never being. Isn't that what you wish, Terry Nicolas? To simply . . . be?"

To his dismay, when Terry spoke again his voice seemed . . . tiny. "Yes."

"The strangest path. You have one chance."

Terry waited a beat, as if chewing on his next breath. Then: "In 2005, a year after . . ." He paused, searching for words. "A year after some very bad things happened in a place called Fallujah, I was seconded to the CIA for nine months, and while I was, met some people familiar with something called 'Voodoo6.'"

"I have never heard this name," she said.

He hesitated, thinking over what he was about to say. Was he breaking rules? Did he give a damn anymore?

"It's what America's MK-Ultra super-brain project became after the core information was declassified. A top-secret operation correlating body-mind information from around the world. The super-soldier project. They called themselves 'Dorsai.' I don't know what that means."

"Go on."

"There was a bit of footage of a man named Adam Ludlum."

Madame Gupta's eyes narrowed. "Adam . . . Ludlum." A spark lit the darkness behind her eyes. Whether she admitted it or not, that name was familiar to her.

"Yes. My friend showed me . . ."

♦ ♦ ♦

Terry Nicolas and Ernie "Father Geek" Sevugian sit in a room without windows, lined with computer screens. Geek rolls his wheelchair over to a twenty-inch flat-screen monitor. "You're a martial arts nut. All that Bruce Lee shit, right?"

"Yeah. So?"

Father Geek grins behind his wire-rims. "So I've got something you've never seen."

"What?"

Geek assumes that owlish, self-satisfied aspect exclusive to people who know they have information you lack. "Well . . . back in about 1987, something really weird happened. You know MK-Ultra was trying to make Jedis and shit. They researched A to Z, got their hands on everything they could find. One thing was a surveillance tape from Westwood, California."

"Surveilling what?"

He shrugs. "Well . . . look for yourself."

He searches to find a video file, and begins playing it. At first the screen is fuzzy, full of crossbars, then alphanumerics. And then it clears, presenting an image of the intersection of Westwood and Wilshire Boulevards. Streams of cars and pedestrians against a backdrop of movie theaters and fashionable shops. Then . . . chaos.

A man comes galloping into frame. Two police officers try to grab him, and with a wave of his arm he sends them sprawling. His head snaps forward . . . and then he keeps going.

"What is this?"

"Guy's name was Adam Ludlum. Computer nerd. Story is he went crazy. There's another piece of footage on him from a restaurant out in Orange County."

The image changes to a western-themed bar. Scratchy video. Patrons sit drinking, flirting, dancing, enjoying themselves. Suddenly there is a ruckus. Several cowboys confront a solitary man, and the air is suddenly filled with tumbling bodies. Terry leans forward. Hits the rewind button. "What the fuck?"

"Indeed. There he is. Nerd from hell, huh?"

Three cowboys jump him, and the man moves so fast it is almost as if he disappears and reappears in the midst of an invisible explosion.

"Whoa!"

"Now this is the crème de la crème."

Back to Westwood. A police officer shoots Adam Ludlum point-blank in the head, and the guy shakes it off and keeps going. The cop looks bamboozled.

"What the hell?" *Terry yells.* "Were those blanks? Is this footage real?"

"Real as your last shit. There you have it. The guy was inhumanly fast, strong, aggressive, and resistant to being shot at close range. We'll assume that bullet didn't carry away critical bits of cranium, but the shock alone should have floored him."

"What happened to this freak?"

"Nobody really knows," *Geek says.* "He disappeared. There are hints that he might have been involved with a paranormal incident in the Bay Area. That information . . . I just don't have."

"Some kind of drug? Uppers? Steroids?" *Terry asks.*

"I don't think so," *Father Geek replies.* "After he disappeared his computer and notes were seized. I only know about this because of MK-Ultra."

"If it wasn't drugs," *Terry asks,* "what was it?"

"Well . . . according to his files, it was some kind of meditation. Some way of breathing and visualizing. And it . . . triggered something in his head."

This is one of the strangest things Terry has ever heard. "Is there any record of what it was?"

Geek grins. "Thought you'd never ask. Top secret. Cannot leave this room. Can't be printed. Can't be shown, either. But . . . I'm rolling down to le pissour *for five minutes, and if you were to accidentally hit that key, something would come up. I believe your cell phone is a Nokia N-90?"*

"Yes. So?"

"I hear it has a digital camera. Just a bit of trivia, with no bearing on the situation at hand. If you were to use said digicam, and I found out about it . . ."

"You'd have to kill me."

"No, I'd have to report you to certain unpleasant people. They, in all likelihood, would do things to you that would make Jack Bauer throw up." He yawns, stretching. "My bladder hurts," Geek says, and leaves. Terry pauses for a shocked and pleased moment, then begins to photograph the screen with his Nokia.

◆ ◆ ◆

"And that," Madame Gupta said, "is how you came to know of Adam Ludlum?"

"Yes. Had you heard the name?"

"In truth, yes." Madame Gupta rose, pacing.

He caught something at that moment. She'd broken contact with him. *She knows more than she wants to say.* It was the first hint of obfuscation he had detected, and it intrigued him.

"I, too, have seen some of this footage. But I have also seen the original material created by Mr. Ludlum. And . . . some of my followers knew him."

"Who was he? Really?"

"A genius," Madame Gupta said. "He read some fragmentary public pronouncements of Savagi and somehow integrated them into a cohesive whole. Quite remarkable."

"Why?"

"Because . . . Savagi himself was taught via an oral tradition, and all that remains are partial transcriptions of his lectures. Savagi's concerns overlapped with those of the martial artist, but were not specific to them."

"So . . . you began as a martial artist?"

Madame Gupta's smile was surprisingly elfin. "No. The martial arts are . . . a byproduct of other knowledge." Her expression suggested that that was all he was going to hear at the moment.

"So you came in touch with the work of this Ludlum guy. I thought that everything was classified."

"Like you, I have my sources. But let us come back to you. You are unique. I know of no one who ever had a 'kundalini trap' remain unintegrated for so long. Over a decade." She shook her head in wonder.

"How long was it supposed to remain?"

"Weeks," she said. "Months at the outside. As I said, it was an experimental program, possibly misapplied by that instructor."

"Did it hurt me?"

She considered. "It . . . delayed you. It will be fascinating to see what happens now. I have something I would like to give you." She rummaged around the office bookshelf, and found a DVD sandwiched between two thick volumes.

"What is this?" Terry asked. The cover was mimeographed, the case of cheap plastic. He guessed that someone had duplicated it on a home computer. The front photo was a close-up of a bearded Indian man with his eyes rolled up toward heaven.

"The only known video of Savagi himself, speaking and teaching students," she said. "Take this with my blessing."

"The interview is over?" The idea triggered . . . disappointment? Fear, perhaps?

"For now, yes. There are . . . matters to which I must attend." She approached him, smiling, and laid her hand on his arm. A kindly gesture? Something else? Her hand was cool and smooth, but in the moment before she touched him, a little static charge leapt from her flesh to his. "But after the first of the year, I invite you to come to me at the Sanctuary. I believe our conversation has just begun."

CHAPTER 13

Hannibal was asleep almost the minute they pulled out of the parking lot. Although the trip home lasted only seven minutes, it felt so much longer, because Olympia had played the evening's events over and over in her mind a dozen times.

Confusion, awe, and . . . hope. Real hope. She had seen something very close to the miraculous, and that was what her little family needed. Hani's response to Madame Gupta, the fact that a woman of such phenomenal capacities had taken an interest in the Dorseys . . . miracles. By the time they pulled into their driveway, his rosebud lips burred with snores. She couldn't wake the boy to feed him, and decided to just carry him up to his room.

Olympia tucked him into his sports car, kissed his forehead, and closed the door.

♦ ♦ ♦

Hannibal dreamed.

The Game was different now. The house was different. Or . . . perhaps he only saw it differently. The exterior was overgrown with vines, and wreathed with Christmas lights. The walls were translucent, and in them he could see piping . . . electrical wiring . . . so much else. And some of the wiring was frayed, broken or tangled.

So much to do. The wiring was burned and melted, but Madame Gupta had been right: there were ways around the damage. Ways to knot and mend things together. And that was a good thing, because suddenly, for the first time in his life, he felt . . . urgency.

There was a reason he wanted to build his house stronger. A reason to repair. A reason to want not to be limited by how bright and sharp the entire world seemed to be. He didn't know quite what that reason was . . . but knew it was there.

Something was coming. Coming faster and faster, something with bright eyes and sharp teeth.

Work. Quickly.

CHAPTER 14

As Terry let himself into his condo, he felt as if he were sleepwalking. Floating. He barely looked at Mark's bedroom door, which was closed. Television and snoring sounds drifted from behind it. When he had first met Mark, the big man had slept as silently as a rock. Now, it sounded as if there were wet, greasy bladders collapsing within him with every breath, wheezing like a dying steam engine.

Time takes everything. Tropical diseases and bullets to the chest and liver just make it all happen a little faster.

Mark. His friend. Maybe his only real friend.

Dying slowly, however much the old soldier might try to laugh it off.

Dying, and hoping he could get even with O'Shay before death had the last laugh.

Terry wandered dazedly into his own room, gazed around as if he had wandered into a stranger's. The spare bookshelves, the cheap stereo system, the closet hung with T-shirts and jeans in laundered rows. A room without personality, or any purpose save function.

He took off his shoes and laid back on the bed, eyes open and staring. When he closed them, colors and lines of light and motion exploded in the darkness, as if he had suddenly entered a new and alien world.

Or been plunged back into an old one he thought he'd escaped.

Flashes: men fighting, screaming, dying with sand in their eyes and mouths, in places with names from the *Arabian Nights*. Mountains and deserts and dry valleys that had been graveyards for Greeks, Brits, and Russians. Brief glimpses of burning vehicles, shattered bodies, and of Terry himself crawling across blast-torn earth, struggling to pull buddies out of a flaming Humvee. Actions he was proud of. People he loved. Sounds and smells he would give his soul to forget.

Explosions, screams, grinding engines, howling wind, commands and prayers, bullets shredding bodies, helicopters sweeping in and out . . .

Men pleading for mercy where there was none to be found.

Nothing personal. Just orders given by someone far, far away, in vengeance for the death of people Terry had never met.

Dear God. What had he been? What had he *done*?

Why could he not remember the softer sounds? Marketplaces, laughter, music, children's games, calls to prayer, dogs barking, sheep lowing, birds singing and squawking . . . surely there were more such sounds. Surely.

And smells . . . braised lamb and burnt rubber. Sweat and high explosives. Shit and burnt blood and perfume and gasoline.

Why did he struggle to remember anything beyond the hard, the dangerous, and the ugly?

One thought. A man. A friend. Sergeant Remmy Jayce, who had saved his ass, saved Pat Ronnell and Lee as well, on one of those terrible desert days.

But he couldn't stay with that memory, dared not, forced his mind away. Desperately sought something to distract him from Sgt. Jayce, who had died screaming on another day, in another land.

Right, Terry?

Suddenly, he remembered the DVD Gupta had given him, and was grateful for the distraction. A Panasonic flat-screen/video player combo perched on his dresser, and he popped the disk in, then laid back on his bed to watch. After opening titles that looked as if someone had created them on an old Atari computer, he was treated to the image of a classroom hung with tapestries and crammed with cross-legged, straight-backed women and bearded, bright-eyed men, facing an old man as thin as a whispered prayer.

His beard was larger than his head, and heavily streaked with gray. His face was a death mask seemingly composed more of will than flesh. Only his eyes seemed totally alive. When he spoke, the sound was slightly mismatched to the movement of his lips, and Terry had the oddest feeling that it was not a glitch.

From the first words, he felt himself sink into the spell, teetering on the edge of another dream. And then he surrendered, and fell without a scream.

◆ ◆ ◆

In respectful silence they sat, enraptured by Savagi's ancient voice. The aged master seemed nothing but wisdom and bone, his nut-brown scalp bare, his black eyes bright. They listened, unmoving, unspeaking, as if seeking to memorize every word.

"*One final time, I tell you the story,*" he rasped, voice barely more than a whisper. "*The tale that was told to me by my father, and to him by his, and his, and his, back to the time of god-kings. Listen,*" he said, "*and learn . . .*"

♦ ♦ ♦

From horizon to sawtooth horizon, the plain was strewn with the twisted, broken bodies of the dying and the dead. Their groans had attracted swarms of human vermin: throat-slitters, thieves, and cannibals, but soon even those vile predators would gather their dreadful burdens and disperse. Death had flooded down from the north, swarming through the defenders like a cloud of locusts, consuming everything in its path. Now the horsemen, charioteers, and foot soldiers of the greatest army this land had ever seen stood to the south, gazing back over the crimsoned plain, a beast of infinite angry limbs and ravenous mouths.

Its leader was resplendent in his robes and armor, a prince of his distant land. The youngest of five brothers, his father had declined to king him, choosing instead to gift him with an army to carve out a realm of his own, sending him south into the ancient lands to do so.

His cold blue eyes scanned the battlefield. What fools they are, to deny the son of destiny, *he thought.* I am the sun and the moon, and will conquer all.

That night, his men celebrated their victory with the women who have always flocked to the tents of conquerors. Their shrill laughter rose above the cook fires, shaming the stars. Those laughs almost, but not quite, drowned out the agonized cries of the captives unfortunate enough to have survived the day's carnage. After long hours of knives, coals, and obscene promises, flayed lips had at last whispered of a hidden city.

Could whatever pitiless gods crouching in nameless hells condemn their betrayal? In crimsoned time, even the stoutest heart grows frail.

Screams had dwindled to sobs, and thence to moans, and then to deathly silence broken only by mumbled pleas and confessions. Save for those pale lipless men tasked with the various incisions and manipulations, the camp ignored what happened in the black tents. As soldiers always have, they drank and gambled and reveled, laying in the arms of strumpets, lying about their feats of arms, laving their fears of the mayhem to come with laughter and song and the illusion of love.

The prince, stern but focused upon his intent, slept alone. Two raven-haired vixens had offered their ruby lips and perfumed loins to him. His officers grinned and elbowed each other, certain he would succumb to their charms, but he did not. He did not condemn his subordinates for their fleshly hungers, but retired to his tent that he might not be distracted by his own.

◆ ◆ ◆

The cries of pleasure and screams of merriment continued until late into the night, only dwindling as the sun was reborn in the east.

The women abandoned the camp, bearing their bundles of clothing and small sacks of silver coins. All were headed in the same direction, east to a calm section of the Wolf River, where boats and oarsmen waited to ferry them south. The women huddled together, moving little for the six hours they traveled. They did not eat, drink, or pass water. They sang hymns to their gods and to the skies and to their lost purity. By the time they reached their destination, they dwelled beyond ordinary human emotions, in some twilight realm where misery and bliss commingled in sacred harmony, as befitted the priestesses they were.

Swiftly, they were escorted through a gate in the city walls, into corridors shadowed by statues and cooled by gardens. Once arriving in the palace, the priestesses were escorted to private chambers, where they voided their bladders, sluicing out the fluids deposited by the men they had pleasured. Every inch of their skin was scrubbed, washed clean by weeping, wailing maidens.

Then . . . they were coiffed and clothed and scented with precious oils, and returned to their holy offices. After further ceremonies they would be married to highborn husbands and given the greatest respect for the remainder of their lives. It was only right, considering what they had sacrificed to preserve their beloved city . . .

Always assuming, of course, that their efforts were not in vain. The fluids they had voided were gathered in silver goblets. Over coals, the fluid was reduced in volume, then each sampling was poured into a separate goblet, each goblet then taken to one of twelve priests.

Twelve women. Twelve cups. Twelve priests. The priests drank deeply, and then as slaves played drum and string, sank into their meditations.

◆ ◆ ◆

In three days, the northerners had found their way through the ravines and twisted mountain roads, past the camouflaged bridges and a maze of dead-end false paths to the city gates.

Their messengers approached the barred portals. Through great bronze horns they bellowed their demands: total surrender, abandonment of arms, and opening of the gates. In words obscene and devoid of mercy they painted images of agonizing death and disgrace for any who resisted the prince's will.

The eldest of the city fathers emerged and replied that if the northerners did not return to their homeland, the army would be destroyed. As might be predicted, the threat was greeted with derisive laughter.

"I have something for you to read," the elder said, and withdrew a scroll from his robe. One of the soldiers took it, examined it, and then offered it to the prince, who seemed amused. The scroll read as follows:

"We have the power to kill anyone, anywhere, at any time. We can kill your father and family at home. Fight us, and nothing will stop us from killing any who serve you or that you care about. We will tell your father you brought this upon them, and that every death is due to you. You will not be the first to die, you will be the last. And everyone you love will curse your name as they perish."

The prince's smile faltered. Had he not heard of a city protected by magic? Had there not been another time, perhaps several other times, when death like this had been promised, and delivered . . .

The elder bowed his head, and without meeting their eyes proclaimed: "To give the prince a chance to reconsider, we first kill only the commanders."

The generals, mighty warriors and fearless all, laughed raucously at such splendid jest, not realizing that the prince was not laughing with them. The greatest among them stepped forward. His sword flickered in his hand. The elder's head fell to the ground and rolled against a stump, eyes blinking as the corpse toppled first to its knees and then onto its side.

They did not see that the prince had half-raised his hand, as if on the verge of demanding that they wait, just a moment, while he considered more fully.

But in the temple, the priests knew what had been said and done. For three days and nights, they had meditated deeply, the scraps of flesh and bits of hair, the smears of sexual fluid now digesting within their bellies.

And in their meditations, they surrendered their sense of self, abandoning their names, and histories, and even their sacred humanity. Passed through the ego-illusion of separate existence until they were joined with all life, all part of the eternal cosmos. And they sought those from whom the skin and hair and fluid had been taken . . . searching among billions of living beings until they found the men who had commanded the invading army.

And intertwined with them, rooted into them.

Joined.

The commanders gasped, stumbled, feeling almost as though a hand had reached through their skin and into their innards.

Sensed something akin to physical violation as the spirit of the priests entered them, spirits guided by blood drawn to blood and flesh to flesh.

Then the priestesses who had baited the commanders with their own bodies served poisoned wine to the priests. A warm, honeyed concoction it was, which the holy men drank without hesitation. The draughts worked swiftly, such that the priests soon fell to the floor, succumbing to terminal slumber as the sirens soothed their heads, whispering of paradise and reciting memorized passages from the forbidden Black Sutra.

And beyond the barred gates, in the fields of the army's endless thousands, the commanders sank to their knees, dying.

And then dead.

For a few moments there was naught but stunned silence. The foot soldiers and archers and charioteers gazed disbelieving at the corpses of the twelve greatest warriors in their prince's command.

They turned to look at the prince, to see what they should do. If at that moment he had displayed strength and fortitude, they might have plunged on and razed the city.

But there was a reason his father had not gifted him with a kingdom, had guessed that he lacked the fiber necessary to lead. Had instead demanded that he prove himself.

And when the men saw how the color had drained from the prince's face, how he trembled and lost his water . . .

Every man knew what the prince's father had known.

Then, as if of one mind, they returned the way they had come, scatterings of gold coins, silver goblets, and precious jewels marking their northern flight.

It is said that the prince returned to his country, a broken, dishonored man. And the city . . . the city was forgotten, and lived in peace for another thousand years, until finally the desert sands drank the empty streets, and even the memory was lost to time.

Until all that remained were scrolls written in poisoned ink.

And in time, those were forgotten as well.

◆ ◆ ◆

Terry . . . blinked. Yawned. Shook himself to full awareness, for a moment uncertain where or even who he was. The DVD had returned to the main menu. He did not know when his attention had wavered, but could remember nothing of what he had seen. Had he fallen asleep? He must have.

And yet . . . it didn't precisely feel as if he had slept. In fact, he wasn't certain what had happened.

He checked the time: it was two in the morning. He simply wasn't tired or sleepy. Stark naked, Terry rolled off the bed and walked into the living room, their makeshift office, and looked at an array of architectural designs. Pulled away the dummy top sheet to study the real plans. Surveillance. Following O'Shay's trucks. Ambush. Covering the drivers and guards in a potentially lethal crossfire as the loot was taken.

The drawings seemed to come to life . . . roads rising off the page like cartoon animations, peopled with tiny vivid human figures. Cars raced, spun, crashed. The guards tried to protect themselves, and were gunned down by Mark, Father Geek, Lee, and Pat.

Especially Pat.

And once it started, Terry did his share of the killing as well. God, yes, he did. As in Fallujah. As in Central America. As in Afghanistan and elsewhere.

He felt every recoil, saw every drop of blood, heard every wet, horrified howl of pain. So clear were they, each and every one, like images out of one of Hannibal's pop-up books, sounds in Dolby Digital, smells like some maniac perfumer's private sampling parlor. Everything so real, so stark. So . . .

He hung his head, sick and sad and lost.

CHAPTER 15

All the next day, Olympia felt as if she were floating on a cloud at CNS, even though an undercurrent of panic blossomed as another resident of the Dead List, a French executive known to have dumped tainted baby formula on the Nigerian market, died crawling toward the phone while her husband dialed 112, the universal European emergency code. The question was: where were the other promised deaths? In a world of seven billion souls, it was overwhelmingly probable that they had simply gone unnoticed. So many places for people to die, without their bodies discovered or means of death determined.

But what she did grasp was that the world had reached some kind of tipping point. Or . . . boiling point. People were anticipating the next day's evil news. Expecting it. So strange for the external world to descend into chaos just when her own personal world seemed to sparkle with hope. Was that some kind of strange cosmic joke? A cruel universal zero-sum game?

No. She couldn't let her mind drift in that direction. All would be well. Her good fortune could not, would not trigger disaster for others.

Could it?

The only thing that day that alleviated the growing sense of dread was the phone call she received at two o'clock in the afternoon, extending a formal invitation to her, and to Hannibal, to come to the Golden Dream's "Salvation Sanctuary." A limousine would be sent to gather them.

Golden Dream, indeed. She leaned back in her seat, thinking. In the scant hours since Madame Gupta had laid hands on her son, Hani had become more responsive and interactive than he had been in years. If this was real, something about the little woman was powerful medicine indeed. But something tickled at her instincts about this, and she trusted that little scratch. Sometimes life was a long and complicated path. Who had first mentioned the Sanctuary to her?

Was it Maria Cortez? Maybe Olympia should thank her.

Cortez was a blogger, working out of Dayline.com, CNS's illegitimate tabloid child. Maria was a first-class talent in a second-tier job. If she remembered correctly, it was Maria's blogging about the Golden Dream centers that had originally struck Olympia's interest in their day-care services.

Olympia took the elevator down to the basement, a symbolic descent into broadcasting purgatory.

Basement: everybody out. Returns, blemished goods, plumbing supplies, and Dayline.com.

There, in a warren of tiny, badly lit office cubicles that would have seemed spartan by *Dilbert* standards, she found Maria's desk, but not Maria herself. Olympia supposed that the offices were so tiny because they wanted the bloggers to work out of their homes, as if the upper-floor employees couldn't stand the sight of them, perhaps from a popular superstition that blogging would be the death of "real" journalism.

So she called HR, obtained contact information, and punched the numbers. Initially reluctant to talk over the phone, Maria finally agreed to a face-to-face meeting.

◆　◆　◆

It took her twenty minutes through angry traffic to drive to the address, an apartment building across from a One Star Ranch barbecue Olympia remembered as having beef ribs that would have choked Fred Flintstone.

Maria lived in a beige two-story building with a Spanish-style roof, something that looked like it would have been more at home in Tucson, Arizona. She parked in one of the visitor spaces, hiked up the outside staircase, and knocked. When the door opened, she smiled at the slightly dumpy woman who answered it, her blue flower-print dress sashed with a black patent-leather belt. "Maria Cortez? I'm Olympia Dorsey, from CNS."

"I remember." Cortez blinked her small, bright brown eyes, as if scanning a mental file folder.

"You said you'd talk to me?"

"I remember that, too," Maria said, and made a decision, widening the doorway. "Come in."

"Thank you."

"I remember you," Maria said, indicating a comfortable-looking chair covered in floral-patterned cloth. "You helped me on the Timons thing." Xavier Timons was a local eccentric who had been arrested for putting change into expired Atlanta parking meters. That had been a great show.

"I was hoping you remembered. And you said you owed me. I could really use it now."

Olympia was still standing.

Maria waved her toward the chair again. "Have a seat. All right—what can I do for you?"

Olympia sighed. "You're on top of this whole Dead List thing, aren't you?"

Maria chuckled. "Is that what they're calling it?"

She nodded. "People like to name things."

"I just got finished being grilled by the FBI. Made me a little nervous about talking on the phone."

Olympia stared. "You're kidding. What did they want to know? Can I record this?" She reached into her purse for her little digital recorder, but Maria raised a hand.

"No. Absolutely not. I might be willing to go on the record—later. But I'll write it myself."

Sigh. "I understand."

"They wanted to know how I was chosen, who I chose, who might have chosen the president . . . stuff like that."

Maria lit a cigarette, puffed at it without apparent pleasure, and looked at Olympia speculatively.

"I don't want to ask you about that, do I?" Olympia said.

"Not if you're as good a reporter as I remember."

"What I want to know is: what didn't they ask that they should have?"

Maria smiled. "No one asked if I got fan mail."

That caught her attention instantly. "Fan mail?"

"And hate mail."

"From where?" Olympia asked.

"All over," she said with a deep draw on the cigarette, followed by a hiss of blue smoke. "Thirty-six pieces."

"Did anything stick in your mind?"

Maria opened a file folder, extracted a sheaf of envelopes. She fanned through them. "This one," she said. She pulled out a blue envelope, handed it to Olympia.

"What is it?"

"About ten months later I got a letter from the parents of a girl named Maya Tanaka."

"Tanaka?" Olympia asked. "Should I have heard that name?"

"Perhaps. I wrote about it a little, but she wasn't in the news. She was a physics student at Columbia, but also something of a guru junkie. Apparently, she dropped out of college, and joined this group called the Salvation Sanctuary."

"Is that a problem?"

"Not really. Her parents thought so. And they couldn't deal with the fact that she'd dropped out of communication with them."

Olympia's brow wrinkled.

"Actually her parents put so much pressure on so many people that Maya finally came forward and answered the questions. Press conference. By the way, she showed up at her parents' house on turkey day, just last year. She said that she was retreating from the material world, had found the answers she was looking for, and was rejecting the values she had been given. She said she had entered a four-year cleansing program, after which she would return to the world."

"How long ago did she enter that program?"

Maria ticked something off on her pink-nailed fingers. "Just about four years ago. I think."

"Did you believe her?"

"She seemed smart, committed, and in control of herself. True believer, maybe. Sense of mischief, as if she knew a secret no one else knew, you know that attitude?"

Olympia nodded. She surely did. "So you looked into it."

"Yeah, I did. There were a few other reports, people who had friends, children, even a spouse or two who had gone into this organization. They've got at least fifty branches in the United States, and maybe another twenty-five overseas. They run the Golden Dream centers—the ones we talked about back when. They're quiet, don't proselytize much, but seem to be similar to the Transcendental Meditation movement—they have a technique for stress or something, and it works."

"Any secrets?"

Maria smiled. "I thought so. A few people hinted at something big that they were a part of, something that would be revealed in a few years. Remember the T.M. people who said they could levitate, and were supposedly training people to do just that? And that when they had a cadre of flying folks they would shock the world? Turns out they were just teaching 'em to do a kind of cross-legged hop."

Olympia laughed. She remembered.

"Well, I figure that these people thought the Salvation Sanctuary had found the secret of enlightenment."

"What even *is* enlightenment?"

"Hell if I know," Maria laughed. "But they seemed happy. Healthy. Really healthy. I noticed a few things. Complexions cleared up, weight lost."

"Not exactly loaves and fishes."

"No, but they seemed to have something. Let's just say that I looked into it a little more." Her chuckle was mischievous. "In fact, I have to say thank you for reminding me about it. Why are you asking?"

Olympia explained her situation, and Maria was all ears. "So you're going up there?"

"I think so. Why not? If you can think of a reason I shouldn't, tell me now. What do you know about the place?"

Maria smiled again. A secret smile. "Beautiful, and valuable. The property is built around an exhausted gold mine, up in the Georgia mountains. I hear the whole thing is worth about twelve million dollars. Three-hour drive, I guess, from Atlanta. No, look, I looked into them, they're nice people."

"What about this Madame Gupta?"

"From what I've heard, nobody ever sees her."

Olympia snorted. "She put on a karate demo at the school here locally."

"Really?" Maria shook her head. "A public demo? That's . . . unusual. I knew high-level members who're not totally certain she exists. That's bizarre." She leaned forward. "What happened at this demo?"

"She demo'd." Olympia shrugged. Not easy to describe what had happened privately, and even if it had been easy, she had a powerful urge to keep it to herself. "Sparred with my guest and kinda wiped the floor with him."

"You go, girl."

"Invited me to the Sanctuary."

"Why?"

"Well, actually, she invited Hannibal. I'm just along for the ride."

"Tell me," Maria asked. "What was she like?"

Like the answer to my dreams. "It's strange. She was like a three-hundred-pound man crammed into a hundred-pound body. Freak calm, like the eye of a storm. Terry, my guest, said she moves like something that isn't human. She looked pretty much like a kung fu movie to me."

"Wires and all."

"No-wire fu, but I kept expecting Larry Fishburne to offer me the red pill." She paused. "The most important thing is that Madame Gupta thinks Hani's special. Called him an 'indigo boy.' And she thinks she can help him."

Maria blinked. "Indigo boy? Help him? That's odd."

"What's odd about it?"

"Well, I did an article about it a while back. 'Indigo child' is a term that bounces around the neurodiversity community," Maria said. "They basically theorize that autism, ADD, and so forth are positive things. Intermediate phases of an evolutionary response to a changing world."

"That Hani is like Wolverine or something?"

"Kind of. Which makes her comment strange. The NDs take the position that the world needs to adapt to the children, not have the children adapt to the world. So . . . what is it that she's helping the kids with?"

"Dealing with the fact that the rest of us are slow?" Olympia asked.

"Pretty much. But the point is that they don't think the kids are broken, or need to be 'fixed.' "

"That sounds pretty good to me."

"Could be. I'll tell you one thing though." Maria tapped her chest. "Instinct. I think that Madame Gupta went there to see Hannibal. I think she's telling the truth. For some reason, she thinks Hannibal is a very special little boy."

◆　◆　◆

After Olympia Dorsey left, Maria slipped a picture out of her desk, a 5×7 glossy shot of Maya Tanaka. She signed on to Facebook, and went to Maya's page. Up until two days ago, Maya had posted several times a day, glowing about the wonderful experience she was about to have.

Well, she must have had that "wonderful" thing by now. But there hadn't been a post since. That might mean nothing at all, but at one time Tanaka had been compulsive about social media. Reporter instinct told Maria that it meant something.

But exactly what, she couldn't say.

CHAPTER 16

The vine-covered pool house was community property, one of the perks of the Foothill Village Homeowner's Association. Olympia had been in the village three years, and the only time she'd ever been in the pool house was during the Christmas parties.

It wasn't that she wasn't social. It was sensitivity about Hani. She knew on some level that this was her problem, her issue. That it wasn't reasonable to wonder about the meaning behind every neighbor's glance, every word, seeking glassy eyes above a synthetic plastic smile. *There but for the grace of God goes my child.* The politely oblique damnation of the *whew, we dodged a bullet* attitude.

And of course, the other side of it. At times it gutted her to watch other people's children, observing them play and laugh and just be kids, damn it, and feeling herself on the verge of tears. Hani tried to get into a party mood, but inevitably either over- or underreacted, laughing raucously or withdrawing sullenly, flashing between emotional poles without finding balance, aware of the mismatch between his emotions and the external world that triggered them.

Always. Right on the edge.

Pity for the wounded child. Sorrow for the wounded widow. She just . . .

But Christmas was a little different, somehow. For some reason, the yuletide brought out a different feeling from her neighbors, as if focusing on their children's joy brought them all together in a different and wonderful way.

No snow on the ground, but a holiday spirit alive in their hearts. She had been working with the decorations and coordinating the gift exchange for weeks. Her neighbors began trickling in, pointing at the tinsel and punch bowl, cooing with pleasure, slapping backs, pulling cans of pop or beer out of the ice-filled tub, tinkling the corner piano, chuckling at the tinseled plastic tree and spontaneously breaking into snatches of song.

She and her retired neighbor Cathy Robbins served frosted Christmas tree cookies, urged Cathy's husband to play harmonica or piano, and danced with the old guys who normally just sat around the pool smoking cigars and complaining about Liberals. She kept one eye on the door, hoping against hope.

Nicki and two girls from her drama club danced and giggled in a corner and played with the inexhaustible Pax, who for all her polka-dotted Great Dane mass was remarkably delicate with children and furniture, almost as if aware of the damage her rambunctious nature might cause. She was downright tender with Hannibal, and when he tried to ride her, she indulged the whim with a level of tolerance dogs usually reserved for puppies.

Then . . . a cry of "Merry Christmas!" and Mark waddled in, his muscular bulk padded beneath a red suit, sunburnt face concealed behind a white beard. "Ho, ho, ho!" he called, aggressively radiating holiday cheer.

Hannibal shrieked in pleasure and ran to Santa, hugging him around the knees as Nicki rolled her eyes. But she was smiling. Hani rarely initiated physical contact with anyone.

Mark and three other men (one in a wheelchair, wheeling with one hand and carrying a white sack over his shoulder with the other) joined the party, and all seemed in fine moods. They handed out wrapped candies and Dollar Store yo-yos and miniature plastic ukuleles, laughing and letting themselves be chased around the room by a swarm of urchins.

The one in the wheelchair introduced himself to Nicki as Ernie Sevugian, thin with red hair and a full face and not the slightest apparent sensitivity about his disability. Terry astonished her, sitting down at the piano and pounding out an entirely plausible rendition of "Grandma Got Run Over by a Reindeer," singing in a hillbilly voice so at odds with his appearance that the entire room dissolved into gales of mirth.

When he and a falsetto-spouting Mark began "Baby It's Cold Outside," Olympia had to sit before she collapsed with laughter. After he was finished, Terry took a bow and sauntered over.

"I didn't even know you could play," she said.

"Neither did I," he replied. He was being mischievous, but then his expression was genuinely puzzled. "Haven't played since I was fifteen. Don't know what got into me. Life is a mystery, isn't it?" His smile was so close. "You must be an inspiration."

"'Erry!" Hannibal said, and dragged Terry back toward the center of the floor.

"What's this?"

"He wants to dance with you," she said, hoping that he wouldn't rebuff her son. Terry didn't disappoint her, lifting Hani to his shoulders and dancing a creditable jig while Sevugian tinkled out "Frosty the Snowman," singing and somehow managing to layer adult insinuation into the lyrics.

Olympia laughed and laughed until she realized she was crying. She wiped her face with embarrassment, then realized Nicki wasn't watching her. No one was, they were all howling and clapping as well. She felt as if she had stepped through a wall of ice into a world of warmth and connection, and at that moment if someone had asked her if she had ever been happier in her life, she might well have honestly said no.

Her family was happy, and safe, and warm.

Dear God. Such a small and precious thing. But her hunger for it was like a fire that had singed and numbed the very nerves that carried the pain.

Terry lifted Hannibal down to his sister, who guided him into a side room. Olympia handed him a cup of punch. "Really well done," she said. "Thank you. You delivered. Big-time." He bowed, without spilling his punch. Sipped.

"Spiked," he said. "Spiked Hawaiian Punch." He slipped into a damned fine Most Interesting Man in the World impression. "'I don't always drink Hawaiian Punch, but when I do . . .'"

She laughed. It was a relief that the kids had their own party in a side room. She could be an adult, for once. "Who are your friends?"

"Oh. . . ." He pointed out his four companions, who were whooping and having fun, except for the one who had introduced himself as "Ronnell." The wiry blond Ronnell lurked around the side, smiling meaninglessly and observing. She didn't like him much, but smiled back. 'Twas the season.

But there was something her mother had said once upon a time. That if you wanted to understand someone, look at their friends. Add up all their qualities, divide by the number of people, and your friend will be right in the middle of the pack.

If that was true . . . what did that say of Terry?

He named them: Lee, Pat, Ernie, and of course Mark. "Just thought I'd get them in on the fun," he said.

Mark was a force of nature, that craggy face concealing a secret sadness behind a wall of synthetic mirth. Lee was a goofball, looked as if he should have been in a cornfield chewing straw in a Norman Rockwell painting. He was the joker in the deck. Sevugian was interesting—prickly, but with a deep vein of strength. The way he'd improvised on the piano, vocally and instrumentally, suggested high intelligence and mocking self-awareness.

Ronnell was another matter. He reminded her of a very polite, soft-spoken piranha. Something in the back of his eyes was not merely cold, but dead.

"This is wonderful," Olympia said, forcing the corners of her mouth up. "How did you convince them?" So . . . three she liked, and one who scared her, just a little.

What did that make Terry?

Terry sipped punch. "Well . . . actually I just let them convince themselves."

Uh-huh. More likely, they were alone for the holidays save for each other, and needed this. A little light music and laughter.

Mark sat in a corner of the main room, performing his Santa routine as a line of kids waited to sit on his lap. "Have you been a good little girl this year?" he asked the next tyke in line, a Muppet-sized Latina blonde.

"You bet!" Mischief danced in her eyes.

"No, she wasn't!" a reasonable replica of the Stay-Puft Marshmallow Boy insisted.

Mark's eyes narrowed. "Know what elves really are?"

"What?" she asked.

"Bad little kids who get dragged back to the North Pole to make toys for the good kids. So watch your butt."

The girl blinked and drew back, horrified. Scrambled off his lap. The Marshmallow Kid howled in mirth.

Father Geek wheeled up behind Mark and punched him in the shoulder. "You are such an asshole."

"My father was an asshole," Mark said. "My grandfather was an asshole. Just upholding a long family tradition."

Olympia laughed, still glowing with recent memory. "I . . . haven't seen Hani like that in a very long time."

Not since twenty-four hours ago.

"He's a good kid," Terry said. "He deserves a very special Christmas."

Was he reading her mind?

"Mistletoe!" Mrs. Robbins chirped. "Better be careful. Merry Christmas!"

The Jackson 5's piping voices proclaimed "Santa Claus Is Comin' to Town," Olympia's contribution to the soundtrack. After two years of Bing Crosby, she'd managed to season it with at least a few R & B memories from her own childhood Christmas gatherings. When a pair of couples began to bop to the rhythm, she raised an eyebrow, and Terry snorted laughter.

"Not this year," he said. She smiled, masking a sharp stab of disappointment. But when the music slowed, he took her hand and led her onto the floor. Two other couples swayed to the music, but Olympia didn't think about them. She was trying not to think about how Terry's body felt against hers, experiencing the contact not as pressure but as heat cascading through her body. He held her frame beautifully, not really much of a dancer but with a fine sense of rhythm and a mastery of motion that translated very well indeed. She remembered. Damn it, she remembered too well.

Somehow they had maneuvered each other under a mistletoe sprig dangling by a string from the ceiling. She didn't think that either of them had planned it, but there it was. Their eyes floated to the twist of green and red, and then to each other. For a moment they were both terribly amused, and then embarrassingly serious.

"Here we are again," he said, and she could see that he was pulling back, trying to give her room to breathe.

Damn it, she didn't want to breathe.

"Shut up," she said, gripping the back of his head and pressing her lips against his. It was innocent at first, then inquiring, and then hungry. They melted into each other and she didn't give a damn who witnessed the blossoming of her hunger, caring only that he tasted and smelled and felt so good, so very good, and it had been such a terribly long time.

CHAPTER 17

We are, as human beings, traveling a road between birth and death. We attempt to somehow blend the dreams of our childhood with the deepest values we will hold sacred upon our deathbeds. Every action of our adult lives should concern itself only with fulfilling our obligations to family, to society, or ourselves in accordance with these two beings, always with us: our child selves, and our death selves. What those two say about our lives is the only thing that matters.

—Savagi, *The Myth of Love*

Her house was quiet, and had been, even as their mutual heat had built, and raged, and finally subsided. Olympia had filled her mouth with pillow and bitten down hard as she crested, convulsed again and again by pleasure that rocked her like depth charges in a night-dark sea. When her eyes met Terry's, she felt a flicker of uncertainty, perhaps even fear. And she heard her own unspoken words reverberating in her mind, almost as if asking for permission, or approval, for her volcanic response. *Is it all right? Am I safe . . . ?*

♦　♦　♦

They had always been startling together physically, like two starving halves of a creature that knew hunger without end, that strove and strove together in endless tidal rhythms as old as the moon and as new as a breaking wave.

Sex just hadn't been enough. It never is.

The yellowish streetlights drifted through the window, casting valleys of golden light and chocolate shadow across her body, her limbs luxuriantly arranged beneath the sheets. She stretched, and grinned at him.

"You're like a big cat." He traced his finger along her thigh.

She purred loudly and reached out to him, pulling him close enough to feel his rising response brush her thigh as their mouths and bodies fused again.

It was more this time, trembled on the edge of a statement, ending in a question for which no man or woman has ever had a perfect answer. Just . . . a yearning for more questions.

And it was only with great effort that, again, she stopped herself from speaking the words aloud.

Who are we? Why are we here?

Are you the one? The one who will hold me and love me through my life? If I give you all that a woman can, now, while I am young . . . will you care for me, let me care for you, hold my hand as we reach the end of our road?

Are you the one?

Then the heat receded, the vast raw vulnerability healed again, and the questions they had asked, the mutual view into each other's souls . . . vanished like an echo in the heart, until both could pretend it had never been there at all.

Terry was the first to find words.

"Everything works," he said. "Especially us." He waited to say the next thing, and a shadow of the deeper questions resurfaced.

"What went wrong?" he asked, eyes shifting, as if sorry he had spoken. After a moment of silence, he laughed at himself, making light of the intimacy they had shared. "Sorry. Is that kind of a girly question?"

His tension somehow relieved hers. She giggled, then became serious again. "I've thought about that for almost a year," she said. And now, something horrible, pale, cold, and dead writhed in her darkness, fought its way to the surface of her consciousness. Something she barely even thought to herself was about to be spoken aloud.

God help me.

"Any answers to share?"

"Raoul, my husband," she whispered, and with that, took a gamble she wouldn't have believed herself capable of.

◆ ◆ ◆

Husband? Terry thought.

Sex as a reminder of death? A denial of it? He remembered his father once saying if you can remember your name immediately after sex, it hadn't been very good.

And another witticism from Captain Dad: if the first thing a woman says after sex is about today, or her past, it's a screw. If it's about the future, it's a relationship.

What if the first thing that comes up is her dead husband, Pop? I suspect that breaks the rules, don't you think?

A long, long pause, and then she dropped the bomb: "I lied about him. Nicki and I both. He didn't die."

The bottom fell out of his stomach. "What?"

"He's not dead."

Questions swirled and collided in his head until they triggered vertigo. Anger. Confusion. And . . . curiosity. "Where is he, then? What happened to him?"

"We were living in Miami at the time," she said, whispering like a supplicant in a confessional. "I was at the *Herald*. He left us," she said. "Just . . . left. Couldn't handle Hani."

Terry was silent. He envisioned it, and realized that it made so much sense of so many different things he had sensed or noticed . . . "So he left. What about Nicki? What did he say to her? How in the hell could he . . ."

"He told Nicki he'd be back in twenty minutes," she said. "Went out for pizza and just never came back. Sent an e-mail saying he needed to work some things out. The next I heard was from his lawyer. We haven't heard from him in eighteen months."

So the entire family pretended that Daddy was dead. Dear God. *Love means pain. Trust means pain. Daddy equals pain.*

"So how . . . when did you start lying about it?"

"It wasn't me," she said, her voice so timorous and guilty she could have been a child. "It was Nicki. She knew the truth, and just . . . freaked out. I kept hoping Raoul would come home to us . . . that I wouldn't have to say anything. But after three weeks, Nicki exploded and told Hannibal that Daddy was dead. He screamed and actually hurt himself throwing his body against walls and chairs . . . and then pulled inside. I didn't have the nerve to tell him the truth. To build up his hope and then have Raoul never come back. The lie seemed easier, somehow. Simpler."

His tongue felt numb. In his silence, Olympia soldiered on.

"I'd been offered a job at CNS, here in Atlanta. I took it. We packed up, moved up, and started over where no one knew the truth."

"How did Hannibal react?"

"He'd been making progress, like someone swimming up out of a deep, dark hole. When that happened . . . he just sank."

She made an awful chuckling sound, laughter without the slightest trace of humor to soften it. Breaking to a sob. "Oh damn, what did I do? What was I thinking? I just screwed everything up, didn't I?"

An entire family, pretending a terrible thing had happened so that they wouldn't have to face an even greater horror. Words failed him.

"Then when you and I . . ."

"Yes," she said, and then fell silent. The silence stretched. Cloaked. The look in her eyes had changed, becoming not anxiety, but challenge. *I told you my secret*, she seemed to be saying. *I told you what an awful person I am. Terrible wife. World-class bad mother. I showed you my wounds. Show me yours.*

Bleed with me.

He felt his mouth open and close, words crowding the back of his throat. He longed to speak, to share his story, to tell her, to have someone who understood who and what he was, and the hellish moral minefield he was staggering across . . .

But he just couldn't. And at that moment, he knew which of them was stronger.

And so did she.

As if to be certain, she waited another minute before speaking. "I think you should go now," she said. "I really think that would be best."

Her body had gone cold and rigid. *I was afraid to trust you*, she had just said, without those words crossing her lips. *I began to want to, so I pushed you away. And I just trusted you again, and that puts me and my family in danger.*

Her family. Her little bulwark against the night, and the cold.

Once upon a time, she had trusted a man named Raoul, and given him two beautiful children. And Raoul had utterly betrayed them all. And she had made a horrible choice to protect her son. As Nicki had to protect her brother.

Mother and daughter locked in a lie that had poisoned the family . . . but just maybe had protected the boy who had once run into Terry and bounced off toward the swimming pool, to be snatched giggling from the air.

Precious, unique little boy.

And now she was a woman who split her heart and her sexuality into two separate buckets. The liar called Terry Nicolas could play in one or the other. Could be either friend or lover. But he couldn't keep a foot in both buckets. That would be too dangerous, by far.

He wasn't certain, but her story might have been the most heartbreaking thing he'd ever heard.

Terry watched her breathing there, curled on her side, staring out into the moonlight. Perhaps for the first time, he really *saw* her. It was strange, but he seemed to be looking at a child within the woman, curled into a fetal position, as if she were pregnant with her own past, more innocent self. Glowing in the moonlight.

Better to be alone than to trust the untrustworthy. Did that include all of humanity, or just men like Terry?

"Please go." Tears choked her throat.

Terry rolled up to sitting position, couldn't think of anything to say, and then slipped on his pants. Then he remembered their frenzied undressing and plucked his underpants off the floor, balled them up, and pushed them into his pocket. Feeling clumsier by the moment, Terry pulled on his shirt and left the bedroom.

The house, the night was so quiet he could hear private conversations from the pool house. Light from the downstairs kitchen cast a wedge in the upstairs hall, where he stood. Nicki's room was down the way, the door open enough for him to see stuffed animals, a makeup table with little pink lights, and wall posters of Tyrese and Justin Bieber. A slightly surrealistic combination, but there you go.

Hannibal's room was kitty-corner to Nicki's, the door open very slightly.

He couldn't help himself. Terry tiptoed down, and nudged the door open with his fingertips. The pale, reflected light widened in a wedge on the room's floor.

Hannibal still slept in a red plastic car with crib-like walls. A bed with raised edges. A crib that pretended to be a Formula One car. At the moment, Hani sprawled blissfully asleep, his trusting eyes closed. His rounded cheeks looked soft and warm.

A crib like a racer. Raised edges, sunken mattress. Why? Style? No. Terry blinked. He was suddenly dealing with an image, something almost as clear and strong as actual sight, of Hannibal in another, ordinary bed. Tossing in his sleep, and falling out of that bed, onto the floor.

That was the reason for the raised edges. Odd. It wasn't just a thought, it was a sight, like a reflection viewed in a window, bleached but clear.

Poor boy. He'd been so startled, awakening with screams. And . . . Nicki had reached him before his mother. Yes.

Terry reached out, came within an inch of touching Hani's cheek, but then hesitated. What was it like to live within Hannibal? Were his dreams like those of other children? Did he understand how he was different?

Did he have the slightest idea how incredibly precious he was?

Strange. In the darkness, Terry's eyes played tricks on him. A paper-thin layer of light seemed to float around Hani's skin. Oddly, when he looked in the room's mirror, the illusion vanished like swamp mist in sunlight.

Hannibal moved. He was asleep, or nearly asleep, but reached up. His entire fist wrapped around Terry's forefinger, holding with a butterfly's gentle touch. For ten breaths Terry stood there, not wanting to pull his finger away.

He knew that touch. It was an *are you my daddy?* touch. A *doesn't someone want to love me?* touch.

No. He could not bear that contact. It was too real. He could lie to the mother. To the daughter.

Not to this precious boy. That . . . could not happen.

Then the butterfly pressure eased. Hannibal released his finger, a tiny smile curling his perfect lips. Then his face relaxed as Hani sank more deeply back into dream.

What are you dreaming, Hani? Do I even want to know?

Terry slipped from the room, down the stairs, and outside, where the breeze nibbled his skin with frozen teeth.

◆ ◆ ◆

Mr. Terry had looked through the windows, and then backed away.

Hannibal had watched him come and go, safe no matter what Terry decided.

Good-bye, Terry. Good-bye.

You'll be back. You'll be my daddy, one day.

The Game was different, since the woman had touched him. Or . . . perhaps he only saw it differently now. Felt it differently. Something was wrong, something irritating him like the taste of sour milk or the squeal of a mosquito, coming from somewhere in the house his family lived in, and somehow penetrating into the Game.

The walls of his mansion were translucent, and in them he could see piping . . . electrical wiring . . . so much else. That odd new growth of vines and unfamiliar trees. And some of the wiring was frayed, some broken or tangled. And he ripped out the walls and began to play with the cables. There was work to be done.

Through one of the windows, Terry's handsome face peered in at him, curious and friendly. He waved but Terry couldn't see him, which was sad.

As he turned back to the wiring, little Indra wandered in, watching patiently.

"That's good work," she said. Her skin was darker than his, like peanut butter.

"Just wait," he replied. So much to do. There was burned and melted wiring, but Madame Gupta had been right: there were ways around the damage. Ways to knot and mend things together. It was strange, but when he did, entire rows of Christmas tree lights lit up, so that he could see what was right.

And sometimes when he did, things got so bright that it hurt his eyes.

And then the little brown girl took his hand. Her skin was warm, and soft, and tingled where they touched. She led him through the bright halls to the room with the control panels, and placed his hands upon them. And he turned the dials, and the lights went down, or became less agonizing (which was the same thing) and after he did that it felt better, and he was able to get back to work.

So much to do. And suddenly he felt that urgency again.

There was a reason he wanted to build his house stronger. A reason to repair. A reason to want not to be limited by how bright and sharp the entire world seemed to be. He didn't know quite what that reason was . . . but he knew it existed.

"Who are you?" he asked.

She smiled sweetly. "They call me Indra," she said. She took his hand, and kissed his palm.

He felt dizzy.

"That's your name," he said. "But who are you? Where did you come from?"

She smiled very mysteriously, and offered no reply.

Indra led him to a room he hadn't seen. In fact, the entire floor was different. Not frightening . . . but the shadows were different, and the lighting strange. He hesitated.

"Come with me," she begged him.

For what seemed like days he refused, but finally she leaned in and kissed his cheek. She smelled so fresh and lovely, fragrant with some spice like at the restaurant where Mommy bought chicken tikka masala. His head spun and he knew he could refuse her nothing.

They stepped through the door together.

The air was warm and moist. He still remembered Miami in summer, and it felt like that, only more so. Like the bathroom felt when he left the shower on for a long time, very hot, and the mirror steamed. Like that.

Indra held his hand. The streets were narrow and crowded with people who looked a little like Indra, but lighter. And they frowned at her as if they did not think her beautiful, as he did. And acted as if they did not want to touch her.

Led him to a house wherein there were people as dark as she, and he. Two men, two women—one lighter than the other, but resembling Indra. Several children who smiled warmly as they entered.

"My family," she said. "My people. We are called *Siddhi*."

◆　◆　◆

Terry checked his watch. It was two fifteen, and despite the fact that he hadn't slept in thirty-six hours, he felt not the slightest fatigue. In fact, despite the sadness of the last thirty minutes, he felt wide awake. Damn it, this wasn't healthy: he was behaving like a meth addict, without the alleged merriment of meth itself. The crash was going to be brutal.

Terry had been in this space before. He was just wired, that was all. Too much was happening, and too soon. What he needed was to burn off the energy. Then, he was certain, sleep would come.

He returned to his condo and slipped into his jogging clothes and shoes, zipped a couple twenty-dollar bills into a denim mini-wallet Velcro'd to his left shoelaces, and then tiptoed out as quietly as possible. Didn't want to wake up Mark, who had had a great night, transformed by Christmas magic from pill-popping G.I. Joe to a dancing bear with a single bound.

Santa.

Who'd have thought?

The night air seemed to have grown slightly crisper, colder, even in the few minutes since he had returned home from O's. There was no one up and on the street, although a few dim lights shimmered in isolated windows. Most visiting cars were gone. Few were parked on the street itself, but on the street leading to the main boulevard a dark blue van was parked between two streetlights. He vaguely remembered seeing it earlier, parked there or across the street, and wondered if the Nazis in the homeowner's association would have it hauled away. Sometimes people abandoned cars or used public streets for long-term parking. It was annoying.

Terry stretched his calves, warmed up his joints with some slow circular rolls, then jogged down toward Nathan Bedford Forrest Junior High School and its quarter-mile jogging track.

A police car slid by as he neared the track. He wondered what they thought about a black man in a track suit at this time of night. Wondered if they had been some of the ones who had harassed O a few months back. If they might have a grudge of some kind.

Ordinarily he felt caution, the desire to move slowly and definitively, so as not to trigger antagonistic behavior. Oddly, a new thought ran through his mind:

I hope I don't have to hurt them.

Now *that* was odd.

The Smyrna PD car slowed, and then continued on.

CHAPTER 18

Maya (illusion) is the lack of discernment of the principles of transformation. This transformation is stopped in the body.

—*Shiva Sutras*, III, iii–iv

The inside of the van smelled like a badly serviced Texaco restroom and felt like a sauna on low heat. The walls were covered with a series of flat-screen televisions. Some displayed the entire housing complex, and while one man concentrated on a series of sound inputs, the other watched the screens. One focused upon a front door. The kitchen. The boy's room. The master bedroom. His eyes roamed from one screen to another in an endless predatory rhythm.

Back to the center quad, where Terry was jogging out and down the street.

"All things considered," he said, "man has a lot of energy. Off for a run."

"Hell, maybe it's another booty call."

"What a stud," the first said without an iota of genuine admiration. He was already scribbling in a journal. Then he turned back to the screens. Then he scribbled again.

♦ ♦ ♦

In three minutes, Terry reached the junior high school track. He rotated wrists, elbows, shoulders, neck, waist, and knees in a series of circles and spirals, a better preparation for running than the typical quad-calf sports stretches. Stretching was for later. After. He took off down the track, noting that he seemed aware of each quarter-inch of contact from heel to toe. Faster and faster he went. On and on he ran. And to a degree he had never experienced, he felt his body flexing and contracting like a single giant sinewy web. Felt the elastic energy storing and releasing, compressing and propelling with every step like a human Slinky. It was startling, like the opening of an entire rubbery universe that a lifetime of athletic training and competition had never revealed.

The next time he looked at his wristwatch, it was after four o'clock. Almost two hours had passed? Damn, it felt as if he'd just started. Flow state was an eerie thing. He ran on. After another hour or so he came to a stop, bent with hands on knees, sweat drizzling to the ground. His hands trembled, vibrated. He could feel his heartbeat in his legs. "What the hell . . . ?"

Terry alternated sets of push-ups and sit-ups. Fifty. A hundred. More. Pull-ups on the edge of a horizontal pipe along the stadium steps until his fingers cramped and his back burned. Superman push-ups, with extended arms, clapping behind his back between every repetition. Burpees, flinging himself in the air for plyometric breakfalls. On and on. He looked at his watch again, unable to believe what he saw. It was six o'clock. Again, it felt as if he'd only begun. "What the fuck is going on?"

Back onto the track he went. Terry started sprinting across the football field again and again . . . and although he could wind himself, thirty seconds of rest completely refreshed him. He simply couldn't exhaust himself. His heartbeat roared in his ears . . . and then quieted.

Then, finally, after another hour, he came to a halt. He laid down on the grass, not because he was tired, but because it was so damned good to feel the blades against his back, to stare up at the sky as morning's light first began to streak the darkness.

A thought came to him, unbidden: *The enslaved person ties his experiences to his beliefs and to his body image. This perpetuates the binding of the person to the wheel of samsara, the constant reincarnation into the illusory world.*

From what unconscious wellspring had *that* emerged? The Savagi video? Something he had missed hearing consciously while sliding in and out of half-sleep?

Possible, but he didn't think so. Had he heard the phrase "*Spanda Karika*" somewhere? That odd pronouncement seemed to carry such a label, but he couldn't imagine why, or where it had come from, or what it meant. It felt like a fragment of something he had glanced at years ago, that had suddenly bobbed to the surface of his memory well.

But . . . why? Perhaps he was simply exhausted.

But that wasn't true, either.

"I'm not tired," he whispered. "Not sleepy. This is just bizarre." He rolled up onto an elbow. "But I'm hungry as hell."

He paused. "And I'm talking to myself."

And at this, he laughed. And damn, that felt good.

♦ ♦ ♦

Terry headed to the local Waffle House seeking breakfast. It was one thousand, six hundred, and seventy steps away, nestled between a freeway on-ramp and a franchise motel with a brown shingle roof and a postage-stamp parking lot. He didn't consciously keep track of the distance . . . the number just popped into his head as he opened the door.

He entered, and sat in an empty booth. Terry unbuckled the little wallet on his left shoelaces and extracted a twenty-dollar bill. He sat with his fingers carefully folded and his eyes half-closed, listening to his heartbeat.

The redheaded waitress sashayed to his table. "Menu?"

"Thank you."

Terry's eyes skimmed across the tri-folded laminate. He inhaled deeply. Looked around at the other customers. Sniffed the coffee. Eggs. Ham. The people around him seemed fat, pudgy, or muscularly stiff. Most seemed strangled in straitjackets of tension.

The food stank sourly. Terry began to feel ill.

"Have you decided?" the redhead asked.

He answered automatically. "I'll have my usual. Ham and cheese omelet, English muffin."

"Sure," she said, and then paused. "Do I know you?"

He smiled up at her. "Would you like to?"

She blushed as she walked away, swaying her hips like a Vegas hypnotist dangling a gold pocket watch. Terry was a little mystified. And pleased.

He scanned the room. People chewed, talking. His hearing seemed sharper and clearer than usual. Perhaps he was merely paying more attention.

He watched their mouths as they spoke. Watched their motion as they walked down the aisles. And suddenly . . . the air danced with a visual tunnel of images detailing their activities since awakening that morning. *That* one displayed the loose-jointed facility of a dedicated yogi. Over there, a man who had injured his back by lifting weights winced when reaching for his orange juice.

A Hispanic couple whispered in a private world, words coupling urgently, intimately. Unbidden: flashes of nude bodies, twining together, glistening with sweat. He felt the driving, fleshy, staccato rhythms as they pounded against each other.

Married. To other people. Although they had showered afterward, traces of the intimate scent remained.

He shook himself. What the hell was going on? The waitress brought his food to his table. "Enjoy," she said. "Everything. You seem like a guy with a healthy appetite."

Well, woof.

She wiggled away, leaving behind her a trailing worm of images: makeup and shower and exfoliation. A rejection by an old lover within the last few days. A fling . . . perhaps two weeks ago . . . with the head cook. She had terminated it, but he still gazed at her with yearning.

Terry picked up his knife and fork. Scrawled on his napkin in pale pink lipstick: GLADYS. And her phone number. "Damn," he said. This was starting to feel like an infomercial for exotic aftershave.

Terry started forking and chewing his omelet. Before he could begin to swallow a strange, sick feeling spread through his gut, and a strained expression twisted his face. He slowed down.

He closed his eyes, and on a floating screen projected against the darkness he watched a yellowish slurry poured from a waxed carton labeled EGGS, spattering onto a sizzling, shoddily scraped griddle. Then . . . a synthetic cheese sauce squeezed from an orange tube. Ham seething with nitrates and sodium, traced back to a farm where pigs rooted in their own excrement.

Terry's eyes widened, and he bolted up out of the seat, staggered and crossed the sidewalk just in time to fountain vomit into the gutter, spattering orange and yellow onto the cigarette butts and twisted candy wrappers. A passing car honked. The other customers stared at him through the window. Gladys rushed out, eyes wide and panicked. "Are you all right?"

He wiped his mouth. "I'm . . . I don't know what happened," he said. "Here. Take this."

He crammed the twenty-dollar bill into her sweaty palm. Gladys stared after him as he staggered down the sidewalk and away.

◆ ◆ ◆

Terry slid into the empty spaces between pedestrians. Every one of them trailed a pale blue wormlike tunnel stretching back to their past.

A stubbled man drinking bourbon for breakfast. Terry could smell the ulcerous breath.

A small pale child walking to school, a bruise the size of a half-dollar darkening his cheek. Flinching away from a man who brushed against him. The flinch was a dodge, a duck, and in Terry's mind flashed a stark image of the boy trapped in a corner, slapped backhand before being allowed out the door to school.

On and on Terry walked. And then ran. Whenever he stopped, he was seeing people's histories, displayed in rapid projection backward. A riot of sounds and voices reverberated in an emotional echo chamber.

His heels thundered against the dirt and concrete. His breath rumbled in his lungs, a sand-papery sound. Surely he had depleted his muscles' glycogen supply by now. Surely his body was beginning to break down muscle tissue for fuel. Or had it gone directly for fat stores? He didn't know, knew only that he felt good, better than he had any right to feel, all things considered.

The change in his physical energy was strange, but the visual hallucinations were so disorienting that he felt like he'd stepped into another world.

Terry wandered, randomly turning right or left at red lights and when he looked up . . .

It was dark.

Terry checked his watch, watching his own reaction as if viewing himself from above.

He'd been running for ten hours, in a total fugue state, barely aware of where he was or what he was doing. He had no idea what part of town this was. Someplace in the outskirts of Atlanta, surely. A warehouse district.

He was walking now. Faintly at first, then louder as he walked east, bloodthirsty cheers floating on the wind, howls of glee or approval or pain. He kept walking, until he reached an image of himself reflected in a store window.

A trick of the light: god damn, he seemed to be *glowing,* and the illusion was like viewing himself through a kaleidoscope. Not visually . . . the visual image was not deconstructed. But . . . the way he felt. Fragmented. As if the thing he called "Terry" was shattering in slow motion, such that he could glimpse another, smaller, but somehow denser and more solid Terry within.

The cheers grew louder. A hundred pairs of feet stomping the warehouse floor.

He walked into a high-ceilinged wood-and-aluminum building so dank with salt-sweat it was like a hot springs. Beefy guys were pounding each other bloody on the matted floor, surrounded by stacks of crates and a ring of jeering, cheering spectators. In circles of electric incandescent light they slammed knees and elbows into each other's ribs and skulls. With every blow, screams of crowd-joy shook the rafters.

A big flat-faced guy with Popeye forearms and a button nose was taking money at the door. He looked at Terry. "You here for the fight?"

"Yes," Terry said. "Here for the fight."

"Fifteen bucks."

Terry bent down and extracted the second twenty from his mini-wallet, handed it to the guy with the flat face, and received five ones in return.

He turned and watched the brawling beef trust.

The money-taker noted Terry's build, his scarred hands and cheeks. "We have a hole in the lineup," he said. "You interested?"

"Interested," Terry said.

The former combatants had been replaced by a new pair. Human fighting cocks, fireplugs with arms and legs punching and kicking as if each had discovered the other in bed with his wife. One wore a buzz-cut, the other looked like an Aryan Mr. T, slathered with prison tats. The one with the Mohawk rapidly gained the upper hand. Buzz-cut was growing tired, and panicking.

There are few things in life worse than being in a fight, losing, and feeling yourself becoming even more fatigued. Watching your opponent start to grin. Beginning to ignore your strikes. Feeding on your fear.

Terry watched. But within the fortresses of faux anger, animalistic muscle, and savage energy . . . lurked the shadows of sad, broken men. Not all . . . some seemed centered and if cynical, at least untwisted. But others cast the shadows of battered children. Skill, hunger, and anger were elements, certainly. But the atmosphere stank of fear.

Images from their lives, stretching back to childhood, flashed to his mind. Absent fathers, schoolyard beatings, alcoholic, impassive mothers, transgressive "uncles." As they washed over Terry, tears welled and then rolled down his face. Mohawk smashed an elbow against his opponent's cheekbone, splitting it and sending the other man's head bouncing off the mat. Buzz-cut groaned and collapsed, and the conqueror raised his hands in triumph, massive biceps and triceps bunching and coiling as if he were smuggling anacondas.

"Who's next?" Mohawk screamed. "Who wants some of this? What asshole is motherfucking next?"

Terry watched through streaming eyes, and it may have been those tears that attracted Mohawk's attention. The fighter sneered at him. "Who's the little girl?" He grinned. "What the hell are you crying about?"

Mohawk, nine years old. Lips smeared with lipstick, crying and crouching in the basement dark. A huge man hovering over him. Looming. Promising an end to pain if only . . .

"I'm so sorry he hurt you," Terry said.

Mohawk wiped blood from a torn brow, sneering. "He didn't do shit."

"Not him," Terry said.

Mohawk's eyes narrowed. "Then who . . ."

Their eyes met in a world of silence. Around them, mouths moved but produced no sound. All he could see were Mohawk's bruises. The tats and piercings. When had that nose first been broken? The left arm had been fractured, probably in childhood. Who had done the breaking?

A tunnel enveloped Mohawk, canceled out everyone around them, and in its light, Terry saw everything. Everything.

"I'm sorry," he said. "But you grew up, didn't you? He can't hurt you anymore."

Mohawk's eyes tightened and then widened.

The guy was thunderstruck. The room fell silent as Terry walked forward, frozen in place as he wrapped his arms around Mohawk's broad shoulders and hugged him. Mohawk blinked, everything save his eyelids frozen in shock.

"Who the fuck are you?" he asked, voice thickened.

"Just a brother," Terry whispered in his ear. "Be well."

He turned and walked out, leaving the entire group staring after him.

◆ ◆ ◆

Terry spent another hour wandering, only slightly more aware than during his prior fugue state. A ways distant, on a side street, he roamed into a section of pavement where the asphalt had cracked to expose the foundational dirt beneath. And there, improbably, a green sprig of sunflower stretched plaintively toward the sky.

Terry sat cross-legged (what a long-ago army base teacher named . . . Mrs. Benjamin . . . called "crisscross apple sauce") in the middle of the empty street, staring at it.

One after another the glass-and-steel boxes of the office buildings surrounding him dissolved, replaced by older, wooden structures.

And then some of those disappeared, leaving stores and houses more spread out, with wide spaces between.

Then those buildings were replaced by peach groves.

And those by forest.

Terry sat on his mat of leaves and ferns, unable to stop crying. He knew that the vision would go deeper, to a world before life. To a universe before stars. There was . . . no end to it all.

Turtles, all the way down.

Who was he? What was true? He was falling, tumbling, with no net to catch him. Nothing connecting him to a universe that seemed to have no actuality at all.

After a time a car rumbled toward him down the street. When the headlights touched him, the driver leaned on the horn. Terry waved it away.

He looked up with huge eyes. "Not this one," he said. "Not today." Oddly, he felt no fear.

"Asshole!" the driver yelled, weaving around him.

Terry could only smile. Asshole. Yes, he certainly was. He tensed his hand, felt the tendons and muscles hardening into a spade-like weapon. Formed it into a fist like a mace, tensing harder than he ever had, with specific constrictions never before mastered, and smashed it into the cracked asphalt. The hardened tar yielded. Again he struck. And again, until it was arrayed in chunks. He tenderly pulled the sunflower up, cradling it like a newborn, which perhaps it was.

With trembling fingers, he peeled away as much of the asphalt as he could, leaving an area as broad as a comic book.

Then he carried the tiny seedling away in his cupped hands, walking down the middle of the street, cars blaring their horns at him.

He did not know how far or how long he walked, only that he was following a green scent in the wind. Finally, he reached a tiny park, a quarter-block of flowers and grass. There, in a shelter amid a cluster of trees, he squatted and dug a hole with his hands, and deposited the precious sprig. Heaped earth around it, and patted it down.

He stood.

It was not important, just another plant among countless billions. There was no reason to care about it, or think it special. No one had noticed its sprouting, and no one would grieve its death.

And yet . . . he had decided to care about it. Just . . . decided.

What a marvelous, miraculous thing, to care. To decide to feel a connection to something else. A simple act of will. *That* was the antidote to nothingness. Simple caring.

No one would notice the little sunflower here, he knew. But perhaps . . . just perhaps . . . he would come back one day, just to see how it was growing.

CHAPTER 19

It is odd the way panic spreads, once a certain threshold is breached. The "End of the World" headline had been repeated around the globe, in every media, like some viral YouTube dancing cat video.

Myanmar tried to conceal the death of its minister of finance, and when the reality came to light it was worse than if they had told the truth to begin with.

From a stronghold somewhere in the mountains of central Africa, the leader of a notorious guerilla faction appeared grinning in a handheld video pronouncing his health. It took only fifty-seven minutes before CNS technicians determined that the dating codes had been falsified.

Not a good day.

♦ ♦ ♦

Olympia returned to an office dominated by a creeping, barely contained current of dread. Around the world in the last twenty-four hours, five powerful and dangerous men and one woman had died by means unknown, in custody and in front of doctors, guards, and scientists. If the threat could be taken seriously, somewhere in the world at least two more unknowns had died in the same bizarre way, and who the hell could say otherwise? To their knowledge, not a security service in existence had so much as a single solid lead.

Who the hell were the "Elite," for God's sake? She certainly didn't believe it was the end of the world, but *something* was going on, that was for sure.

"*As has happened thrice before . . .*" What tradition spoke of three apocalyptic events in human history?

"*On December 13, our high holy day.*" Whose "high holy day"? The twelfth was the "Feast of Our Lady of Guadalupe" but that was the closest she could get.

"I heard about it all over the radio," Joyce Chow said, interrupting Olympia's thoughts. "The manifesto is all over the Net. Everybody's connected the dots."

"And?" she asked.

Joyce took another sip of coffee. "Making elephants and unicorns. The markets are starting to wobble. It isn't good."

"That makes a total of thirty-one dead?" Olympia asked.

"At least. There are rumors that the numbers are much higher."

Sloan poked his bald head into the room. The fringe of red hair gave him a disturbing resemblance to Bozo the Clown, though she had never mentioned the comparison to a soul. "Conference room in five."

The first news stories hit, connecting conspiracy theory Web sites with the original list, reports of dead leaders, and attempts at cover-up. Panic had begun to boil up around the edges of the calm conversation and polite smiles and neutered news bulletins.

Joyce Chow's face dominated the wall-sized projection screen. "According to WikiLeaks, at least twenty individuals on the infamous 'Dead List' have actually perished. It is unknown how many others there might be." Olympia looked back and forth from her friend to the screen, disoriented by seeing the familiar face so grotesquely expanded. "The stock market today took another dip, and some analysts worry that unless this situation resolves, it could enter a tailspin that makes the 2008 crash look—"

Sloan turned the television off, looked sourly at Joyce, and then cleared his throat. "This is what we're up against. We need to jump ahead of this curve. I've arranged for an exclusive video feed, and it cost me a lot of favors."

A test pattern followed, and then a flicker of colors. This was replaced by a PowerPoint message saying that the footage they were about to see was classified.

"Oslo, Norway." A heavily accented voice. For this one, English was perhaps a third language, behind . . . Swedish and German, she thought. "I will narrate the autopsy footage obtained from sources in Sweden. Arms merchant Thor Swenson died recently in a road accident. That is the official story. But there is more. As you can see . . ."

Olympia gasped.

A naked male human corpse lay upon a steel pallet. The body was misshapen, as if half the bones were broken, the splintered fragments poking through pallid skin. He looked as if someone had stuffed him into a piñata and beaten it with a bat.

"What in the hell could do that?" she muttered. "Electrocution? Poison? Some kind of torture?"

"We have no idea how it was effected," the discordant voice continued. "Only that it happened. There are difficulties, since his body was mutilated in an automotive incident. To complicate further, his corpse was entangled with that of his secretary, so that it became difficult to determine which wounds were pre- and which postmortem."

Olympia tapped her pencil against the desk. "Have you inspected dental records? Medical records? Seeking . . ." She searched for words. "Some sort of mechanism? Something could have been implanted during some procedure requiring general anesthesia."

Sloan nodded approvingly. "That's good. As far as I know dossiers are still being compiled. There are no obvious points of commonality in terms of their timetables in the previous month."

Office-mate Christy Flavor chimed in, but Olympia noticed that she seemed to be struggling to maintain calm. "And is this the same as the Mexican television show? Quinones? Was that his name?"

"Ramone Quinones, the drug lord. As far as we can tell it is the same. The information is still being coordinated."

Olympia watched through her fingers as, with clinical dispassion, Thor Swenson's epidermis was pulled away from the underlying fascia, glistening muscles examined and split and probed.

She closed her eyes, trying not to gag as the dispassionate voice described injuries as if reading ingredients from the side of a bottle of disinfectant.

♦ ♦ ♦

When the voice concluded she opened her eyes again. The images had vanished from the wall. Luckily the pastry dish was empty. She might have thrown up if that cherry-filled blintz had still been oozing on the plate. Sloan glared at the empty glass disk, ran a finger across it to pick up a little sugar glaze, and licked the frosted digit wistfully.

"I don't want you to think like citizens. I need you to think like reporters. Or like kids playing a game. It isn't quite real."

"What . . . do you mean by that?" Olympia asked.

"Like a kid's game. Specifically Clue. Remember that no matter what the story, the answer is always the same: it's Colonel Mustard, in the basement, with the lead pipe."

A few hollow chuckles.

This isn't real. It isn't real. Or if it is, it is some kind of horrible trick. It will end. We will all wake up. And then . . . and then Madame Gupta will heal Hannibal, and everything will be right with the world.

"I need your logic, not your emotions. Nobody knows what's going on here, but my instinct tells me that somehow, human beings are at the root of it. Maybe using machines. Maybe . . . something else. But there is a some-one, a somewhere, and a how. There is a motive and a means. Somewhere." He paused, glaring into them, as if trying to infect them with his will.

"I have something you need to see," he said. "Just came in from a station in Arkansas."

"What is it?" Olympia asked carefully. She had just about convinced herself that the whole thing was some kind of terrorist act, designed to create panic.

No one could kill the world.

Could they?

"Just another tiny thread coming unraveled," he said. "This is what happens when you let yourself forget you're a reporter." That sardonic edge to his voice, the thing she'd always noticed that no one else seemed to hear, was a blade. More terror than irony.

The male and female co-anchors on the next news program looked nervous, not hiding their fear at all. Hogging the story, she thought, like when her network's stars in combat and hurricane zones made their own danger the focus of the broadcast. But this time, it didn't look like theater. It looked like a reason to run and hide.

"So, again, Premier Mumbai is dead—" the male anchor choked out. Olympia flashed back to J-school recordings of Walter Cronkite announc-ing President Kennedy's death in 1963, which had given her chills—as the broadcast now did again, but for very different reasons. President Kennedy had died before she was born, already a symbol. This was her era's trag-edy, monstrous because it was just getting started.

The newscaster's hands trembled, fumbling with a few pages of a script, but recovered quickly. He wasn't a main anchor; Olympia didn't know his face.

"There are already reports of riots in the streets of the capital—the army out in great numbers. Mumbai was accused of using his military in an ethnic massacre in '03. We have several credible reports that he'd been hiding in the main vault of the national bank when struck down. Further reports—and we're waiting for a video feed from a security camera—including the U.N. observer's account from inside the bank—maintain that he was alone at the time."

His emphasis on the last word made it the point of his story. "I repeat—President Mumbai is dead. Precisely as it was predicted on the Dead List. Precisely."

Neither anchor spoke for some time.

"Anything to add, Lucy?"

Lucy, the co-anchor, had painted a plastic mask over a barely restrained rictus of terror.

"I . . . I'm supposed to read this bulletin, Frank." Her hands trembled like a malaria victim's. "But I'm not sure I should. I've been thinking about all of this, and maybe it's time to put aside trivial things."

She paused for a beat. He tried to act as if it was a joke, smiled uncomfortably at the camera. "Uh . . ."

"Have you accepted the Lord Jesus into your life, Frank? If these were the last days, would you be ready to meet Him?"

Frank's face was creased in one of those *holy shit, this woman is a loon* expressions. The screen went blank for a moment, and then they cut to a commercial.

Sloan turned it off. "Wasn't that lovely?"

Good thing it was the end of the world, Olympia thought, or Lucy would be so fired from Little Rock or wherever that station had been. And she marveled at how easily, how logically, the phrase "end of the world" had crept into her mind.

CHAPTER 20

Nicki had decided not to accompany them to the Salvation Sanctuary, preferring to attend her drama club's three-day Shakespeare camp for the first few days of Christmas vacation. She'd spend the night with a friend, engaged in an all-night "Memory Bash" running lines from *The Taming of the Shrew*. Olympia had wanted to protest. This was a time when a family should be together, but Nicki wasn't impressed at all with the horrendous news, had erected her own fortress of denial, and seemed happy to be with friends.

And Olympia was grateful for that, and for the fact that Hannibal was oblivious to it all. And if she could shoulder the entire burden of anxiety for her family, she would happily do so.

Big Sister had kissed Hannibal goodbye, told him to enjoy the helicopter ride, and dashed off when the school van honked for her.

Olympia was just finished dressing when the doorbell rang. "Be right there!" she called down. "Hannibal, are you ready?" She expected no answer, of course—*one day,* she told herself, *one day,* and followed up immediately with direct observation.

He was brushing his teeth, eyes dreamy, when she entered the bathroom. "Sweetie, you need to hurry a little. Today might be a pretty important day. I think that's our ride."

Instead of speaking his reply, he sang. "Okay."

She ran downstairs, and answered the door to find a smiling, square-jawed Germanic woman with blond cornrows wearing an immaculately tailored blue chauffeur's uniform.

"Olympia Dorsey? I'm Maureen Skotak, your driver."

"Yes," she said. "Be just a second. Hannibal, honey!"

Hannibal was already coming up behind her, grabbing her dress, squinting up shyly at the woman with the Dick Tracy jawline.

"This is my son, Hannibal. Hani, this is our driver."

"Maureen," she repeated. She smiled and extended her hand to Hannibal. Hannibal looked at the hand and then up at his mother, hesitating.

It was a notably longer hesitation than he had given Terry on their first meeting.

"It's all right," Olympia said.

He shook hands. The driver smiled again, Olympia smiled. Somewhere beyond their bubble the world was wobbling at the edge of something almost unfathomably hideous, and everybody was smiling. Wasn't that nice?

"Well," the driver said, "we have a chopper to catch!" A helicopter ride to spend a few hours with a remarkable woman. A medicine for madness, just in the nick of time.

They walked out to a white Rolls-Royce limousine, Hani's small hand in hers. Maureen held the passenger door open.

Nicki retreated into the house. Olympia watched as the front door closed, wondering if Nicki's first independent steps were just the beginning of losing touch with her daughter. Her own relationship with her mother had never stabilized after her father's death, after they had moved from Liberty City. After the excessive life insurance he'd purchased to buoy a drowning cousin had bought a new home and a college education, and destroyed the woman who had once seemed so lithe and lovely, she'd withered into bitterness and finally death.

But long before her mother died, their relationship had cooled to ashes. She would *not* let that happen with Nicki.

No. Never. Not after the last three terrible years.

But what if some catastrophic event yet to be felt tangled traffic, triggered an evacuation, and somehow prevented her from seeing her daughter again? The thought felt too damned plausible. Olympia stared at the closed door.

Maureen swung around to the driver's side, then dropped the partition and looked back at them. "Buckle up, little man. Someone very important is waiting to see you!"

The interior of the car was black leather and stainless steel. It was beautiful, comfortable, and functionally elegant. She sank into the seat, sighing, and fastened Hannibal's safety straps.

They pulled out of the driveway, and then the complex. Vaguely, Olympia noted the cable truck, still parked at the curb outside the complex. It had been there, with minor shifts from one position to another, for five days. Someone must have been ordering a lot of HBO.

◆ ◆ ◆

Their limo moved out onto Atlanta Road, heading east toward the 85 freeway. "There's a PlayStation back there, and a bar with ginger ale," Maureen said cheerfully.

That, Hani understood immediately. Needing only a little help from Olympia, he booted up the PlayStation. Sonic the Hedgehog bounced onto the screen and promptly commenced hopping hedges.

"Do you work for the limo company?" Olympia asked.

"No," Maureen replied. "I work for Madame Gupta."

"You're one of her . . . what? Students? Acolytes?"

Olympia caught the edge of a cool, remote smile in the rearview mirror. "No. Just handle odds and ends."

The limo cruised along the freeway for ten minutes, then pulled off. Eight blocks through an industrial district took them to a fenced helicopter pad the size of the Foothill Village basketball court, marked like a rifle scope.

"All out!" Maureen chirped, and oddly, again Hani didn't complain or resist. Olivia had never been in a helicopter before. It was smaller than she would have expected, and the body juddered as she stepped up into the passenger compartment. She tested her weight, then decided that the yielding she felt from the steel and Plastiglas was part of the design. Hannibal's grin was as wide as the horizon. They climbed into the back of the 'copter, which was almost as plush as the limousine, although the buckles were more elaborate, almost like a webbing.

The pilot welcomed them aboard, and checked to be sure they were safe and comfortable as Maureen strapped herself into the third seat. The rotors began to turn. "Here we go!" she said, heavy jaw softened by a broad smile as the chopper lifted off the pad.

"First time in a helicopter?" she asked.

"Yes." Olympia turned to her son. "Do you like this, hon?"

"Up, up, and away!" Hani said.

"How far is it?" she asked.

"Twenty minutes," Maureen said.

"Twenty minutes to a new life," she said, surprised that she would speak her thoughts aloud. "Just a helicopter ride. You'd think there would be more drama."

Maureen chuckled heartily, loud enough to be heard above the rotors. It occurred to Olympia that there seemed an element of theatricality about that guffaw. "Madame Gupta takes care of her people."

"Who owns the Salvation Sanctuary?" A perfect name, she thought. Sanctuary. Salvation. Yes.

"We do," Maureen said. "Two hundred and forty acres."

"Wow," Olympia said, looking down over the patchwork of industrial parks beneath them, yielding to freeways and rolling green acreage. Her worries about what she had seen at work floated behind her.

Instead, she took in the ivory-speckled foothills of the North Georgia mountains, and then the peaks themselves. Hani seemed at peace, perfectly happy just watching the patterns swirling past beneath them. Circles and squares and even spirals of green and brown. The patterns seemed comforting to him.

Chaos swirled at the edges of logic. Reality was less solid than we like to think. What was it that Joyce Chow had said about money? She called it her favorite illusion. It was trust, belief, shared faith. And the instant the faith was gone . . . the entire pyramid of dreams would collapse.

"The retreat was built atop an exhausted gold mine by a silent movie star in 1914, went into collections in '48, and was purchased from the state in 1999. We've made extensive changes."

Now she reckoned they were approaching the Salvation Sanctuary itself. High walls topped with razor wire. The very center of the grounds was an elaborate circular hedge maze, looking like a page out of a Dell puzzle book. She could see what looked like a spa or pond at the center of it. Hani studied it carefully, his lips moving in silence.

"Why so much security?" Olympia asked.

"Not only do we need privacy, but our library has some of the rarest and most expensive books in the world, an estimated value of fifty million dollars."

"Wow!" Hannibal said.

"That's exactly what I said the first time." Maureen laughed. "Wow." She smiled that shovel-jawed smile again.

Olympia blinked a bit, but managed to get her unease under control. Probably just the unaccustomed vehicle. Maybe it was just excitement. The sense of possibility.

The helicopter descended.

CHAPTER 21

"Where exactly are we?" Olympia yelled against the helicopter rotor's incessant *whop-whop-whop*.

"North Georgia mountains," Maureen said. She didn't seem to be raising her voice, but somehow they could hear it anyway. "The Salvation Sanctuary is located in one of the most beautiful and peaceful spots in the Southeast. Blue Ridge Mountains, Cedar Mountain, in particular, to the west, and the Horseshoe Appalachians to the north. It's great here year-round."

Olympia had grown up in a concrete village. Lived and worked all her life surrounded by stone and steel and glass. The endless expanse of natural green, dappled with white, was soothing even before she had placed a foot on the ground.

"We have miles of nature trails, winding through old hardwoods and pines. Do you jog?"

"Sometimes," she said.

"Good. Madame Gupta believes a healthy body is a doorway to a healthy mind and spirit. You can trot beside the streams, or sit at spring-fed reflection pools or quiet coves and never hear anything louder than a blackbird." Maureen's voice was oddly flat, as if she were quoting a tourist brochure.

"Sounds lovely."

"Like barbecues?" she asked. "We have fire pits. Three outdoor hot tubs. A world-class library. We have it all."

♦ ♦ ♦

As the door opened, Maureen helped Olympia out into the mountain air, at least ten degrees cooler than it had been back in Smyrna. The sky above was too blue for snow, but a few drifting flakes would not have astounded her. A slender, pale young man in a gold robe greeted them. The joy radiating from his face both warmed and comforted her. "Welcome!" he said. "We've heard so much about you. Waited a long time for this."

The adulation was disorienting. "I'm supposed to be a writer, but I can't think of words right now."

"No words are necessary," he replied, and helped Hannibal down. She noticed that Maureen had seemed to melt away, leaving her to the newcomers.

A guard in a very traditional security officer's uniform waved them through a gated road, smiling broadly. Their guide led them in a clockwise fashion, pointing out buildings around the rim. "Administration," he said. "And our dojo. And just a little farther on is the library."

At a slight distance, a group of people in civilian clothes headed toward the hedge maze. A woman in a gold robe led them, lecturing and gesturing languidly.

"Who are they?"

"Devotees from around the world," he said. "We see hundreds a month. They come to study, hoping to glimpse Madame Gupta, or to gawk at the library."

"They research in your stacks?" she asked. He was leading her toward a brown two-story building with an adobe-tiled roof, about the size of a typical McDonald's.

"Oh no." He laughed. "Outsiders never get to touch those."

The notion struck Olympia as profoundly sad; books so few could read or touch. "Oh!"

They hurried on. The tour group, consisting of a dozen or so, passed murmuring like a flock of geese. For a moment she thought she recognized a woman in the group. Was that . . . *Maria* . . . ?

◆   ◆   ◆

Maria Cortez saw Olympia, but did not acknowledge her recent guest. She had recognized the possibility that they would encounter each other, but that couldn't be helped. She had last been at the Salvation Sanctuary four months ago, and knew where she was going and what she needed to do.

"And if you come right this way," the tour guide chirped. "We'll try not to get lost in the topiary maze."

They walked on. Maria continued to observe Olympia and her son, Hannibal, from the corner of her eye, but kept her head down and said nothing.

◆   ◆   ◆

Olympia and Hannibal were led to the main library building, two stories tall with a tiled roof. The broad double doors opened into a reception area. Through walls of two-inch-thick glass they peered into an astonishing private book collection: two stories high, wide as a college auditorium, and crammed floor to ceiling with volumes, some protected behind Plexiglas panels.

"Could we . . . ?" she asked, expecting to be turned down.

"Of course." A woman's voice, from behind them. Olympia turned as Madame Gupta glided toward them, smiling broadly. "Greetings," she said. "Welcome to my humble home."

"Wow," she said. "And the Taj Mahal is a Motel 6."

"Wow!" Hannibal finally said. Sang, actually, a musical quality entering the single syllable.

Madame Gupta knelt down, her saffron robe barely touching the ground. "Hello, young man. I don't expect you to answer me, but I think we're going to become great friends. I certainly hope so."

Hannibal didn't meet her eyes. He was counting books through the glass wall.

"Would you like to go in?"

"How many?" he said, staring straight ahead.

"Thirty-two thousand, nine hundred, and forty-six," Madame Gupta said. "We almost never let outsiders in. But you, young man, are no ordinary visitor."

She ruffled his hair, and stood. She took a deep breath of bracing winter air. "I never get completely used to it myself." A twinkle lit her eye. "Would you like a personal tour?"

"I'd love it," Olympia said.

"How about right after we go to the lab?"

"That would be fine," she said, but the bibliophile in her soul felt a keen stab of disappointment. Then she remembered why they were there, and what her son stood to gain. Gupta believed in Hannibal, and after all the bad news Olympia had gotten from his teachers, that was a very good thing to hear. *Hannibal can't sit still, can't focus, can't complete work on a schedule,* she'd been told. Madame Gupta, at last, thought Hannibal could . . .

Could what, exactly?

"Was it difficult to get off from work?"

Yes, Sloan had been irritated. But he had children of his own, and an office filled with panicky employees. In some ways, he had seemed relieved to have a problem small enough to solve. "No. I mean, yes, but nothing is more important than my boy. If you can really help him . . ."

"We believe so, yes," the smaller woman said.

"That's all that matters."

She led them through a panel in the glass wall, so cunningly concealed that Olympia hadn't noticed the fault line. The door had to have been unlocked by some means she didn't understand: a hidden camera or perhaps a magnetic passkey. They proceeded through a passage next to the library to a bank of elevators in a lobby formed of steel, glass, and dark, warm, earth-toned woods. A banner above them read: SANCTUARY.

Yes. *Sanctuary.* She appreciated that. They had reached Sanctuary. A place of healing and safety.

". . . is also the meditation complex," Madame Gupta said. Olympia realized her mind had wandered. She hoped she hadn't missed anything important. "Here, we train, test, and prepare our followers for the rigors to come."

Olympia felt a bit of mental dazzle-fog slip away. "Rigors? Is there risk?"

Madame Gupta placed a comforting hand on her arm. "Oh, no. Not in the training. Not for Hannibal, ever. Our missionaries sometimes encounter resistance."

They slid down a level, and Madame Gupta ushered them out. They passed through a hall lit by soft glowing tubes overhead, walking past a series of doors with broad, clear windows. Through them Olympia could see five young men and women wired to a series of machines with beeping displays, perhaps a variety of fancy brain-training machines.

"What is all of this?"

Madame Gupta took a deep breath, and let it out slowly. "You have heard people say we use only ten percent of our brains?"

Olympia felt a bit of caution. Was this the opening for a Tony Robbins sales pitch? "Yes, I've heard that."

The little woman smiled. "Well, that's not neurologically accurate. It's a myth, really."

"Then why do people say it?"

"Well, it's probably a statement of our potential in terms of optimal organization. What we think we are capable of at higher levels of integration. But one thing that we can actually say with confidence is that we really have little idea of what human beings are capable of accomplishing. No one does."

"I can believe that," Olympia said.

"What do you think evolution is, my dear?"

"Survival of the fittest?"

"Well," Madame Gupta said. "That is what people say. Not quite what Mr. Darwin had in mind, however, and Mr. Darwin had neither the first nor last word on the subject."

Olympia laughed. "All right. What is evolution?"

"Darwinian evolution stems from the observation that there is great variety in life. And some of those variations 'fit' better with the world around them than previous incarnations of a particular species." Odd. That almost sounded like she was quoting something, rather than accessing an integrated memory, a little like Maureen's recitation of the Salvation Sanctuary's attractions.

"It isn't just being bigger or stronger?"

"Oh, no," Gupta said. "Not at all." Her tone of voice had changed. She was back to the warm maternal flow again. Olympia decided that she had been imagining things. "Now, the challenges faced by a child like Hannibal are clear. What is not so clear is that there may be equal and compensating advantages. Autism is often seen as a socialization issue. A difficulty in communicating with the external world. A lack of capacity to read body language or facial expressions or divine rules of behavior and interaction that seem automatic to the rest of us."

"Advantages?"

"The world is changing, Olympia. All the time. And our children will face a very different landscape than what we ourselves traversed." *A changing world indeed,* Olympia thought. But the horror of the mysterious killings felt far from her mind, merely gentle whispers drowned out by Madame Gupta's voice.

"It would stand to reason that some changes we consider problematic might actually be strengths. These strengths may only be revealed in a world we cannot currently imagine. A writer named Thom Hartmann thinks children designated with attention deficit disorder may simply be hunters in a world full of farmers. Those who prefer patterns to human interaction may simply have a male genius for organization."

"Isn't that sexist?"

Gupta laughed. "Oh . . . everyone believes there are differences between men and women. We just can't agree on what they are, or what they mean. I would only consider it sexist to say those differences limit all behaviors for all people, or places one gender above the other. Labels offer little: we mustn't mistake the label for the thing itself."

That was a little New Agey for her. "What kind of abilities?"

Madame Gupta leaned forward and dropped her voice, her eyes

twinkling. When she spoke, for the first time Olympia detected layers of accent below the American affectation. British. And . . . Indian? "That is what we brought you here to discover."

◆　◆　◆

The next elevator was concealed within an office, as if protected from casual eyes. Their descent lasted fifteen seconds, after which the elevator opened into a caged storage area. Beyond were raw rock walls and the impression that this level of the Sanctuary had been deliberately left a little rough, to preserve the old mine's natural atmosphere. She could hear water trickling in the walls, trailed her hand across the uneven rock surface as if trying to read Braille. The rock floor beneath her had been smoothed by countless feet over a century of wear before the newcomers retrofitted man-made caverns with tile and incandescent lights.

The basement lab was delightful to Hannibal—lab animals, lights, and fawning attendants. Toys! His grin was so wide she almost expected the top half of his head to fall off.

"What is it you do here?"

A round-faced technician whose name tag read ROY addressed her. "We have the facility available to measure mental and physical abilities on an extremely advanced level."

"Like at the center in Smyrna?" Her memory of the little laughing woman leaping and tumbling on the jigsaw mats returned in a flash. It was hard not to just swoon with awe and gratitude.

Roy laughed. "Oh, no, far beyond that. We fund those centers all over the world. Over two hundred of them."

"Two . . . hundred? Why? How many are the size of the one in Smyrna?"

"Few of them. The Smyrna facility is close to the Sanctuary. But why? We're looking for very special people," he said. "Like your little prince here."

Hannibal burbled with happiness at the attention. "I'm Hannibal!" he said.

Olympia forgot to inhale, suddenly realizing she was holding her breath. "He said his name!" Had he ever done that? Spoken his name aloud? Surely, surely . . . but with tears flooding down her cheeks, she realized that she couldn't remember when. And that might have been the most terrible thing of all. From the time her eleven-month-old son began to have difficulties meeting her eyes, the moment that his pediatrician had said the word "autistic" when he was twenty-five months old . . . from the time that Raoul had fled the boy who might never catch a ball, might never ride a bicycle, let alone drive a car . . .

This might have been the best moment in seven years of strangled hope.

The technician was talking, and she'd not heard a word of it. ". . . that's unusual, isn't it? I've read the reports. Mrs. Dorsey—"

"Please, call me Olympia."

"Olympia. We can't promise anything. But I can tell you we've had excellent results, some of which we've yet to share with the outside world." A glittering *something* surfaced in Gupta's eyes, like a diamond in a pool of oil. Then it submerged again.

"Why?"

"We have . . . proprietary processes, based upon knowledge and models of the human body-mind connection not yet accepted by Western science."

Olympia's head spun, then centered again. She had the odd sense that she was being buffeted by a storm, a cyclone, and that only by being in harmony with Gupta could she remain in the calm center. She so desperately longed to escape the travail that she longed to crawl into the little woman's sheltering arms and sob with relief. "I don't care about that. I care about my boy."

Gupta smiled warmly. "That was what I was hoping. Would you allow him to participate in an experiment?" The word "experiment" jarred, but Gupta's face was open and inspiring of trust.

"What sort of experiment?"

◆　◆　◆

Even before they entered the next room, the muscular, dank zoo smell told her what she was about to encounter. The walls of the subbasement lab were lined with toys, reminiscent of developmental blocks and puzzles one might find at a preschool. What was the gamey aroma, then?

"Hi!" a female tech said. She looked like Roy's rounder, jollier sister. "Hannibal! We've been waiting for you!"

"What is this place?" Olympia asked. The odd toys, the animal scents . . . her recent fabulous mood wavered.

"We pretty much run a petting zoo here," Roy said. "This is just where we pen them when we need medical testing." He laughed. "We don't hurt any of them. Nothing like that."

Desire to believe was a powerful thing. After all, it *could* be true.

"Well, we believe that part of what seems to be random communications, or suboptimal communication, are actually mental outreaches on a completely different level of consciousness."

Olympia felt her brow wrinkle, an odd sensation. "I don't understand."

"Neither do we." He grinned. "But sailors used the wind a very long time before we understood pressure gradients. Understanding is the booby prize. Do you want to understand love, or experience it?"

Olympia felt warmth creeping around her collar. She wanted . . .

"The real question," he continued, "is: can we use it?"

"Can we?"

"That," Madame Gupta said, "is what we're going to find out."

A lab-coated tech with Hi! I'm Mike! stitched onto his shirt appeared through a door in the back, holding the furry hand of a healthy, wide-grinning, and bowlegged black chimpanzee. The chimp made a kissy face, and then chittered. "This is Serge!" Mike said. "Serge, say hi to Hannibal!"

Serge bounced up into the tech's arms. Hannibal vibrated with delight.

"Have we your permission?" Madame Gupta asked.

"Is it safe?"

"Oh, completely," she said. "We'd just like him to look at some pictures, listen to some music. Nothing to worry about."

The tech smiled. "Serge is on loan from a facility in New Mexico. Very gentle, loves kids. Here." He let the friendly chimp clamber onto the boy, and the two of them embraced. Serge played huggy games immediately, which delighted Hannibal.

Mike gestured to Olympia. "Ma'am?" he said quietly.

When she responded, he gestured her over to a station. On a featureless bust next to a computer screen rested a golden mesh cap. Mike peeled it off the bust and held it up. "This is a harmless, noninvasive scan system we'll use to monitor Hannibal's brain waves. Do I have your permission?"

"Why do you need to do that?"

"Well, partially to be certain that Hannibal's brain wave patterns remain within a safe range."

"Safe?"

"No activation of the amygdala," he said. "No sharp beta waves, representing fear or anger response. Want to make sure that neither of them ever experiences excessive stress. Safer than a roller coaster."

"I . . . would appreciate that."

It took mere seconds for him to slip and strap the cap into place. Hannibal barely noticed.

"There's more," he confided. "We've identified simpatico brain wave patterns, and if Hannibal and Serge manifest them in similar amplitudes, then we have the best chance of . . . ah." He was suddenly distracted and pleased by something on the screen. "Very good. I think we have a 'go.'"

Despite her momentary misgivings, Olympia was now only curious. "What are you doing?"

"Something very, very clever."

Madame Gupta had been watching the exchange with a Yoda-like smile. Olympia almost expected her to start scrambling her sentences. "I'm going to leave you in Michael's very fine hands," she said. *Leave you, I will.*

"You're off?"

"I will see you again before you depart. And Hannibal?" The boy glowed up at her.

"Hannibal," he said. Twice in a day! Could the miracle she'd prayed for since Hannibal's diagnosis finally be unfolding? *Easy, girl. You just got here.*

Madame Gupta stroked Hannibal's cheek. His smile was radiant. "A very good afternoon to you, young sir." She winked at Olympia. "A very interesting lad, indeed."

Madame Gupta glided out the door, lowering the air pressure as she did.

Mike grinned. "We'll say good-bye to Serge now. He's going to be busy, and we're sending him back to the zoo this afternoon, so say good-bye."

"Bye," Hannibal said.

Olympia shook her head. "He's said more since he saw Madame Gupta at the school than he has in the previous year."

Mike took Hani and Olympia down a hallway. Out through a garden corridor wreathed with vines that seemed to grow out of the rock, but actually were rooted in cunningly concealed planters.

"Do you like it here?" the tech said.

"Oh yes, very much."

"So do we."

Olympia felt dazzled and dizzied, the computer screens and toys and smiling faces threatening to spin her like a merry-go-round. She reeled, off-balance, struggling to remain calm. "What exactly is this place?"

"Not just a research center," he said. "But a home. And a nexus for meditators from all our centers around the world."

"What pays for all of this?" she asked.

"We have benefactors. People who believe in the work we're doing."

"And they fund it?"

Mike scratched his head. "Well . . . there's more to it than that, but you're on the right track."

They traveled another corridor, this one narrower, and lit with corkscrew fluorescent bulbs. Where were they now? Certainly no longer under the library building. Had they been traveling counterclockwise?

Hannibal was just gawking and trailing his hands along the ridges and valleys of the rock walls, enchanted.

"Now," the tech said. "This is where a lot of the work gets done. We teach meditation here, and . . . other things."

"Other things?"

He smiled mysteriously. "Yes," he said. "You'll see."

He opened a door into a room filled with plush chairs and couches and wide black-rimmed video monitors.

They sat Hannibal down at a black couch positioned in front of a computer screen. The couch was warm and malleable, like a divan-shaped balloon filled with Jell-O. "Squishy!"

Olympia tried it for herself. She sank, and then buoyed back up almost as if she'd dropped into a colony of friendly jellyfish. "Yes! It's squishy! What is this?"

"It's sort of a water-couch. Hundreds of individual cells filled with water and maintained at body temperature. It molds to his posture. Madame Gupta's own design. Feels amazing, doesn't it?"

He adjusted some dials, and the translucent image of a chrysanthemum blossomed on the high-def screen in front of him.

"Hannibal, do you like the flower? Nice flower?"

Hannibal squinted at it, displaying little apparent enthusiasm.

"How about this? Spider-Man?" The familiar red-and-blue web-slinger appeared.

Hannibal's smile expanded.

"How about this?" A soccer ball! Hannibal clapped in delight.

"He loves soccer," Olympia said.

"Soccer it is! All right, Hannibal, just watch the soccer ball, all right?"

The boy nodded and leaned forward toward the screen, riveted. The overhead fluorescents paled him, accentuating his cheekbones, and made him seem older than he was.

"What is this?" Olympia asked.

"We're scanning him. Our technology uses brain scans to reconstruct images, and it helps us to measure activity and find ways the brain is working. Identify approaches to improve function."

"Really?" Olympia felt numb, but forced the feeling away. Her face was a mask, her responses curt, because the schoolgirl inside her was squealing. Her own childish enchantment worried her. Hannibal needed her head firmly planted on her shoulders, not floating away with bedazzlement. But that was so difficult when her instincts roared, *This is the best thing that's ever happened* more loudly with each passing moment. Other specialists had studied different parts of her boy—his physical health, his psychological health, his intellect—but Madame Gupta was the first to see him as a whole. In all these years, Madame Gupta might be the only person who could see her child at all. If not for Olympia's mask, she might have dissolved into tears.

It was all just too much. "That's wonderful," she said, embarrassed by how lame the words seemed.

"Yes, it is. So. Let's get this going."

The soccer balls multiplied, twisted, and spun on the screen. "Serge!" Hannibal said, pointing to the balls with delight.

The chimp? "What, darling?" she said.

"Serge!" he said.

Olympia was confused. "What is he saying?"

The tech bit his lip and squinted, seemed a little baffled, even upset. But when he noticed that Olympia was watching him, he shook himself and relaxed.

Olympia's numbness broke. Was something wrong?

"Concentrate, Hannibal," he said. "Please look at the balls. Just think about the balls . . ."

Hannibal watched, apparently delighted with the black-and-white spheres while Mike worked his magic.

At last, Mike sighed. "Fabulous! That was very good."

"He did well?"

"A whole lot better than that." He shook his head. "I think Madame Gupta will be tickled pink. I'm sending this on to her."

Olympia hugged her boy. "You did great, Hannibal."

"Serge?" Hannibal asked. "Is Serge good?"

"He's asking about the chimp," Olympia said.

Some emotion she couldn't name flitted across Mike's face.

"Serge," Hannibal repeated.

She finally understood what her boy was asking. "Now that he's finished, can we go back and play with Serge again?"

Again, Mike's expression was impenetrable. "You'll have to talk to Madame Gupta about that. This way, please."

◆　◆　◆

When they returned to the lab room, the techs were standing, applauding. Madame Gupta wore one of the widest, brightest smiles Olympia had ever seen. She embraced Hannibal, and he beamed. "Scrumptious," she said. "In fact, I don't believe we've tested a subject with higher potential."

The techs applauded and whooped. Olympia was dazzled. "So . . . ?"

"So we'd like Hannibal to come back. In fact, we'd like to invite you to come and stay with us for several days."

"When?"

"As soon as possible. Why not immediately? I think we could promise your boy the best Christmas he's ever had."

Christmas away from the memories locked in their walls at home? At a vacation retreat in the mountains? She wanted to say yes, but of course she would have to talk to Nicki first. It was all happening so fast. "I'll have to think about that."

"Please do."

Hannibal tugged on her wrist, and she remembered his request. "Could we see Serge again before we leave?"

Their Afro-Indian hostess shook her head with infinite regret. "I'm sorry, but he is no longer in the public portion of the facility. As we said, we're preparing him to return to New Mexico." She smiled. "But, we would like to serve you a fabulous lunch, and then your helicopter awaits for a trip back to Atlanta."

"Thank you very much," Olympia said, and allowed them to escort her out.

◆　◆　◆

Hannibal was not happy. The game had been a wonderful one, something he had never experienced. What terrific pictures! Soccer balls, yes. But Serge was hiding there among them, peeking out at him, grinning at him, calling to him. He'd felt that connection.

Then he'd heard voices telling him to *relax, relax*. For his heart to slow down. Odd music, music that Mommy couldn't hear, calming him. Slow. Slow.

Then a whispered suggestion, something he couldn't remember, but it made him feel funny. And then . . . Serge was gone. Just . . . gone.

Hannibal couldn't feel the connection anymore. It was like looking at the television when the screen was dead. Nothing. He was not happy about this.

He hoped Serge was all right. Certainly, Serge was all right.

Maybe if he was a good boy, they'd let him see Serge again, so he could be sure.

CHAPTER 22

Terry was thirty minutes late to the shuttered warehouse east of downtown Atlanta. He knew the Pirates would be impatient for his arrival, and didn't care even though there was a part of him that knew he should. Being late anywhere could lead to grim consequences, making his friends doubt his commitment.

One way or another, he was about to have an argument. Terry could feel it. There was scant chance that this would be a happy conversation.

When he lifted the aluminum roll-up door and shut it behind him, he felt the irritation instantly.

His four compatriots clustered in a corner of the empty warehouse, watching a long-lens video of three trucks leaving Dobbins Air Reserve Base in Marietta, Georgia, sliding out onto Cobb Parkway, and heading south toward the freeway.

"Right on schedule," Terry said, and the others turned and nodded. So far, argument averted.

"And there's not a lot of reason to believe it will change New Year's Day," Mark said.

Terry grunted. "So that's it. The gems will come in, and slide back out. We divert the convoy in South Carolina, and we'll have . . ."

Father Geek made rapid calculations on his iPad. "I do believe I can promise you seventy seconds."

"That should do it, I reckon." Mark stretched, yawning fiercely.

Geek nodded. "Yep, that should do it."

Terry leaned back against the wall. "And if anything goes wrong? If they fight back? I mean . . . we don't know for sure that the guys driving the trucks even know what they're carrying."

"You mean, what if they're not bad guys?" Geek asked.

"Yeah."

Ronnell grinned, and it wasn't a pleasant sight. "Then they may not be bad guys, but they're definitely having a bad day."

Mark squinted at Terry. "You got a problem with that?"

Ah. The argument had arrived just in time.

"Yeah, actually," Terry said. "I'd like to put a little more thought into nonlethal alternatives."

"We've been over all this, Terry." Mark drummed his fingers on his thigh. "What's up with you?"

"Just thinking. It's like we said: there are lines you can't step back across. I want to be sure we're not doing that." He felt a shiver. "It's cold in here."

Mark and Father Geek exchanged a strained expression.

"And . . . what about cops?"

Father Geek seemed on stronger footing now. "Assuming they will reach the fire road at four o'clock, we'll blow the Wilson Farms water tower at three forty-five. That should attract all the police and highway patrol for thirty miles."

Terry wasn't convinced. "And if it doesn't? I mean . . . if we miscalculate, and there are highway patrolmen on that stretch of road, and they take issue with the barricade, what do we do?"

"We move forward," Mark said.

"'Move forward,'" Terry repeated. "That's such a nice, antiseptic way to phrase it."

Pat moved forward, narrowing the distance between them. "What are you saying?"

Then the words he knew were coming tumbled from Terry's mouth before he could dam them up. "I don't think I can do this."

"What the fuck?" Mark's whisper, low and ugly.

"A little late for that, Boy Scout," Pat said coldly.

"No," Terry said. "You're wrong. It's not too late. For any of us."

A frozen moment of time, like the hollow between a lightning strike and a thunderclap. Mark was the one who said what they were all thinking. "Terry, this isn't going to end well."

"I reckon you're right," Terry said. "But someone has to speak the truth. And the truth is that the five of us have a choice. And my choice is to walk away. I have nothing to say to anyone outside this room."

"We're supposed to just believe that?" Pat asked.

"Yes," Terry said.

"And you expect us to just let you walk out?" Lee's voice rose to something very near a squeak.

"No," Terry said. "But I wanted to give you the option."

"What the hell do you mean? What kind of option?"

Terry sighed, already sensing the hopelessness of it. "We need to think about who we are."

"What?" Mark flicked two fingers in a signal, and the Pirates approached more closely, squinting as if examining some kind of previously undiscovered species of insect.

"Why do you want to do this, Geek?" Terry asked.

"Do what?"

"Hijack O'Shay."

Father Geek glared, eyes frozen open and locked on Terry. "I want the money."

"No, you don't. You want a reason to get up in the morning." Now Geek lost his basilisk gaze and blinked. "And you, Mark . . ."

"What the hell are you talking about?"

"You talk payback, but that's not all this is about. As XO, you were the best tactical mind I've ever known. And how do you walk away from that? Just what are you supposed to do? You became your job. And without your job, you're left without an identity."

Mark glowered at him. "You're out of your mind."

Terry managed a wan smile. "That doesn't make me wrong. And you, Pat?"

Ronnell sneered, fiddling with his onyx-handled Colt .38, popping the cylinder open and snapping it shut again. "I think you'd better stop now."

"It's too late for that," Terry said. And so it was. And they all knew it. That particular genie was out of the bottle. "It's been too late. But it's not too late to stop this."

Pat stopped playing with his revolver. "All right, Grasshopper. What's up with me?"

"You said it. The only thing you were ever best at was killing people. You liked it. You got to do it legally."

Something glittered in Pat's eyes, gleaming like a Cheshire cat's teeth. "You need to watch your step."

"Why, Pat? Are you going to kill me, too?"

"Shit happens."

At another time, someone might have laughed. Not today. "You're hoping something will go wrong, Pat. You want something to go wrong, so that you have another opportunity to do the thing you love, and at the same time claim that it's a shame that it happened."

The air was dead still. Mark spoke in a hard, level voice. "What if it's true, Boy Scout? What if all of it's true? What if the money isn't the point?

What if kicking O'Shay's ass isn't the point? What if what we want is to be who we are? What we were selected and trained to be? What would be so wrong about that?"

"Nothing. For any of you, if that is who you really think you are. But I can't do it. I just can't."

When Mark spoke again, his voice was smooth. Deadly soft. "Why not?"

"Because I don't need this," Terry said. "I thought I did. I don't. I don't need the money. Or the revenge. Or the thrill. Or even my brothers, if this is the only way to earn their friendship."

"What are you asking?"

"I'm out. If you're going forward, God bless you. I'm not a part of it."

"You can't just walk away from something like this," Mark growled.

"Yes," Terry said. "I can. And so can any of you. *Any* of you. You can change anything except your essence, and none of you know who that is. What that is. Do this . . . step across the line stretching right in front of us, and you're doing something that can't be undone."

"You can't just walk away," Mark said. Lee and Pat moved to bracket him. Even Father Geek wheeled around behind him and locked the door.

But despite his actions, Terry could tell that Geek wasn't so sure. "There's something different about you, Terry. I'll give you that. I can feel it. But some things never change." He smacked his balled fist into his thigh. "These legs . . . I can't get them back. But enough money means I'm not a freak anymore. I'm a charming eccentric. Enough money . . ."

"Stop it," Mark said. "Just stop. It's not about reasons. I don't care about that, and you know I don't. You can't walk away from this."

"Geek was right," Terry said. "I've changed. You need to see that, I understand now. It's all right, Mark. It really is."

Mark looked at him, and it was clear that he didn't comprehend. Not at all. For the very first time, something like unease touched his face. "I think you need to see how serious we are," Mark said, and nodded almost imperceptibly at Pat.

And that was how it started.

From Terry's point of view, the "worms" appeared again, seething tunnels like time-lapsed photos of his four partners in crime as they approached and surrounded him. He saw every action's root before it flowered.

As expected, Pat attacked first. Almost placidly, Terry leaned out of the way as Pat lunged at him with a tire iron, nudging an arm with his finger to keep Pat from whacking Mark. He collided them with each other, tied them into knots.

He was curious about a lunge from Lee, and poked Lee's shoulder with a fingertip at exactly the right moment, at the instant Lee transferred balance from one foot to another, and was functionally like an ice-skater balanced on the tip of one skate. The Okie spun helplessly away. Without conscious effort or intention Terry always seemed to be in the right place, with the right balance, moving at the correct speed, at the right moment.

The Pirates moved at what should have been an incomprehensible blur, but was as clear as ice. Terry was moving slowly, but they smacked into each other, tangling themselves into knots of arms and legs. He actually protected Lee from Mark when Lee collided with the XO's greater mass and nearly bounced off into the corner of a desk.

Father Geek wheeled at him, knife in his right hand and then his left and then his right, targeting Terry's legs, his South African "Piper" skills whipping with speed that should have been a blur . . . only for the first time it wasn't. It seemed to Terry as if his mind had a hyper-fast shutter speed, every individual "frame" seething with an almost overwhelming amount of information, *Blade Runner*–level density. If he focused he could isolate an individual frame and gain clarity, but in the process miss the overall dynamic pattern. He could know where the hands were, but not precisely where they were traveling and at what speed. Or the speed and direction, but not the precise location.

So . . . strange.

But whichever it was, some part of him knew where and when to be, and acted instantly. He kicked with perfect timing, striking Geek's elbow so that the arm rebounded and Sevugian almost stabbed himself. In the moment of confusion, as Geek spun his wheelchair in a circle, Terry push-kicked his shoulder and the chair flipped onto its side.

Then the "worms" receded, and he stood alone in the middle of the room, his four erstwhile opponents sprawled in various postures of semi-consciousness.

Mark stared up at him, too dazed to speak. Terry was delighted, filled with almost childlike glee.

He bounced over to Father Geek, sprawled on the ground. "Are you all right?"

Geek flinched away as if Terry was a sack of cobras.

Only then did he realize what he must have seemed like. How they must have felt.

"I'm sorry," he said, and meant it. "So sorry."

And he walked to the door. It was locked. He gripped the knob. Twisted and exhaled. And exhaled. And exhaled.

The knob broke. The door opened. Terry laughed. And left.

♦ ♦ ♦

For a moment there was silence in the room. The Pirates picked themselves up off the floor, groaning.

Mark wagged his head like a huge, sick Saint Bernard. Stunned. "What . . . in the hell . . . was that?"

Pat growled. "I'll cut his nuts off. I swear to God. He's dead."

Mark helped Father Geek back into his chair. Sevugian just sat there, thinking back on what he had just seen and heard. And entirely uncertain of what it all meant.

CHAPTER 23

On the pretext of seeking out a restroom, Maria Cortez had managed to slip away from the tour group. That excuse had worked for her four months earlier, the last time she had visited the Salvation Sanctuary.

She found herself in a section of the easternmost building, the one labeled ADMINISTRATION. Most of it was deserted, but she went directly to an office she had identified months ago as a place where decisions were made.

Very carefully, making sure she was unobserved, she removed the black plastic rectangle of a Sony VOX digital recorder from beneath a chair, where it had been secured with a wad of plumber's putty. She checked it, found it was still operating. Maria allowed herself a satisfied smile, checked to be certain she hadn't put anything out of place, and slipped out of the room. . . .

And directly into the path of a security guard. Tall, slender, straw-haired, loose-jointed, muscular. His badge read TONY KILLINGER, CHIEF OF SECURITY.

"Hold up there, ma'am," Tony said. "What are you doing here?"

Maria slipped into her most obsequious body language. *I'm dumpy. Harmless as a hamster.* "I'm sorry. I think I got separated from the tour."

Tony squinted at her. "I've seen you." His Southern accent was very pronounced. Mississippi or the Louisiana delta perhaps. "Didn't you take a tour here, just a few days back?" He pronounced "here" *heah.*

"No," Maria said. "It's been months. I find this . . . what you are doing here . . . to be very interesting."

"I'm sure you do. No offense now, but I'm afraid you're gonna have to show me your purse."

"Why?" Maria said, fighting a stammer. "You have no right."

"I got every right you can think of, señorita," Tony said calmly. His eyes were bright with interest. "In fact, it's my responsibility. This here is a private area of the Sanctuary. There are valuable books and documents top to bottom. I have what you'd call an obligation to the folks I work for."

She began to tremble, and deliberately breathed deeply, seeking to quiet her nerves. "No, I won't."

He finally seemed to notice that he was looming over her, and stepped back a bit. "Well, if it's a personal thing, maybe you'd like it better if I called for one of our female security folks. We have a little lady named Maureen Skotak who might suit you just fine."

Maria pretended to consider. That bought her some time to think, which was always a good thing. "If you have to. If it is so important to you."

"Yes," Tony said. " 'Fraid it is, ma'am."

She handed over the purse. He combed it, then handed it back.

"You see? Nothing. May I have it back now?"

Tony looked at her. And then back at the office. "I think I need to search you," he said.

"No!"

He smiled. "Again, if you would prefer to be searched by a female officer . . ." He touched his epaulet's microphone button. "Maureen, come to the main house, if you please . . ."

"No," Maria said with all the firmness she could muster. A mental line in the sand. "I simply don't give you permission."

There followed a long and increasingly stressful pause. Then Tony said: "You'll have to come with me."

◆　◆　◆

To Olympia's surprise, when they emerged from the underground labs they were under the castle, not the library. Hannibal was delighted with the apparent "trick," and Madame Gupta affected an appropriately mysterious air.

Their tiny hostess escorted Olympia and Hannibal counterclockwise around the Salvation Sanctuary, past the dining hall and back toward the library. Olympia found herself wishing she could be here in the springtime, she wondered what birds and butterflies might swarm about when the garden bloomed. "It's so beautiful here," she said.

"Like it here," Hani said chattily. "Don't want to go."

"And you've seen only the surface," Madame Gupta said. Her voice and face were suffused with wonder.

"What is it you think you can do for Hannibal?" Olympia asked. "Do you think you can help him . . ." She cursed at herself for almost saying *be normal*. "Fit in?"

"No," the little woman said.

That answer seemed to stop her heart. "No?"

"No. Far more than that. I believe your son is what many would call a genius."

That word unfroze her world, started her walking again. "Genius?"

"Genius!" Hannibal crowed.

Olympia's face felt paralyzed in a taut smile. This was what happened when you were afraid even to hope. Dear God, she prayed the woman wasn't using the word lightly. She'd seen the "genius" autistic children with their spectacular artwork and prodigious piano skills, felt envious of the parents who at least knew what they had traded normality for, could show evidence that their children were so much more than their deficiencies.

"Have you given more thought to Christmas?" Madame Gupta asked. "Have you plans?"

Olympia was again swept away by the fantasy. She'd barely had a moment to think about Christmas, much less plan. "Just . . . a little tree, presents . . . I've already done my shopping."

Madame Gupta smiled. "We would give you a wonderful suite. A thirty-foot tree, the most beautiful tree you've ever seen."

"But you aren't Christian, are you?"

Gupta laughed. It was a beautiful, warm, welcoming laugh. A jolly Mrs. Elf laugh. "Christ wasn't Christian, either." She smiled. "I believe in seizing every conceivable opportunity to celebrate. And would do everything to make this the most spectacular Christmas Hannibal has ever had. And presents . . . what would you think of offering Hannibal the most wonderful present in the world?"

"Wh-what?

"A new and better life."

Olympia felt dazzled again. Could think of fewer reasons to fight the feeling. "How long would this miracle take?"

Madame Gupta's nut-brown face creased as she considered. "The process has already begun. Can't you tell the difference already? Give us ten days. Total. Then Hannibal would return to his world. Imagine him being able to join the other children after Christmas vacation. Playing with them. Attending a normal school."

The word "normal" tweaked her, but she tamped down the reaction.

"Play," Hannibal said.

Olympia felt herself wavering: a different world, a world with hugs and eye contact, a world where she knew what her own child felt and thought. A better world. She had never, probably *would* never say that aloud, but there it was.

"What would I have to do?"

Gupta spanked her hands together. "We will send our helicopter to get you. Just let us—"

"*Get your hands off me!*"

Olympia recognized that voice instantly, and whipped her head around. Could it be Maria?

One of their golden-robed escorts focused on the approaching knot of tense-faced people. "What is going on here?"

"A security matter," the tall guard said. "I caught this woman exiting Madame Gupta's private office."

"That's not true," the woman said. God, it *was* Maria! "He lured me here."

Olympia pulled Hannibal closer to her.

Maria saw her, and the expression on her face was that of a drowning swimmer sighting a lifeguard. "The girl I told you about, Maya Tanaka, has disappeared," she said. "I'd been tracking her through her Facebook posts, and the day she said she was going through this special ceremony was her last day posting."

Madame Gupta looked at Maria with sympathy. "There is more to life than social media. She is simply . . . busy."

"And where is she now?"

"On her way to our facility in Brazil. Nothing sinister has occurred here, my dear. She will be back after the holidays, and you are welcome to speak with her then."

Gupta sounded so reasonable, so conciliatory and calming. And yet . . . Maria was terrified. Why?

"Mommy . . . ?" Hannibal said.

"Please, ma'am," Tony said to Maria. "This is an internal matter."

"What did she say?" Olympia said. "I know this woman. Please let her speak."

"Show me Maya's airline ticket," Maria insisted. "The e-mail reservation confirmation. Do that, and I'll go with you quietly."

Tony struggled to restrain himself. A glance passed between him and Madame Gupta, a private communication. "Please," he said, "escort Mrs. Dorsey to the library, while we see to this lady's request."

"I would like to leave," Maria said. "Look. I have no books or sacred objects on me. I just want to leave. Please. Help me." She locked eyes with Olympia. "What if your son wanted to leave?"

"This is absurd," Madame Gupta said. "Our guests are welcome to leave at any time."

Olympia's heart had dropped into her stomach. Had the madness engulfing the outside world penetrated here as well? Was there no sanctuary anywhere? A mixture of anger and grief numbed her.

Madame Gupta seemed to have come to a decision. "And what precisely is the nature of our problem?"

"I caught this woman coming out of your office," Tony repeated.

For a moment there was a standoff, with Olympia, Hannibal, and the entire group motionless as statues. The hair at the back of Olympia's neck flamed, and she could hardly breathe.

Then Gupta smiled.

"Well," she said, "if we can be certain that this young lady has nothing belonging to the center . . . I suppose she can go."

Maria gripped Hannibal's hand for dear life. "Helicopter!" he said, trying to pull away. "Hani wants helicopter ride."

Maria dropped Hannibal's hand, and grabbed Olympia's. Held tightly in that desperate, clammy grip, they walked toward the gate. The blogger was scared. She could tell that Hani was, too.

And now, she was as well.

"We'll be happy to take you back in the helicopter," Tony said.

Maria looked pale, panicky. Seemed to be silently pleading with Olympia: *Please don't leave me*. Hannibal's arms slipped around his mother's waist and he clung in confusion. Madame Gupta's gaze shifted from one to another and then to Tony. Anger radiated. But at who? And for what? "Please, Ms. Dorsey. This is not . . ."

Whatever happened, at whatever cost, she would not leave Maria in this place. The rest could be sorted out later. "Maria," Olympia said quietly. "Did you bring your car?"

"Yes. Please." Her eyes pled. "Let me drive you back."

Madame Gupta seemed unsure of what to do. Her eyes shifted back and forth between the two women. A few members of the visitation group were drifting closer, perhaps drawn by the commotion. Then Gupta smiled brilliantly, and motioned that the security man should step out of Olympia's way. And in that moment Olympia slipped back into the eye of the storm. Perhaps, hopefully, this was all just a misunderstanding.

All the way to the parking lot, Maria stayed very close to Olympia and her son. "Were you in trouble back there?"

Maria nodded. "I think so. Yes."

"What had you done?"

"I can't talk about that, but I swear to God I didn't steal or break anything." She stopped, and for a moment the newswoman she was peered through the panic. "What do they want from you?"

"I don't know. They wanted to help my son."

"I don't know what is going on there, but people have disappeared."

Olympia blinked. "Who? This girl Maya?"

"There's talk a few others have dropped out of sight. A man named Corwin Kimball. His communication with the outside world dwindled and then just stopped. Three days ago."

"What are you saying? What happened to him?"

"No one seems to know. Thank you. I don't know if I should have been scared. They seem so gentle . . ."

"That security man didn't seem particularly gentle," Olympia said.

"Tony? Yeah, he's a prince. If I was you, I'd look a little closer before I trusted the little guy to them."

You'd better believe it, Olympia thought. She felt a pang of sadness; the potential death of a dream she'd just discovered.

Their car pulled out of the lot. Strapped into his seat, Hannibal sobbed and squealed back over his shoulder as Madame Gupta, her acolytes, and security men dwindled behind them in the dust.

CHAPTER 24

A half-hour after dropping Olympia and Hannibal off at their home, Maria drove up to the covered parking shelter of her own apartment building. The night was upon her, and the frigid December rain fell like a veil of mourning. By the time she had locked her car, climbed the steps, and entered her apartment, her skin felt numb. Fingers trembling, she locked the door behind her.

That was too close. I need a new job.

But somehow, despite the nightmare scenarios of torture and rendition into black site cells that had raced through her mind at the Sanctuary, she was back at home. Safe.

Her aquarium burbled at her, and her gray tabby Ming-Ming rubbed against her legs in both greeting and reminder that his bowl was empty. She fed both fish and feline, that the latter might be motivated to ignore the former a little longer. Then Maria slipped into her black leather office chair, extracted the digital microrecorder from the little pouch sewn into the belt-line of her pants, and hooked it to her desktop computer with a micro-USB cable. She popped a Dos Equis out of its refrigerated six-pack and then turned on the recorder.

The VOX function guaranteed there was no dead air, making it fairly simple to scan through the files, looking for something interesting.

"Electrical usage . . . off the grid . . ."

"At auction for seven thousand . . ."

"A bus coming from Tallahassee . . . CNN is interested . . ."

Most of it seemed to be standard stuff, accounting and discussions of doctrine or procedure or ordering material for the laboratory. Bill payments and bank accounts, tourism and supplies from the local town.

Her computer executed a series of steps designed to download the audio files to her Mac. She dumped over a hundred of them into an iTunes playlist. Most were quite short, the VOX function flickering on and off for even the most casual conversation.

She chose the largest file with a recent date. Forty minutes, two days ago. Maria highlighted the file and then clicked the play button.

A voice she recognized: Gupta's. Not the motherly, warm Gupta, or the gleeful urchin she had heard of. Cold and calculating as a machine. *"The current situation continues to develop. The only problem is that we haven't enough reliable projectors."*

Maria frowned. Projectors? What in the world was a "reliable projector"?

"And the boy?" another voice, a man she didn't recognize.

"The highest rating we've ever seen." Gupta again. *"But we are all agreed that, if necessary, the mother will have to be excised."*

"That's a lie, actually." She recognized that voice as well. The bayou twang of the security man. It took a moment for her to realize that the voice wasn't coming from her computer.

Gupta's security goon was behind her. In her house. A moment of shock, disconnection, in which ear and brain simply didn't agree on what was happening.

"But she really is a ruthless bitch, ain't she?"

Fingers like pliers bit into her shoulder. In spite of the pain, she twisted in her seat, and looked back and up into Tony Killinger's narrow, smiling face.

Maria whipped around in the swivel chair. Tony's hand pressed flat against her chest and pushed once, sending her crashing back against the wall.

"She don't seem that way to the world, of course. But I know her much, much better than most. From the day she first walked into J-block up at Georgia State, I knew what that little twist was."

Maria felt like she was somehow simultaneously freezing and melting under his gaze. Her chest ached where Killinger's palm had pressed. "What . . . ?" She couldn't quite wrap her mind around what he was saying, what was happening. "She was in prison?"

He tapped her cheek with the flat of his hand. "No. That was me. Another story. She was there to teach meditation. At least that's what the board thought."

She fought to find words. Her reporter's mind searched for a question that might make sense of this dark and terrifying corner of the world into which she had somehow blindly stumbled. "Why was she there, then?"

"To find someone like me," he said, grinning. "She knew what she needed, and went shoppin'." He squatted in front of her, teeth gleaming.

"Ever see one of the big cats in the zoo? Lions and tigers and such? I mean up close? They look so purty, and soft. Here, kitty kitty." He came so close he was practically resting his forehead against hers, his lips only a breath away from a kiss. "And they look at you, and all the time you know they're working it out."

"Working what out?"

"How to get from behind those bars. How to get at *you*. And . . . it's nothing personal, you hear? They aren't sick, or bad, or twisted. Their tiger mommies didn't abuse them, and society is not to blame. And God didn't make no mistake. That's . . . their nature. Everything else . . . the bars or balancing on a ball at the circus, or smiling at you from a box of corn flakes . . . that's all the illusion. We. Us. All of this we wrap around ourselves to forget that we're tigers, too. All of that is illusion."

What was he saying? And why? Panic fought with logic as she strove to untangle facts from fantasies, reality from madness. If she could just understand quickly enough, surely there was a way out of . . . whatever she had stumbled into.

He paused. "There's a story called 'The Lady, or the Tiger.' Ever heard of it?"

She nodded. High school lit class. A boy named Caleb had read it aloud.

Damn, where had *that* memory come from?

"That poor sonofabitch had to try to figure out which door was which, and whether the princess who said she loved him would send him to his death. What people like you don't realize is that the story cheats. See, the trick was that the title wasn't referring to the doors. It was referring to the princess."

"What?" Her head spun. "I don't under . . ." and then she did.

"I don't like the idea of killing a single mother," Tony said, the very soul of reason. "I was raised by a single mother, bless her heart. Sort of a holy thing. It just seems . . . wrong."

"H-how . . . ?"

His smile was almost kindly. "That's the thing about the drive to Atlanta. It's slow. Slower than the choppa. Gave me time to get here and wait."

The fact of his presence was so grave that it seemed to shut her mind down. "Get out . . ."

His fingers clamped onto her wrists, suddenly applying pressure so great she felt her ulna and radius grinding together. She was about to scream, but he whispered, "Shh," and she knew the agony would only in-crease if she made a sound.

His next words verified this. "Please, don't make a mistake. Because it'd tweak me to kill a mother who has done nothing but attempt to pro-tect her little boy, don't think I'd have the slightest hesitation to wring your nosy neck. None. Never cottoned to reporters. Especially ones like you who puts her fancy little proboscis where it don't belong. Like the ones who write about, you know, bad cops who stick drug dealers in holes, back in the swamps. Stuff like that."

"What do you want?" She shuddered.

"You just give me the recorder."

She did. He crushed it underfoot, and then scooped up the pieces and dropped them into her fish tank. The guppies and silvertip tetras scattered in all directions, trailing bubbles.

He smiled again. "I suppose that there are . . . notes. Addenda. So forth."

"No," she said. "Nothing."

He smiled. "Such a pretty liar," he said, and deftly slipped his arm around her neck and twisted until she was blinded with pain, as if struck by an axe blade composed of solid light.

She passed out.

When she came to she couldn't move anything but her lips and eyes. From the corner of one eye, she could see Tony in her kitchen, blowing out the pilot light on her stove, then turning the gas on. He had been rum-maging around, and had found a package of novelty birthday candles left over from a nephew's party. "Hey, you're awake!" he said when he saw her watching him. "These are fun, ain't they?" He planted two of them on the dining room table, and lit both with a Bic. "Happy birthday to you, happy birthday to you . . ." he sang merrily.

Humming, he lifted her body and carried her outside. She was still con-scious, thinking, *Maybe if I don't move he'll think I'm dead. Maybe if I don't move it won't sever my spinal cord. A hospital can set my neck . . .*

Then he dumped her down the stairs, so that she tumbled like a broken doll, competing the damage his *hishigi* neck lock had begun. He contin-ued to hum the birthday song, passing her on the stairs. She wasn't quite dead yet. If he had looked more closely, he would have seen her lashes tremble, and a tear drip from her left tear duct and flow down her fore-head toward the roots of her hair.

He walked past her, then paused. Bent down. "I let the cat out," he said. "I'm not a monster." Then, still humming, he trotted down the stairs to his car, which was parked on the street half a block away. He slipped behind the wheel, and waited.

Maria's lips trembled, worked several times without sound. Then a whisper:

"Help . . . me . . ." She heard a meow, and her gray tabby Ming-Ming licked her face, his rough tongue an irritating comfort. "Help . . ."

Then . . . the window above her exploded. Flaming debris rained down on her. Maria's scream was barely more than a whisper but she screamed for as long as she could, and then gratefully accepted the dark.

CHAPTER 25

An hour later, Tony Killinger was back at the Salvation Sanctuary, walking through the lab with Madame Gupta, who radiated danger like a slow-mo nuclear blast. He could swear that he smelled it on her like musk. He had known that scent of hers, intimately, soon after joining her ranks, experiencing for a short time something he would not have believed existed in a human form. Then after a few amazing weeks, as if she had sampled him and found him wanting, she had withdrawn the intimacy and simply behaved as if she had turned the page of a book, patted him on the cheek, called him a dear boy, and warned him never to speak of what they had done in her bedroom again.

"What happened?" Gupta asked. "You will tell me, and you will tell me now."

"The woman was found in your offices," he said. "I was taking her to security."

"Did you search her?"

"As much as I could," he said mildly. "I ain't the one who turned this place into Disneyland for bat-shit tourists. I warned you that would make things more difficult."

"You flirt with insubordination."

He laughed. "Flirt mah ass," he said, allowing a little more bayou into his voice. "Hell, ah French lick insubordination every damn day."

Her smile was thin. "You are not afraid of me? After all you have seen?"

For a moment a flicker of anxiety did touch him. He'd seen her kill, and control, and felt her reach into his mind in the throes of passion, flipping switches he'd never known existed at all.

But something was dead inside Tony Killinger, and even Madame Gupta's magic couldn't bring it back to life. And dead things did not feel fear.

"I'm just a wild and crazy guy," he said.

Gupta stared at him a long time, then turned to a golden-robed man with a thin face and a fringe of red hair around a sunburnt bald spot. "The boy is as he seems, Mike?"

Mike nodded. "Absolutely. The tests are irrefutable. There was no dangerous change in Hannibal's core patterns, but the chimp died."

She seemed dubious of the good news. "No change at all?"

Mike shook his head. "Nothing substantive. And that is without training or precedent. In other words, we may have found an apex projector."

"How many do you think he can link and . . . effect . . . without damage?"

"It is impossible to know," he said. "We've never seen anything like him. Every other acolyte projecting a killing wave has died. Hannibal's pulse didn't even accelerate."

He fast-forwarded the video image. They watched the digital recording again. And then . . . a gurney entered the room, bearing the motionless body of Serge the chimp. He resembled an ape-shaped rag doll stuffed with knotted rope.

Gupta seemed pleasantly surprised. "This is a complete result. More than satisfactory. The steganography?"

Mike fiddled with his controls, and the soccer ball image appeared. "This is the image that produced the best effect. As you'll notice, the true image was fractured and then hidden. Double masking. But something odd happened."

He slowed the spinning image down. And slower. A flicker. And then a quick glimpse. And then he froze, focused upon Serge.

"As you can see," Mike said, "the image of the chimpanzee was implanted far below the normal threshold of conscious awareness, at a rate of one frame per two seconds flashed at one-sixteenth of a second."

"What is the minimum threshold for vision?"

"Absolute?" Mike scratched his head. "Well, that was determined in an experiment in 1942. Hecht and Shlaer, I believe. They were trying to detect the minimum number of photons detectable by the human eye.

"They dark adapted the subjects for almost forty minutes, then a stimulus was presented twenty degrees to the left of the point of focus, where there is a high density of rod cells."

"What kind of stimulus?"

"A circle of red light. Diameter of ten minutes." He glanced at her with an unspoken question. When she didn't speak he said: "A minute is one sixtieth of a degree."

Killinger sneered inside. Fucking brainiac. He rather hoped Madame

Gupta would give him the assignment to break Mike the Geek's arm one day.

"Yes," Gupta said smoothly. "Continue, please."

"Good, good. Well, this ensured that the light stimulus fell only on what is called the 'area of spatial summation.'"

"What?"

"Nerve rod cells connected to the same nerve fiber."

"What did they determine?"

"That the emission of only ninety photons was required in order to elicit visual experience. However, only forty-five of these actually entered the retina, due to absorption by the optic media. Furthermore, eighty percent of these did not reach the fovea. Therefore, it only takes nine photons to be detected by the human eye."

Now Killinger hoped it would be the guy's neck. Would he get to the point?

Gupta's left eyebrow arched. "A small miracle."

"It may only take one photon to excite a rod receptor."

"And?"

"And the boy saw it. He *saw* it. Consciously."

He shifted the video image onto the boy, then started real-time playback. "*Serge,*" Hannibal said.

"See that? He's very clearly referring to the chimpanzee he had met previously. He recognized his friend. And asked for him again, after the exercise was concluded."

Really? That actually was interesting. Damn.

"Yes," Gupta had to admit. "He did. What does this mean?"

"We've never seen anything like Hannibal. He can be unresponsive unless some internal trigger finds interest in externals. But there seems to be an operating pore, some kind of wormhole between that unconscious and his conscious mind, like something that might be achieved by an extremely advanced meditator or martial artist."

Gupta waved her hand impatiently. "And what precisely has that to do with our project?"

"Well, he is producing the delta wave forms of deep sleep, but in a configuration ordinarily found in states of high excitation." His finger traced a squiggle on the screen. "The lesser levels of that wave-form conform to the usual flow-state, or the 'dissolution of the subject-object relationship.' That is the doorway state, of course."

"Yes," she said, her voice touched with impatience.

"And there is an energetic threshold at which this seems to interact with the external world to produce this allocational kundalini effect. A macro instance of 'spooky action at a distance.' Quantum entanglement. But that effect occurs on a subatomic level. Somehow, this technique creates an effect on a macro-level linking. We don't know precisely how."

"You've focused this energy on the image."

"That, according to testing, has been the best way. Something almost like an area code. And this boy can not only deliver that killing pulse to people on the Dead List." His lips twisted in a smile. "But note this . . ."

Mike's fingers spread out the touch screen, expanding Hannibal's head.

"Yes?" she said.

"Note again that the boy's own brain waves suffered no disruption. That is why we accidentally allowed Serge's destruction. Hannibal experienced no discomfort, so we never knew it was happening. There was no necessity to hurt the boy, or . . . kill him."

"You mean . . ."

Mike nodded enthusiastically. "Under our guidance, he's a perfect weapon. The mother must agree to bring him back."

"And if she doesn't?" Tony said.

"We have little time," Gupta said. "I suggest that we remove the mother from the equation."

"Is that necessary?" Killinger asked, surprised that he had spoken aloud.

"And if it is . . . have you a difficulty with this? I had been led to believe you suffered no such compunctions."

Tony Killinger smiled coldly, killing whatever tender instincts had threatened to surface in his heart. "Ah think we've come a little far for that," he said. "Be no trouble at all." She stared into his eyes a long moment. Too long. He felt that *frisson* of anxiety again, swiftly submerged but unmistakable. He would do it, or she would kill him and find someone who would. "And now I think I'd best get ready for tomorrow morning's little exercise."

She nodded, apparently satisfied.

"I believe his name is Kimball," Madame Gupta said. "And I thank him in advance for his sacrifice."

CHAPTER 26

♦

In a room upon the third floor of the Salvation Sanctuary's defining land-mark a young man awakened from deep sleep, dreams of childhood and fleeing forest creatures sloughing away like thin syrup. As he had carefully arranged, the first sight to meet his eyes was a silver-framed painting upon the wall, flower and heart symbols arrayed in overlapping and concentric mandalic patterns, designed for meditation and contemplation.

The young man breathed deeply two hundred times, as he did every morning and every night, with an additional three hundred counts during the day. This gave him a daily total of seven hundred conscious breaths. It took no more than a little awareness from time to time during the day to bring the total to a blessed thousand, the goal of those on Madame Gupta's Million Breath program, designed to lead one to full Awakening within three years.

He had completed five breaths before he remembered his name: *Corwin Kimball.* Another ten before he remembered where he was, how he had come to be here, and what this day would mean. This would be a day like no other. Nothing in his life would ever be the same again.

The mandala patch displayed a meld of chrysanthemums and lightning bolts. As he stared at it, in his imagination the lines became dynamic rather than static. When he closed his eyes, they danced in the darkness.

At eight forty-five came the rap of knuckles against his door. Corwin Kimball opened his eyes. "Yes?"

The unpainted wooden panel opened, revealing a tall, thin woman in a golden robe belted with braided white rope. Corwin recognized her im-mediately, of course: Sister Solitude, her broad face and heavy jaw set in a smile, eyes filled with light and love.

"It is time," she said. Although ordinarily her voice was rather nasal, this morning it was so suffused with joy that it, and she, seemed almost beautiful despite the strong jaw and coarse complexion.

Corwin took a last breath, exhaled harshly, and then swung his legs over to the floor. His naked toes gripped at the woven reed mat beside the bed, a hint of asceticism within Castle Delonega's appalling luxury. He savored the contact, even the chill. He stood, donned his yellow robe (not golden, like that of Sister Solitude, not quite yet), and sashed his waist with a white belt that might have seemed more appropriate in a martial arts school than a place of more blissful discipline.

"I'm ready," he said. Sister Solitude—not her birth name, of course; all the adepts, all the Golden Robes, had taken new names, appropriate to their new stations in life—nodded, and held the door for Corwin. He slipped on his sandals. Took a dish of ramen out of the microwave, thought about eating it, then decided to leave it atop the little box for later. There were dirty dishes in the sink, but he'd either come back and do them later, or leave them for the staff.

Was that wrong?

Before passing the threshold, he looked back at the place where he had slept for the last year.

He would miss them: the books, the incense burner, the thin mattress on which he had spent so many solitary hours. He wished to sear their images into his mind, feel the texture of the floor, even listen to the music of the water pipes in the walls.

There was a last time for everything.

◆　◆　◆

Corwin left the castle and took his final walk through the maze, a memorized warren of twisting paths that skirted the grotto then took him south to the library building. And beneath the library, the original opening to the mine. It was said that there was an additional entrance beneath the castle, that in fact the entire area was honeycombed with connecting passageways, but Corwin had no personal knowledge of such things, and could not say.

The Sanctuary was nearly deserted now, buses arriving late last night to take most of them to a sister center in Louisiana for the holidays. But not so long ago, the Salvation Sanctuary had been full. Devotees had strolled contemplatively through the maze, past the topiary lions, in the shadows of the rosebushes. The aromas still fascinated him, drew him no less today than they had from the very beginning.

Step . . . breathe.

Step . . . breathe.

Contracting his abdominal muscles in rhythm with each step, compressing, creating an exhalation. Allowing it to expand again, allowing air pressure to fill his lungs. *Active exhalation, passive inhalation.* As Madame Gupta instructed. As the great Savagi had taught before her. Still, he smiled at this small miracle, thinking that in fifteen years of yoga practice no other teacher had even hinted at this secret, or explained what it meant in the arena of calmness, mindfulness. So long as one could maintain such a pattern, stress could not devolve to strain, which was the real destroyer. And when a devotee dedicated himself to the path, did the things he was told in proper sequence and trained himself to yield but not break . . . this was the path to adulthood. Awakening. Perhaps even that elusive spiritual quality called enlightenment.

Such a small thing. Such a lovely gift from Savagi, the greatest man who had ever drawn breath.

More than anything in his world, Corwin wished to be worthy of that gift. And by the very fact of being chosen on this most important of days, he knew that his feet were firmly planted on the righteous path.

A willowy figure presented itself, by some trick of the light seeming to hover before a cluster of yellow roses. A sweet, kind face, and a slender, strong body held with the kind of feminine grace that, once upon a time, might have triggered an entirely unbrotherly response.

Savagi did not demonize sex, as did lesser gurus. Amongst the casual devotees, carnal relationships were common if not encouraged. And among the advanced, bonded pairs were frequent. But the intermediate phase was delicate, and could be disrupted by the quest for physical pleasure. Better to seek joy.

Pleasure is in the body, Savagi had said. *Happiness is in the mind. But joy is a thing of the spirit.*

He, Corwin, was in that awkward place, had been, would continue to be until this critical day was past. When it was over, he would be out in the world again, sharing the word of Savagi, and the health practices of Madame Gupta, with all of creation. And at that point it would be permissible, even encouraged, for him to enter into intimate physical relationships. After all, they were building community. Crafting the future.

And at that time, he knew, Maya Tanaka, the golden-skinned girl at the rosebush, would rank high among those he would desire.

"You, too?" she asked. Her green eyes were so very bright.

"Yes," he replied. "Pray for me."

Her answering smile was brilliant. "You don't need my prayers," she said. "You're the strongest of us."

"We always need prayers," he replied, and extended his hand. The touch of her fingers struck little sparks in his heart. If he turned his head sideways, squinted just *so* he could see the flux and flow of her aura . . .

Perhaps just an illusion of light. Perhaps not. It mattered little. It was possible that he would be sent to Costa Rica. He'd heard that Madame Gupta had established a pod there. Maya had also been chosen for the day's ceremony. Their souls vibrated on the same frequency. It was possible that they were soul mates. If that was true, then one day, perhaps soon, they would be together.

"Be well," he said.

"Be well," she replied.

As he passed through the garden his thoughts returned to Maya Tanaka. That . . . was a distraction from the task ahead. Again he concentrated on his breathing, balancing every step to create a contractive exhalation, defocusing his eyesight slightly to deny single-point focus, that disciplined state to which he now so naturally defaulted.

Behind him Sister Solitude touched his shoulder lightly, guiding him toward the main building. For just a moment, he felt irritation. He was going. There was no need for guidance. He was far beyond that.

The brown brick central building's double doors opened, and the senior security guard smiled at him. Security wore blue robes, or shirts, as opposed to the gold robes of the spiritual staff, the purple-suited tech staff, or the white robes of the aspirants. This Blue Robe was a prim man, with brown hair and pale skin, as if he never saw the sun. Tall, but so perfectly proportioned that he somehow seemed shorter than he actually was. His name was Tony Killinger. Killinger rarely smiled, and never seemed to laugh. If Corwin hadn't known the idea was absurd, he'd have thought the other security people were afraid of Tony Killinger.

There was a vaguely martial feeling to Tony and the others. Police, perhaps. Only six Red Robes in the compound, providing special security and protection for Madame Gupta's priceless library of occult books, including *La Très Sainte Trinosophie,* Aleister Crowley's complete *Equinox,* and Savagi's legendary *Transformations.* Corwin understood the need, but wished it was unnecessary. Perhaps he could help birth a world beyond dishonesty. In fact, at that very moment, he committed to creating that world. As unworthy as such reactions might be, the Blue Robes made him uncomfortable. Far be it from him to question Madame Gupta's wisdom, but still . . .

"Stairs to the left," the big man said, unnecessarily. The Blue Robe paused outside the threshold, as if it were a barrier, then seemed to ease his way across it.

The parquet tile floors were clean but worn, probably had been last replaced thirty years before, an odd contrast with the rest of the building. Corwin entered the elevator and descended two hundred feet, into the mine's cool depths. As the doors slid open, the laboratory sounds grew from a whisper to a babble.

This was the meditation lab, the place where ancient spiritual practices met the scientific measurements of the future. Biofeedback, neurofeedback, CAT scans, and biometrics whose names he couldn't imagine. Together they churned out gigabytes of data concerning body fat, reflex, digestive efficiency . . . as well as all the measurements that composed the modern lie detector: galvanic skin response, pupillary dilation, heart rate, respiratory depth, and so much more.

Binaural sound synthesizers, designed to induce the same levels of trance state ordinarily experienced only by Zen monks. Patterns of light and even scent generators, controlled and measured in feedback loops, giving even the least aware among them a concept of his progress on the internal voyage.

Corwin had gone far, far beyond the need for such things. That was clear by the fact that it was he, Corwin, who had been chosen to begin this next phase.

"Are you prepared?" Master Bishop said. Bishop was a tall, purple-robed, broad-shouldered black man with a McCartneyesque English accent. A man of strength and compassion, even if his external demeanor was often a bit distant. He seemed to be the leader of the Purple Robes: technical people who looked like they would have been more comfortable in white lab smocks.

"Yes," he said. "I am."

Corwin was escorted to a locked door. Sister Solitude pressed an app icon on her cell phone, and the door clicked open. Beyond it was another flight of stairs, descending into a darkness relieved by the flick of another switch.

A short flight. The lights at the bottom were just whispering to life as they reached the last step. Corwin glanced up and down the corridor.

Thirteen doors. Most were dark, but light shone from beneath the farthest to the right. He had heard that the tunnel ran from the mine all the way northwest to the castle, but he could not vouch for or against that idea.

"Everything is in place," Bishop said. "We want everything perfect for you."

Sister Solitude unlocked and opened the door. Corwin almost cried with joy as he stepped through. The room beyond was simple.

In fact, there was almost nothing in it at all, and no windows. No furniture, save for a steel coffin.

"Here," Master Bishop said. On a hanger next to the door was suspended a yellow mesh jumpsuit, webbed with sensors.

This routine was all very familiar to Corwin by now. He stripped off his robe and stepped into the suit, the mesh snug against his thighs and chest as black Velcro straps were lashed into place.

The tile was cool against his toes, his heels, the balls of his feet. He flinched a bit as the sensors were zipped up against his chest. They tickled against his nipples.

Suddenly, and unworthily, he was thinking of Maya again. *Banish those thoughts,* he said to himself. *Madame would not be pleased. Not now.*

Later perhaps. He allowed himself the thinnest of smiles.

"Remember," Sister Solitude whispered, smoothing the suit into place. "Think of a chrysanthemum."

He nodded, and now, just now, the first feather of nervousness touched him. He looked at the steel coffin, and something old, something of his previous life, whispered to him.

You don't want to get into that, it said. *You really, really don't want to do this.*

"I'm ready," he said, lying to his inner voices. Master Bishop opened the top of the coffin. As he did, Sister Solitude quietly attached cables to Corwin's wrists and ankles.

Despite its outer appearance the box wasn't really a coffin, of course. It was actually a float tank, holding eleven inches of water within which was dissolved eight hundred pounds of Epsom salts, a supersaturated solution on which a human being could bob like a cork.

He slipped into it, the water almost skin temperature, warm against his nakedness. The yellow mesh was, he supposed, more measurement than modesty.

Corwin reclined, looking up as the lower section of door was closed, leaving only the portion over his face. Master Bishop and Sister Solitude smiled down at him in the darkness, their faces so filled with light and love that they seemed, at that moment, almost angelic.

"This is your moment," Master Bishop said. "You know what to do." Then he closed the panel.

Darkness. Corwin had been in the box before, of course, and always previously suffered a bit from claustrophobia and light withdrawal. In fact, one way or another those conditions had plagued him most of his life.

But Savagi, through Madame Gupta, had taught him that all fears are different forms of the primal terrors of death and separation. Cut the root and the flowers die.

He was not afraid. Corwin was no longer the man he had been, the boy he had been, and he owed it all to Gupta and the long-dead master Savagi. And perhaps the Other as well, the man who had made so many discoveries, and died a martyr.

The darkness was complete long enough for the first stirrings of panic . . .

And then light blossomed.

Eight inches from his face, an LCD monitor flickered to life. The light rose slowly, so as not to cause discomfort. Corwin floated in a sea of luke-warm salt, relaxed as an infant in the womb, exhaling and then allowing his body to welcome in the murmuring air.

He had not noticed precisely when the sound began, but it was now weaving its web around him, facilitated by hidden speakers. A comforting whisper seemed to arise from the water itself. He could not quite make out the voices, but a year previously he had been allowed to listen to an isolated audio track, back when he had just begun this sacred journey. Voices male and female exhorted him to *relax, give in,* and yet paradoxi-cally to focus. It was walking the line between these, resolving the apparent duality that gave power. That pierced the illusions of maya.

He laughed at the pun. His Maya was no illusion. She was a woman of flesh and blood and . . .

Corwin felt himself sinking. Calming. Focusing and releasing. There was the paradox, the thing that he had never understood until experiencing. It did not make sense, but then again, not every truth did.

For an instant, he felt as if he was pressing against a membrane. On the other side of that membrane was . . . what? A person. A man. He had never seen this man, but had a sensation of someone of power and privi-lege. Someone . . . that face. Had he seen it somewhere, on a news pro-gram, perhaps?

Why would he be thinking of a man he had never met, and whose name he didn't know . . . ?

♦   ♦   ♦

Even now, over a hundred and twenty years after the first execution by electrocution, there is disagreement about what, precisely, kills the victim.

Corwin Kimball had been wired for three thousand volts and six amps. Electricity seeks the fastest way to the ground. Skin has a relatively high resistance rate, so it goes deep, into muscles and veins into the brain, sinuses, and eye sockets. Eventually, the brain's respiratory centers are affected, and the heart fibrillates violently. If the event is badly mismanaged, the body can literally *barbecue* like a roast pig.

If Corwin had been capable of observing what was happening to him, perhaps he would have been able to answer the argument.

But he was not, and could not. And in truth, that was the only mercy that Corwin Kimball received on that balmy December day.

CHAPTER 27

◆

Tony Killinger and the woman sometimes known as Sister Solitude, and more often as Maureen Skotak, entered the flotation room. They removed Corwin Kimball's corpse from the tank, and detached the wires from ankles and wrists. It was a little wrinkled from the water, and singed where the wires had connected. Wet and glistening, they stowed it in a body bag. Just before they zipped it up, the woman spoke. The former Sister Solitude's broad jaw seemed somehow more prominent in her current red uniform. "They really don't have any idea, Tony?"

In his time, Tony Killinger had been both a police officer and an inmate of the Georgia State Corrections institution, indiscretions in the former having led directly to the latter. Despite a heavy Louisiana drawl, he spoke with great precision, as if he might have had a speech impediment in his youth. He was strong enough to lift the body without apparent effort, save for a slight reddening of his pale complexion.

"Would you get in this damned box if you knew? Watch the feet."

They lifted the body onto a cart, then rolled the cart out and through the halls.

Tony produced a key and opened a gate, leading to a refrigerated steel-lined room. Twenty-three identical body bags were lined up side by side on the floor, covered with thin frost. The woman sniffed. "How much longer?"

"Until January," Tony said.

"And then?"

"Then escrow clears, and we get paid."

They left the room, and the door closed behind them, leaving only the darkness and the dead.

Corwin knew nothing, of course. But if he had retained life and consciousness, he might have noticed that the bag next to him contained the former Maya Tanaka. And he might have found it ironic, if not pleasing, to know that they had indeed found their way to one another, in the end.

CHAPTER 28

According to various news sources, all the survivors of the original Dead List remained under high security. They had been exhaustively scanned. Nothing unusual or dangerous had been detected in any of their bodies or behaviors. Regardless, one by one, they were dying in the same grotesque fashion, as well as a few individuals whose names had not been on the original list. As well as, most assumed by this time, yet unnumbered or unidentified others.

International lawyers and diplomats worked overtime, all backdoor channels sizzling. It was a period of unprecedented international cooperation on the one hand, and explosive tensions and suspicion on the other. Everyone saw the current situation as someone else's gambit.

But whose? And what was the endgame?

At her desk at CNS, Olympia Dorsey scanned the news synopsis flowing across her screen, searching for information relevant to her own concerns. What had happened at Madame Gupta's? Was Maria telling the truth? She didn't actually know the woman well . . .

On the other hand, she didn't know Gupta at all, not really.

One bit of local news popped out at her. A death. Flagged as important because of the direct connection to the Dead List.

But before she could follow that thought, her phone rang. "CNS," she said.

She recognized the growl on the other end instantly. It was "George," the same man who had called eighteen months before, providing information about crack dealing in Smyrna. She wasn't certain, but she suspected he was a Fed strangled by bureaucratic red tape. "You want to check your e-mail," he said. "It's from an account called Mailvault. The password is your son's middle name."

She didn't wonder how he knew Hannibal's middle name. "George" had access to information far more secretive.

"Why are you doing this?" she asked.

The man on the other end of the line sighed. "Just . . . seems like the right thing to do."

"All right," she said. "Hold on."

She opened her e-mail. Clicked on one from a Mailvault address. Typed in the password "Kai" and then clicked on a link.

Eight split-screen images appeared. Several were just names, but two of them were live human beings.

"What am I looking at, George?" she asked.

"There were eight targets on today's list. There were suspected criminals, but also heads of state, and a general. Two of them agreed to be under constant medical imaging surveillance. They are all exhaustively protected by their respective governments, but also we're videoing the whole process. At least, we . . . were." Some fluttering in his voice froze her stomach.

"What happened?"

"You'll see in a moment," he said. "What you have there is the record of the last ninety seconds of one life, and the last . . . hundred and eighty seconds of another."

Another nested box popped up in each picture. Thermal-coded scans of human brains.

"Who is this?" she asked.

"Do you really want to know?"

At first, the question irritated her. And then she tasted her sour stomach in her throat. "No. Maybe not."

Graveyard laugh. "Here we go. Notice that the temperature in the pineal gland just began to rise . . ."

Crimson invaded the picture. "Whoa . . ."

"And then . . ." he said, "the entire nervous system goes 'Merry Christmas.' "

The screen brightened. The man's muscles bunched tight, tighter, contracted so violently, that several actually tore away from the insertion points.

The room spun, and then steadied. She realized she'd been gritting her teeth until her jaw felt sore. "Is this in real time?"

"No. Slowed by a factor of ten. But at the last second there was a steep, steep spike, and . . ."

The screen went white.

She blinked and drew back. "What happened?"

The sensors protested. "Now watch the time code. Just about the time the first one was peaking, the second began to heat up . . . and there it goes."

The scan was chaotic now. Something terrible had happened in both brains. The temperature began to drop again. Before it cooled both men were dead, twisted by violent spasms into pipe-cleaner origami.

"What does this mean?" she whispered.

"We don't know. These two died under supervision, and we have confirmed reports of three others, with no word at all from three more. We're assuming death. From what we can see, timing is uneven, but many were clustered around nine a.m. Eastern Standard Time."

Olympia felt a chill. "It's almost as if it isn't a mechanical effect."

The voice on the other end of the phone wasn't machinelike at all. The answering tremor was too damned human. "An explosive, some kind of nanotechnology . . . all of the strangeness people have been talking about. All those things could be timed, and precisely. There is an odd . . . *casualness* about this. As if there was a human factor more directly involved, an . . . organic quality to the whole thing."

"George," she said. "Is that your real name?"

He paused, then said, "No. It's Cody."

A violation of their unwritten agreement. A tacit acknowledgment that some things simply didn't matter as much as once they had. "Do you have any idea at all what is going on? I mean . . . if this is real, what does it mean? How is it being done?"

For a moment the only sound over the phone line was breathing. Then Cody spoke. "We have a thousand leads, and not a single solid clue. All I have right now are questions. I'm sending you another file. And this one . . . well, put on your headphones. I don't want someone listening over your shoulder."

Another encoded e-mail popped up on the server. She clicked, and produced a document entitled EYES AND EARS ONLY.

The document was mostly an embedded video, but these words were written at the top: DECEMBER 18, WASHINGTON. MEETING IN WHITE HOUSE BRIEFING ROOM.

The image was blurred, as if it had been captured on an iPhone. The room was filled, awaiting a press conference. A panel of very tight-lipped men and women faced them. President Brenda Correll stood at a podium to the side, severe in a dark suit and judicial expression, perhaps officiating. Olympia had voted for Correll, but the razor-sharp debater and former governor seemed shaken, and not at all the cool, unflappable campaigner who had motivated Olympia to donate more money than she ever had to any other politician.

A man Olympia did not recognize was speaking. "Fact: world leaders, key people in military, arts, and society are dying and we don't know why."

"Fact," the woman next to him continued. "People are dying, but dogs, cats, trees . . . other people nearby are not affected. This is something that is targeted at specific human beings."

The first man spoke again. "However, this unknown mechanism does not meet the criteria of an infectious disease. There is no virus or bacteria, no known vector to move something from one person to another. There are diseases that move through the air like pneumonia; there are diseases that spread by contact with bodily fluids like Ebola. This does not meet either criteria."

A third panelist spoke. "Something is selectively killing people, but it is not a disease. It seems to operate independent of distance. It is not that there is some place where it began, and spread outward from that locus, according to the rules of epidemiology. This is not a plague. People have died in steel-reinforced cages locked in sealed vaults. One man died in a nuclear submarine, a mile below the surface of the ocean."

A shocked murmur from the room. "We don't know anything that can do that across arbitrarily long distances, penetrate lead or steel and kill human beings selectively. Those are the facts as we have them. There is no mechanism, even theoretically, that can do what has been done."

More murmuring, half-formed questions, anxious hands raised and then lowered.

And then a voice. "Well, you know . . ."

The camera turned around, focused on the back where a man about six feet tall with a shock of gray beard and a roundish belly stood and repeated: "If you look at it from the point of view of information, quantum mechanics, and DNA, there is at least a framework. There is one mechanism that might be able to do it. One device."

President Correll's voice: "Professor—" (something or someone had obscured the sound of the name), "precisely what machine or technology do you have in mind?"

"Precisely," the bearded man said. "The mind. The human brain. Question: what makes us human beings and not chimpanzees? Our DNA is ninety-six percent the same as chimps', but the four percent difference contributes to what we do with our brains. It makes us what we are, makes every individual human being what they are. So the DNA isolates us as a species and each of us as individuals.

"The mind and the physical brain have some interaction we still argue about—we know that somehow a thought triggers a physical action, say the lifting of an arm. But exactly how? We don't know. And . . . if we can affect things within our bodies, can we do the same outside them? These are questions for a philosopher . . . perhaps."

"But it opens a door," Correll said. "Is that what you're implying?"

"Yes. The next piece is what is called 'Quantum entanglement'—the fact that on a very, very small scale, things that have touched, or been a part of each other, continue to interact after separation. Well, you know, this is something that Albert Einstein, Nathan Rosen, and Boris Podolsky wrote about, what has been called 'spooky action at a distance.'"

"This is just absurd," the female panelist said.

"The entire situation is absurd," the bearded man replied. "And yet, it is happening. You can't describe this in terms of medicine, technology, or disease or poisons. No way to kill at a distance, no way to achieve the kind of precision we have seen. Not with any known technology.

"So . . . I suggest we deliberately throw out what we think we know. Start at the other end of the spectrum. And ask what is required to do what has been done, even if we cannot or will not believe in any theory as to the means of accomplishment."

"And you're saying," Correll said thoughtfully, "that the smallest number of moving parts would involve human DNA, some . . . undocumented capacity of the human mind, and something we have yet to understand about this 'entanglement.'"

"Precisely," the professor said.

The room exploded into buzzing conversation, and above that roar Olympia could hear the president say: "Get on that. Find out everything that man knows. And by the way, this has been declared ultra–top secret and does not leave this room."

The video winked off. She swallowed.

"Well . . . do you believe any of that? I mean, isn't that Area 51 stuff?"

"As you can see, it's kitchen sink time."

When you have eliminated the impossible, whatever remains, however improbable, must be the truth.

Who had said that? Stephen Hawking? Sherlock Holmes?

"Well, thank you, Cody. A lot to think about. If you get anything else you can share, please do."

"I will."

She sighed. The end of the world might have been on her screen, and she was supposed to work on a story about traffic lights. "I have to get back to work. Today's a rush. Not even time to start the Crock-Pot. Pizza tonight."

"You can still get pizza." He laughed. "Way things are going, that's something you might miss in a couple of days. Enjoy it."

No pizza? Somehow, that notion was so incredible that it penetrated the bubble of calm that held back her panic. Didn't pop it, not quite . . . but she noticed her hands were sweating. "Now you're scaring me," Olympia said.

CHAPTER 29

Olympia grabbed her stuff from her desk and headed into the editorial room. As they gathered, she noticed that her coworkers looked more ragged and haggard than they had just a few hours previously, as if some *elixir vitae* had been drained out of them.

"Thank you for coming," Sloan said. His Bozo hair was tangled, as if he had combed it with his fingers. "Two things. First, I regret to tell you that a member of the CNS family, blogger Maria Cortez, died yesterday in a gas explosion . . ."

Olympia heard nothing more for at least thirty seconds. Maria . . . dead? What the living hell? She realized that she had started to read that story when Cody called. Olympia held her breath: this was simply too enormous a coincidence: it had to have something to do with the Salvation Sanctuary. But what?

She felt numb, sick, overwhelmed. Something about the disappearances? Was this a child abuse situation? Missing cult members?

And . . . dear God, Hannibal. She had almost put Hannibal directly in their hands. God only knew what they wanted.

She wanted to leave the room, to have a chance to think through all of this. She had an almost overpowering urge to talk to Terry about it. He had been at that first meeting. He would have an opinion. But she had ordered him from her house and bed. She couldn't.

But he loved Hannibal. He would want her to . . .

The ongoing chatter pulled her back to the room.

". . . will keep you posted as to the time and location of memorial services.

"Now on to other business. We received a note that the president will be making her . . . last public statement before . . ."

He couldn't quite bring himself to say it. *Before she gets twisted into a knot? Before the end of the world?*

"Does anyone have any idea at all . . ."

The television screen flickered. The seal of the office of the president of the United States appeared. And then it disappeared, and the POTUS herself appeared. She looked wan, hollow-eyed, as if she hadn't slept in a month.

"My fellow Americans," Correll began. "The message I have to give you is unique not only in my own life experience, but so far as anyone knows, in the entire history of the human race."

"Shit," Joyce Chow whispered.

You have no idea, Olympia thought, remembering the White House briefing and the professor's metaphysical theory.

"As you know," the president continued, "ten days ago, a message was published on an Indonesian Web site. The origin of the message is a matter of intense speculation by intelligence agencies around the world, but so far, at this time, no one has been able to identify the source."

"I don't like where this is going. Come on, we must know *something,*" Joyce said.

Did she, Olympia, know something? Could the pieces she held be anything but insane supposition? Was it suicide to speak, or murder not to?

". . . some unknown form of assassination technique has been employed. The following illustration is the current best guess. I offer this theory for a variety of reasons. Your government has been trying to understand this most difficult situation. We are committed to protecting our citizens from the fear and chaos that would inevitably accompany a sense of unfettered risk. And there is another concern. A hope that somewhere, someone listening to these words might know something that would help us understand, and counteract, what has happened here."

"Here we go," Sloan said.

The screen blossomed with animations illustrating the president's words.

"There is an entire science of nanotechnology," she said, "the production of machines on a microscopic level. The size of bacteria, or viruses. The current best guess is that such assassination nanobots have been developed, and introduced into the bodies of the people on the list. Possibly including myself. How? There are several competing theories. Through food, perhaps, or even through the air, if someone has devised a method of guiding machines the size of gnats at a distance."

That sounded almost as far-fetched as the professor's take, which might have been debunked—at least as far as she was willing to say publicly. Did the White House even believe its own theories? But then . . . she remembered legitimate scientists speaking of nanotechnology, and its potential did sound almost magical. So it *could* be true, but . . .

"Say, what?" two of the reporters muttered, almost simultaneously.

"Jinx," one said. And that was followed by a nervous twitter. Olympia wanted to slap the living hell out of someone.

"Extensive examinations have revealed no such nanocytes, but that is not in itself determinative. We have stealth technology for missiles, planes, even submarines. It is possible that someone has found a way to cloak the existence of such creations. The possibility of guiding them at a distance is suggested by the precision targeting involved. Every one of the killings might have been the result of nervous system disruption of a nature we have been unable to duplicate or explain . . . or prevent."

President Correll stopped. Her hand twitched toward her forehead, and then settled back down. Sloan froze the image.

"Did you see that?" he asked.

"That," Olympia said, "is pretty frightened body language. She thinks she's dead on Christmas Day."

"She's the one who's been scanned. They can't find anything. She's terrified."

"Pretty calm and cool on the outside," Christy muttered. "Holy shit."

Yeah. Holy shit, indeed.

The video came back to life. "The current theory is that by techniques currently unknown, such nanocytes have been introduced into the bodies of the selected targets. That they then navigate through the bloodstream to the cerebellum, sending a signal to every muscle in the body, triggering lethal contraction. Effecting hemorrhage, and the breaking of bones. Massive doses of relaxant have been given, to no effect, and in one case, resulting in cardiac arrest. The cure was as deadly as the disease." The president paused, a thin sheen of sweat gleaming on her forehead.

"Yeah, freaked out," Christy muttered.

"Wouldn't you be?" Olympia asked.

"I'm already pissing my shorts."

The president continued. "So . . . certain aspects of the triggering suggests such a signal. Of course, there is another body of opinion that suspects the assassination is timed with some unknown mechanism, perhaps nuclear decay, or microwaves, or a soluble wall around a biotoxin."

"Could we get Neil Tyson to comment on this?" Christy asked.

"If the latter . . . and the nanocytes have already been introduced into my body, then there may be no effective countermeasure. But if the former, then my advisers believe it might be possible to block such a signal, or to counter it. For obvious reasons, it would be unwise to further discuss our plans, but it is important that you, my fellow Americans, know that all that can be done is being done."

She knows there's nothing she can do. Knowing the government was helpless was one thing, but seeing was another. Olympia's heart was a steady drumbeat in her breast.

"As part of those countermeasures, I must tell you that I will no longer be in communication with you for at least the next seventy-two hours. All that can be done is being done, but part of what I can do is to ask you, the citizens of this great country, to dig deep into your hearts and resist the urge to panic. We have faced many threats together, and have come out the other side stronger, more secure in our union, and in our faith in God." And now, finally, she managed a wan smile.

"That," Sloan whispered, "is a woman who thinks she's already dead. I'm starting to wish I'd voted for her."

"If you have any information or know of someone you believe may, please send anything you may have to the following Web address. And . . . have faith. And if, by chance, this is the last time I speak to you, it has been the greatest honor of my life to serve as your president."

And the picture went black, except for the URL of a government Web site.

"Holy shit," Sloan said. "Well. What do we do with this?"

"Contextualization?" Olympia asked. "Helping people remember other events of equal stress that we survived?"

"Run with that," Sloan said. "Maybe contrary theories. Encourage lateral thinking."

"End times," Christy said. Her blue eyes had a strangely watery look to them, and she was beginning to chew on her lower lip.

"Please," Sloan replied. "We don't need that."

"No," she repeated, spine straightening. "No. I won't be quiet. It's time we look at this. It's time that we admit that God has been unhappy with us, that it might all be coming apart."

For a moment they were all too stunned to comment. Then the editor spoke through clinched teeth. "Christy. Please leave the room. Please leave *now.*"

Olympia's friend glared at him defiantly, and then grabbed her things and left.

Sloan's glare chilled the room. "And that goes for any of the rest of you who want to talk about things like that. We are holding on by our fingernails here. We need logic, not . . . not superstition, god damn it! Another fucking word . . ."

Olympia brooded, until finally what she was thinking boiled over. "There is something. I think we need to look at Maria Cortez's death."

"What about it?" he said, curious.

"She was looking into the disappearance of a girl. A physics student who vanished while following up research on a . . . a . . ." She paused, trying to decide how to put it. "A possible cult."

His face tightened. "A cult?"

"There is a group up in the mountains north of Atlanta. They seem to believe in miracles . . ."

He sighed. "What religion doesn't? Adam to Xenu. I've told you, I don't want this—"

"Actually, Xenu is spelled with an X," Joyce Chow said. Sloan's glare could have frozen a welding arc.

Olympia pushed on. "No. I was up there, and they . . . they said that my son was what they call an indigo child, and had him talking to a chimpanzee."

The room tittered nervously. Sloan gritted his teeth. "Talking . . . to a chimp?"

"And Maria was there, and they were trying to arrest her. This woman who does martial arts tricks let her leave, but . . . but a day later she's dead."

There was a pause. Then: "Olympia, I think you need to leave," he said.

"No, you have to listen to me. The greatest—"

Sloan's façade of calm dissolved, revealing a white-hot core of anger and fear. "Olympia—get the hell out! Leave this meeting. Leave this office."

"Grant—I can't. I really think that—"

Spitting, furious, terrified, he roared: "Olympia, damn it, get the hell out of my sight!"

"I'm just trying—" She could hardly recognize her own voice.

"I do NOT have time for this bullshit. Leave. Just . . . consider yourself on Christmas break. Now." Stunned into silence, she gathered her papers and left.

Christy Flavor stopped her in the outer office. "What happened in there?"

"Armageddon," she replied.

◆ ◆ ◆

Olympia grabbed her purse from her desk, slipped on her coat, and headed out to the parking lot. Liquid ice spattered against her umbrella. Even as she walked the raindrops morphed into sleet.

She noticed that almost a third of the parking spaces were empty. She heard sirens from two different directions, and wisps of black and gray smoke curled from the roof of a burning building near the horizon.

The Christmas decorations seemed muted by the freezing downpour. This changed in turn, finally turning to real snow.

Olympia pulled her collar more tightly around her slender throat. The falling snowflakes seemed like crystalline butterfly wings, somehow colder than she could ever remember snow feeling, as if they singed her flesh with every caress.

Hurrying, she got into her Kia and closed the door. Locked it with an odd sense of urgency about the task. The system was breaking down, she could feel it. But maybe Sloan was right. Maybe she didn't need to be at work: she needed to be with her family.

Olympia pulled out of the white-dappled lot, and into the flow of traffic.

CHAPTER 30

Olympia's first stop was the Golden Dream center to pick up Hannibal early. News of Maria's death had crystallized her thinking: no matter what the truth might ultimately be, she needed her boy closer to her.

Nicki was still in drama camp rehearsing *The Taming of the Shrew* and wouldn't be home until later, but she wanted Hani in her sight.

The traffic along Atlanta Boulevard was sparse and increasingly . . . irritable. Drivers seemed to keep shorter intervals between themselves and those around them. There were more irate expressions, more raised middle fingers, and more flashing red lights. Whining sirens. In combination these caused the traffic to delay, leading to more irritation, a downward spiral. The world in microcosm.

She pulled into the parking lot, noticing that there were fewer cars than usual. Probably Christmas vacation.

There were few students in the dojo itself, and the slender, broadshouldered instructor whose name she could never remember was teaching just three boys and one girl. When he turned to face her, he seemed a little puzzled. "Hannibal is in the back," he said. "And Mr. Ling would like to see you."

She nodded, and walked into the back of the building, past the rows of classrooms. Again she was struck by the fact that the center seemed almost a ghost town, and wondered about that.

Ling's office was the very last door down the hall, and on the way she peered through door after door, a niggling sense of alarm building until she saw Hannibal with several other kids in a room filled with super-sized Lego blocks. Mr. Ling was coaching them through building some kind of communal castle, and her boy was having great fun.

How would he react if she told him he was never coming back? At the very least, she'd keep that to herself until she had a chance to think things through more carefully. Maria had been in trouble at the Sanctuary. Maria had contributed to the Dead List. Maria was dead. Someone was killing people using nanotechnology, unless . . .

Ling came to the door. "Ms. Dorsey!" he said. "I'll be finished here in a moment. Could you wait for me in my office?"

"Certainly," she said. "Can you bring Hannibal with you?"

"Of course." He smiled. He seemed the same warm, gracious man he had always been, not a hint of guile about him. Or any of them.

She waved at Hani and headed down the hall to Ling's office, a simple matter of a desk and a pair of folding chairs for parents during conferences. She sat, thinking back over her association with the Golden Dream facility, wondering if it was coming to an end.

She had to find out more about Maria's death. A horrible coincidence at a time of terrible stress? She didn't know what had come over her in the CNS offices, the wild and bizarre speculations she had made, based on nothing but the rantings of a bearded stranger and the disappearance of a girl who had probably not actually disappeared at all.

The office radio was a satellite job tuned to *Kids Place Live,* the only station Hani liked. There was a song on the radio about not stepping in what the cat had thrown up, and despite her dreadful mood, the absurdity of it made her chuckle. The hosts' young, fresh voices seemed more shrill, slightly less buoyant than usual, but perhaps that was her imagination.

She was allowing herself the luxury of thinking about dinner. A tactic to avoid thinking about her job, and her upcoming apology to Sloan. God, she was going to have to crawl a little, but it was better than—

The door behind her opened.

"Mr. Ling," she said, and then turned. "I'm afraid that I have some bad news—"

"So do ah, darlin'." Tony Killinger's voice. Her mouth opened to speak, and then scream, when she saw the Taser baton in his hand.

But too late. It crackled in the instant before it touched her skin, and then she was screaming in her head, but nothing came out of her mouth at all.

CHAPTER 31

"A man with no trace of the feminine in him, with no duality at all, is a man without tenderness, sympathy, gentleness, kindness, responsiveness. He is brute-mean, a hammer, a fist. McGee, what is a woman with no trace of the masculine in her makeup?"

"Mmm. Merciless in a different way?"

"You show promise, McGee. The empathy of kindness is a result of the duality, not of the feminine trace."

—John D. MacDonald, *Bright Orange for the Shroud*

Madame Gupta knelt in her meditation room, alone, mind floating back to decades past. Thinking of the child she had once been, a girl long gone.

Once, that child had possessed family. Once, she had been loved.

Theirs had been a small home in Mysore, a city in India's southwestern state of Karnataka. She would not have known they were poor but for the mockery of her schoolmates. Would not have known she was different but for the constant reminders of the darkness of her skin, and the word "Siddhi."

Her mother had told her why she was darker than their neighbors. Why they were shunned. What the word "Siddhi" meant. That centuries before, the Portuguese traders had brought Bantu slaves to India, and later abandoned them. That the Africans had not been able to go home—that they had made their world in among the Hindus, keeping their own gods and spirits. "Siddhis" they were called, and "Sheedi," "Habshi," or "Makrani." And that while "Siddhi" was often used as a curse, it had another meaning.

It also meant power. Magic.

"That is who you are, little one," her mother said. "That is why they will fear you."

◆　◆　◆

Her two acolytes stood at the edge of the silk-draped, wood-paneled room for thirty minutes, waiting for her to sense their presence and return to the world.

"Yes?" she asked.

One of the Gold Robes cleared his throat. "There is a message for you from the laboratory." A fine young man, he was. Sincere. Oblivious. Totally unaware of the true nature of the activities in the underground.

She nodded, and arose from her seated position almost as if floating. The Gold Robe handed her a cordless phone. She pressed the intercom button, which was wired into a private communications network.

"Yes?" she asked.

She recognized the voice on the other end. Maureen, one of Tony Killinger's security persons. A damaged woman, but useful. All human beings were damaged. It was the nature of life. But that did not mean they could not be fulfilled, if proper use was made of them. "Tony has the boy and the mother."

"Good," Madame Gupta said. "Be certain that everything is ready for their arrival."

She exhaled happily. It was too soon to celebrate, but things were going well, very well indeed. The boy was beyond special. He was possibly . . . unique. But the mother was expendable if necessary. On the other hand, it would give Gupta no pleasure to kill the woman unless it was absolutely necessary.

Motherhood is a sacred thing.

"Is it positive news?" the earnest young Gold Robe asked.

"The very best," she replied. And smiled. "God is good."

CHAPTER 32

Olympia Dorsey had awakened from a dream of wolves and caves, of foaming jaws and red eyes, and her children screaming behind her. And while the agony of the tearing jaws was a terrible thing, her awakened world was even worse.

Olympia found herself riding in the back of a van, her wrists zip-tied in front of her. Hannibal sat on the bench seat behind her, silent, staring, eyes wide. His jeans and the white T-shirt beneath his denim jacket were rumpled and stained with something that looked like vomit.

Please, God, no.

By the time the van arrived at the Salvation Sanctuary the day had grown dark. The blackened window glass was chill to the touch in spite of the hot air blasting through the ventilator. The exterior temperature plummeted as the sun weakened. The van slid into an underground parking garage, gliding like a shark slipping into its subterranean lair.

"Please, ma'am," Tony said. "Time to get out."

"Why are you doing this?" Olympia asked, desperately fighting the urge to beg.

"All will be clear," he said. "In good time."

Hannibal let them help him down from the van, doughy and unresponsive. Had they drugged him? Would they have needed to?

Olympia recognized the woman who approached them now: Maureen, their bullfrog-jawed erstwhile driver. Smiling, she took Hannibal's hand. "Hi, Hani! Remember me?"

He didn't try to draw his hand away, but refused to meet her eyes. Hannibal looked up at Olympia, who held his other hand, her face drawn. Olympia tried to hold onto him with her bound hands. The man called Tony brandished a Taser the approximate size and shape of a standard flashlight. The one that had rendered her unconscious at the school.

"Let go of his hand," Tony said quietly. "Or I'll fry you like a catfish, right in front of the sprout. Sight of you twitching and jumping 'round like a toad on a griddle would probably last quite some time. Don't you think?"

Oh, God. Had Hani heard that? Was the image already emblazoned in his mind, playing in an endless loop on some interior monitor? Rage pushed back the terror long enough for her to whisper, "What kind of man are you?"

"The kind that gets things done," he said with a twinkle in his voice. "Also the kind who tells the truth. And the truth is that ah don't want to hurt your boy. But ah will surely do whatever I need to do to get what I want. Now, if you cooperate, you'll see him right quick, in . . . oh, about two hours. We'll take good care of him."

She felt as if someone was standing on her diaphragm, and struggled to keep from dissolving into total panic. Tony's fingers dug into her arm. She saw . . . no options at all.

"Please," she said.

He nodded. She bent over to Hannibal. "Go with these people. Mommy will see you soon."

"Soon?" Hannibal asked. He looked up at Olympia, confusion and fear in his eyes, yes, but at least he'd made contact.

At the moment there was nothing either of them could do, and if they were going to hurt her, she didn't want it to be in front of him.

"May I? Please?" she asked Killinger, desperate.

He nodded, and she knelt in front of her son, caressed his hair. "Go with them now, Hani," she said, hoping that he wouldn't hear the agony in her voice. "Mommy will see you soon."

"Hani be good," he said, a single tear welling from the corner of his right eye. And then he was led away. She was relieved that he didn't fuss to agitate their captors, exposing him to God-only-knew what other traumas—immediately followed by a rush of cold terror at the idea that she might never see her son again. That this was more than a nightmare come to life—it was the end of her world.

Tony lifted her up to standing. "That was intelligent. Let's see a little more in that vein, darlin'." He walked her around the circular path clock-wise, toward the castle. The grounds seemed to be deserted.

"Where is everyone?" she asked.

Tony smiled. "Most of the folks here believe this is just a yoga center. Wouldn't be healthy for them to learn more. They were transferred to a sister center down in Baton Rouge. Mah home turf."

"Learn more about . . . what?"

Tony's grin widened. "That's the good part. There's a part of you that really wants to know, ain't there? And that curiosity will be satisfied, just you wait a spell. Hell, little lady, you might even be able to write the story, one day. Wouldn't that be something?" There it was, dangled, the *hey, you might survive this!* suggestion. The pitiful part was, even though she knew it was bullshit, some part of her wanted desperately to believe.

"I don't know what you're talking about," she said.

"You will," Tony said. He walked her to the admin building, and from there to an elevator. Although he was slender, and even genteel in his way, Tony seemed to suck up all the air around him. She couldn't breathe. At one point she braced herself to resist, and he sensed it before she could do anything at all, his fingers biting into her biceps like a pit bull. He shook his head, just a little: *don't try it.*

Nicki, she thought. *At least they didn't get Nicki.*

Yet.

CHAPTER 33

Foothill Village was quiet as the battered blue Chevy van with a white SHILO DRAMA CLUB placard on the driver's side pulled up and dropped Eva Nicole Dorsey, known generally as Nicki, off in front of the house she shared with her mom and brother. She punched her code into the lock pad, waited for the whir, and entered the house.

"Mom?" she called.

No reply.

"Mommy?"

Nicki Dorsey peeked into the kitchen. Despite the Kia Soul squatting in the driveway, no one was lurking there, waiting to surprise her. The living room was graced by a rather mournful four-foot fir tree in the corner. They'd tried to cheer it up with a can of Presto-Flok, and tressed the poor thing with white tissue at the base. Six or seven red- or blue-wrapped presents sat at angles awaiting Christmas morning, more wistful than festive.

Most of them were addressed from Santa to Hannibal or from Santa to Nicki. Nicki had one addressed to Mom hidden in the back of her closet.

A scratching sound at the back door caught her attention. Paxie, their ever-absent neighbors' polka-dotted Great Dane. She smiled, some of her discomfort leaving her immediately at the sight of the big, sloppy grin. Nicki poured kibble into a steel dish and water into a plastic one, and carried them both back to the sliding glass door leading to the patio. As usual, Pax had climbed the back stairs and was fogging the glass with tongue and doggie breath. Nicki set the water dish on the mantel, unlocked the glass door, and opened it just enough, then picked up the water dish again and nudged the door the rest of the way open with her foot.

Paxie whined and backed away with wide-eyed, worshipful thanks as Nicki set the food down. She scratched the Great Dane's head, went back into the house, and closed the door most of the way to the frame.

"Anyone here?" A forlorn hope. Nothing. No one. Irritation creased her face. This was not new. Ever since Mom had gone undercover on the cop/

drug dealer thing, it seemed that career and Hannibal took up 90 percent of her mother's time and energy, leaving precious little for unimportant little things like Nicki. The sick thing was that Mom had risked her neck on that story, but the expected promotion had simply never material- ized.

"Shit."

Nicki flipped open her phone and dialed. Nothing but a buzz, and then it went to voice mail. *"You've reached the telephone of Olympia Dorsey. Sorry, but I'm busy saving the world. I'll have my blue tights off and be back from my secret identity as soon as the crisis ends. Please leave a message."*

Nicki's frown touched her voice. "Hi, Mom. I'm home. You promised you'd be home. Where are you?"

She went back out onto the front doorstep and looked around the housing complex. Twenty or thirty condos clustered around a central pool and rec area. Too many retirees, but a couple of cute guys who at- tended her school lived on the diagonal, and when the weather was warm they invited their team over for shirts and skins basketball, and that was always entertaining. Was Mom visiting someone in the complex? They didn't have any real friends here. No one close, but maybe someone at the homeowner's association had demanded Mom explain why the trash cans were always put out the night before instead of in the morning.

Nazis.

"Where are you?" she muttered. "Where is Hani?"

She snapped her phone closed, went back into the house, and grabbed a single-serving pouch of Dole pineapple juice out of the refrigerator. She turned on the television, slipped in the Elizabeth Taylor version of *The Taming of the Shrew* on DVD, and began to watch. Pax settled down on the floor beneath her feet. She didn't even think about it until the Great Dane nuzzled her dangling hand, then she realized Pax had pawed the sliding door open.

She scratched Pax's cool nose, happy for the company. Mom didn't like Pax in the house, but screw it.

Nicki owned six different versions of *Shrew* (including the rare BBC one with John Cleese!) on DVD and VHS. She'd heard a rumor that Lena Horne and Harry Belafonte had done a version at Harlem's Apollo Theater, supposedly available through specialty video shops. In six months of searching she'd yet to find a copy but continued to try tracing it down. If it existed at all, she'd eventually find it. But in the absence of such a gem, she'd enjoyed watching Taylor and Burton spar the very most.

But wow. Horne and Belafonte? That would be freakin' magic.

◆ ◆ ◆

Nicki sat mouthing dialogue, a beat ahead of the screen. It was difficult, demanding two different levels of memory: for the original text, and for the edited versions used in all films. Regardless of any changes, Elizabeth Taylor did a star-turn and Richard Burton returned her verbal sallies with brio.

Or was it gusto? One of those two.

Again and again she looked at her phone, expecting a familiar ring tone, a call that did not come.

Then . . . the front doorbell chimed.

Her lips crinkled in irritation. "What is that? What now?" She got up, slouched through the hall with a mouth full of Pringles. She slipped the chain on the door and opened it wide enough to see. A stranger stood there. White guy. Looked a little like the guy who played Thor, but with shorter hair and a scarred upper lip. She wiped her mouth. "Yes?"

His hand pistoned out, striking the door flat-palmed so that it jolted taut and snapped the chain. It smacked her in the face, smashing her backward across the threshold to fall flat on her butt, mouth open in a stunned O, so shocked she could barely believe what had happened to her.

In that moment the entire world narrowed down to a tunnel, everything outside the clear walls of that tunnel crawling in slow motion. And within the tunnel in a terrible, focused cone of attention, lived a girl named Eva Nicole Dorsey, and a man with a flashlight-shaped device. Nothing else mattered, nothing but her and the man standing over her.

The man who looked like Thor leveled his arm, and electrical sparks climbed the outside of the flashlight. A Taser. Fear was a coppery taste in her mouth. Then . . . a black-and-white-spotted blur as a hundred and twenty pounds of Great Dane launched herself teeth-first into Thor's arm. Thor's scream was a blend of outrage, surprise, and shock. "Get this fucker off me, Shilling! Damn!"

Shilling, the second man, was shorter, wider, and built like a power-lifter. His Taser crackled, sparks twining the flashlight shape as he thumped Pax with it. The Great Dane flew back, howling, and smashed against the wall, nails clicking against the hardwood floor. Shilling Tased her again, then kicked her in the head. Pax yelped and slumped.

"You okay, Marty?" Shilling asked.

"Jesus," Marty said. "Where the hell did that come from? They weren't supposed to have a dog. That little bitch . . ."

They turned around . . . and Nicki was gone.

"Shit! Where is she?" Marty said.

"She didn't get past me," Shilling replied. "Lock the fucking door."

They did. And then went back and checked the rear window.

"Nicki!" the bigger one called. "Eva Nicole Dorsey! You need to come out now! Look what you made us do! You hurt my friend, and your mother is going to be very unhappy with you."

♦ ♦ ♦

It had taken all of ten seconds to run to the upstairs hallway and pull down the attic's trap door. Mom hated it when she stood on the clothes hamper to reach the first step, but now that bad habit was a lifesaver, allowing her to vanish without the obvious evidence of a chair, stool, or ladder to betray her. The cord that ordinarily hung down could be pulled up after her. Despite the closed trap Nicki could hear Marty clearly, calling in a mild voice, pretending solicitude and acting as if he gave a damn what her mother thought or felt. She was hurt, dazed, and terrified, crouching there among the Christmas presents and boxed old clothing with her heart in her mouth. She could hear Marty and Shilling searching through the house. She checked her pockets, and only too late remembered that her cell phone was downstairs on the couch.

Light slanted in sideways through the latticed window covers. She heard the intruders thumping around down below, and scuttled back, trying to remain above them where she could hear.

She bumped into an orange-and-white corrugated cardboard U-Haul storage box. It had no top on it, and looking down she saw, nested in the bottom right corner a smaller box, a novelty gift, a flying alarm clock. Looked rather like a beanie, with a propeller on the top. She remembered the television infomercial: at the selected time it would rise from the base and zip around the room, squawking, until the victim arose and captured it. She stifled a laugh that threatened to spiral into a scream. This was a gift for her. Mom had noticed that she had bleated with joy at the commercial. Mom had noticed. She wasn't just an appendage to Hannibal.

Mom had noticed.

Nicki shook violently, the tears an unstoppable waterfall now.

Police sirens whined to the north. Fire trucks to the south. End of the world fever.

"Oh crap, oh crap."

"Come out now," came the voice from somewhere beneath her. "And we'll take you to your mother. Your brother needs you!"

"Hannibal." She groaned. It was a lie. She knew that. An obvious, stupid lie. And yet she felt her heart respond. *Hani needs me . . .*

She heard them coming up the stairs. Stalking back and forth in the halls. Checking everything, and everywhere.

The attic's dust seemed to respond to the action below, every footstep rousing another small puff of swirling motes. It took every bit of strength and will in her one-hundred-and-eighteen-pound body not to sneeze.

The hatch opened. As the men clambered up Nicki crawled back against the wall, pushing boxes out of the way with kicks and thrashing arms. "Stay away!" she sobbed. "Get away. Help!" The last word rose to a scream.

Thor smiled at her. "You made me do this," he said, thrusting the Taser forward.

She convulsed, muscles locked together, the world spinning into an agonized Tilt-A-Whirl. She felt the contents of her stomach lurch into her mouth, found herself choking on wet vile sour mash. Watched helplessly as her lunch spilled onto the floor. Helpless as she collapsed cheek-down into it.

And quivered there in her own stink, unable to move.

The men looked down at her. "Shilling," Marty said. "Kill her here?"

"No," answered Shilling. "Back the van up to the house, Marty. We'll take her out through the garage. I think there are ways we can use her. Get cooperation from Mom. Maybe even little brother."

The smaller man shrugged. "I can tell you, I'm still a little creeped out by this whole thing."

They carried the paralyzed girl down the stairs from the attic. When they reached the ground floor, Pax was starting to stir.

Shilling snarled. "Kill that fucking mutt."

Marty shrugged. "How about a little juice, pooch?"

He Tased the Great Dane again, until she convulsed and spewed kibble. They laughed.

A groaning, twitching Nicki was gagged and bound at her wrists and ankles with plastic ties. Marty stood in front of the door while his partner went outside to get the van.

Nicki began to stir. Marty leaned close. "I know you're scared. Hell, I'd be scared, too. But I really don't blame you for what you've done. What you need to know is that there's a way for you to come out of this alive. But you have to cooperate."

The garage door opened. Nicki heard the van roll into the carport. "Now, when we transfer you to the van, maybe you're not as smart as you look, and think there's a chance that you might have the opportunity to make a sound. You might think of trying to attract a neighbor. What you need to know is that if you do that, I will hurt you. Badly. The other thing you need to know is that I will come back and kill whoever you attempt to signal, even if they don't see you. Do you understand? Nod if you understand."

She nodded, more frightened than she had ever been.

He hustled her up, and opened the door leading to the garage, gun in hand. There was a blur as indistinct as a hummingbird's wings, simultaneous with a crunching sound, and Marty dropped like a sack of sand.

Then . . . Terry stepped through the door, so calm and relaxed and unexcited that she thought it was a dream. He glanced from her to the man he had just rendered unconscious. She gargled at him, the sound somewhere between a scream and a prayer.

"Sorry," Terry said. He hooked one thumb under each side of the plastic band binding her wrists, pulled, and . . . it just popped. Did the same thing with her ankles.

"What the hell is going on? I saw the other guy come in through the garage, and . . ." He paused as if trying to find a way to phrase it. "I knew there was trouble."

"Don't know," she sobbed. "I don't know. I think they have my mother. They have Hani." That last word, her brother's name, was a despairing wail.

"Who are they?"

"They didn't say. I think they have something to do with the police story my mom did." She choked out an explanation about the barbershop and the crack dealers. Her teeth chattered as she did, and she was surprised to be able to get it out.

And just as surprised by the kindness and compassion in his eyes. "Did they say where they were holding them?"

"No. We can't go to the police. Not around here," Nicki said.

"The drug story. That's what you think?"

"It's what I know."

"Then we'll find some other cops. It was just Smyrna PD, right? Right?"

Slowly, she nodded her head. "Just Smyrna."

He locked eyes with her. "I won't let anyone hurt you. I've got very, very good instincts for bad cops. I promise."

She was terrified, but desperate to believe. "Okay."

"We have to get out of here. Now."

In the hallway, the broad inanimate lump of the stunned Great Dane began to stir.

"We have to take her," Nicki said. "We have to."

"We can't take the damned dog," Terry said.

Fear left her, replaced by indignation. "Pax saved me. If we don't take her, I'm not going. Go screw yourself."

"You kiss your mother with that mouth?"

She set her feet, hands fisted at her hips, all of the unreasoning terror transmuted into anger at the wrong target. "You're not going to treat her like some . . . some malt-horse drudge!"

Terry stared at her, mouth open. "What the hell?"

Nicki suddenly realized what she'd said. "It's Shakespeare." Hysterical laughter tickled her throat, and she bent over, laughing and crying and then clamping control back down. She took a breath. "Listen. If we leave Paxie, they'll kill her. They'll have her put down, and you know it's true. I can't let that happen to her."

He considered her words. Then he sighed in surrender. "All right. We take the dog."

That small victory gave her strength and hope. "Where are we going?"

"Where can we go? The local Smyrna police were corrupt." Maybe. Maybe just a few. But it would be safest to assume they'd have to go a county over to find real help.

"We can find police over in Fulton County. That should be all right."

They got into the kidnappers' van and took off. The streets were glaring with flashing lights, the air stringent with smoke. Stores were crowded, and shoppers pushed baskets piled with canned food and bottled water.

Nicki's sad, wise gaze lingered on the chaos. "Everything's coming apart," she said. "What's happening?"

"I don't know," Terry said honestly. "But we're going to do what we can."

"If the police have my mom . . . why would other police help us?"

"Because most cops are pretty good," he said, pulling out onto Atlanta Avenue. "And that's what good cops do."

CHAPTER 34

"Where's Mommy?" Hannibal asked. He rocked back and forth in front of an easel in the underground lab that stank of animal sweat and fear, blinking rapidly.

"Don't worry," Mike the tech said. "She'll be here."

"Where is Nicki?"

The techs looked at each other. Then to Maureen, who seemed to have assumed much of the role of supervisor. Stepmother. Babysitter. Something. "She's . . . at Christmas camp, hon," Maureen said. "She didn't want to come."

Hannibal didn't look up. He sat slightly hunched, hands fiddling with the butcher paper mounted on the board, playing with one of the dozen crayons on the tray beneath it. Eyes focused forward. "You're lying."

"That's not nice," Maureen chided.

"Lying isn't nice," he said. "Where's my mommy?"

Her flat, rectangular face creased into a smile. "You'll see her soon."

Hannibal picked up a green crayon and began to draw squares. Without looking up he said, "If you hurt my mommy, I'll hurt you."

The room seemed to inhale and hold its breath. Hannibal kept rocking.

The techs watched Hannibal drawing, almost as if he hadn't said anything. But they understood perfectly well that this extraordinary boy had been brought here for very specific, violent purposes. And the idea of pressuring such a human weapon was discomforting at the least.

The door opened and Madame Gupta entered, gliding as smoothly as an air hockey puck, Olympia in tow. Gupta motioned to the female attendant, and she stepped aside.

"Hello, Hannibal. I've brought someone with me I think you want to see."

Hannibal rose and ran to his mother, hugging her around the waist. A happy reunion. Olympia looked around the room, desperate, seeking an ally anywhere. They watched her as if it was a world's-end PTA meeting, all smiles and love and creeping horror.

Gupta cleared her throat. "I think there's something you want to say to him?"

Olympia glared at Madame Gupta, as if she had decided she would only be pushed so far. "I need a few minutes with my child. Is that all right? Hannibal, do you think that they should give us a little time?"

Hannibal pointed at Maureen without turning his head. "She's a liar."

"I know, honey," Olympia said. "But I won't lie to you. I'd never do that."

"Liar, liar, pants on fire."

Madame Gupta motioned for Maureen to leave the room. Olympia sat with Hannibal at the drawing.

"Hani," Olympia said. "Let's just pretend the rest of these people aren't here."

"Not here."

"It's just us," she said.

"Where is Nicki?" he asked. "They said she didn't want to come."

What should she say? Agree? Hope that her girl would avoid this terrible place? Or did she want Nicki's presence, thinking that at least then she would know her girl-child was still alive?

She didn't have time to answer. "Nicki will be here," Madame Gupta said, and then repeated: "She will be here."

"Really?" Hannibal said, not looking at either of them. His intonation was odd. Almost a dare.

"I think so," Gupta said. "But if she decides not to come, we'll have fun anyway, won't we?"

"Nicki wants to be with me," he said coldly, as if talking to the paper.

"Sometimes big sisters have other plans."

"Nicki wants to be with me," he insisted.

"Perhaps—"

Hannibal cut her off. "Do you know what a liar is? The other woman was a liar and you made her leave. Do liars have to leave?"

Madame Gupta recoiled, taken aback. Olympia was almost as startled: she had never heard Hannibal say so much at any one time.

Gupta gathered herself quickly, the moment of imbalance swiftly remedied. "You should talk to your mommy, Hannibal," she said. "You need to cooperate with us, or we won't be having much fun."

She looked at Olympia and narrowed her eyes. "In fact, I can promise you that if we don't have cooperation, you and Hannibal will have no fun at all."

Olympia kept her face neutral. Something about Hannibal's answer heartened her, but this was not the moment to reveal it. "What do you want me to do?"

"Tell him to do as we ask," she said. "We'll play some games, and then you'll all go home. And he will be healed. Can't you tell the difference already? My commitment is to his growth. The world needs children like Hannibal, and I've dedicated my life to their development."

"Liar, liar, pants on fire," Hannibal chanted.

Her smile remained in place, but her face tightened. "Talk to him. For your own sake." Olympia noticed something else, for the first time: Madame Gupta was wearing thin, transparent plastic gloves. In fact, everyone in the room was. Had they worn them on the previous visit? She didn't think so, but couldn't be sure. But the question was: was this something important? Were they afraid he had something infectious?

"And Nicki?"

"She'll be here," Gupta said. "One way or another."

She shut her heart to the thrust of sudden, maternal terror. There was a child right here, right here, who needed her. Here, now, she could do nothing to help Nicki except pray. Pray that she didn't fall into this evil woman's hands, that somehow disasters global or intimate would pass over her child, leave her baby unscathed. Or that there was some way, by some miracle, that whatever terrible fate might await them, her children could survive and only she, Olympia, would suffer the consequences. Please. There had to be some way out of this.

But . . . didn't she have to understand a trap to figure a way out of it? And she understood almost nothing about any of this.

"Are you all right, honey?" she asked.

He didn't look at her, lost in his drawing again. He glanced around, transfixed by a pen in a technician's vest pocket. "Pen!" he cried, pointing. "Give me pen!"

The tech looked from Gupta to Hani and back again. Gupta nodded, and he gave Hannibal a retractable ballpoint. Hani clicked its button a half-dozen times, and then concentrated on the picture again. Progress with the pen was faster and cleaner than the crayons. A house was taking shape. "Missed you," he said. "Miss Nicki. Want to go home."

She sat beside him, sighing. She felt unutterably weary, as if she was filled with a thousand pounds of wet cement. "We can't do that, not yet. I want you to do what they want you to do."

"I can play the game," Hannibal said. "Yes."

She felt a small, happy, evil laugh. *All right, you bastards. You want to play? Let's play.* Who was *that* voice? She didn't recognize it, or have any real idea why it was happy. But she knew something: they were cautious of Hani. Perhaps even . . . afraid of him. Could that be possible? What in the hell was going on? "All right. Then we're going to play."

She turned to the guards.

"All right. We'll play their game, and then we'll go home."

They seemed uneasy. She didn't know why, but realized that they didn't want her to know. And that she could use that fact.

"Don't lie to me," Hannibal said.

"You're right," she said quietly. "You're always right. We'll play their games. And then Mommy promises to do everything she can to get us home. Will you play?"

"Hani will play."

Olympia had never loved him more than at that moment. Instinct told her that she had something. Some kind of leverage, if only she could see it, damn it. Figure out what the hell it was. She drew herself up, and stood as tall as she could to deliberately look down on Madame Gupta. "What do you want from him?"

The little woman smiled placidly. "Nothing more than what he has already done. We are engaged in great research. One that will benefit the entire world."

Olympia wanted to spit. "So you kidnapped us out of a love for humanity?"

"No," Gupta said, almost sad. Almost. "No. I forced your hand because your son is a prince, and you let your fear stop him from ascending his throne."

Olympia watched Gupta's brown face, looking for the lie. "What happened to Maria Cortez?"

A moment's confused hesitation, and then: "The woman who transgressed upon our property?"

"Did you kill her?"

Gupta's eyes widened, innocent. "She is dead? I was unaware. I assure you it had nothing to do with us. What happened?"

Olympia forced calm into her voice and face. "Nothing. You only want to help Hannibal."

She could feel the truth within Gupta's lie. There was something honest here, but also a grave falsehood. And she knew that hope killed. That it was hope that Madame Gupta was extending to her, and that she must not sample the tainted goods.

"Very good," Gupta said. "Begin."

Hannibal positioned himself in front of a screen.

"Hannibal. My little prince. Now, the last time you were here, you concentrated on a picture of a soccer ball . . ."

"It was Serge!" Hannibal cried, delighted. His mood had shifted suddenly, totally.

The techs look at each other, as uncomfortable as Hannibal was delighted. What the hell?

Even Olympia was confused. "I saw the image, and it was a soccer ball, hon."

"Serge," he said petulantly.

Madame Gupta's face tightened in frustration. Her technicians selected another image for the screen. Daisies this time.

"Do you like this picture?" the tech said.

"Doggy," Hani said. Her heart hammered. Something floated up close to the surface of Olympia's understanding, and then sank again.

"And what about this one?"

Mike changed the image. Mickey Mouse.

"A man. Mommy! We saw him on TV!"

Something cold and feral squatted in the pit of Olympia's stomach. Again, her heart glimpsed the shape of something her mind could not hold. What the hell was going on?

"It's all right to pretend, Hannibal," Mike said. "Let's just look at the mountain, please."

"Please, Hani," Olympia said. "Do what the man said."

He paused, his little face screwed up tightly as if trying to think. But again, for some odd reason she couldn't put her finger on, she had the sense that Hani had already made up his mind.

CHAPTER 35

Terry's van pulled off the freeway into a Denny's parking lot. "We're in Fulton County," he said. "Should be far enough. I don't know what is going on . . ."

"I told you. I told you," Nicki said. "Mom was working on that story about the Cobb County cops shaking down drug dealers."

"All right," Terry said. "We'll deal with this."

They left Pax in the van and walked into the diner. He scanned the room, picking up information from everyone in sight, an unfiltered flood, just unfocusing his gaze a bit to receive a riot of twisting, intertwined snakes of personal history, drawn from some unconscious sorting of their bodies, postures, interactions, voices, and dining preferences. It reminded him of the series of labels illustrating Sherlock Holmes' deductive prowess on the BBC series, only there was no language involved. It was all visual . . . auditory . . . and tactile, as if their nervous systems were joined.

He knew these men. Had always known them.

"These are good cops," Terry said confidently.

"How do you know?"

"I know things," he said.

They sat down at a side booth. He counted eight uniformed officers at multiple tables. Terry observed them. Their fitness, focus, interactions. Everything seemed fine.

"Can I get you something?" the waitress asked.

He inhaled. Among the myriad smells of fried fat and artificial flavorings, he could detect the oily citrus smell of fresh-cut citrus peel. "Just orange juice," Terry said. "You, Nicki?"

"I'm not hungry, thank you." He didn't blame her. She had to be wondering about her mother. Dealing with the shock and disorientation of an attempted kidnapping. If O had researched or run a story on drug dealers, and been targeted for revenge, this was deeper than anything he could imagine. If on the other hand she was safe, and the dealers (bad cops?) had tried to grab Nicki to gain revenge, or leverage . . . this situation might be resolvable, if they could find allies. If he could find someone to hand her over to, someone willing to protect her.

"Maybe something to drink?" the waitress persisted. She looked more concerned than irritated.

"Is the orange juice fresh?" Good girl. She smelled it, too.

"Yes, it is." The waitress smiled. "We're kinda famous for our fresh-squeezed."

"Please."

♦ ♦ ♦

Father Geek had spent the last six hours breathing increasingly stale warehouse air, burrowing into his computer. Mark sat drinking beer and trying to drown out the voices that said he would have to kill his friend. The others glowered or stalked in circles or drank beer, radiating anger, nursing their various contusions and abrasions.

"This had better work," Mark said. If he could find Terry, maybe they could talk. Work things out. Before Ronnell did something that couldn't be reversed.

"It will," Geek said. "The trick is that you have to start high enough in the chain and go downward. I have a hole in Homeland Security. A couple of years back I was part of a team sprucing up their cyber defenses, and let's just say I stole the keys on the way out the door."

That was Geek, all right. Good man.

The screen capture was an image of Terry, wanted in connection with the public threat to the president, assumed to be armed and exceedingly dangerous.

Ronnell grinned. "Something like this could get a guy killed." He laughed. None of the others laughed with him.

"He was a friend, Pat," Lee said.

The smaller man's smile chilled unpleasantly. "Choose more carefully next time."

And that, to a T, was Pat.

The others looked to Mark, seeking leadership. Shit. He had to step up, whether he wanted to or not. "I agree that we can't take a risk. He's going to talk. Somebody took him to Jesus. We've got to either find and neutralize him . . . or have someone else do it. We've broken no laws as of yet, so if he talks before the first, we pick up O'Shay and his people later."

"Unless he talks about the flight itself," Geek said.

"That's possible. And if that happens we're dead in the water. We haven't received any stolen property. I doubt anyone could make a conspiracy charge stick at this point, and that's important to remember."

"Let's do it." Father Geek pushed the button.

"And if the gendarmes take him out?" Lee asked. "Folks are a little nervous."

Mark sighed. "Then I'll get fucking drunk."

"I'm buying." Ronnell grinned.

♦ ♦ ♦

Terry and Nicki approached the table with the four cops. One was eating a chicken pot pie that looked homemade and smelled delicious.

These are not Smyrna PD. They are good cops.

"Excuse me, please, officers," he said, hands relaxed and in plain sight. "This young lady has something to say to you."

"Yes? Can we help you?" the first officer said. Then he raised his hand. "Just a second."

He cupped his ear. The officers looked very tired. Terry wondered if the call had something to do with him, and tensed.

"What have we got?" the second guy said.

"Another fire on the south side," the first guy said, and sighed. "Shit. It's coming apart, man. I'm sorry." *It's coming apart.* That seemed to have become a catchphrase. He'd heard it a dozen times in the last day.

The cop looked more than merely tired. "Tired" was a distant blip in his rearview mirror. This man was so exhausted the skin on his face seemed bleached gray.

One of the others tried to smile. "What can we do for you, young lady?"

That was odd. Something fluttered around the edge of Terry's visual field when the officer spoke. He hadn't noticed it until that moment, but there was a darkness around these men, as if he was viewing them through muddied water. But the instant this officer had spoken to Nicki, the "mud" thinned. There was more light. As if he was looking into the heart of a good man, mired in his own fears and anxieties, who had made a genuine effort to lift himself up and be of service to a young girl.

A good man. A genuine peace officer. What was it he had just seen, or sensed? Was it something visual at all, or was his mind playing with him again? Was this what people referred to when they spoke of "auras"?

"My mother is an employee at CNS," Nicki said. "She's been working on a story about police corruption in Cobb County."

They bristled: *cop pride.* "Yes?"

"I think they took her."

One glanced to the other. "Took your mother?"

She nodded.

"Did you report it?"

Nicki was losing patience. "Didn't you hear me? My mom was writing an article about crooked cops. What's wrong with you—"

Terry shushed and maneuvered her back behind him. "Officers, it's true that there were men in her house."

They seemed a little more interested, the fatigue beaten back by professional curiosity. "You were there? Excuse me, sir. Who are you?"

"My name is Terry Nicolas. An hour ago this child was Tased unconscious by men who then attempted to abduct her."

The cop's eyebrows beetled together. Instant focus. The two of them had just dropped into another category. A crime had been committed, by someone, the instant he said those words. "And you are related to this young lady exactly how?"

"I'm a neighbor."

A couple of the other officers were starting to pay more attention.

"A neighbor," the cop said. His badge said OFFICER MITCH BASKINS. "I see. And what exactly did you witness?"

Terry was aware of the flush of focused interest, a shift from clear to rusty red in that odd visual field distortion. Threat assessment? Good cop tactics. He deepened his breathing, as if telling himself to stay calm.

"I was in my apartment. I saw the girl come home. She was dropped off by a car."

Mitch the cop smiled thinly. "Do you normally pay such close attention to your teenaged neighbors?"

Terry felt something growl inside him, but tamped it down. "I'm . . . friends with her mother. It's a community, and we watch out for each other."

"Takes a village." A thin smile. "So what happened?"

"A few minutes later two men approached the door."

"Cops," Nicki said. "They said they were cops."

"Were they wearing uniforms?"

"No, they were out of costume . . ." Nicki said.

"Plainclothes," Terry said.

"Did they show identification?"

"Yes. At least I think they did. Badges in black folding cases."

The cops exchanged glances. "Go on." The officer was fully engaged now.

"I saw them push her, and enter the house."

"Did you call the police?"

Terry hesitated. "No, I didn't."

"Why not?"

"I don't know," Terry said. "Can't say. I just acted."

The cops looked at each other. One said: "Were you in the military?"

"Afghanistan, Iraq. Other fun places."

"First Marine Expeditionary Force," the cop said.

"Out of Pendleton?"

"The very same. Oorah."

"Hooah," Terry replied, the army equivalent. They laughed.

"All right," the cop said. "So what happened?" The others at the table seemed to relax a bit, approving, or at least understanding. Band of Brothers.

"I watched the house from my kitchen window. After a while, the garage door opened. One of the men came out and moved his vehicle into the garage."

"And what did you think?"

"I thought that they might be trying to move Nicki out of the house without anyone seeing."

The cop squinted, seemed dubious. "Bit of a leap, wasn't that?"

"Possibly," Terry admitted. "But I was correct. I crossed the street, and slipped into the garage before the door came down."

Now, finally, he had their full attention. "I . . . heard them say to bring the girl out, and I . . . intervened."

That reddish tint to his vision sharpened. Oh, yes, he most certainly had their attention now. "You assaulted them?"

"I used sufficient force to free their victim." Phrasing was everything. "And found the girl, who had been rendered unconscious."

"Write down your name," Mitch said. "And her address."

Terry and Nicki did as they were asked, and handed it over.

The cop studied the result. "Where are these men now?"

"I left them at the house, unconscious. We got the hell out, in their vehicle."

A raised eyebrow. "Why?"

"It was handy." They were looking at him *very* curiously now.

"I'll check this out. Do you mind?"

"No. Please."

Mitch took the slip out to the car, which was parked in the lot right outside.

The other cops assumed an attitude that seemed some odd intersection of suspicion, solicitude, and fascination. "Please sit down. Now, young lady . . . you said that your mother was taken. You saw this?"

"I didn't say she was taken," Nicki said. "I said that I *think* she was taken. There's a difference."

Despite the seriousness of the situation, Terry had to bite his lip to keep from smiling at that answer.

"All right," the officer said, conceding the point. "What makes you think that they took her?"

"And my brother," Nicki added.

The cop nodded. "And your brother."

Terry could see Mitch out in the parking lot, staring into the little tactical laptop hinged to his dashboard. He had typed briefly, then paused. A startled look spread over his face. He looked up at the diner, then down, then up again . . . then picked up his intercom.

The hair at the back of Terry's neck flamed.

Something was happening, and it was affecting the men around him. One at a time they touched their fingers to their ears, and when they looked at him, their eyes hardened.

The people around Terry began to shift. The cops were starting to pick up on the fact that something was wrong out in the parking lot. Mitch somehow seemed to be larger, more solid, as if he had both swollen and increased in density. He got out of the police car and came back into the diner, his hand resting on the butt of his service revolver.

The younger cop was still talking. ". . . and you rendered them unconscious. With your hands. You one of those karate guys? MMA or something?" The cop was still smiling at him, but his eyes had frozen into gun barrels. In addition, the diner was becoming quiet.

Terry watched the cops around him as they began to bracket him. Every one of them seemed surrounded by a muddy, bloody whirlpool. Black shifting toward red, until the air resembled a swath of Ukranian flags. "What's wrong?" he asked, already certain he knew.

"What do you mean, sir?"

The other cop had reached the table. "Sir. Step away from the table."

He had his service weapon leveled directly at Terry's chest. From kitchen to cash register, the room went deadly silent.

"I see," Terry said.

Nicki paled at least two shades. "Terry . . . ?"

"Don't worry," Terry said. "Everything will be fine."

He stood.

"Sir, you are under arrest."

"For what? Assault?"

The barrel of the Smith & Wesson .38 was as huge as a train tunnel. "For threatening the security of the president of the United States."

Somebody had hacked Homeland Security. *Father Geek. You son of a bitch*. Terry closed his eyes, the corners of his mouth ticking upward in comprehension and grudging admiration.

"Place your hands behind your back, please, sir."

Terry sighed. Relaxed completely, slumping his shoulders in surrender. And then . . . he moved.

But only in his mind.

In his imagination, the air around him became a choreographed ballet of twisting bodies and reaction probabilities. Responses. Men diving, raising guns, lines of fire, patrons diving frantically out of the way, anticipating a hail of bullets.

A thousand possibilities, a million responses.

The world became like one of those rotating mirrored disco balls, each facet revealing a new potential reality.

RESPONSE: A twisting evasion in response to a grab. It ended with a cop pointing his sidearm at a woman and child.

RESPONSE: Another movement option, in reaction to a looping punch. The sequence of twists, chops, and deflections ended with a whirling breakfall that shattered a cop's collarbone.

RESPONSE: Another movement option as a cop leaped at them like a defensive lineman flinging his body into a running back at the five-yard line. A pile of twisted, groaning customers and cops. Nicki shrieking with a broken arm.

RESPONSE: (In between each fractured bit of perception, the others in the diner were moving toward him, away from him, piling through the door, scrambling over the counter, injuring themselves and each other in the process . . .) Terry's inner vision swirled and swarmed with motion, blindingly fast and simultaneously slow as melting ice—dodge, deflect, position cops between each other so that they tangled each other's arms and legs; grab Nicki; hip throw one cop into another—and then, miraculously, he was through the press.

Blue sky.

He'd found the sequence he had sought. Terry smiled, and began the dance.

Now in actuality rather than imagination, the diner transformed into a cacophony of screams and splintering furniture. At every moment he was shielded by a falling or fleeing body so that the police were unable to shoot without risking the life of a civilian or brother officer. Terry flowed through the openings and around the obstructions, all the while carrying Nicki under one arm like a squirming, squealing sack of potatoes.

A continuous flow of motion. Uninterrupted. Fluid. Moving with the speed of a rock falling in a vacuum. Down the aisle between tables and finally through the door, slamming a young cop back into the others as he cleared the threshold.

"Come on!" Terry yelled.

He was all the way to their van before he realized he still had Nicki tucked under his arm. He dropped her, whipped the door open, shoved her in, sprinted to the driver's side, jumped into his seat, slammed the key into the lock, gunned the engine, and peeled out. They were around the corner before the first cop made it out of the restaurant. Pax slimed the side window with saliva and warm breath as she barked and howled at their pursuers.

♦ ♦ ♦

"God damn it!" Mitch tripped over his partner, sprawled to the snow-speckled ground, and bounced back up. Blood streamed from his nose. "Did anyone see what he was driving?"

"A van, I think," a pedestrian said.

"A station wagon?" another ventured.

"What color?"

"Green?" the first said.

"Blue?"

"Shit!" Mitch was now almost hysterically frustrated. He had bloodied his own nose in the melee. If he thought about it, the guy had kicked all of their asses without doing extreme damage to anyone in the process. What in the hell was that? What kind of freak were they dealing with?

"This is car twelve-oh-three calling a code two," the cop said into his microphone. "Be on the alert for a van, color blue or green. Or a station wagon. Color blue or green. Heading west. The driver is an African-American male, wanted for questioning by Homeland Security in relation to the threats and recent spate of assassinations . . ."

♦ ♦ ♦

Terry slowed after turning left onto Dixon Lane, slid across three lanes of traffic, and turned left onto a residential street. Three minutes of zigging and zagging took him to another major boulevard, where he spotted a covered parking lot. He pulled into the driveway, got his ticket from the machine, and sought a space in the deepest shadowed pocket of the second level.

"W-what are we doing?" Nicki asked, teeth chattering with adrenaline.

"We have to change vehicles. Now. There are satellites, and you'd better believe Homeland Security is on the job."

"Why are they after you?"

"I have friends with a nasty sense of humor." What had the Pirates wanted? Him arrested? Killed? How did that help them . . .

And then he realized. If he was killed outright, they were free and clear to continue their plans. If he was captured, all they had to do was destroy evidence of conspiracy, and either O'Shay would go down, or they'd be free to find another way to take a whack at the bastard. And Mark always had backup plans.

Terry drove into the long-term parking section, then spotted a space and slid in. He unscrewed the license plate. Then he began searching for another vehicle.

"What are you looking for?" Nicki asked.

"An old car," he said. "Something last century."

"W-why?"

"Mechanical locks. Easier to . . . ah! Here we go."

A big powder-blue Chevy was parked between a Fiat and a little silver Prius. Late 70s, he figured, and just about perfect. He jimmied open the door, and then performed some wire yanking and crossing magic. The ignition responded with a roar.

"Wow," she said.

"Get Pax!" Terry said. Nicki squealed with delight and ran back to the van, slid the door open, and let the Great Dane bound out. Pax lumbered in, followed by Nicki. Ninety seconds later Terry had paid his ticket and rolled out onto the boulevard.

He parked on a side street and improvised a screwdriver from his pocket knife to switch license plates. Nicki watched him. "So what do we do now? How do we find Mom?"

"I don't know." He sighed. "I'm not sure. But they're looking for us. Maybe the people who grabbed your mom. Maybe something else."

"I'm scared."

"Good time to be. So am I." And . . . he was. He felt it. Something was changing inside him. He had been running at breakneck speed for three days, and all of that fatigue was tumbling toward him like an avalanche. Whatever fire had sustained him at such an amazing level was starting to recede. His hands trembled on the wheel. Adrenaline dump, or something even worse. He struggled to keep Nicki from seeing it. From a state of feeling like Superman, he felt like Clark Kent the night after a kryptonite-enhanced bachelor party.

Luck was with him. Nicki had noticed nothing amiss, apparently still in awe of his diner display. This would be easier if he could keep her from panicking. "You're scared? It's hard to believe anyone who can do what you did would be afraid of anything." She stared at him with some emotion balanced between awe and disbelief. "Where did you learn to do that? Are you like Morpheus or something?"

"I took the red pill, that's for sure." The weariness foamed up like clouds of boiling ink, dampening light. But if he focused . . . there were still little sparks in the darkness, and he dove into them. The moment he did, he felt lighter again. On some deep level he reckoned that he was tapping into emergency reserves, that there would be a price for this, a price to be paid in full measure. But later. Please God, later.

Not now, while Nicki needed him. "Where did I learn to fight like that? Here and there . . . no." He stopped. Shook his head. "That's not true. I learned it from a very remarkable woman."

"This Madame Gupta Mom raved about?"

"Yes." A light seemed to flash on in his head. "And . . . she might be just who we need to protect you. She just might have an answer for us."

"Can we go to her?" The sense of hope had blossomed in her as well.

"Yeah. I think I can find her. I think that's exactly what I should do."

License plate secured, the two of them got back into the vehicle and peeled out.

CHAPTER 36

A smiling, plain, and boyish Filipina calling herself Sister Blossom escorted Olympia and Hannibal to their apartment. Sister Blossom was accompanied by three unsmiling guards.

"And this is where you will stay while you are with us," Blossom said. "Isn't it pleasant?"

Olympia looked over the room quickly. Noncommittal on the outside, internally she noted that the decor bore an uncanny resemblance to their own house, the same earth tones and glass, a sofa that matched the tan rollaway in her living room, and windows with the same dark brown drapes. The implications were ugly. She turned to Sister Blossom. "What is your job here?"

The Filipina smiled blissfully. Whatever was going on here, this woman knew nothing of the evil, of that much Olympia was certain. "It is my pleasure to provide for our guests."

Olympia watched Hannibal run into the living room and immediately turn on the flat-screen television perched on a burnished-oak media stand.

Just like theirs.

Brightly colored animals performed various athletic feats and breakdance moves, competing in an endless video game loop. Hannibal was enchanted, more engaged with his environment than usual. By far. "There are others like us here?" she asked, trying to keep her voice casual.

Information is power.

Sister Blossom's smile made her plain face almost beautiful. "Oh, from what I've heard I don't think there's anyone quite like this little man. You'll have fun." She said the last in a conspiratorial tone.

"Are you aware that we are held here against our will? That my son and I were kidnapped?" She focused in on Sister Blossom's face, looking for any shift of eyes, tic of mouth, shift of balance. Nothing. The woman was a null. "Does this even matter to you?"

Sister Blossom took Olympia's hand and peered into her eyes. "I know that it feels that way to you. But we are more than flesh. Your spirit cried out for us, for what we can offer you, and what we have to offer your son."

Olympia gripped her hand. "I'm not sure you are hearing me. We have been kidnapped. Men came to the Golden Dream community center and took us at the point of a gun. Do you understand?"

Sister Blossom's smile never wavered, but two small vertical creases appeared between her brows. Confusion, not anger. "I'm sure you remember things that way. But you are mistaken. In time, all things will be clear. You asked us for help—" When Olympia opened her mouth to protest, Blossom raised a chiding finger. Olympia wanted to slap her.

"If not in this life, then in another. This is what I know: you are only to be here for a few days. You'll be home before New Year's. And after that time, your son will be whole. If you wish to remain with us, we would love it. But these things are delicate. It isn't about you. It is about what is good for your boy. Wouldn't you agree with that? Isn't that what all mothers want?"

Olympia was aware that she wasn't quite communicating. "Mothers want a lot of things," she said. "I'm starting to think what I want doesn't matter much." This was not a bad woman. This was that very rare and dangerous being, the True Believer. And that made her even more difficult to predict, let alone bribe or persuade. "I'll cope."

Sister Blossom seemed relieved, as if she had finally taught a recalcitrant kitten to use the litter box. "Well then. You'll see. Your boy is very special.

"Come on, Hannibal. Let me show you something." Hannibal allowed himself to be led to one of the bedrooms. "This is yours!" The posters on his walls were scenes from *The Lego Movie,* as well as various superheroes and Pixar films. She'd seen them all before. In the same arrangement.

Hannibal seemed ecstatic again, oddly engaged with his environment, eager to examine everything. From time to time, he looked up to the corner of the room. Then he stared up into the corner, and pressed his hands against his ears.

Odd.

Olympia's throat tightened, and when she spoke her voice was low and hard. "You were in our home." The anger and fear felt as if her scalp was frying. How long had these terrible people spied upon them? This had taken time.

"Yes. Isn't it wonderful?"

Olympia's voice went dead. "When were you in our home? What are you up to? What is this all about?"

Sister Blossom wagged her head, almost as if talking to a naughty child. "I think it might be best if you rest. Don't agitate your boy. See if you can get him to take a nap. He has a big day coming up. A big, big day."

Sister Blossom closed the door. It clicked shut behind her, followed by a low machine sound, like a bolt being geared into place. Hannibal stopped running around the room. "Not home," he said. He pressed his hands against his ears again. "Looks like home," he repeated. "Not home."

"No," she said. "It's not home."

Hannibal looked sad. Scared. Hurt. He squeezed at his fingers until his knuckles whitened. Something was hurting him. A sound? She couldn't hear a thing. "Where is Nicki? Want my Nicki."

"I don't know if we want her here. We just want her safe, and this isn't safe. Come on, hon, let's look around."

They began to examine the space. The living room window looked down on the courtyard and the topiary maze.

"Animals," Hannibal said.

"Yes. Animals. I wonder if we can get out to see them?"

She tested the window. It was sealed. Reinforced. She suspected that she might be able to break it, if that would accomplish anything. Right now, she didn't see how it would. She put that out of her mind for the moment, and began inspecting other aspects of their not-home away from home. The corners and walls, the living room minibar, the bathroom and microkitchen. Was there anything they could use? Anything that offered escape, or communication? There was a phone line, but no phone. Was there any way to tap into it?

She bet Terry would know.

Hannibal threw his arms around his mother's neck.

"This is not our home," he whispered to her.

"No, it's not our home."

He looked directly up into the corner of the room. "You're hurting me!" he screamed at the wall, small fists screwed into his ears. "It hurts!" He made more sounds, but they were unintelligible, just rage and fear and pain. He sprinted in circles, slamming into the wall before Olympia grabbed and held him. Hannibal writhed and struggled in her arms, panting like a little steam engine, eyes wide and wild, but no longer fighting to escape.

She cried with him, shushed him, something cold and primal and hard as a diamond sparking to life in her heart.

If you hurt my boy, she promised. *I'll see you all dead, so help me God.*

◆　◆　◆

Madame Gupta stood in the control room, watching with fascination as Olympia quieted her son. "Are they settling in?" she asked. A memory flickered to mind: her own mother, comforting her on a night of flame.

She pushed the memory away.

"Yes," Sister Solitude said. "The woman has questions."

"What was Blossom's assessment of the boy?" Madame Gupta asked. "What if we . . . removed the mother?"

"It would depend on how it happened," Maureen Skotak said, small mouth above her broad jaw working thoughtfully. "If he thought we were to blame, he might shut down completely."

"And given the fact that we brought them here, it is unavoidable that he might hold us responsible."

Oddly, she was relieved by that answer. She would have her goal, but if it was possible for the woman to survive, that would be a good thing. But . . . she *would* have her way. "And there is little chance that the boy would be able to function if . . . compelled."

"I don't think so," Master Bishop said, Cockney accent lending musicality to the words. "Survival stress would seem a barrier to conscious delta-state. And that is the doorway to the abilities." He paused. "I think. And there is another matter. He seems to be able to detect the electronic monitoring equipment. When we turned the camera on a few minutes ago, it seemed to hurt his ears."

That was of interest. She herself prickled a bit when those hidden cameras were switched on, but she'd assumed her sensitivity was unique. "How is that possible?"

"We don't know. It may emit some sort of low-level tone. Something we couldn't detect."

"He didn't hear it in his home, did he?"

"There is no sign he did, no. Several possible explanations come to mind. One is that the equipment is of a different make or model. Another is that it was installed improperly, and broadcasting an unshielded signal detectable to a child's ears."

Or . . . it was something else. Hannibal was changing. And that was both good and something to watch very closely. "Is that all?"

The technicians shared a worried expression. "Yes, there is another possibility. We want this boy because of his special sensitivities. And a few days ago, you triggered something in him, what you called a 'kundalini trap,' designed to help him focus and align his capacities at a greater level, yes?"

Gupta nodded her head slowly.

"Well . . ." Master Bishop swallowed. "It's possible you were more successful than you knew. He might be consciously aware of things that most people register only on the unconscious level. It is certainly irritating him, and I think that will reduce his effectiveness."

She was pleased. Their thinking trailed but mirrored her own. "What do you suggest?"

"I suggest that they are in a locked room, on the fourth floor of a secure building, in a guarded enclave, miles from any help. We can afford to turn the monitors off."

Madame Gupta regarded Bishop. Then slowly, she nodded. "I see. This increases our need for the daughter . . . the additional leverage could be valuable. We can . . . punish the girl without leaving marks upon the mother. That would increase her motivation to cooperate. Given that, I believe we will have a positive result."

The tech cleared his throat. "Have you ever considered . . . ?"

"Considered what, Master Bishop?"

"Well, considering what we're asking him to do. What we're . . . *teaching* him to do . . . have you considered that there may be risks associated with pushing him too hard?"

She leaned her head slightly to the side. "Risks? I would be concerned more about what will happen if we don't succeed. In that instance, I can promise that an eight-year-old boy will be the very least of your concerns."

And with that, Madame Gupta turned lightly and left the room. But she was glad that they could not read her mind.

This was a most unusual boy. Beloved son of a fascinating family. Olympia Dorsey and her own mother would have understood each other.

And that thought disturbed Gupta more than any she had entertained for a very long time.

CHAPTER 37

The energy of the universal vibration within the unawakened person enslaves him. Whereas this same energy liberates the yogi.

—The Spanda Karika

The stars played peekaboo with gray-edged, cloaking clouds. The air swirled with flecks of ice. Ignoring the cold, Madame Gupta walked clockwise around the outside of the maze, returning to her castle. She tapped a four-digit code and the front door opened. Another code, and her private elevator lifted her to the top level and opened again, depositing her in the foyer of her personal residence.

If a museum exhibit of Indian and African art had selected for images of family, workers, and celebrants of little-known spiritual and physical practices, it might have resembled her furnishings. Statues carved in polished driftwood or scraped stone or beaten metal. Beaded tapestries displaying images of dark-skinned African people with their hands raised to heaven, arrayed against the silhouette of an incongruously Indian palace. The walls were hung with flat sculptures made from iron and some kind of plastic treated to look like bronze or steel, each of them with wide mouths and open eyes, all seeming to represent a single family or members of a larger tribe.

The furniture was a similar blend of earth tones and steel, balanced on an edge between luxury and austerity. It might have seemed incongruous without her human presence. Somehow, it all connected in her.

She sighed and made herself a cup of herbal tea. Sipped it. Then went to a small room decorated with an ancient bronze of four-armed Kali and her necklace of heads. And sat. Closed her eyes. Slowed her breathing. And slowed it again, and then again, until respiration was barely detectable.

Darkness seethed behind her closed eyes, like clouds of oil suspended in water. And then light in the darkness, as if weaving a golden cocoon around her heart.

A cocoon that birthed a forest, within which she knew every tree, every bush. And from those familiar branches hung decorations beyond count-ing, as if she walked through an infinite Christmas tree display, each tree burdened with chakras, mandalas, and constructs of sound and light, delicate glassy structures resembling diatoms, like creatures swarming in the stygian depths of the sea, shining in her inner world.

And as she walked, the years fell away, and again she was a child.

Indra. Little Indra.

What a good little girl she had been.

◆ ◆ ◆

She heard things, felt them, saw memories preserved like insects in amber, echoes of emotional prehistory.

Her family lived in the shadow of a great palace, a gold and crystalline citadel perched on the hill above the common folk, but at the very tip of that shadow, where there was no wealth, no luxury. There lived a dark-ness of another kind. Of the spirit, and of the flesh. Her father worked on the grounds of the palace, but when he returned at night, cloaked in fatigue, none of its splendor returned to their hovel with him. None of them ever traveled into the light with him.

Father was darker than Mother. Indra and her siblings and cousins were different, darker than the brown-skinned people around them. There was a word for that difference, and the word was "*Siddhi*."

"Why do they call me names?" she asked her mother one night. "Why won't the girls play with me?"

"We are *Siddhi*," she said. "Many years ago, traders brought your father's Bantu ancestors from West Africa as slaves. And abandoned them here. I am of his people now. We have no other home, but many here think us unclean, unfit."

"Are we, Mother?" The softest questions cut the deepest.

"No, darling," her mother said. Mother was so beautiful, her light copper skin only a little paler than Indy's own. She was Brahmin, had been disowned by her family for marrying Indra's handsome father. Tears sparkled in her eyes. "No one knows where the name '*Siddhi*' comes from. Some say it is related to '*sahibi*,' an Arabic term of respect like 'sahib.' Others that it comes from '*Sayyid*,' the name of Arab captains who brought your people here. They are ignorant." She spat, angered. "They know nothing of the old ways. It comes from the term for powers derived from deep knowledge of mind and body. I knew your father was magic the mo-ment I met him." The shadow of a dreamy smile softened her face. "And they are afraid of you, because they know you have strength."

"I feel very weak," little Indra said.

"Never fear," her mother said, and kissed her forehead tenderly. "In time, you will find what you need to walk this world with power. You will make them pay, my little Indra. Anyone who ever hurt us. Anyone who ever hurt you. You will make them pay."

And her mother taught her things, things to focus her mind and cleanse her heart. To find stars in the darkest night. A glimmer of hope in the midst of chaos and pain. To focus her breathing, and create tunnels of attention that blocked out the confusion. At times they lacked food, but every day there remained the discipline of the mind and heart, the only gift that her mother had to give.

"Where did you learn these things, Mother?" Indra asked.

Her mother would not answer at first, but over weeks Indra asked and asked, and finally her mother answered her. "I learned from my grandfather," she said.

"The one who disowned you when you married Papa?"

"Yes," she said, tears sparkling in her eyes.

"What was his name?"

"Savagi," her mother said. "His name was Savagi."

♦   ♦   ♦

But the day came when her father was accused of stealing silver from the palace, and of fighting with the men who tried to arrest him. She only saw him once more after that terrible day. He wept in his cell, unable to hold her except through the bars, telling her mother not to bring Indra to see him again.

There was no adequate repayment for that. Or for the things her mother was forced to do to support them. And even though she was willing to dishonor herself to feed her children, because they knew she had married a *Siddhi,* the men who came to her bed paid few rupees, and hunger was a sharp-fanged, gnawing beast in the night.

♦   ♦   ♦

Was it disease? Or a crowd with torches? She could not remember. Despite all the power of her deep and questing vision, a gap existed in her memory. There were scattered images: flaming brands, angry faces, hands pulling her from her mother's ravaged body.

Blackness. A scream she recognized as her brother's. Then no sound from him, no sight, ever again. Alive? Dead? She did not know.

All she remembered then was thirst, crawling in the streets begging for water, her hands stained red with blood. Hers? She didn't know.

In her memory there stood a building with a blue flag. Or was it red?

No, red and white stripes against blue. A British flag. And gates opening, and a man with a camera filming her, and arguments about what should be done, and what something called the *Bee Bee See* would want.

She tried to whisper: *water.* Even though she knew that water would only postpone death for short while. She was . . . broken.

But the people in the building with the flag, the people who had traveled the streets with cameras, took her in, and that was the last she remembered for another time.

There was pain. But also comfort, and clean sheets on a hard bed. And faces that did not hate, and hands that did not hurt.

A new life began there in the place where the people with cameras lived while they took pictures and made films. And in time little Indra was healthy enough to perform tasks around the building, which she did with a feverish energy, hoping and praying that she would not be sent back outside.

By some miracle, she was not. She remained there for months. Over a year. A woman in the building was surprised, shocked perhaps, to learn that Indra could read, and more to realize just how well, and they began to look at her differently, and spoke to her of different matters.

And one day they asked if a small lost *Siddhi* girl would like to go to a place called England.

If she would have clean sheets and good food, yes, she would. There was a time of papers and officials and, she thought, money and gifts changing hands. And then the trips by car, and small plane, and then by a large plane, in the company of one of the men with a camera.

And all of this was so new, and so strange to a small child, and she was grateful for all he did, so grateful when he brought her to a home almost like a palace, with her own room. And sent her to school with other children who spoke bad English, but learned to improve.

It was all so mysterious, and so wonderful, that it was years before she understood that he should not have come into her bed at night, nor done the things he did once there.

It took years. Not until he brought a young white woman home for his wife, and Indra was sent away to a boarding school, and she spoke to the other girls of how her life had been, did she understand.

And then . . . she hated.

◆ ◆ ◆

And she poured that hate into the books and lessons and lectures at the school. Knowledge, Francis Bacon had said, was power. And how she craved power. With power she could strike back at the people who had crushed her life, who had taken everything, who had given her dignity and snatched it away.

Power, she understood. Power she would have.

She remembered everything she had been taught, her mind keen as a diamond's edge. But the lectures faded into each other, as if they were water pouring from myriad pitchers into a container the size and shape of Indra Gupta. A plump shape, a plump face of studious inclination, round wire-rim glasses perched on her plump little nose. She was alone most of the time, with no friends. She wanted none. She now understood what happened if you trusted.

With precious few exceptions, all the lessons and teachers flowed together. One was a Mr. Bland, a balding man with comb-over hair. His class, his intense face, she remembered. Remembered both because of what he said, and the fact that she suspected that, behind his lectern, he stroked himself as he lectured and looked at her. "And Marxist theory suggests that power collects regardless of the specific system of government. Two thousand years ago, it was Egypt. And then Greece. Then Rome. And then England was the greatest power in the known world. Now it is America. And then? Who knows?" Bland peered out at them, owlish in his horn rims. "It may be China. Or, the era of nations may be passing. But what we do know, can be certain of, is that money is the most fluid form of power that has ever existed, and the rulers of the future will not be bounded by geographical lines . . ."

Indra Gupta's sixteen-year-old mind was transfixed.

In time she graduated with honors, and found herself turned down for job after job for which she knew herself qualified. And finally an old Indian man named Sanjay gave her a chance. She had the sense that he would not have wanted her for a daughter, or as marriage material for his son, but that he had a certain amount of sympathy for a refugee from his own homeland. "We have a position as data analyst available," old Sanjay said. "It is an entry position, but then, all things considered, that should be acceptable, shouldn't it?"

All things considered.

Gupta seethed, but agreed.

The valedictorian found herself working in the back of an office, scanning sheets and computer screens for errors made by her intellectual inferiors.

Months passed. Years. She watched as others . . . white, male, Christian,

British, sometimes all of these at once . . . were promoted over her, even if they often needed to come to her for help. Resentment simmered.

Every night she would return to her efficiency apartment in London's East End, and there she cried herself to sleep. She had found, in a magazine called *National Geographic,* a picture of the palace that gleamed like gold in the night, and kept it in a frame on her dresser. She watched it as she went to sleep at night, pretending that just out of frame, down at the bottom of the picture, was the house where she and her family had once lived, the last place in this world she had ever smiled.

◆   ◆   ◆

During the Brixton race riots of 1981, her skin caused her to be mistaken for one of the Afro-Caribbean immigrants who had triggered the outbreak of hatred and violence, and Indra was savaged again, losing consciousness as she had in childhood.

She remembered staggering through the streets, not knowing who or what she was, yearning to die. And at that moment something awakened within her, something that was not Indra.

I am Shakti, it said. *And I will keep you alive. Follow me.*

Onward she had staggered, above herself, watching with a kind of placid horror at the marionette she had become. Poor little Indra, child of pain, had become this bleeding, mindless rag doll composed of meat. Controlled only by the voice of a goddess in her head now, no longer remotely human.

Weeping blood, she had collapsed in front of a line of armored police officers. Awakening in a hospital, Indra learned that she was being treated for contusions, abrasions, and STDs. The nurses managed to imply that, while they were forced to admit that her wounds had been the result of the riot, in all probability she had acquired the STDs on her own.

She heard them, but didn't hear them.

Shakti heard.

Shakti replied in blistering words that sent the nurses fleeing from the room.

Indra was far, far away. It was as if some part of her had become untethered from her soul, drifting up and far away. Perhaps dead. No, not dead, but no longer in this world.

By the time she returned to her data analyst position, the Shakti voices had receded, but she had changed. She could no longer remember a single dream she had ever had in childhood, seemed only a machine designed for survival.

Survive just another day. *One more day. Kill yourself and end the*

pain . . . tomorrow. Shakti's voice, returning to keep her alive. Then returning to the darkness like a beast shambling to its cave. But today, and
today, and today and all the todays she could manage were for life, for the
living. One more today, on the forlorn hope that some tomorrow would
be better than yesterday.

Please. Any sign in the gray fog of her life. The smallest sign.

Before all of her tomorrows became another endless today.

For seven more years she worked in the bleak, dark basement office.
The company had taken on some government contracts, and from time to
time, they proved of minor interest, small bright spots in the gloom. Her
supervisor's name was Gladys. Only a year previously, Gladys had been her
assistant.

"Here, Indra," she said, bringing her a file and a videotape. "These have
been declassified."

"What are they?" the girl asked.

Gladys grimaced. "Originally, American CIA and NSA files. They sat
on them for a while, then began to share with other agencies. Our MI6
wasn't very interested, and farmed out the films and some academic analysis
to lower-clearance instruments."

"And now us." The plump Afro-Indian data analyst sighed. It didn't
sound promising at all.

Indra Gupta looked at the video. At first she was bored. This was something from an American television series, perhaps. It looked like a man
free-running through traffic, tossing people every which way. The man's
name was said to be Adam Ludlum. The name meant nothing to her.

She was interested, but not engaged. She looked at the data. And finally
something tweaked her interest, caught her attention. This . . . was real,
not stunt work or special effects.

This was *real*. She was transfixed.

Indra stayed up late that night, studying the documents. And there was
a name in the documents that she knew.

The name Savagi. Adam Ludlum had been his student.

Her interest intensified. There were descriptions in the notes. Apparently, Ludlum had been trying to find a central theme to all the world's
most powerful meditation techniques, and had naturally drifted to her
great-grandfather's teachings.

For the first time in memory she felt excited. Began to cross-reference
the documents in bound black journals, working until late in the night
without the slightest sense of fatigue.

One day she went to 96 Euston Road in London, the home of the British Library. She gawked as she entered the massive brown brick building, nineteenth-century architecture housing the largest library of the twentieth. Standing in the presence of over 150 million books, journals, newspapers, manuscripts, and sound and video recordings . . . the collected knowledge of humanity stretching back four thousand years was a bit overwhelming.

She stood in line to speak to one of the assistant librarians in the metaphysics and esoterica section, still gawking at the endless row-mazes of files and books twisting off along unimagined corridors representing the life work of countless hives of scholars and artists.

Indra felt as if the elephant god, Ganesh, lord of wisdom, was standing on her chest.

"Excuse me?" the slight woman behind the desk said. "Can I help you?"

Indra managed to focus. "I understand that in your rare book section you have some material on a man named Savagi."

The librarian brushed a strand of pale hair from her face. "Savagi? I don't believe I've heard that name."

"He was a mystic," Indra said, almost apologetically. "Died in 1967, I believe."

The librarian's mouth twisted as if Indra had asked entrance to their pornography collection. She rose and consulted a microfiche. "Well, now . . . let me see. The central library apparently has a copy of a book of his entitled *Transformations,* but it isn't available for circulation. Are you affiliated with a university?"

"No," Gupta admitted.

"Well . . . hmm." The librarian paused. "There is a commentary on *Transformations* that might be of interest. Would you care to examine it?"

She nodded her head, barely able to speak, and was led back to the stacks, where she read all day, even seeing a few photos of the man who was her great-grandfather, a wise and powerful man. His books were unavailable, but along with the commentary there were a few other articles and pamphlets written by his students, as well as chapters in books that mentioned him and spoke of his work . . . often in cautionary tones and with phrases like "blasphemous commentary on *Ahmara Rishi'a Yama Sutra*" and "moral jeopardy" and "darkly controversial."

She began to create her own notes. Those original films of the mysterious-Adam Ludlum were linked to files and scanned photocopies of notebooks attributed to the same man. This "Ludlum" had studied Savagi's work on the far reaches of human consciousness, cross-referencing meditation systems—chiefly visualization and breathing—with martial arts techniques, constantly using Savagi as a reference, and seeking . . . what?

According to the notes, Ludlum sought physical and emotional control, and judging from the video, he had succeeded. What had this Ludlum been? A computer nerd, a geek, much like herself. Overweight, a smoker, one of the marginal people crammed into cubicles all over the modern world. And he had transformed himself into some kind of Olympic-level athlete in what . . . a year?

Impossible.

But if it was true, if it *could* be true, then this was her heritage. A gift from the great-grandfather who had never held her, never loved her, never cherished her. Had apparently driven her mother into the streets. But his spirit still lived, she was certain. And if she could make that spirit proud, she would have made a connection with him, one that might sustain her.

And she desperately needed to be proud of *something* in her life.

♦   ♦   ♦

In the months that followed, Indra Gupta devoted an average of three hours a day to staring at geometric patterns, breathing slowly enough to risk hypoxia, and chanting phrases gleaned from the articles . . . and remembered from her mother's nursery songs. Something within her blossomed. Following her great-grandfather's instructions and Ludlum's notes she learned to control her mind's interpretation of external data, to separate complex sounds into layers and manipulate them mentally. To burn away elements of her visual field, so that she fell helplessly into a field of white.

And there, she saw her father . . . so handsome and smiling, white teeth brilliant against his black skin. And her mother, brown and lovely, and fierce. Both dead and gone and in some strange way . . . *hungry*. And expecting something terribly wonderful of her.

"*The world is chaos,*" her mother had said. "*Our minds desperately seek order, and sacrifice their power thereby.*" Was that another maternal aphorism? Or was that Savagi's? She was no longer certain. "*When you learn to step beyond the illusions that hold back chaos, you have found the doorway.*"

But that doorway was not self-sustaining. It required energetically aligned intent to keep it open. And when at last fatigue overcame focus her parents disappeared, the blank white walls and halls dissolved, and she was back in her tiny apartment with its grimy walls and windows open to streets filled with the hopeless and homeless.

All was as it had been . . . except for one thing. She saw, and was uncertain of what she had seen. A smudge smeared the wall, in the precise location where her visual field had begun to peel away reality. Indra rose from her chair and reached out, afraid to touch it, afraid not to.

And when she did, the spot on the wall was warm. Almost hot. At least ten degrees warmer than the surrounding paint.

And at that moment, she felt something awaken within her, and smile. *Why, Shakti. Wherever have you been?*

♦ ♦ ♦

The very next day she sought out a yoga school on Felsham Road, in fashionable Putney, sandwiched between brown brick buildings. The room was rimmed with fifteen-centimeter-square wooden cubicles within which pairs of shoes and sandals, and neatly folded bundles of clothing were tucked away, awaiting their owners. The walls were covered with posters of improbably flexible, waifish women and muscular smiling men balancing like acrobats or twisting their lean bodies into curlicues while maintaining beatific expressions.

She greeted the woman at the front desk, a white lady in a beautiful black leotard that displayed broad shoulders and a flat stomach. In her forties, perhaps, but admirably well preserved. "Hello," Indra said, smiling as warmly as she could. "My name is Indra Gupta. I request instruction."

"My pleasure," the instructor said. "I'm Sarah. Do you have experience?"

"Not in physical exercises, no. Some of the mental principles."

Lean and severe as a prima ballerina, Sarah looked at Gupta's dumpling-shaped body, and sniffed. "You are African?"

"Indian."

She looked at Indra's skin with disbelief. "Where do you come from?"

"Mysore. Other places."

"Isn't that interesting?" the woman said, as if she found it the opposite. "There is a great yoga school in Mysore, taught by a man named K. Pattabhi Jois. Ashtanga. One of the very most difficult forms of yoga."

"Of Hatha yoga." The physical gymnastics were not the highest form, but they were the aspect with the clearest feedback as to accomplishment. The least room for hallucination.

"Of course. It might be better to begin with something simpler. Easier."

"No. I would like you to begin with the end," Gupta said.

For the first time, the teacher displayed puzzlement. "The end?"

"What is the highest level of Ashtanga?"

Sarah's otherwise smooth brow wrinkled. "I . . . don't know. I think there are five or six levels. I never learned more than the first. And . . . I'm afraid even that might be inappropriate for you."

Gupta concealed her irritation. "I wish to join your class."

The instructor bit her lip. "Well . . . did you bring workout leotards?"

"Yes," Indra said, and extracted her newly purchased pair from her bag.

"Oh. Danskin. Charming. I didn't know they made them in your size."

Anger flared, but Indra Gupta kept her face immobile.

She changed in the locker room, and some of the other students concealed polite disbelief.

The students were distributed across the mat: standing, stretching, and talking in hushed voices as Indra entered. A garden of beautiful, toned, muscular bodies. Gupta felt like a sack of wet meal in a field of flowers.

The teacher appeared, slipped a headset over her tightly braided hair, and stepped up onto a raised, carpeted platform at the front of the class. "All right. We have a new student today. Her name is Indra, and I'd like to welcome her."

They responded with polite applause. Some congratulations and words of encouragement. The teacher began class, moving them through poses with names like Surya Namaskara and Utthita Trikonasana. Indra struggled. And then . . .

She began to visualize, looking at the instructor and the other students. Following her breathing. Her heartbeat. She found the little girl image within her, and linked it to her adult self. And found her elder, the old woman she might one day be upon her deathbed, withered and worn with experience sweet and bitter, who spoke in gravelly tones she imagined similar to Savagi's. "The body is our greatest snare. It is created by our minds, but its hungers are so primary that it convinces us that it is the reality, our souls the illusion. The truth is just the opposite. Let your spirit guide the mind, and the mind then guide the body."

She grasped the line of light within her darkness. Tied it into a knot, in the shape of a woman performing a sun salutation.

Her back was stiff. She could not touch her toes.

"Every muscle in your body is controlled by either your conscious or unconscious mind. The doorway between them is the breath, the only process that is both voluntary and autonomic."

Indra lay in a humiliated heap. Ignoring the mocking voices in her head, she picked herself up again. The instructor approached her, lean face compassionate at last. "Really, dear, this class might not be for you."

Sweat beaded on Indra's skin as if the walls were covered with heat coils. "No . . . I can continue."

The instructor was worried. Both for Indra and herself. "Our insurance . . ."

Gupta managed a smile. "I'm fine. Fine. Please."

She got up. Centered her breathing. Visualized, and focused again. The class continued. Whorls of energy, like glowing fingerprints, coiled from the students around her and danced.

The echoing waves of respiration, the endless eternal rhythm of inhalation and exhalation from the sweating, straining students enveloped her.

Forget your body, her great-grandfather said within her. *Form the shape of the motion in your mind. Where the mind goes, the body follows.*

She wove her thoughts into a tunnel as narrow as a pencil.

Gupta struggled back to her feet. The sweat was rolling off her body. Sarah glanced back at her time and again, incredulous and then fascinated.

Indra wobbled . . . and then righted herself. Her body began to blossom like a Morning Glory. Her eyes were focused through the wall.

The instructor droned. "Feel your heels sink into the ground, feel the alignment of your skeleton, the air traveling through the empty places . . ."

Gupta finally managed to catch her balance. It felt as if her feet were anchored into the mat, and now she was bending and twisting with remarkable ease.

Savagi's voice again: *Your body is tight and stiff for one reason: it holds fear and grief. The body is a black bag holding the emotions you have yet to own. It tightens like armor, thinking it protects you, but if you release the pain, you return to the potentials of youth.*

"Release . . ." Gupta groaned, feeling that she might collapse into the hollows of her own bones.

Images flashed to mind, thoughts that she could not summon consciously. She saw images of being burned out of her home. Crying, running. Fear. Sanctuary.

Hell, masquerading as heaven.

Transform your fear, which paralyzes. Transform it . . . into anger. Into rage. Destroy the object of your pain. Set yourself free.

The little girl screamed. The entire crowd disappeared. She stood alone, in an abandoned world of stained walls and shattered houses.

Then, the buildings crumbled to the ground. And then began to grow, sparkling like gemstones. Beautiful. A crystal kingdom through which she walked, alone.

Then . . . children came running out of the doorways, the alleys, laughter and song, holding her hand, covering her with kisses . . .

♦ ♦ ♦

Discipline in the class had begun to break down. The measured focus of the advanced students was giving way to astonishment at the chubby, awkward-looking girl whose flesh seemed to possess an ancient and uncanny memory. Sarah was gawking openly by now.

"The advanced version of that pose is generally considered one beyond the ability of . . ." Words failed her. She stepped down off the raised platform. "Try this."

Not realizing it, she had begun to compete with the little round brown woman. But Indra was oblivious, an empty vessel of total concentration.

Sarah performed a standing bow pose, Dandayamana Dhanurasana, balancing on one leg, the other pulled up behind her, curving far enough for the sole of her foot to touch the top of her head. Indra reflected it as through a mirror that miraculously removed distortion. Her body sagged, but within the extra meat her legs and arms and spine described a perfection of motion that belied the flesh. Murmuring, the students began to follow her lead.

Like a field of flowers they were, all aligning with the sun . . . and Indra was that sun. The instructor was physically beautiful, an athlete. An artist.

But . . . Indra Gupta was the source of all light. The air about her shimmered in the humid room. When she moved, they moved.

Other students peered through the door. Finally the lights dimmed.

"Sarah? It is time for our class." They looked from the lean woman to she who by all rights should have been ungainly, and marveled. "Is . . . is this your teacher?"

Sarah emerged from her yoga trance, and stared at the clock. Three hours had passed. The students shook themselves out of it.

Some seemed almost afraid, and made their excuses, streaming out the door.

The instructor hurried the others away, and locked the door. She and a dozen others remained. Sweat and condensation streaked the window as if a tropical storm had raged within.

Sarah folded her legs lotus style and sat before the plump and shining girl, face shining. "Who are you?"

"My name is Indra Gupta."

"Why did you come?"

A pause. Indra felt something within her, a swelling of great purpose. Then she said: "I came to teach you."

CHAPTER 38

Olympia lay shivering on the living room couch of her faux condominium, tamping down the daymares, focusing on everything she had learned and done in the last hours, trying not to fall into panic or depression. So far as she knew, she was all Hannibal had, and if they were to survive this, she had to find calm within the storm. She thought deeply, constructing a model of the entire grounds in her mind. Wishing that she could commit it to paper. Hannibal had screeched, pointing up in the corners of the room, where tiny glass lenses poked through the plaster, if you looked closely enough. Then he had stopped shrieking. What had that been? Intuition told her that something had hurt his ears. Perhaps surveillance equipment? And did his silence mean that the surveillance had terminated? She suspected so, but dared not take the chance.

Not now. Later perhaps.

She had long been frustrated by Hannibal's inflexibility in certain arenas, but one of the doctors had clarified things for her: autistic children make rules, and insist on playing by them. *If you can learn his rules, you can enter his world.*

She had tried, and Hannibal had responded by teaching her a memory game. He would walk with her through a canvas of his imagining, and challenge her to remember where they were and the bits he had told her of their surroundings. And in her desperation to communicate with him, she had learned. Just a bit, but she had learned.

She imagined the Salvation Sanctuary's grounds, a clock-dial surrounding the maze garden and inner fountain. The library and the castle at six and nine o'clock. What she could remember of the underground laboratories, stretching from the castle around to the library and main building.

The roads leading to the Sanctuary. The van's windows had been tinted, but she could see a bit at the edges, when the light was just right. For instance, she had known when they drove through the town of Dahlonega. A central traffic circle had been circumnavigated, sending them along a smaller road and eventually to the route leading to the Sanctuary, the parking lot, and helipad.

The doorbell rang. The map she had been constructing in her mind fell to pieces. Olympia steadied herself, and answered the door. She would play the game of pretending to give them permission to enter. It seemed to pacify them. And she desperately needed her captors to remain calm.

The guards entered, pretending to be concierges. They were Abbott-and-Costello types, except Costello was thick with muscle rather than chubby, and Abbot was black, with an English accent. "We came to see if you needed anything."

"Is there a menu?" she asked with studied and deliberate naiveté. "Or can we get you to shop for us? Can I make a run to the store?" She seemed both friendly and plausible.

Costello wagged his head. "No, we'll be happy to do that for you."

She sighed with what she hoped sounded like relief. "I'm so grateful. I really want to just concentrate on helping Hannibal. Can I have my cell phone? I need to call the office, let them know I'm taking Christmas vacation."

Abbott smiled this time. "I'm sorry, we've found that it is best not to allow guests access to their usual communications channels. This is a very delicate process. I hope you can understand."

She hoped her expression would be considered bright and chipper. "Sort of like an intervention?"

The security man seemed pleasantly surprised. Almost as if others had not understood. "Yes. Just like that. You have to understand that your relationship with your husband was part of the dynamic that created Hannibal's prison. We can't allow you to have your usual activities. It's all for Hannibal."

Her relationship with her husband. They knew. Of course they did. How long had she been under observation? She felt raw, violated. They had been in her *home*. Olympia Dorsey had never been a violent woman, but at that moment, she could gladly have committed murder.

"It's hard," she said earnestly. "But I'd do anything for my boy."

"Good," he said. "So. Would we like something to eat?"

"A couple grilled cheese sandwiches?" she said, thinking to herself that a food server might be the perfect person to ambush, yes indeedy.

After they left, she visualized the steps from the elevator to the door. Another piece. The security at the front door.

Who was at the door? How much security? What did they know about what was really going on here? Were they at fault, or innocent dupes? Victims themselves? And in the final analysis . . . did it matter?

Her lips curled in a hard frown. "No, it doesn't matter at all," she said, tiptoeing into the apartment's family room.

There, Hannibal watched television, as he had since he first stopped shrieking at the corners of the room. He seemed lost in the chaotic cartoon images, thank God.

She prayed that he was unaware of the extent of their peril. Prayed that he could find mental and emotional sanctuary in his painfully narrow and brittle focus.

It was the first time she had ever been grateful for that terrible gift.

A single tear rolled down her cheek, unobserved by neither of the two people she loved most in all the world.

CHAPTER 39

"What are we going to do?" Nicki asked, her breath fogging the glass. She gazed out of the passenger window as the station wagon slid past manger displays and dancing neon reindeer. Behind her, Pax panted humidly against the back of her neck.

"We have to find help."

To either side, threads of smoke rose from the woods and rows of houses, wafting to the dark, cold clouds above them. Sirens wreathed the air, so constant that she barely noticed them anymore. "Everything is coming apart, isn't it?"

"It seems like that. Do you have any relatives here in Atlanta? Close friends of your mom?"

"No." She stared at him. "She had her job. That was about it." She changed the subject clumsily. "The cops in the diner. How in the world did you do what you did?"

"Someone gave me a gift," he said.

"That Madame Gupta person?"

"Yes."

Nicki was quiet for a while. "Mom said she was a miracle."

"Sure seemed that way to me."

By now, Nicki was near tears. "Do you think she could help us? Would help me?" Her voice cracked. Nicki realized her lower lip was trembling. She could not let that fear and frustration out. If she started crying, she'd be unable to stop.

Terry considered. "I'm not sure. What I'm pretty sure of is that you'd be safe there. And she can help me understand what is going on in my head."

"Mom said they were going up there, but I didn't get a chance to ask her about it. I hope it was wonderful." She shifted in her seat. "Do you think Madame Gupta would take me in? Is she nice?"

He smiled, warmed by the memory. "She's a lot more than that."

"Would you take me there?"

"Yes."

"How do we find her?"

His fingers hugged the wheel in a white-knuckled death grip. "We'll find her."

◆ ◆ ◆

Terry pulled off the freeway at a spot he chose more by instinct than logic, and cruised darkened streets. Few stores were open. Many looked as if they had been closed for days. Signs on windows: THE END IS COMING. And LAST CHRISTMAS SALE.

"Holy shit," Nicki said.

"Sounds just about right."

An entire block of businesses were blacked out. The residential neighborhoods they passed seemed darker than any other Christmas he could remember, scant on holiday cheer. Doubt had begun to devil him and then he found something . . . the long, beige, two-story silhouette of a vacation-emptied high school. Dark windows.

"Here," Terry said. He pulled into the abandoned parking lot and parked in a shadowed enclave between two aluminum sheds. Studied the main building. "Let's go," he said finally.

"You're going to break in?"

"Yep."

Terry walked around the periphery, every sense alive. He chose a window, worked the point of his belt knife under the window, and slid it up. "Not exactly Fort Knox."

He climbed up over the sill, and helped her up behind him. He pulled a narrow black Maglite from his pocket and pushed the recessed button, casting a pale saucer of light around the room.

"What are we looking for?" Nicki asked.

"The library, I think."

He used the light to navigate through the halls. Nicki followed, creeped out by the darkness, the interplay of light and shadow, even the abandoned Christmas decorations. On the walls: MERRY CHRISTMAS! HAVE FUN!

Nicki stared at it as if contemplating her own tombstone.

"Do you think they could be right?" she whispered.

"Right about what?"

"About this being the last Christmas."

"No," he said. "I don't believe it."

She walked closer to him. "You're a nice man. I'm sorry about how I treated you."

Terry grinned. "Oh, I'm an asshole. I'm just not the kind of asshole you thought I was."

"Thank God."

"No," he said. "The other guy."

They reached the library. "See if the Internet is on," he said.

"Over here," she said, waving him to a row of Macs. She finally seemed perky, as if a ray of optimism had pierced the fog.

"Good. Leave the lights off."

He sat down and booted up. Went to Google, and entered "Madame Gupta."

Information scrolled. "Okay. Let's see. We have a small Wikipedia article. Hmm. Indra Gupta. Born 1952. A question mark. Came to United States in . . . all right. Ah! Her American residence is in the retreat known as the Salvation Sanctuary in the Georgia mountains. No link."

He typed in "Salvation Sanctuary." And a few moments later Google provided a list of possibilities. He put quotes around it, added "Georgia" and received a much smaller list.

"I'm not seeing much," he said, focus pushing back the disappointment. "Place is secretive. I'm guessing they have some kind of Web scrub."

Nicki leaned into the screen's pale light. "Look. These are big sites. Articles by reporters, and all they say is 'somewhere in the Georgia mountains.' You believe they didn't actually go there?"

He liked the way she was thinking. "No. A couple of them describe it. What are you saying?"

"They're reporters. They were asked not to say more."

"Yeah, you're probably right. What do we do?"

"Think like reporters," she said. "Look for smaller sites. Look for followers talking to their friends."

He ruffled her hair. "You . . . are a clever girl."

He scrolled down to a spiritual blog on Huffington Post. "And . . . here we go. The town of Dahlonega, lovely little bed-and-breakfast named . . . Long Mountain Lodge. Close enough to hike to the sanctuary. What's hiking distance for you?"

"Five miles or less?"

"Lady gets a prize."

He typed "Dahlonega, Georgia" into Google, and received a map in return. Studied it. "Seventy miles from here. Still want to go?"

"You really think Madame Gupta can help us?" she asked.

"She wanted to see me. She wanted to help your brother. She may be the most remarkable person I've ever met. I think she may be exactly what we need."

"Then hell to the yes."

CHAPTER 40

The doorbell rang again.

Olympia steeled herself, then donned a happy mask. "That's the door," she said sweetly. "Just a minute! Come on, Hannibal."

"Food!" Hani screamed.

She went into the bathroom. Looked around for something she'd seen earlier: a bottle of Listerine mouthwash on the sink. She wondered what her captors were more concerned about: gingivitis or bad breath? She poured a stream of astringent amber fluid into a glass, and drank. She answered the door.

The waiter was a fine-looking young man who looked like a church choir's lead tenor. "Dinnertime. Hungry, I hope."

She smiled, then as he closed the door behind him, Olympia spit the mouthful of Listerine into his face. He screamed, clawing at his eyes, and she smashed him in the face with a lamp.

He collapsed to the ground, moaning, and rubbing at his face and head.

She had watched the entire act of violence without feeling the civilized guilt and regret she would have expected. Damn, but that felt *good*.

She grabbed Hannibal, who had been watching without comment or change of expression. "Come ON!"

She snatched the key card from the guy's neck and slid it through the slot on the side of the doorknob. The little light on the plate switched from red to green, and the lock clicked. Holding her breath, Olympia twisted the knob and opened the door, very gingerly sticking her head out. The hall was empty. She went to the elevator, pushing the wheeled meal cart in front of her, almost as if she thought she'd be able to use it as camouflage. Pushed the button. "Come on, come on, come on . . ."

Ding! A guard exited and she abandoned her intended soft-shoe and rammed the meal cart into him. As he lurched against the wall she snatched the Mace from his belt and sprayed a stream of white foam into his eyes and up his nose. He screamed, gobbling inarticulately, rolling on the ground, consumed by a world of pain. Adrenaline numbed panic or concern for his injuries, and she hit the ground-floor button.

"Damn you!" he shrieked. "Oh, shit! Eyes! My eyes!"

"Don't look, Hannibal," she said.

She needn't have said a word. Hannibal was almost like a sack of potatoes, dissociated, not engaging at all. The Hani she had known just last week, with her once again. A sob caught in her throat.

The door opened, but this new guy was a normal Yellow Robe, not a gold or blue security guy, and he was willowy and innocent, his eyes wide.

"I'm sorry," she babbled. "I'm sorry. Help me. We have to get out of here."

His wide-eyed confusion seemed genuine. "You . . . want to leave? No one is forcing you to stay."

She thought fast. "That's not true. Someone is disobeying Madame Gupta. It's . . . the security men. It's Tony."

"Security?" His eyes sharpened.

Pay dirt. Perhaps she could exploit the tensions she'd detected between the security guards and the followers. Wheels turned, and her mind whizzed. "You know they're not like us. Like you. Or me. Or Hannibal." Create rapport. Get him thinking "us." "You have to get us out of here. It's what she would want. Can you get us out?"

"Security," he said, lips twisting in a kind of triumph. "I knew there was something wrong with them! They were so mean when they rushed the rest of us out of here."

"Out?"

"Yes. They're bussing us to a facility in North Carolina. Something about a gas leak. Bastards!" He seemed to remember there was a child. "I'm sorry!"

"Bad word," Hannibal said, not meeting their eyes.

"What's your name?" Olympia asked.

"Torrence."

"Can you help us?"

"Come on," Torrence said.

Relief and gratitude flooded her veins. Finally, someone she could trust. Torrence knew his way around, might know his way out. This could be . . . the answer to her prayers.

Torrence led them through the building to an employee parking lot. It was a ghost town, only three cars in a garage built for thirty. "I'll drive you out. There has been some pretty strange shit going on here. I don't know what to think about it, but I can promise you that we aren't like that. It isn't what we're about." He directed her to the backseat of a battered blue station wagon.

"I know," she said. "Please. Hurry."

He backed out in a squeal of wheels, almost hitting a yellow concrete pillar, then spun the wheel and left the underground parking garage, driving along the concrete lip outside the main fence as if heading clockwise to the helipad. "They've canceled the tours, even for the devout. Locking things down, furloughing out the aspirants."

They rolled up the underground parking lot to the gate. Two men met them there. The taller one smiled. *Oh God,* she thought. It's Tony Killinger, a step ahead of them. "Hello, Torrence. Where are you going?" Olympia noticed that his right hand was behind him.

"I'm leaving," Torrence said, gritting his teeth as he did.

Killinger looked at the woman and boy huddled in the back. "These are our guests."

"They'd like to leave."

"Well, now . . . that's not possible right now." Tony scratched his head, an oddly disturbing *aw shucks* gesture. Was he putting on an act for the acolyte? His faux folksiness made him feel more dangerous. Olympia's heart, strangely calm before, thumped back to life. "Some . . . things have been stolen, and we need to question her."

Torrence put on his stubborn voice. "I'll take her to the sheriff's station."

"No, we'd prefer to handle it right here." Tony sighed. Then his hand came out from behind his back—holding an automatic pistol which made a *phutt* sound as he fired a single round into Torrence's face. Olympia screamed as his brains splashed into the backseat next to Hannibal. She pulled a frozen Hani against her, turning his head away. The security man pushed the corpse over, and nudged himself in behind the wheel.

He smiled at Olympia, who sat with arms wrapped desperately around her shrieking child.

"Now ain't that a shame, darlin'?" Tony said. "See what you made me do?"

CHAPTER 41

Oh beloved, put your attention not on pleasure or pain, but
between these.

—*Vigyan Bhairav Tantra*

The interrogation room was sterile, all white walls and shelves and knife-
edged incandescent shadows. In the middle of the room, anchored to the
floor, was a single chair that reclined to a table. Olympia was forced down
and strapped in. An overhead light glared down on her like a blind, un-
blinking eye.

Two people entered the room, wheeling a table carrying a beige rectangular container of dimpled plastic. They parked it next to her.

"Who are you?" she asked.

They said nothing. One removed the top from the container, and she
glimpsed various glittering implements of intimidating design. The men
reclined her, and she felt the contents of her stomach pushing their way
up into her throat as if she was being squeezed by a giant hand. Her head
spun, and it was all she could do not to scream.

"What are you doing?"

They continued reclining her until her head was lower than her feet.
Then they draped a cloth over her nose and mouth and eyes. It smelled like
Febreze.

"Wait! Wait! What do you want to know—?" The words were inter-
rupted by a gush of water over her face. She bucked and writhed, screaming
and choking.

Drowning! I'm drowning! All the tissues of her throat and sinuses contracted and clogged, everything in her brain screaming *drowning!* And
panic, raw primal survival fear such as she had never known seized her
entire body like a wet fist. Shook her until all thought and emotion save
terror simply tumbled out of her head and heart. Then not even terror, just
a mute scream of survival as she strained against the bonds convulsively,

bucking and twisting and pulling, vomiting and choking on water at the same hideous instant.

They pulled the cloth away, and looked at their watches, counting seconds.

Olympia sucked in a mouthful of air, gobbling incoherently. "Wait. Please. There's been some kind of mistake—"

The cloth was slapped back over her face, and watery hell descended with it.

The anguish continued endlessly, and all the while not a single question was asked, no requests or demands made.

Then, when she was exhausted, hollowed out, too numb to do anything but accept death like a deer dazed and limp in the tiger's jaws, she was allowed to rise to a sitting position. The cloth was peeled away from her face, and she was allowed to gasp a few breaths. Almost tenderly, they patted her face dry. And then the two torturers left.

The room was empty and silent. Olympia heard nothing but her own breathing, felt nothing but her fevered heartbeat.

Then . . . Madame Gupta entered the room, wearing a clinging silk cheongsam. Her face was smooth, unlined, suffused with compassion. Olympia wanted to kill her, but what was disturbing was that she felt a tickle of a terrible urge to beg forgiveness for her sins. "I am genuinely sorry that we had to do that to you. You seem a good woman, a good mother, a woman honestly concerned with the welfare of her children. There is no finer thing in life. My own mother would have understood you very well indeed. She died for her children. I hope you will not have to die for yours." Gupta's manner was sympathetic, plausible, seductive. No overt threat at all. It was obscene.

"Why did you do this to me?" Olympia fought to control the sour tangle of fear and rage that tightened her voice.

Be careful. Very, very careful. This woman is insane.

Or worse.

Gupta hung her head. "I am sorry, but it was necessary to convince you that we were serious. You would not want this happening again, would you?"

"No . . . no . . ."

Madame Gupta loomed over her. "And even more, you wouldn't want such a thing happening to Hannibal."

Olympia's world flashed red, then white, before her vision cleared again. "You wouldn't."

Gupta's long fingers twined together. "I can understand why you wouldn't want to believe it, but it is critically important that you believe that I am indeed most sincere. I will indeed do whatever is required to accomplish my aims. I will free Hannibal's mind and spirit from its prison, and to do that I will need your full-hearted, enthusiastic cooperation. Or at the very least, a lack of obstruction. I can accomplish what I want even if you . . . or your daughter . . . are dead."

Another sledge blow to her heart. Help her son? Why? What was in it for Gupta? Why was it so important? She sensed that truth and lies were intermingled so closely that she needed to parse every word, search every phrase, if she was to find truth. "Leave Nicki alone, or . . ." She tried to be strong, to demand, to pretend indignation, but instead heard her voice collapse. "Please."

"The 'please' is nice." Gupta smiled. "It is an acknowledgment of our relative status in this matter. And I appreciate that you have not blustered, or made demands. It suggests that you are intelligent enough to grasp your situation."

"What do you want?"

Gupta smiled. A kind, wide smile. "We just want to help Hannibal reach his full potential. He is an extraordinary child. And with my help . . . he will become an extraordinary man. There is no telling what he might accomplish."

"Who are you?" Olympia asked. *And what do you really want?* A time would come for that question. But that time was not now.

"The woman who is going to help your son reach his full potential." Gupta leaned closer. "Whether you . . . or your daughter . . . will be alive to see it is totally up to you."

Or your daughter. Oh, God. "Where is she?"

"We are locating her," Gupta said. "You will be together soon." That sounded like the truth . . . but not the whole truth. Irritation had tightened Gupta's eyes. Had they tried to acquire Nicki? And failed somehow?

"You are, I believe, a reporter. Who. What. Why. Where. When. How. In time, all will be revealed. Those are the questions, aren't they? In the news business? Your business? You will want to know. The world will want to know, and in time, it may be revealed. It is possible. And if it is, you will be the one who was there. Would you like that?"

The trap was almost complete. If they'd had Nicki, the jaws would have been closed. But with her daughter free . . . there was a prayer. Olympia was helpless, but not without hope. "Where is Hannibal? What are you doing to him?"

"He is in another room. A much more . . . comfortable room. Watching cartoons, I believe, with our friend Maureen. He is a lovely child. A very unusual boy." Damn it, if this bitch said that one more time, Olympia was going to try her best to strangle her, regardless of the consequences. "I will teach him, I think."

"Teach him what?"

"What he needs in order to embrace his destiny."

"His . . . destiny?"

"There is only one question you have to ask. And that question is: will you be there to see it? His destiny . . . my destiny . . . cannot be denied. There is nothing you or anyone else can do to stop it. But you have a choice."

"What choice?"

"To live or die. To be there for your son in the flesh, or to be only a dwindling memory, as he embraces a new life. A new mother. Children do that, you know. It is a survival trait. They . . . forget. Do you want him to forget you? Forget . . . his sister?

"I lost my parents when I was young. Cannot remember their faces. Our family was scattered. I have, somewhere, a brother and a sister . . . if they survived. I have never been able to find them."

"No," Olympia pled. "Not my daughter! Leave her out of this! She doesn't know anything that can help you."

"Strange, isn't it?" Gupta said, ignoring her. "Already you have forgotten your pain. But while the water was pouring you forgot about everything in the world but your next breath. Your desire for air."

"What do you want from us?" Olympia asked.

"And now, minutes later, you are concerned only for your son. And your daughter." Gupta's smile was saintly. "You are a good mother." The horror of it was the part of her psyche, growing in the back of her mind, that craved this harpy's approval.

"Where is my daughter?"

"Your house is being watched. When she returns, we will know. What happens then is up to you. She can be brought here. Safe. She can be brought here, damaged. Or she can die there."

"What kind of sick bitch are you?"

Gupta seemed to have too many teeth in her mouth. Sharp teeth. The Indian accent that normally was nothing more than a slight twinge at the edge of aural perception was more alive now. "The kind of sick bitch who accomplishes her goals."

"What do you want?"

"I enjoy James Bond movies," Gupta said. "The color. The adventure. The British Empire lives again! But I am not a villain in an imperialistic fantasy. You will know only what it is critical for you to know. And that is that you must answer this question, and answer it honestly."

"What question?"

She leaned forward. Her breath was sharp with some spice Olympia did not recognize. Turmeric? "Are you a good mother? Will you put aside your personal feelings to provide nurturance to these young people who need you now more than ever?"

"Yes."

"Good. Good." She unclamped Olympia's bonds, then turned and whispered into a handheld communicator. A black-handled knife glittered on the cart of torture implements, and Madame Gupta's back was turned to it. Silently, Olympia's hand stole toward the blade's handle. But the moment her fingers brushed against it, Madame Gupta changed somehow. Her back to Olympia, something had shifted. Not anger. Not alertness. Almost relaxation, like someone anticipating pleasure.

Olympia froze, then recoiled as if physically struck. Her heart trip-hammered.

"Remember," Gupta said. "Orphans I understand. I was an orphan. I might even prefer to deal with one. The choice is yours."

Olympia was so deeply afraid that she could not separate herself from the emotion enough to feel it.

"But," Gupta said, turning and plucking the knife from her nerveless hand. "Perhaps you do not comprehend the extent of my determination. I think a demonstration may be in order."

She looked at the guards. "Tell them to kill the girl."

Olympia could not even speak. Gupta left the room, wheeling the cart out in front of her. The door closed.

Olympia snapped out of her paralysis, sobbing, what fragile strength she had mustered collapsing into panic. And then she screamed. "No! No! I'm sorry! I'm sorry! Don't hurt my baby!"

◆　◆　◆

Out in the hall, Tony frowned. "'Kill the girl.'" He seemed to roll the words around in his mouth. Taste them. "Are you serious?"

"Perhaps." Madame Gupta seemed deep in thought. "If we were to bring her here, and cut her throat in front of her mother and brother . . . I suspect resistance would cease."

"Maybe." He looked at his employer, perhaps wondering how serious she was. "But . . . well, we don't have her yet."

"Where are your men?"

"They . . . haven't reported back. There seems to have been a spot of difficulty."

Gupta's face tightened, and then relaxed. "Secure her," she said. "Bring her here. And then we will make our decisions."

CHAPTER 42

After their last stop at a gas station, Terry drove on I-95 north for about seventy miles, through punishing bumper-to-bumper traffic all the way.

"Is everyone leaving town?" Nicki asked.

"I don't know, Nicks-Nicks."

She stuck her tongue out at him. "I used to hate it when you called me that."

"And now?"

"You're just a minor annoyance."

He grunted. "Ouch. That's harsh."

She grinned. "'If I be waspish, best beware my sting.'"

"Will you please cut that out?"

◆　◆　◆

Caught in traffic, they inched along, then turned onto a smaller road and began to make better time. Passed between rows of trees, a four-lane highway headed up into the mountains. With slow-motion urgency, light snow flurries drifted toward the ground.

He hadn't many memories of snow. Most of his childhood had been spent on military bases in warm climates: Okinawa, Guam, Texas, California. Most of his adulthood in hot ones: the Middle East, Central America, Africa. "Merry Christmas," Terry said.

"What?"

"Merry Christmas," he said. "It's snowing. Don't you like snow?"

"Nope."

He snorted in disbelief. "What kind of Georgia girl are you?"

"There's not that much snow around here. But anyway, I'm a Miami girl."

"Then why aren't you in Florida?"

"We left right after Dad . . . died," she said. Her hands pressed at the soft ringlets of her hair, as if checking to see if they were in place.

Holy crap, he thought. *She doesn't know I know.*

"And we're stuck, because Mom can't get a job in Florida as good as the one she has here."

"How old were you when you left?"

A pause.

"Ten."

Terry's eyes widened. "Ten years old. Three years. Isn't it time to be a Georgia girl?"

"Kill me now."

"Do you have friends out here? Things you like to do?"

"Sure."

"Then what's so bad?"

A faux English accent: "'There's small choice in rotten apples.'"

Terry winced. "I'm dying here."

She smiled. In the backseat, Pax barked, communicating in a universal doggie language, tail wagging furiously. "Pax has to go," she said.

"My opinion, precisely."

"Very funny."

"Oh, you mean poop." He nodded. "All right."

He spotted a sign directing them to a rest area just three miles ahead, and six minutes later, they pulled off to the right. An elderly white gent in a black Stetson leaned against a white-and-red camper shell, smoking an unfiltered cigarette. There was a Marlboro Man leanness about his chest and cheekbones. He looked more like he belonged out on the plains roping longhorns than anywhere near a city, but here he was.

"Howdy."

"Howdy," Terry replied.

"Bad traffic."

"Yeah," Terry said. Pax and Nicki were romping on the rectangle of manicured grass. Pax found a likely spot and squatted to release a steaming yellow stream.

"Almost waited too long to get out," the smoker said.

"Out of Atlanta?"

The Marlboro Man nodded and tapped his cigarette with his fore-finger. Ash floated in the wind. "I don't know if there is anywhere at all to go. Not anymore."

"You really think it's that bad?"

The man turned his head and hawked and spit. "Worse. Worse than anyone is saying. The ones in the news are just what's leaking out. I've heard millions have died in India and China. Just . . . keeled over and went back to Buddha."

The cars honked at each other. From some distant place came the sound of metal cracking against metal. "What do you think it is? Some kind of natural thing? A weapon of some kind?"

The man shook his head. "End times. Fags getting married. Muslim in the White House and Jews controlling our government. It's all in the Book. Read the Book. 'Afore it's too late."

He regarded Nicki with Pax. "Your girl?"

"Watching her for her mom."

The man nodded. "Nice girl. I'd say be careful, but I'm not sure that matters. Not anymore."

He looked up into the sky. "It's gonna open. A flaming sword. 'So he drove out the man; and he placed at the east of the garden of Eden Cherubims, and a flaming sword which turned every way, to keep the way of the tree of life.' "

"And what is this 'tree of life' we're going to be denied?"

Marlboro Man gave him an owlish expression. "Life," he said. "It's all ending. And we ended it. And the angels will drive us all away."

Jesus Christ, Terry said to himself. *This is the way the world ends.*

"It'll be the last thing any of us see. The very last." The smoker took a last drag of his cigarette, threw it to the ground, and ground it underfoot. Then lit another, the match briefly flaring to sharpen his profile. "What do you think? Would you rather see it, or just have it happen in your sleep?"

"I guess I'm the kind who wants to see it."

"Me, too." The old man grinned, a bitter expression Terry couldn't decipher. "Well . . . you take care."

Terry managed a smile. "Thought you didn't think it mattered."

Nicotine-stained teeth in a somber smile. "Might be wrong."

The cowboy got into the camper and pulled away. Pax's nose was suddenly snuffling Terry's leg. "Who was that?" Nicki asked.

Terry watched the camper's taillights disappear into the traffic stream. "He never said."

♦　♦　♦

Two hours later, they pulled onto a smaller road, toward a town that looked like a Fort Lauderdale tourist trap transplanted in the Georgia mountains. Their lane was slowing, but the opposite lane was speeding up. Not a good sign.

When they got closer, they saw cars being turned around, heading back south toward Atlanta. An even worse signifier: the borders were being sealed. "Uh-oh . . ."

"What do you think this is?" Nicki asked.

"Trouble," Terry said as they reached the barrier.

CHAPTER 43

It seemed to Olympia that all hope depended upon the significance of what had *not* been said. No one had said: "We saw you Mace our guard." No. Security had discovered her, but up until the very last moment, it seemed that she had been a beat ahead of them. Improbable as it seemed, it was just possible that there was no surveillance of their room.

And if that was true, if it was even *possible* that it was true, then it was worth trying again.

She and Hannibal chewed at rare roast beef sandwiches with a hint of horseradish in the mustard.

Hannibal was very quiet. Not hysterical. Not crying. He had seen a man's brains blown out of his head, and the sight had induced something akin to somnambulism. He seemed to have slid into some distant place inside his head, and she was afraid for her boy, didn't know how to reach him.

But where words would not suffice, perhaps actions would.

For Hannibal's sake she pretended to savor every bite, but tasted nothing. What had happened in that room, with the chair and the straps and the water and the soft words from the insane woman had burned away her taste buds, and it was entirely possible that the simple pleasure of food and drink might have been banished forever.

She rose. "All right. They always give us ninety minutes before they come back. If we're going to do this, we have to do it now."

"Yes, Mommy."

"Do you trust me?"

"You're silly," Hannibal said, without looking at her. "You are a very silly mommy."

She looked at him. Although he still declined eye contact, this was more than he had said for a very long time.

"I wonder about you."

He giggled.

The bedroom windows looked out on the maze and the interior of the clock-face underlying the entire Sanctuary's design. Olympia pulled the blanket off the bed and stripped off the sheets. They were good, twelve hundred thread-count Westport sheets, but by stabbing a fork through the edge she was able to start a rip, and then tear the entire thing in two. She looked around the room and decided on the clock radio on the dresser next to the bed. The cord was attached to the wall, not plugged in. She wrapped the cord around her fist, set her foot against the wall, and pulled with all the strength in her good, long legs.

Pulled until the bite from the cords against the flesh of her palms was so strong she thought she would have to quit. Then the cord came loose, and she stumbled back.

Olympia wrapped the clock up in the half-sheet, then twisted and knotted the sheet until she had a flexible mace. The window wasn't thick, but it was sealed. She looked out across the courtyard, out across the maze, and saw no one. She had to take the chance. She whirled the weighted sheet around her head and smashed it into the window once, twice. The third time the glass cracked, then spiderwebbed and shattered. She knocked the shards out and then leaned out herself to take a look.

The adjacent room seemed quiet and dark.

If what the unfortunate Torrence had said was true—that the security force was moving people out, then there was a chance this might work. The apartment next to theirs might be unoccupied.

Hell, it might even be unlocked.

Olympia took a deep breath, leaned out, and whirled the knotted sheet again. It took four attempts before the glass on the adjoining window broke, then another ninety seconds got most of the glass shards out. Chunks of pane fell down to the garden below them, making blessedly little noise.

While walking around the edge of the maze she had looked up at the castle and seen the narrow ledge under the windows, and she relied upon it now.

Yes. No more than four inches wide, and she was four floors up. A fall was probably fatal, and even if by some miracle she survived, her chances of helping Hannibal would have evaporated.

The next window over was only about three feet away, just slightly farther than she could stretch her arms while holding onto her own window. She examined the frame, plucked out another sliver of glass, and realized that she couldn't be as picky on the far side. Olympia ripped the other half of the sheet into quarters, and wrapped her hands.

When she stuck her head out again, the snow was falling harder, prickling her cheek and brow. Taking a deep breath, she stepped out onto the narrow ledge, gripped her window frame, and flung her right arm out feeling for the next room's raised metal frame.

There. She had it, but could feel glass under the sheet's merciful buffer. Olympia knocked the glass out and grabbed the window frame. She was completely outside her room now, balanced on the narrow ledge, trying to press her stomach and chest into the wall as tightly as possible. When she shifted her grip, her feet slipped and she almost fell, one arm pinwheeling before it slapped against the frame again and her bandaged fingers found purchase. Exhilaration, the simple joy of taking some kind of positive action, was intoxicating.

She caught her breath for five seconds, then managed to find a new grip that gave her better balance. She used her right arm to pull herself against the stippled wall, then got her left hand between herself and the wall to grab alongside her right. She changed grips again and finally gained the position to step through the window.

A bright ribbon of pain told her that she had sliced her leg, but the gash was only a quarter-inch deep, and she had the sheets to bandage it.

The apartment was empty, dark. The same size and shape as hers, but furnished much more simply, and with an extra wall where it had been divided into a dorm for perhaps four students.

If anyone had been in residence recently, they had abandoned the room leaving few clues: unwashed cups in the sink. A dish of ramen atop a microwave, cooked but uneaten.

Now came the critical part, and she prayed she was right: that no one would bother locking an empty room. That was half of it, and she was right. With a twist and a bit of pressure the front door opened.

Now came the next part, and for once luck seemed to be with her: the doors were indeed locked from the outside, with a bolt instead of a key. She slid it back, crying with relief.

Hannibal hadn't even noticed she was gone. He was still watching robots transform into trucks and planes on the television. She picked him up, and he didn't fight her. His arms circled her neck, his breath soft and sweet upon her cheek.

Tiptoeing back to the door, Olympia poked her head out. Nothing. She scurried down to the end of the corridor, and the door was locked. "Damn."

The roof access on the other end of the hall was open. "Come on."

"Okay."

The two of them crept up the stairs. Up two levels, including one that said PRIVATE RESIDENCE, NO ENTRANCE. Madame Gupta's quarters. She felt a chill as they climbed past that level, smiling in Hannibal's face, whistling past the graveyard. The door at the top of the sixth-floor landing was stuck. For a moment she despaired, but then it opened.

"Thank God."

They made it out onto the roof. Snow twirled down from a darkened sky. She looked for a fire ladder. Anything. Nothing. She looked down over the edge of the roof, and saw something heartening: on the north side of the castle, a fire escape rose up to the fourth floor, but no farther. She looked around frantically, and then remembered the fire hose they'd passed in the stairwell. "Wait here."

She went back into the stairwell and unreeled the hose, uncoupling it from the spigot. Carried it out and tied it to a stanchion at the roof's edge.

"Baby," she said softly. Snowflakes crusted his eyelids, and he blinked against their twinkling. "I don't want you to look down. Can you do that?"

" 'Es."

She tied the fire hose around his waist and braced herself, lowering him two floors to the fire escape landing. He landed there and looked up at her, his round, dark face shining with love.

Olympia tied off the other end of the hose. "Come on, girl," she whispered to herself. "You can do this. You have to do this."

And hand over hand, she lowered herself off the edge of the roof. "It's just a climbing wall," she whispered to herself. "Just Atlanta Rocks!"

Suddenly, two Gold Robes appeared, walking along the path beneath them. She hung there, holding her breath, back and shoulders and biceps aching. Hannibal stared down at the maze.

Faintly, she heard: "And the others? What happens?"

"I don't think we want to think about that now."

"Someone needs to," the woman said.

"It's the woman and the kid I'm worried about."

The reply was almost reverent. "Not just a kid. *The* kid, maybe. The way Madame talks about him, you'd think he was the Second Coming."

"That's not what bothers me."

"No?" the woman replied. "What bothers you?"

He paused. "What if she's right?"

They disappeared around the corner. Olympia breathed a deep sigh of relief, and lowered herself the rest of the way.

Her breath scalded her throat, and her arms felt as if the skin had been peeled away, and the muscles sandpapered. This was the hardest thing she had ever done, by a painful margin.

But despite the fatigue, the words she had just heard haunted her. *What if she's right?* What in the world was so special about Hannibal? Why was he so important? She knew that if she could solve that puzzle, it might mean survival. And if she couldn't . . .

"Love you, Mommy."

She held him tightly, self-doubt crushed by his answering embrace. They crept down the rest of the fire escape, the snow falling thicker and harder. Their breath curled in front of them like plumes of exhaled smoke.

"If we get a car, they'll hear it. If we walk, we won't get as far. What do you want?"

"Quiet," he said. Looking directly at her.

She hugged him, and he let her. "We walk, then."

They could take the walk around the maze . . . or go right through it. She'd been decent with maze books as a kid. From the window, it didn't look too complicated. There would be places to hide, and relatively easy ways to avoid accidental encounters. There were four entrances, one in each cardinal direction. They crept from the tower across to the maze without incident, but a voice drifted through the snow just as she passed the Ganesh elephant topiary marking the maze's western entrance.

". . . and if we finish by the first of the year, I'd reckon . . ." a man's voice. A second set of footsteps, but no voice to accompany it. She didn't recognize the voice. And she had slipped inside the maze before they were close enough to see her.

"Maze!" Hannibal whispered.

She held her finger to her lips. "Yes, maze. I think we go right here."

"Yes, Mommy. Right." They crunched softly through the snow, now a four-inch carpet of frozen white. The maze was composed of seven-foot-tall evergreen shrubs of some kind, cloaked in ivory. The walls were about two feet thick with a four-foot pathway marked off by the twists and turns.

They reached a hedge lion, rearing back with white mane and frosted head, roaring silently. The path forked: *left or right?*

"Left," Hannibal said.

"No, right," she said.

He shrugged, and she took him right . . . and the path dead-ended in another twenty feet.

Sheepishly, she retraced her steps and turned left. Hannibal was humming. When the snow began to fall more briskly, he started catching flakes on his tongue, licking them happily out of the air. "Hani was right," he said.

Yes, indeed. Hani was right.

Had it not been for her frying nerves, the hedge maze would have been beautiful. Olympia heard another voice, too indistinct to make out the words, close enough to have been inside the maze or outside. She just wasn't certain.

Closer.

No, it was someone *inside* the maze, a single set of footsteps. Someone talking on a cell phone?

She pulled Hannibal back into the shadows, and wrapped her hand around his mouth. Blessedly, he seemed to understand exactly what she needed from him, and did not struggle.

The phone-talker was a woman, the big security woman with the square jaw. Maureen? She had just finished a phone call, and flipped it closed as she plodded by, humming, never seeing the two refugees crouching in shadow behind her.

As soon as Maureen was gone, they hurried forward, and within a few steps came to another split in the path. Hani had seen the maze from the helicopter, and from the window. Yes, she had as well, but she had begun to suspect Hani's memory was superior to her own.

"Which way?" she whispered.

Hani's thin outstretched arm pointed to the right.

He was correct. Two more twists and they were in the center of the maze. A concrete pond bracketed by a pair of marble fish spitting water at each other. Low floodlights rotated colors from gold to green to blue as she watched. "Pretty," Hannibal whispered. It might have been. At another time in another mood the snow-crested hedges and sculptures, the pool and cascading lights might have been wondrous. This wasn't that time. She pulled him onward.

Hani was correct at every turn, and they emerged at the maze's east end three minutes later.

She kissed him. "Good boy."

She paused, looked left and right and listened hard, and when her heart stopped leaping they snuck up to the guard's gate. The road was fenced and chained. If they tried to climb that fence, they'd be right in plain sight, helpless and trapped. She went north around the inside edge of the fence until they reached a stand of trees. One of them was climbable, and its branches reached right over the fence.

Beautiful.

"Hold on tight," she said, and he wrapped his arms and legs around her so tightly it seemed he wanted to become part of her again. In the last hour she'd had more contact with Hani than he'd allowed her in the previous six months. For another such hug, she would climb the Empire State Building, and roar at the world like Kong.

Pretending she was again on the Atlanta Rocks! wall, Olympia climbed the tree. She stopped to calm her breathing, then shimmied out over a branch. It scraped at her legs, bit at the cut on her leg, and she had to stifle a cry. Then she rolled down, holding onto the branch until her hands held all her weight and Hani's as well, and her numbed fingers lost purchase. They fell, and as her feet crunched through the snow she deliberately tumbled facedown to protect the precious cargo clinging to her back.

When she opened her eyes, Hani had dismounted, crouching beside her, staring into her eyes with adoration. " 'Ommy."

"I'm all right, Hani."

Distantly, down the slope, Dahlonega's lights twinkled and shone below them, a Christmas display in miniature.

"We can make it, baby." Her breath puffed out before her in little clouds. "We can make it."

As they descended the slope, behind them, the first alarm bells were sounding.

◆　◆　◆

Olympia and Hannibal slid, staggered, and crunched their way down the slope southwest of the Salvation Sanctuary through the thickening snow toward a distant Dahlonega. How far did they have to go? Five miles? Six? They weren't dressed for this kind of cold. What would the temperature do to her stamina? Hani's? Whatever it did, it wouldn't stop her, wouldn't stop *them*. She swore that to herself as indistinct shouts of alarm drifted from the gate behind them. Clanking. Cars leaving. Flashlight beams sweeping through the darkness.

"The snow is bad. But it might cover our tracks, if we're lucky."

"Cold," Hani said.

She shucked her coat and bundled him in it. Carry him? No, he was eight, and strong, and seemed eager to use that strength. "Here." A house not fifty meters distant, smoke curling from a brick chimney, lights in the windows. If they could make it that far, there might be safety.

They banged on the door. "Help! Help us, please."

A pause, and then a voice from inside. "Here, here . . . what's all the fuss?"

"Please let us in. We're freezing."

The door opened fractionally. The man who opened the door would have to stand on a case of Wheaties to see eye to eye with a cricket. "Yes?" he said.

His hair, what there was of it, was as white as typing paper, even his bushy eyebrows. Behind him, a Mrs. Cricket appeared and shared his evident curiosity.

"Please," Olympia repeated.

And miracle of miracles, the door opened to admit them.

CHAPTER 44

Mrs. Cricket's name was Margerie, and Jiminy's was Franklin. As they entered, Olympia scanned the room, looking for signs that they were alone, or safe. A Christmas-themed picture of young adults holding babies on the mantel. Shelves filled with books, and a smaller rack half-filled with DVDs. A rifle on a rack over the fireplace. Could she get her hands on it? And ammunition?

"We have a fire," Franklin said. "Come in. Your boy must be a Popsicle. Come in!"

"Thank you." She was shivering. "Do you have something warm for my son?"

"We have cocoa," Franklin said. "All he can drink."

"I'll just be a minute," Margerie said.

Hannibal wandered around the room in a rough counterclockwise circle. Couch, fireplace, bookshelves, past the kitchen door.

"Here by the fire, hon," Olympia said.

Hani grinned. "Warm." He dawdled, running his finger along a long row of ancient *Encyclopedia Britannicas* as he wandered over.

Olympia rubbed her hands briskly. "Do you have a phone?"

"Yes. Of course. What happened to you?"

Hannibal shook his head. Just a bare left-right-left, but for Hani, that wag was as good as a neon sign.

She improvised rapidly.

"My car hit a deer. I spun off the road. Need to call the police."

Margerie brought a pitcher of cocoa and a pair of mugs. "Here you go, sweetheart. Have all you want."

"Where was the accident?" Franklin asked.

"Mile down the road. We waited in the car until it got cold."

"The engine stopped?"

"Yes," she said. "I hit a tree."

"I thought you said a deer," Franklin asked.

"A deer," she replied. "And then I hit a tree."

"Poor darling," Margerie said. "Here's the phone."

Olympia called 911. Busy signal. She thought of the chaos that had consumed the world, and understood. "Is there a local police number?"

"It's on the refrigerator," Franklin said. "I have to tell you that things have been bad. Even with just the weather, they've been bad. But with all this end of the world craziness . . . I just don't know."

She dialed again, receiving another busy signal. She looked at Hannibal. He mouthed the word: *Nicki*.

Finger trembling, Olympia Dorsey dialed Nicki's number.

CHAPTER 45

Nicki sat scrunched in her seat in the car, enjoying the steady stream of dry, warm air from the heater as Terry went into the 7-Eleven, seeking coffee and a tourist map, something that might display local roads.

Standing on the backseat, Pax began to bark in her ear. "Ow!" she said, jerking her head out of the way. "What is it, girl?"

Then she realized her phone was buzzing. She turned it on, and her ring tone thumped with the bass of a song so old she barely remembered caring about it. The number was unfamiliar. "Hello? Hello?"

The line was full of static. "Nicki? Baby? Are you all right . . . ?"

The phone crackled and popped, battery dying. "Where are you calling from? I'll call you right—damn! I mean, darn!"

Fighting panic, Nicki realized she had a possible way of calling her mother back. Nicki dug in the glove compartment, hoping to find a compatible charger . . . and found Terry's phone. And next to it, the battery. She frowned. Why would he take the battery out?

She fumbled and clicked the rectangular battery package back in. After a moment of searching, the status window displayed two bars! She squinted, dialed the number, and punched buttons. "Mom?"

"Baby?"

"Mom, it's me!"

♦ ♦ ♦

In the warehouse eight miles north of downtown Atlanta, Father Geek had been slumbering by his computer screen, deep in a dream of childhood, running through narrow Johannesburg backstreets that kept transforming into Fallujah's cobblestones. He was yanked out of it when the screen blossomed into a grid with a radiating green dot beeping against the map of a mountainous area. "What . . . ?" he said groggily. And then: "Well, lookie here!"

The others were sprawled on cots around the room. One at a time they muzzily rose to their feet. Mark rolled over and up, his face heavily creased, wiping at the snail-trail glistening at the corner of his mouth with the back of one meaty hand. "What is it?"

"I think Mary's little lamb just wandered back into the fold."

"Ooh, I love lamb," Pat said. "Let's go shoot it."

♦ ♦ ♦

"Mom?"

"Baby?"

"I'm here."

Her mom's wonderful voice, staticky or not, was still the sweetest thing Nicki had ever heard.

"Are you safe?" her mom asked. "Where is 'here'?"

"We're with Terry."

"Is that Nicki?" Hannibal squealed. "Want Nicki."

"Thank God." Then she paused. "We? Who is 'we'?"

"Me and Pax."

"The dog?"

"Where are you?"

"On Lookout Mountain."

"So are we!"

Her mom sounded near tears. "What kind of miracle . . ." A honking sound. "Listen. We're at . . . what is the address here?" A muffled conversation. "One triple two Rebel Way. Give the phone to Terry."

"He is asking directions in the store. Here he comes!"

He approached the car, carrying a bag of groceries. When he looked carefully through the window, his face flattened with shock. "Oh, shit! What did you do?"

She blinked. "Mom called. My cell signal sucks. My network is no good. But yours is great."

He glared at her.

"Did I do something wrong?"

He snatched the phone from her. "Olympia?" Terry said.

"Terry?"

"Where are you?" he asked.

"Outside Dahlonega. One triple two Rebel Road. Can you get here?"

"As fast as we can. Are you with Hani?"

"Yes. He's fine," she said. "Just . . . get here."

Roughly, Terry thumbed off the phone and ripped out the battery.

He looked as if he wanted to scream at her, and the sudden shockwave of anger took her totally by surprise. She'd never seen anything but kindness or intensity from Terry, but this was anger, deep and savage. Almost as if there were another face beneath the human, struggling to reach the surface.

Then . . . he took a deep breath and calmed down. And the emergent face was gone. "Listen. I took out the battery so that . . . certain people wouldn't know where I am."

"Why?" Nicki felt confused. Were the people trying to kidnap her tracking his phone as well?

"Too hard to explain."

"Well . . . I'm sorry. It's out now. So you're safe?"

"I can hope so," Terry said. He punched the address into the car's portable GPS unit.

She glanced at it nervously. "Can they trace us through that thing?"

"I don't think so," Terry said. "I never gave it my name, so I don't know how they'd isolate me from all the other GPS systems on the road, even if that's technically possible. Maybe if they had my identification number or something."

The GPS spoke in John Cleese's fussy butler voice: "*Take a right turn just ahead, if you can remember how to do that, sir.*"

Nicki tried to laugh, but failed. She had put them in danger! "I'm sorry," she said.

"It's all right," he replied. Once again he was calm Terry. Centered Terry. In-control Terry. "We'll make do."

Then with a whipping motion of his wrist she wouldn't have expected to shred a paper bag, he smashed the phone against the steering wheel. It splintered like a cracker. He tossed the wreckage out of the window. She stared at him, expecting the angry face again . . . but no. Nothing but softness and concern.

"You just wanted to talk to your mom." He sighed. "I'd give anything in the world to talk to mine one more time."

Her eyes shone at him as they drove away into the night. But Terry's eyes were worried.

♦ ♦ ♦

Olympia and her new friends sat around the fireplace, the flames popping and crackling and begging for marshmallows as yet unproduced. Somehow, a new and unnamed tension had entered the situation. "Your friends are coming?" Franklin asked.

"Yes."

"That's good," Franklin said. "That's good."

He looked at Margerie. She nodded, and he crossed his legs, his foot bobbing rapidly.

"Did I hear you say something about the Sanctuary?" Margerie asked.

"Yes," Olympia said. "We were there for a tour last summer. Have you been there?"

"Yes," Margerie replied, but left it at that. Olympia thought she saw Margerie's eyes shift to Franklin and back again, but wasn't certain.

Before Olympia could formulate her thoughts, the phone rang. "Excuse me," Franklin said, and picked up the phone. "Yes?"

He said something she couldn't hear. His body tensed. His back went to Olympia and Hannibal. Hannibal stared at the television screen. It seemed to be a rerun of *Gilligan's Island,* with the professor once again creating laptop computers out of coconuts and seaweed.

"The television isn't good," Margerie said. "The local station . . . nothing but bad news. Everyone's scared. Frankly, I'm surprised that you got up the road. I'd heard it was barricaded."

"Some of the smaller roads weren't blocked."

"Not really a great time for tourism, dear."

"No. To tell the truth, we rented a cabin last summer, and I hoped to make it there, maybe have a chance to wait things out. It's getting frightening down in the city."

Franklin was talking animatedly on the phone. Quick gestures and a mobile face. Although she couldn't make out the conversation, and he was turned away from the living room, Olympia's ears burned.

"Thank you," Franklin said. He hung up the phone and returned to them.

"So you wanted to get away from the city," Margerie said. "I can understand that. Nothing down there."

"How long have you lived up here?" she asked. That phone call. What had the message been? Their faces were unreadable.

"Six years now," Franklin said.

"What brought you here?"

"Our grandchildren," he said calmly. The kind of quiet, calm voice one uses with hysterical children.

"Oh?" She hoped her voice was as mild as she intended.

"Yes. They were nearby. We came to be with them."

"Franklin had just retired," Margerie said. "He was dealing with job stress."

Franklin smiled ruefully. "Oh, you can tell the truth."

"Well, it's your story, dear," she said. "If you want a thing told right, you should tell it yourself."

"My health had collapsed," Franklin said. "I was a writer in Hollywood." That condescending voice was gone. Now he was back on more comfortable ground, talking about his own hard-won experience.

"Is that hard?"

"Not if you enjoy idiots, butt-kissers, and tons of money," he said.

They all laughed. Maybe she was imagining things.

"Oh, that's an exaggeration, I'm sure," Franklin said. "It wasn't that much money once you average it over the months of waiting."

Olympia looked more closely at Margerie. "Haven't I seen you before?"

Margerie smoothed her hair. "Oh, my, only if you watch old television commercials."

"That happy grandmother?"

"Yes. Granny Lee."

Hannibal sang, "'Hot dogs. Armour hot dogs. What kind of kids eat Armour hot dogs . . .'"

Margerie blinked. "Oh, my goodness. He saw that? That must be on one of the retro channels. Nick at Night, perhaps."

"He remembers everything."

Margerie laughed. "Yes, that was me. It was silly, but I was happy to get it. Hollywood can be kind of hard on ladies of a certain age."

"So you came out here from Hollywood to be with your grandchildren?"

"Well, our grandchildren encouraged us to come out. I guess that's the same thing."

A horrible possibility collided with Olympia's growing sense of calm. Calm lost. "They . . . were at the Sanctuary?"

"Yes, dear."

From the corner of her eye, she saw Hannibal's mouth tense into a worried frown. Without turning away from the television set he mouthed: *get out.*

"You said there were stress issues. Were they able to help you?" Olympia tried to keep her voice from sounding leaden and panicked.

"More than I can say."

"Was that them on the phone?" she asked mildly.

"Yes." A pause, then: "You really shouldn't have taken the book, dear. Where is it?"

"There is no book," she said.

"Franklin?" Margerie asked, curious.

The older man seemed infinitely regretful, but also reproachful, as if irritated that Olympia was forcing him to be inhospitable. "Our guests have light fingers, honey. They took something that doesn't belong to them. Our friends up the hill asked us to keep our eyes open." He looked disappointed in his guests, as if he considered this new information a personal betrayal. "And here they are!"

"You don't understand," Olympia said. "That's not the truth."

Franklin wagged his head. "The good folks at the Sanctuary just want the book back."

"That's not what they want," Olympia said. "They want my son . . ."

"Now, now," Margerie cajoled. "I'm sure they just want the book back. Probably won't even press charges. They're really the very nicest people."

Olympia got up. "Hannibal? Come on. We're going."

"It's very cold out there," Franklin said.

"We're going."

"Well, I can't stop you, dear," Margerie said. "But you'll have to leave the book."

She spread her arms, a *search me* gesture. "There is no book. They're lying. We were held captive. Madame Gupta is a monster."

Franklin turned to his wife. "They said she was emotionally disturbed, that she had been abusing the boy. Child Protective Services released her to their custody in an effort to save the family."

The corners of Margerie's mouth sagged. "Is that any way to reward people trying to help you?"

"We're leaving now."

The old man lunged and grabbed her arm. She wrested herself away, and he lost balance and tottered back against the wall with a thud, sliding down. His expression was more surprise than shock or pain, but still . . .

Olympia and Hannibal fled out into the snowstorm.

♦　♦　♦

In the warehouse, Lee, Pat, Mark, and Father Geek grabbed weapons and equipment: flash grenades, radios, and five beautiful Ares SCR laser-sighted rifles, .223 caliber with sixteen-inch barrels and black hardcoat anodized finish. Lethal, accurate, dependable . . . and legal in all fifty states.

Geek guided the loading and preparation, then roared: "All right! We're out. The number faded again. Short call. He probably thought we wouldn't catch it."

Mark tied his shoes, then paused. "Maybe he traded phones with some-one. He's using a burner, and this is a decoy."

Geek shook his head. "If that's true, why would he take the battery out? Why only talk for thirty seconds? No . . . I think that's our baby boy, and I think he made a mistake."

"Everybody makes one," Mark said. "He was mine, and it's time to undo it."

He looked around at the others. "All right. Dahlonega. That's sixty miles north. A decent place to hide out. If he stays put, we should be able to get within a couple hundred feet of him."

"So . . . he's somewhere in the Georgia mountains."

"I wonder what he's doing there?" Mark asked.

Pat sneered. "He'd better be picking out a grave."

"Give it a rest," Lee said. "This is bad enough as it is."

Mark and Father Geek exchanged troubled expressions: this wasn't what they had wanted at all.

But damn it, it was sure as shit what Terry had given them.

◆ ◆ ◆

Olympia and Hannibal stumbled through knee-deep snow, down the mountainside toward the distant lights. "Cold," Hannibal said, his breath puffing in wispy white clouds.

"I know, baby," Olympia said. She peered through a stand of saplings beneath them, able to make out a road. Two sets of headlights heading toward them. Other human figures in the woods, glowing fingers stab-bing out into the swirling snow.

"Come on!"

Holding Hani in her arms she waded through calf-deep frozen white, despair beginning to seize at her before she saw a rectangular blue shape half-covered in white: a child's sled, a Christmas present left out in the night for her to find. Perhaps Franklin and Margerie's grandchild. No doubt the manufacturer's specifications would consider it too small for the two of them, but to hell with that: this was another small wonder on a day she would take any miracles she could get.

Olympia pulled the sled out and faced it downhill, deposited Hannibal in her lap, and pushed it into motion. A red-and-white steering rope had been looped to the front end, and she was able to swerve it this way and that, picking up a little speed as they slid. Snow fountained up from the blades and into their eyes and mouths, numbing her fingers so that she couldn't feel the rope cutting into them as she wove left and right, threading trees. It was a glorious moment, a moment she might have enjoyed had this not been the worst night of her life. The frustrated voices of armed and angry men grew fainter behind her . . . until they crashed into a snow-covered shrub.

At least, she thought dazedly, as she spit snow, it hadn't been a rock.

"Whee!" Hannibal squealed.

"Whee. Whee, baby." She desperately forced merriment into her voice. "We're having fun. We're having fun . . ." She chanted the words over and over again. "We're having fun."

Then she heard a woman's angry voice to her right. "They're over here!"

"Come on!" Olympia yanked at Hannibal's sleeve, pulling him to the south.

They tumbled down the slope, earth and sky whirling around them. Their destination: the frosted gingerbread houses below that had seemed so close . . .

Air, ground, trees . . . all a thumping tangle and then they hit something soft and were still. Where were they . . . ?

When her vision cleared and she looked up, a man was looming over her, a gun pointed directly at her face. "Where is the boy?"

Suddenly a powder-puff explosion of ice and snowflakes on the side of his head. His feet slipped out from under him, and he fell.

"Bingo!" Hannibal laughed. He'd hit the security man with a snow-ball! Before he could get up and correct himself, the two escapees were back on the sled and flying down the slope again.

A gunshot behind them. Olympia flinched as she felt something like a white-hot wire scraping across her arm, a sharp gust plucking at her sleeve. Behind her, a thud and a gasp. Then a man's roar: "Damn it, we need them alive!"

◆　◆　◆

Their sled hit a road, skidded across, and then slammed into another tree. "Oof!" she groaned as they spilled onto the ground.

She stumbled up as two vehicles approached from opposite directions, pinioning her with their light. A man got out of one, and aimed his gun at her in the swirling snow.

She held Hannibal, wheezing clouds of vapor.

"I'm sorry, baby. I'm sorry," she chanted, as if saying the words could make things right.

Then—

"Mommy!" Nicki called.

The gunman turned around, but as he did the other vehicle slammed to a stop and from the corner of her snow-blind eye she saw someone vault across the hood of a car, blink-fast, like a gymnast vaulting the horse. The gunman had only begun to turn when feet slammed into the side of his head. The light was too bright to see clearly, but the two collided with a cracking sound. Another man appeared from behind them, but as soon as her eyes focused on him he dropped bonelessly, crunching face-first into the snow.

And . . . Terry emerged from the light, extending his hand to her. "'Come with me if you want to live.'"

She stared at him, teeth chattering with adrenaline, cold, and disbelief. "They're trying to take my son, and you . . . you're quoting *The Terminator*?"

Terry had been grinning, almost like a kid who has just used a new favorite toy.

"Are you out . . . out of your . . ." She broke down, tears choking her throat, and collapsed into his arms.

He blinked. And then the almost childlike glee dissolved, and he finally seemed to understand how inappropriate his words had been. "Hey, hey. I'm sorry. I was just . . . being an asshole, I guess."

Olympia's legs wobbled with anger, relief, and a wave of gratitude strong enough to drown thought. They hugged, and she kissed him desperately hard as Hannibal clung to his leg. "You," she whispered in his ear, "are the very best asshole in the history of the world."

"Come on," Terry said.

In a fumbling welter of hugs and kisses Olympia and Hani piled into Terry's powder-blue Chevy. "You're all right!" Olympia said, embracing Nicki. "Thank God!"

Pax slobbered over her cheek, and curiously enough, that was what finally convinced her she wasn't dreaming.

She and Hannibal clung to Nicki like crazy, and the three of them cried and kissed and huddled. And in the back of Olympia's mind, she thought: *Hannibal is hugging! Touching! I've never seen him like this. What did that woman do to him?*

"Mom!" Nicki sobbed. "I was so scared." Olympia held her daughter's face, gazed into it as if trying to memorize it, hugging her until their tears smeared each other's faces, and then hugged more.

Never let you go. Never let you go. Never—

"What the hell is going on?" Terry said. "What are you doing up here?" His face twisted in a snarl. "We have to get to the Salvation Sanctuary."

She froze, and then gripped his shoulder. "Are you out of your mind?"

"What?"

"That's where we just came from," she said.

"What precisely are you saying?" Terry said, his voice like grinding gears.

"It was Madame Gupta."

Terry recoiled as if she'd slapped him. "Madame . . ."

"Look out!" she screamed.

Another car came roaring in from the side, and smacked against the back end of their Chevy.

The wheels broke traction, and they did a 180.

◆　◆　◆

The world drowned in syrup as Terry sorted the variables and calculated his options. Bizarrely, an old Bill Cosby routine popped into his mind. *Turn in the direction of the skid . . .* He did, the fishtails broad and frightening, then smaller and smaller until the rear wheel found traction and chewed its way back onto the road. He floored it, making up for the lost time as the attackers roared in pursuit.

He couldn't exactly see the roads, but Terry navigated as if he could see clearly despite the night and the snowfall.

Olympia and Nicki were both terrified, but in the front seat beside Terry Hannibal squealed, "Whee!"

The cars to either side slammed into fences and plowed piles of snow, fountaining white. "Hold on!"

He pulled the wheel left and then right, and their Chevy wove around an oncoming truck, missing by inches. The car behind them slammed into it. Metal buckled under the impact, screaming like a scrap-metal dinosaur caught in a crusher. The two vehicles rammed against the metal barrier, the impact separating them so that the truck blocked the road . . . and the car disappeared into the ravine.

They trundled up the dark, narrow, rutted road.

◆　◆　◆

At the Salvation Sanctuary, Tony Killinger set the phone in its cradle. He felt a mixture of irritation and fear. Oddly, some part of him enjoyed that combination. "I see. Set a cordon."

"What do they say?" Madame Gupta asked.

"We weren't able to stop them."

"I am less than thrilled at your arrangements," she said coolly.

He had heard that tone of voice, seen that expression on her face the moment before she cracked the skull of a guard who had stolen from them. Fool. He'd known too much for them to turn him over to the police, and that left them no choice. He, Killinger, was not in real danger . . . yet. But a few more mistakes could change that. And that was amusing. Feeling a bit like a kid poking a hornets' nest with a stick, he said: "And I warned you about tryin' to keep security while tourists are strolling around. All those holy-roller meditation assholes, too. It was your call."

Her eyes narrowed. "That was very close to impertinence."

"It was truth."

She studied him. "You aren't afraid of me, are you?"

"Not particularly," he said. He smiled. His eyes met hers levelly.

"Why not? You know I can kill you."

He laughed and shrugged. "So can a baby with a hand grenade. Yeah, sure. I also know that you need me. And that the better your project works, the more you need me."

"And if that situation changes?" she asked.

He smiled. "That kinda depends on which of us tweaks to that first."

Madame Gupta very nearly smiled in return. One predator could appreciate another. "Seal off the mountain. I suppose it is a good thing that she does not know exactly why we wanted her son. With the current chaos, even if they manage to file a report, soon the police will be too busy to respond. Very soon."

"Yes, ma'am," Killinger said, saluting.

"Find them."

She left the room.

Master Bishop turned to look at him. "You really aren't afraid of her?"

The Cockney accent seemed a little thicker, perhaps with worry. A black man who talked Limey. He'd never really gotten used to it. Tony laughed. "No."

"But she really can kill you?"

"Or anyone else."

Bishop shook his head. "Then why not . . . ?"

Tony smiled. "If you're afraid of dying, you're in the wrong fuckin' business, old son. Now get on it."

♦ ♦ ♦

From his perch at an elevated turnout, Terry peered down the road at a roadblock below. Police and private cars swarmed like ants at a picnic, a symphony of red-and-blue flashing lights. Corrupt cops, or just good men protecting their community?

This . . . was getting complicated.

"What is it?" Olympia asked.

"I think it would be risky to assume that Gupta hasn't coopted the Dahlonega Police Department. The roads are blocked. I don't know what they want with Hannibal, but we can be pretty sure they don't want us communicating it. They might be willing to shoot, and I can't risk that."

"What are we going to do?" Olympia asked.

"Hole up until I can think of something." He pondered a moment, and then a thought occurred to him. "I saw a hunting cabin on a road back a couple of miles. I think we can get there, and hunker down."

"Will we be safe?"

"As safe as anyone's going to be. They won't expect us to double back, so that's exactly what we'll do."

CHAPTER 46

Olympia watched Terry pull their Chevy in beside a single-level log cabin with a stone chimney and broad bay windows. He peered at it from three directions, as if trying to extend his senses into the darkened rooms, perhaps imagining that he could hear and see and feel what was happening within. "I think its empty," he said.

He then pulled into the driveway more deeply, until they were well back from the road. Out of sight. Almost a quarter-mile from the main route. "Wait here," he said.

"I'm not going anywhere," she said.

He exited, crunching down on the snow then moving smoothly toward the side door. Pax jumped out and bounded behind him, kicking up snow as she pranced.

"Mom . . . ?" Nicki said.

"Yes?" Olympia couldn't keep her eyes off their protector. At that moment, Terry seemed like living proof of God's love.

"Terry is like, way cooler than I thought."

Olympia nodded. "At the very least."

"At least," Hannibal said.

♦   ♦   ♦

Terry peered in through the windows on the garage. An orange Jeep Cherokee squatted in the shadows. He broke the window on the back door of the house, waited a moment to be sure there was no response, and then reached through and unlocked it, entering the cabin. He cast a Maglite beam around the room. Nothing on the back porch, but on the kitchen refrigerator he found, clipped to a square magnet, a picture of a bearlike Caucasian male, fifty years old with capped teeth, surrounded by cubs and mate. Pictures of a happy summer fishing and hunting.

All . . . *summer* pictures.

"Excellent," he whispered. If this was a summer retreat, there was scant chance of an embarrassing winter encounter with the owners.

Muttering prayers and happy curses, Terry headed back out to the car.

♦ ♦ ♦

Three cars had driven along the main road a quarter mile away, their lights poking through the falling snow like silver fingers. Searchlights? Friends? Foes? Did Gupta's people know where to look? Had they been spotted? Wouldn't it be smarter to just keep moving . . . ?

Her mind spit out those and a thousand other questions before Terry crunched his way back to them.

"Well?" Olympia asked. "We must have doubled back. I think I passed this cabin on my way out of the Sanctuary."

"Dollars to doughnuts it's a summer vacation cabin," he said. "I think we have a clear shot until about May."

"That had better be long enough."

"That's the damned truth. We can't be seen from the road," he said. "We have power, and food in the freezer. I say we call this home. Hannibal? What do you think?"

"Not home," he said.

Olympia smiled. "For a little while?"

"Little while," Hannibal said.

"All right, then! Everybody out."

Like the tiny band of refugees they had become, stiff with cold and fatigue, Olympia, Nicki, and Hannibal pried their way out of the car and headed into the house. "Let's get a fire going."

Nicki was excited. "I saw a wood pile outside."

"I don't think so," Terry replied after a moment's thought. "We can use the oil heater, I think."

"Why?" Olympia asked.

"Smoke," Terry said. "We don't want someone over the hill seeing smoke coming up and wondering why Bubbah Wilson is here out of season. Maybe bring over a pie or some Christmas cookies. For the same reason, we're going to put tin foil over the windows, so that light doesn't show."

"I thought you said we can't be seen from the road." Her teeth were chattering, and it wasn't from the cold.

"That's true," Terry said, "but someone might be cross-country skiing, or snowshoeing, or just looking from across the mountain. We'll take no chances."

She nodded, understanding. Now that she was out of the cold, she was warming enough for the numbness to ease. Her bra was soaked with anxiety sweat, and when she didn't talk she had to clinch her teeth to stop their burring. Now, for the first time in what felt like days, she felt a measure of safety. The appreciation and relief she felt were more than words could have expressed.

"Come on, Hannibal," Terry said to the boy. "Can you help Terry?"

"Can help Terry." Flapping his arms in an endearingly awkward manner, Hannibal accompanied Terry to the kitchen.

It was, Olympia thought, a man's kitchen, organized not sensually but by some sense of order that existed before the kitchen had been stocked. Perhaps by alphabetical most-common-usage rules. There was no sense of an emotional personality about it, and it seemed more like a tool bench than a place where food was created for hungry families. More show than function. She bet the refrigerator was filled with frozen dinners.

Somehow, that mismatch of form and function reminded her of the Salvation Sanctuary. Spiritual books and spiritual topiary and inspiring gardens and dazzled aspirants.

And a rotten, toxic core.

Everything in its place, and a place for everything, whether or not it related directly to anything positive, or even anything sane at all.

◆ ◆ ◆

Terry found the aluminum foil in a drawer between neatly placed wooden spoons, a plastic bag filled with something resembling jumbo chunks of Purina Dog Chow, and a rubber band–wrapped packet of steel ballpoint pens. They were industrial strength, sturdy as railroad spikes, like something designed for astronauts. Pressurized ink cartridges. Everything neat and tidy.

Hannibal seemed to appreciate the kitchen. He searched behind Terry and found a freezer bag filled with animal crackers in the refrigerator, and jumped up and down with simple childlike joy that said all the troubles of the last days had, at least for this moment, been forgotten. Terry enjoyed seeing the kid like this. He didn't know what O and her son had been through, but the clues he had extracted so far sounded horrid.

"He's right," Nicki said.

"About what?" Olympia asked.

"That these people aren't coming back for a while. But we need to be careful."

Nicki squinted at her. "What happened to your arms?"

Olympia covered the bruises, as if embarrassed. "I'll tell you later. Let's see if there's a phone here."

So O didn't want to tell Nicki something . . . or didn't want to remind Hannibal of horrors of the recent past. Or was choosing her moment to tell the story. Something.

Hannibal spilled the animal crackers onto a kitchen counter, and began to sort them: horse shape, lion shape, giraffe shape, and fish shape, all in different columns.

With Hannibal safely busy, Olympia and Terry searched drawers and cupboards and closets, seeking to own their temporary shelter as best they could. He found the keys to the Cherokee in the kitchen drawer next to the sink. He was definitely switching vehicles. The electricity was still on, but the phone was dead. "Maybe they turn it off for the winter," she said. "Let's get some food going. Heat going. We don't know how long we'll be here."

"Got any ideas?" Terry asked.

She gave him a tentative smile, warming and widening even as he watched. "Sit back, Terry. We have the makings of a Christmas feast. I'm hungry enough to eat a moose."

♦ ♦ ♦

Ninety minutes later, they were eating a simple meal drawn from a collection of freezer bags: chicken, lentils, and fresh biscuits. They scarfed the food down as if they hadn't eaten in days. The cabin smelled like normalcy, like family, as if they had borrowed some of the joy and safety on display in the photos.

The windows were all foil-sealed, and the clan was gathered around the kitchen table, the stove providing enough heat to make things toasty.

"Reminds me of a Christmas I spent with Mark in Afghanistan," Terry said, stifling a belch. "We sealed up the windows of an abandoned shepherd's hut and had ourselves a party."

"Dancing girls?"

"Some pretty cute goats," he said. "I think Mark fell in love." That left his mouth before he could stop it, but as soon as the words were spoken, they were regretted. Mark. Geek. Shit. His best friends in all the world. Probably looking to kill him.

"Mom . . ." Nicki said. "Are you going to tell us what happened to you?"

"All right . . ." she said, and told them. For Hannibal's sake she skirted details of the waterboarding, saying only: "And then they punished me."

"How?" Terry asked, knuckles paling as he gripped the table's edge.

Her voice almost broke. "I'd rather not talk about it now." Her eyes begged him not to demand particulars in front of the children, and he relented. Under the table, she reached out and squeezed his leg.

By the time she was finished telling her story, Terry was staring at her with new and deeper respect. "Jesus." This woman was a freaking *boss*.

"Just like Tarzan!" Hannibal said.

Nicki hugged her mother. "Mom . . . you rock."

Olympia laughed shakily. "I just want to say something. We don't know what's coming. We don't know why what has happened has happened. But I wanted to say, right now, that I am as grateful as I've ever been in my life. Everyone in the world I care about is in this room, right now, right here. I don't take things like that for granted anymore." When she looked at Terry, the heat in her gaze rocked him. It was possible that no one had ever looked at him like that. That level of love, gratitude, trust.

It was . . . humbling. Exhilarating. Whatever he had done to earn it, he wanted to do it more, and right *now*.

"Terry," she said. "Nicki said that there was someone after you?"

"I think so, yes," he said.

"Why?"

"Some friends and I were planning to do something . . . bad. And then I changed my mind."

She was confused. "What?"

He shook his head. *Not now.* As one who had recently asked for privacy, she seemed to understand. "Why? Why did you change your mind?"

And that question he was willing, if not quite able to answer. "Ironic as it seems now . . . Madame Gupta." He shook his head. "So . . . what did she want?"

"I don't know. Just . . . crazy cult stuff, I'd guess. End of the world fever."

"Hannibal?" Terry asked.

"Terry?" the boy said, voice flat. He had seen more emotion, more interaction out of the kid in the last hour than in the previous year. And now he was whiplashed back into that emotionless response. Poor brave little soldier.

"Can you help me, kiddo? What did they ask you to do?"

His eyes never left the table. "Pictures. People. Monkeys."

Olympia shook her head. "I saw some of them. I didn't see any people. Just . . . I don't know. Colors and patterns."

Terry sighed. "Well, we may never know. We'll get out of here, and tell the authorities . . . assuming there will be anyone left to tell."

Nicki had turned on the television. "Mom! Terry! The tube is working."

They huddled around. A snowy news broadcast. A CNS feed. "That's Joyce Chow," Olympia said. "I work with her."

The image was shaky, the broadcaster's round face glum. "I wish I had good news. What we know is that no one who was on the original Dead List has survived, or at least made public appearance since the date they were projected to die. This image, of the major general of Indonesia, was shown the day after his reported death, but computer analysis of the tape suggests it was actually made the day before."

The screen flickered, and the image of a twisted, shattered body appeared. The face was a Halloween mask, distorted, bleeding from mouth and nose and ears, eyes wide with terror and agony. "Jesus!" Olympia screamed. "Who okayed that?"

She grabbed Hannibal and tried to cover his eyes but he slithered out of her grip, transfixed by the television.

"Nicki, turn that off!" The girl started toward the set, but before she could touch the control, the image changed back to the newswoman.

"Okay, wait," Olympia said. "That producer should be fired. Hani, are you all right?"

Hannibal seemed unfazed. In fact, more disturbingly to Terry, he seemed eager to see more.

What the hell had happened up there?

"Where pictures?"

"Those aren't good pictures," Olympia said. "You'll have nightmares."

He didn't respond to that. Instead he seemed fascinated by the image of Joyce Chow as the reporter said something Terry couldn't hear.

"She's scared," Hannibal said.

"We're all scared, hon."

"Hannibal's not scared. You're here. Terry's here."

"Hey!" Nicki said.

"Nicki's here."

He hugged her, then grinned up at them. "My family is here. Everything is good."

Olympia and Terry looked at each other. What in the hell do you say to *that*?

Chow continued. ". . . President Correll has not been seen since her last press conference, and we do not know her status. If she is alive and well— and we sincerely hope that is the case . . . then she is scheduled for death tomorrow."

Joyce Chow doffed her glasses. Her hands were shaking. "We do not know what this means. If she dies . . . if the most heavily guarded woman in the world can be . . ." She paused again, unable to speak the thought. "The promise is that this terrible thing will continue, and continue, until . . ."

Someone in the studio said something unintelligible. Terry could not make out the words. A man's voice.

"Sloan," Olympia said. "Must be subbing for the producer. Things must be bad over there."

Chow's forehead glistened. "Tomorrow is Christmas Day. Ordinarily this is a time for joy, for communing with the ones we love, for sharing warmth and hope. Because of circumstances beyond our control . . . perhaps beyond our imaginings . . . there may be nothing to celebrate tomorrow. Or ever again."

Tears streaked her face. "I have children. I think of them. Yes, I am afraid to die, but the concept and finality of death has always been tempered by the promise of renewal. But this winter is said to last forever. And a storm cloud such as many of us have never known . . . perhaps such as humanity itself has never known . . . hovers over us, and we tremble beneath its wings. We walk through the valley of the shadow, and it seems we are alone."

Olympia looked at Terry, whose expression was sober indeed. "I know her."

"Those who published the original Web site have disappeared. No one knows who they are. I do not know the inner workings of the world's intelligence agencies, but I have heard they have reached out to universities, to news agencies, to private citizens asking for help in identifying those who might have caused . . . or know the cause . . . of the calamity which threatens to engulf us."

A pause.

"But I speak now to those responsible, or who know who or what is responsible. I cannot believe in a God who would simply wipe the world out in such a way, although there have always been millennialists. Catastrophists. Apocalyptists. Always. And always, I believed they were wrong. My God is a God of love."

"She's never talked about her faith before," Olympia said. She was crying.

Terry slipped his arm around Olympia, and she gripped his hand.

"This may be a matter of human agency . . . or it may be divine, or something beyond our ken. I grant that human beings seem unable to do anything to stop this. And I ask for mercy. Tomorrow is the date upon which we celebrate the birth of the Prince of Peace. Whether he was born that day, or if it is merely the day upon which we celebrate it, coopted from pagan rites, is not a matter of interest to me at this moment. What is important, is that I believe humanity has striven to be loving, and kind, to know what is and is not true, to understand itself as deeply as a being can without a cosmic mirror. We have certainly sinned . . . but we have also loved. I ask for mercy. I ask . . . I beg . . . for a Christmas miracle. This is Joyce Chow, saying . . . good night, and good luck. And . . . Merry Christmas."

Nicki turned the television off. They stared at the darkened screen.

"I don't know what is going on out there in the world," Terry said. "But we're together, and that counts for something."

"That's a small miracle," Olympia said. "And if you can gather enough small miracles together, sometimes you can make big ones. Let's just gather every one of them we can. Like . . . like stringing pearls . . ."

Her voice broke. Nicki hugged her, and then Hannibal, and then Olympia looked up, tears shimmering in the firelight, and Terry joined them. The four hugged each other intensely, snuffling and shuffling a bit, and then finally came up for air.

Terry spoke first. "Now . . . the police, fire departments, everything will be busy tomorrow. We can either stay here . . . see what happens. Or we can try to come down from the mountain."

"And go where?" Nicki asked.

"And go where?" Olympia echoed. "Damned good question. Terry— you said that people were looking for you."

"Yes. But Nicki triggered the phone miles from here. We should be safe."

She sighed. "Then . . . let's stay here. It's beautiful here." Their fingers twined.

"Let's see if we can get ready for bed. There are rooms, and beds, and I want everyone to be comfortable. Tomorrow is Christmas!"

Hannibal grinned. "Christmas!"

◆ ◆ ◆

By eleven o'clock, Hannibal and Nicki were headed for bed. "Night, Mommy," her boy said. "Tomorrow Christmas! Hope Hani gets lots of presents from Santa Claus. Can Santa find me here? I hope so."

The family looked at each other. Nicki looked devastated. "That's more than I've ever heard him say at one time."

That comment caught Olympia by surprise. "I thought he talked to you."

Nicki looked down. "That's what we pretend." She tried to smile, but it wavered. "If he only started talking at the end, how sad would that be?"

Nicki seemed disconsolate. Olympia hugged her. She looked up at Terry. "I wish . . ."

"What?" Terry asked.

"I wish I hadn't been such a bitch to you, Terry."

He laughed. "That's all right. You were just trying to protect your mom."

She tried to find something to say, but words failed.

"Right," she said, and on tiptoes, pecked his cheek. "Night."

And retreated to her room, Pax trotting at her side. Terry started stacking logs into the fireplace, positioning them carefully. Olivia watched him, surrendering to a sense of calm and familial warmth she hadn't experienced in . . .

When exactly had she? In Liberty City? With her deteriorating, widowed mother? With Raoul, who must have signaled that he was leaving long before he actually left?

Was it possible that the answer was . . . never? "I thought you said we shouldn't have a fire."

He frowned. "I think it will be all right at night. I think."

As the light and warmth filled the room, she felt as if she was melting into him. "It's nice."

"We deserve a little something, I think."

She nodded. "Thank you for taking care of Nicki."

"My pleasure," he said. "Maybe I saved her. But I'm starting to think that all of you saved me."

She paused. "Where are you sleeping?"

"Out here by the fire. The kids have their room, and you can have the other one."

She nodded uncertainly.

"I made a mistake," Terry said. "And then I very nearly made an even worse one. One I wouldn't have been able to come back from."

"Trusting Madame Gupta?"

He shook his head. "Yes. I would have delivered Nicki to that bitch gift-wrapped."

The heat and light washed over them in waves, warming Olympia as if her heart had been locked in an ice cave. "What about these friends of yours? What were you about to do, and why didn't you do it?"

"We met in Iraq," he said. "We were doing something ugly that got uglier."

"What do you mean?" she whispered.

"Remember when those Blackwater operators got butchered in Fallujah in 2004?"

"Some men were ambushed? Hanged?"

"Yes," Terry said. The firelight transformed his face into a mask of shifting flat planes. "And worse. A lot worse. On March 31, 2004, four Blackwater employees by the names of Scott Helvenston, Jerry Zovko, Wes Batalona, and Mike Teague were ambushed and killed. A pretty pissed-off mob of Iraqis burned and mutilated their bodies and dangled them from a bridge. Our commander-in-chief went ballistic, bless his pointy little heart. And he sent in troops on a general punishment mission."

His heavy voice lulled her into a near-trance, as Gupta's had. She could almost smell the explosives in the air, hear the gunfire, feel the terror.

"But what the public didn't know was that embedded within the general chaos were smaller units, tasked specifically with the obscene murder of the men we believed responsible for the attack."

Olympia drew back from him a bit. "Obscene . . . *murder*?"

"Yes. A twofer. Revenge, and sending a message. The kind of thing America just doesn't do. But our commander-in-chief wanted it done. So men were tasked from several different groups, selected by our . . ."

He searched for a word. "Let's just say our *history*. We were selected, told what was expected, and dropped into the killing zone."

"They knew that you and your friends . . ."

"Would do whatever it took," Terry said.

"And . . . ?"

"And we did what it took," Terry said. "It was the kind of thing you don't want to ask about, Olympia. The kind of thing you don't come back from. We crossed some kind of line. Together. And after we left the service, the five of us kept in touch. There are shielded Web sites where vets do that."

"You . . . did a bad thing?"

Terry nodded. "By any civilized standard." He paused. "There is this expression called 'the outer darkness.'"

"Yes."

"We just called it 'welcome to the suck' and left it at that. You don't shake that off. It lives inside you. Hungry. Like an animal you've penned up. If you build a great race car, you want to race it. Study medicine for twenty years, you want to heal someone. And if you practice war . . . and find out in the most intimate way possible that some part of you craves it . . . you want to go back."

Go back? To something so soul destroying? All she could whisper was, "Oh, my God."

"And we pulled off a little something extra while we were there. You see, while we were . . . working . . . one of the jihadists thought he could end his pain by telling us about a cache of diamonds Saddam had hidden in statues in one of his palaces."

"Did it?" She paused. "Did it end his pain?"

Terry couldn't meet her eyes. "No." He paused. "It didn't."

For a moment she wondered where his mind had gone, and then was profoundly grateful she had not the slightest idea. Her savior. Suddenly, the universe had no moral center. Nothing was real, or certain, and "good" was merely a concept.

No. Her children were good. Love was good. And this man, whatever he might have done, was good.

He stared into the fire as if counting sparks. Finally and with great apparent effort, he shook himself free of the memories.

"But we did look into it, the ten of us, and it was true. And we devised a scheme to divide the loot, and smuggle it back into the U.S."

"Did you?"

"No," Terry said. "We were betrayed by a man named Colonel O'Shay. He misdirected a pickup chopper so that we were late to a rendezvous. By the time we get there, they'd hidden the shit, and said they were afraid we'd double-cross them. Swore that they'd give us our share. Yeah, right."

"What did you do?"

"We waited. Waited for them to rotate out. And the guy we were counting on to get us the location died in a firefight in '05, and we thought we were screwed permanently. But Lee—"

"Who?"

"One of our crew. You met him at the Christmas party."

Straw haired. A little puppy-doggish, dominated by Mark and Terry. Yes.

"Turns out that the dead man had mailed a diary home to his family. Maybe he knew something was coming. Seems that even double-crossers get crossed. Anyway, one of his crew got ahold of it, and found some coordinates that related to one of Saddam's son's desert hideaways. Took them ten years, but they'd never stopped looking. And we'd never stopped watching. They found the loot, and we waited for them to make their move. And finally they did. Father Geek—"

"Who?"

"One of our merry crew. Real name is Ernie Sevugian. You met him, too. Injured his spine in Iraq, sits in a wheelchair now, smartest guy I've ever met. He got through their security, found out when they were planning to move it."

"When?"

"New Year's Eve. And fly it into Dobbins Air Reserve Base on New Year's Day. We knew that six months ago. It was going to be Dobbins, Edwards in California, or one of two bases in Texas. One of us was salted near each of them, a year and a half ago, while we waited to see which way they'd jump."

"A year and a half . . . ?" she said. "So you and Mark . . . ?"

"That's right. We were here on business. And when Geek got the last piece, we concentrated operations here."

Comprehension dawned. "You were going to steal it back."

He grinned. "That's exactly right. And were prepared to do whatever it took."

She paused. "What if they wouldn't just . . . give it back?"

"Whatever it took." His smile was a wolf's. She wanted to back away from him, but managed to stay in place.

"What then?" She could barely breathe.

"Then I met Madame Gupta. And she showed me who I really was."

"The . . . the Shakti whatsis? The . . . uh . . . cunnilingus trap?"

She realized what she was saying a moment after the words slipped out of her mouth, and felt a deep wave of embarrassment and . . . need. She wanted to touch him. But was afraid to at the same moment.

"Kundalini." Terry laughed. "It was like all my yesterdays became my Now. Opened the door to tomorrow. Suddenly, I could see what I've always sought. I saw myself sitting at her knee, learning, for the rest of my life. And knew that the hijack—getting those diamonds—was the wrong path."

"And?"

"And my friends disagreed. And now I find out that she's . . . just another kind of monster."

"What do you think she wanted?"

"She saw something special in me. Something in Hannibal."

Olympia nodded, but in her heart and mind, the images of all Gupta had done for Hani, and of the nightmare she had put him through, warred until it was hard to even think. "She says she wants to help him. To . . . recruit him." Suddenly she wanted to scream, and only the fear of frightening her children caught it in her throat.

"But for what?" she croaked. "What does she want? What does she want to teach him, or what does she want him to do? He's just a . . . a boy!" She suddenly squawked, as if someone had let the air out of her, and she collapsed into Terry. Perhaps the strength that had sustained her for so long had suddenly drained away, and she just sobbed in his arms, until whatever poison within her had, at least temporarily, been nullified by gentleness.

"More than that. But I don't know if we'll ever know. Tomorrow, we'll see what's next. Try to get down out of the mountains and away from them."

She watched the fire crackle. "Fire has always seemed alive to me," she said quietly. "It eats, and breathes, and moves, and makes children." She tried to smile, and failed. And then spoke the thought she had struggled so hard to repress. "What if the world really is ending?"

"Then it doesn't matter where we are," he said.

"I'm glad we're together," Olympia said.

"Me, too."

She got up, and walked to the door of her room. She looked back at him. For a moment she was about to ask him to stay with her, make love to her in an ancient ritual of reassurance as old as our first chittering ancestors in the treetops.

"Terry?" she said.

"Yes?"

"That thing in Fallujah. Was that . . . the worst thing you ever did?"

He hesitated for a moment. "No."

She swallowed. "What was?" Her eyes were very steady on him.

"Happened about six years ago," he said. "In some mountains in Central America. I was there with some guys, pruning back some guerrillas. We needed the cooperation of the locals, and one of our men . . ." He paused, as if trying to find the right way to say it. "One of our guys, Sergeant Remmy Jayce, had been one of us in Fallujah. He was a wild man, and sometimes that's just what you need."

"But not this time."

"No. Not this time. Jayce got drunk. Raped the daughter of a local headman." He inhaled, then let it out slowly. "They demanded that we turn him over to them."

She had to work her mouth a few times before anything would come out. "What did you do?"

"We . . . *I* turned him over. He was a long time dying." He met her gaze evenly.

"Jesus," she said.

"Yeah," Terry said. "He saved our asses in Iraq, and I gave him up in Central America, and the last thing he said to me was that it was okay. He'd fucked up, and knew it."

"And . . . that made it worse?"

"Yeah. That made it worse."

If she had been considering asking him into her bed, that door had slammed shut. He was a massive, solid shape near the firelight, indistinct. Barely human.

"You were friends?"

Slowly, almost imperceptibly, he nodded. "Right is right," he muttered. "Right is right."

This man, this good man had given up a friend to avenge a wronged woman. And even though that friend had forgiven him, he could not see the good in what he had done.

He stared at her like a wounded animal.

"Need to be alone," he whispered, his voice such a rasp that she could barely understand him.

Alone with his memories, and his thoughts, and his regrets.

And . . . she saw him. Perhaps for the very first time, really *saw* him. Wondered that he could have done so much, so many terrible things, and still retained any vestige of the very real humanity . . . and even chivalry . . . he had exhibited. Wondered how in the hell he had managed to preserve his heart.

And she wanted him. But for the both of them, that moment had passed.

"Merry Christmas," he said. "Sleep well."

"You, too."

And she closed the door.

♦ ♦ ♦

Terry lounged around for a time, gazing into the fire as if seeking meaning from the flames. Fire was alive, in its way. Olympia had said that, and he agreed. It breathed, it ate, it reproduced. Fire and man had co-evolved, each becoming more complex and powerful in the company of the other.

In its eternally shifting light, could he make any sense of what had happened? Could it speak to him?

If it could, what would it say?

He didn't know how long he sat there, but the crackle and shifts of light were hypnotic. At last, discontented with the shape of his thoughts, Terry stood, stretched, yawned, and circumnavigated the room, preparing to shut down for the evening. Suddenly, he felt the fatigue that adrenaline had kept at bay for . . . how long? How long had it been since he'd slept? Two days? Three?

Hannibal had apparently shifted the site of his cookie-sorting activities to the dining room table. Lions and tigers and bears, oh my, all in their edible rows. He chuckled and popped a predator shape into his mouth. Chewed. Slightly stale, but sweetening as he ground it to paste.

The boy had found several folded sheets of butcher paper and colored pencils. He had begun a drawing of a house made of boxy rectangles. There was a sense of order about it, a feeling of design or depth that impressed Terry. What a kid. What a remarkable kid.

He smiled, a sudden idea occurring to him. He puttered about in the kitchen for a minute, tending to his notion, and then dragged his dead ass to bed.

Sleep fell like a storm.

CHAPTER 47

Three hours of heavy traffic had brought Mark, Father Geek, Pat, and Lee to the first roadblock on the road to Dahlonega.

"Sorry," the uniformed officers in plastic ponchos and snow coats said, pointing a flashlight into the passenger compartment. "We can't let you through unless you're residents."

"I understand," Father Geek said. "Forgot my papers. I'll be back." He smiled and turned the Expedition around.

"What are you doing?" Mark said.

"Becoming a resident," Ernie Sevugian replied.

Geek turned into a gas station and booted up his computer. Humming, he hooked his laptop to a portable printer, made some adjustments, and loaded up a custom program. A few keystrokes and he was on a secure Web site stocked with a variety of driver's license models, and quickly found Georgia's.

Humming, after a quarter hour's work he had positioned photos of himself and Mark onto the template, which randomly generated license numbers to match. He looked up addresses in Dahlonega and gave one to himself under the name "Fred Kelly" and another address to Mark under the name "Karl Astaire." He liked musicals.

He gave Atlanta addresses to the others under randomly chosen names, discarding the possibility of "Rogers" and "Charisse" as entirely too cute.

Entering the Georgia DMV database was trickier, and if it hadn't been for the access to Homeland Security, might have frustrated him. But it was always easier to go top-down than bottom-up, and took no more than a half hour to find a way to insert the necessary information.

He printed onto card stock installed with the proper hologram emblems, laminated them, and slid the result into his wallet. Mark did the same.

He looked at it: not bad. It would hold up to a simple roadside check, and maybe a little better.

They were certainly about to find out.

"Scary," Mark said in admiration.

"I'm a scary guy."

An hour later they were back at the same roadblock, talking to the same officers, who didn't remember them at all. "Sorry," the officer said. "We've had to close the area to everyone but residents."

Geek smiled. "Residents," he said. "With guests."

He displayed his driver's license in the wallet, then pulled it out and handed it over.

Geek felt only the slightest flutter of tension as the cop studied it. "You, too?" he said to Mark. Mark showed his wallet.

The cop grunted. His attitude had changed. "All right, Mr. Kelly. And these are your guests?"

"Absolutely," Geek said. "We just figured this might be a good time to be out of the city."

"Times like this, you start asking yourself about what is really important in life, you know?" the cop said.

"Ain't that the truth." Pat smiled flatly. "We know what's important, and we're going after it."

"Well, Merry Christmas. Feels so strange to say that."

"Merry Christmas, Officer," Mark said.

And they drove through the checkpoint. Geek wouldn't have admitted it to anyone, but he hadn't breathed smoothly for about five minutes.

"Well, that was kinda interesting," Lee said. "Didn't even check the computer."

"Better safe than sorry," Geek said.

"Where was the last blip?" Mark asked.

"About twelve miles from here."

"I think he's still here," Pat said. "Why the hell would he leave?"

"Because he figures we picked up his scent?" Geek said.

"Maybe," Mark said. "But I don't think so. I think he thinks he's as safe up here as anywhere."

"What do you think is really going on?" Geek said after a silent mile. "I mean . . . do you think the president is going to die today? And if she does . . . and the rest of it is true . . . isn't all of this just bullshit?"

He was gazing out the window as the landscape slid by: Christmas decorations with an increasingly desperate air of joy about them. Geek hadn't been home for Christmas in so many years he barely remembered eggnog.

"What if she dies?" he said after a few minutes. "Tell me." His hands

were anchored to the wheel, and his face was drawn and overly strained.
"And then the others die? What if we're all about to die, every lousy one
of us? What if we really have fucked everything up, and are paying for it
with . . . everything? If this is the end?"

"What of it?" Lee asked.

"If this is the apocalypse, do you really want your last act before you
meet God to be icing some motherfucker?"

"Jesus," Mark said. "Shut the fuck up."

And they drove on.

Mark finally spoke again. "What would you do, if you thought this
was it? I mean . . . if you really believed it?"

Father Geek shrugged. "Well . . . the implications are pretty huge. An
apocalypse, I mean a miraculous one, not an asteroid, or Godzilla. Something that implies divinity, or what they used to refer to as an 'act of God,'
right?" He paused, considering. "I've lived a lot of my life assuming there
wasn't anything out there. If there is . . . and He's watched what people
have done, I don't wonder He's not pleased. I guess . . . I wouldn't do anything to piss Him off any more."

"And if it was too late for that?"

"I guess I'd just try to have the best Christmas I could. I'd wish I was
with someone I loved. Try to make things good for her."

Geek looked in the rearview mirror, considered his allies and accom-
plices. Hard, dangerous men. He glanced at Mark, the tactical knuckle-
dragger. Something in Mark's eyes reflected a tiny bit of softness, some
feeling rather than mere thought.

"Just . . . don't," Mark said.

"Hell, no," Geek said fervently.

And they drove on through the drifting snow.

CHAPTER 48

Hannibal awakened slowly, anxiously. His dream had threatened to turn into the Game, the altered Game, with the beautiful house slowly over-taken by forest. He knew that in the forest was the girl, and although he didn't understand, he knew that he didn't want to meet the girl, here or anywhere else, and that she was coming after him.

He didn't want to be there anymore. And he didn't know how to pre-vent it, since no matter what he did he had to sleep. Waking was better but eventually, no matter what he did, he would sleep.

Hani looked around himself and saw an unfamiliar room. "Mommy?" He said. "Nicki?" Then: "Terry?"

He levered himself out of bed and walked to the dresser, and touched it. Strangeness. He opened the door and tottered into the living room. He opened and closed each drawer he passed, in turn.

Cutout paper snowflakes hung from the ceiling. "Have Yourself a Merry Little Christmas" played on a staticky radio, and the smile made his face hurt. His entire family awaited him there. Nicki and Mommy and Pax . . . and Papa Terry! Christmas cookies were heaped on plates in the dining room. Hannibal danced up and down with joy.

Nicki, Terry, and Olympia held clumsily wrapped packages out to him. He ran and jumped into Nicki's arms.

"Merry Christmas!" the three of them called.

"Merry Christmas!" he called in reply.

He hugged them, smooched and held them, and then tore open the presents. Nicki was glowing.

"And these are for you," Terry said to Nicki and Olympia, and handed them packages wrapped in aluminum foil.

Nicki radiated joy, but Mommy looked a little sad. "I didn't get any-thing for you," Olympia said.

"I don't remember the last time I had Christmas with a family," Terry said. "That's pretty much the best gift I could have, right there."

He kissed her like people kissed in movies.

Nicki gasped. "Mom!"

Olympia leaned away from Terry and grinned. "Shh. Go away. Nothing to see here."

♦ ♦ ♦

Terry felt as if his eyes were hungry video cameras, soaking in every expression of pleasure, every squeal of glee as they opened the packages and discovered heartfelt makeshift presents within. For Nicki a DVD of Joss Whedon's *Much Ado About Nothing,* filched from the wall case. A bouquet of winter-blooming camellias gathered from a small self-sustaining garden in the cabin's sun room for Olympia. And for Hannibal, one of the kitchen pens. A Uni four-color multifunction pen, sturdy as a railroad spike. For Pax, a thawed beefsteak from the freezer.

Best of all, Hannibal bounced and glowed as if he'd been given the keys to FAO Schwarz.

"Terry . . ." Hannibal said. "Thank you. Thank you."

If in Terry's life he had known a moment sweeter than the hug that followed, it was entirely beyond his capacity to recall it.

♦ ♦ ♦

The day was glorious, as if the tribulations of the outside world could not touch them. The ground was blanketed with white, and they engaged in snowball fights, sledding, and creating a small but sturdy army of snow elves, half of which were promptly demolished by an enthusiastic Great Dane. Good old-fashioned fun. An eye of calm amidst the storm.

Olympia leaned against Terry. "So . . . do you think we can risk going into Dahlonega? I'd like to lay in some supplies."

Terry could imagine an entire world of problems with that idea. "I'm not sure you should show your face around here."

"We still need the supplies," she said.

Nicki perked up. "I'd like to go!"

He considered. They really could use some fresh fruit . . . maybe some other things as well. "All right . . . I'll go by myself. They obviously know who you are, so we can assume they'd recognize Nicki. It doubles the risk. I think it might be better if you give me a list."

She found a scrap of paper in one of the kitchen drawers, and scrawled out her requests with Hannibal's pen. Terry found himself enjoying the simple play of muscles in her toned, lovely forearms as she wrote.

Uh-oh.

"Here," she said and held the list out. "If you can find a convenience store, that would be great. If a grocery store, there are a couple of other things we can use. But there's one thing I didn't put on the list."

"What's that?"

She put her arms around his neck. She stood on tiptoe, pressed her lips against his, and warmed him with the slightest, most discreet pressure of her hips. Then she whispered in his ear, "Hurry back, soldier, and report for booty."

"Roger that."

They kissed again, far more thoroughly this time.

"Mom! Terry! There are children present!" Nicki squealed, as Hannibal clapped delightedly.

Terry broke the kiss, grinned at the kids. "'For I am rough,'" he said, "'and woo not like a babe.'"

Nicki goggled at him. *Yeah. Got ya.* He shrugged modestly. "There's a *Complete Works of Shakespeare* on the shelf."

Terry ruffled Hannibal's head. "What can I bring you?"

"Bring me Terry," he said. "And animal crackers. They stale."

Nicki came over to him. Her liquid brown eyes were so vulnerable, so open and trusting and loving that he could hardly meet them. "I don't know how all of this is going to turn out . . ." she began.

"We'll be fine," he said.

"Will you please shut up? I just wanted to say something."

"All right."

"'My tongue will tell the anger of my heart, or else my heart concealing it will break.'"

Terry winced. "What does that mean?"

She shuffled a bit, breaking eye contact. "It means that I say what I'm thinking. And that means that sometimes I said some mean things to you."

"It's all right," he said.

"No. It's not. Because it's like you said last night. What if this is all that there is? And what if it's almost over? We could be dead tomorrow. Or worse. And I need to tell you that . . . if there was going to be someone who would be with Mom. Be with *us*. To be kind of like a dad . . . I'd pray to God it was you. No one else but you. I love you, Terry."

He blinked. Hard. His own relationship with his father had been one of respect and awe . . . but he was not at all certain Captain Nicolas had ever said those three simple words, "I love you." Could that be possible? Then he realized that he was forcing back tears. "That might be the best thing anyone ever said to me."

She brushed his cheek with her lips. "Come back."

Then, suddenly shy again, Nicki backed away. She and Hannibal held each other, and Pax panted by their side, exhaling vaporous clouds of doggy breath.

◆ ◆ ◆

Terry slid behind the wheel of the Cherokee. The engine turned over on the third try, and he let it run for ten minutes to let things warm up. While he waited he searched the glove compartment: a package of gum, a flashlight, a disposable Samsung TracFone with half a charge. A map of North Carolina. He slammed the door shut and pulled out of the drive, vapor gushing from the tailpipe.

Terry drove the Jeep slowly down the road, looking both ways at every opportunity. The roads glittered with virgin snow, and his wheels crunched through the icy surface. A few small streams of smoke rose from chimneys dotted across the valley. The world looked like a Hallmark card. Terry found Christmas music on the radio, and sang his heart out.

◆ ◆ ◆

It took twenty minutes of careful grinding along icy paved and unpaved roads to reach Dahlonega. Hiding his face beneath an Atlanta Falcons football cap, Terry made his way slowly through the sparsely populated streets. A police car cruised past. The officer looked at him, and he waved. The officer nodded back, unenthusiastically, a haunted expression on his pale flat face.

Terry pulled into the parking lot of a Piggly Wiggly market. THE FIRST TRUE SELF-SERVICE GROCERY STORE! a faded sign declared. The streets were quiet. He parked and got out of the car. A banner above the doorway read OPEN ON CHRISTMAS DAY.

Ho, ho, ho.

He entered, and took a cart.

"Merry Christmas!" a clerk called. He was an amiable, ugly young man with great energy. He reminded Terry of Kermit the Frog, except for the part about being green and amphibian.

"Merry Christmas back atcha," Terry said. "Sorry you have to work today."

The clerk grinned. "Earning double time, man! Picking up a few last-minute things?"

"Yep." Terry noted the sale signs. Everything seemed to be a bargain. "Having an end of the world sale?"

The clerk barked laughter. "You know that my boss buys into that crap? He gave me double time to come in, just dumping his cash. It's like Tarzan throwing Cheetah off his back before he jumps for a vine."

"Colorful, if slightly confusing image. What if he's right?"

"I'll spend it fast."

"Do that."

Terry rolled his cart down the aisles, looking up and down the rows carefully. Nobody, save for one other shopper, an elderly woman in a caterpillar-green sweater pushing a creaking cart with wobbly front wheels.

He quickly gathered his items, and took them to the front register.

"Find everything you wanted?" the clerk asked.

"Nope," he said. "But everything I needed."

"Mick said it best." The kid grinned.

And together, they broke into spontaneous song. "*'You can't always get what you waaant . . .'*"

They laughed. Damn, it felt good to laugh. Terry felt it had been too long since he'd had anything to laugh about, and let the mirth roll out of him like a river.

Behind him, the creaking of unoiled wheels.

The old woman had pushed her shopping cart up behind them. She tried to smile, but her makeup was skewed, messy, overdone. Streaked. Her socks were mismatched: argyle blue and solid yellow.

"Are you all right?" Terry asked.

She smiled, the smile too bright by half. "All right. It's all right."

"Really. Are you?"

Her lip trembled.

"Go on ahead, won't you?" he said, making a space for her.

"Thank you," she said. And then almost as if she'd already forgotten she'd said it, she repeated her words. "Thank you."

The clerk rang her things up. As he did, she looked shyly at Terry. "You're a kind young man. Do you have someone?"

"Excuse me?" he asked. There was something in her eyes. As if she had spent the morning peering into the mirror, searching for the girl she had once been. He had the sense that every old woman did that, searching for something gone forever. "A sweetheart to be with. You shouldn't be alone. After all . . ." She smiled brightly, with small, brown, evenly-spaced teeth. Too brightly. "This is the last Christmas."

"Yes. I have someone." He wasn't sure what she meant. And then he understood.

"I'm a survivor," she said.

"Excuse me?"

"Cancer survivor."

He found a smile. "Congratulations. How many years?"

"Seven," she said. "It came back."

His good mood darkened. "Oh. I'm sorry."

"I'm a widow woman," she said. "I prayed for a miracle. I told God I didn't want to die alone. He misunderstood. I didn't mean for the whole world to die with me."

She touched the counter, as if dizzy and needing a steadying reference point. "I'm sorry," she whispered. "If this is my fault, if this is all me . . . I'm so sorry. Please forgive me."

She took her groceries and tottered out of the store.

"Jesus Christ," the clerk said.

"No," Terry replied. "The other guy."

They rang up Terry's items in a silent store.

"Thanks. Be well."

"You, too." The clerk's Christmas cheer had evaporated, and Terry could think of no way to revive it.

◆ ◆ ◆

An icy breeze greeted Terry as he reached the sidewalk. He looked down the street and saw the old woman wheeling a cart along, pitiable in her isolation and despair.

He wondered if she needed, or would accept, a ride. Terry put his stuff into the car, then froze, a terrible realization striking him like a stone. "Oh shit oh shit oh shit" he said aloud, thinking, *Oh my God. I forgot. I was thinking so hard about the woman that I handed Kermit my damned debit card.*

He started the engine and pulled out of the parking lot. Looked both ways down the empty street. "Maybe it's nothing," he muttered to himself. "Maybe Geek missed it."

Terry continued to drive, slowly and carefully. And then . . . an SUV barreled around the corner, squealing and throwing up snow as it did.

The battered green Geekmobile was instantly recognizable.

"Shit!"

He swerved to the side and made a right-hand turn. "Even if that's something, they don't know what I'm driving. They didn't see me pull out of the lot . . ."

That faint hope vanished when the Expedition plowed around the corner, coming after him full-tilt boogie.

Cherokee and SUV slid, spun, and squealed through the empty streets. Patches of black ice broke his traction twice, and he slewed, rear wheels slamming against the curb before they dug in and shot him forward again. He was gaining on the Pirates when he turned left into a dead-end alley blocked with orange construction signs and an abandoned cement truck. No way out.

The Pirates pulled in behind him, blocking the alleyway. Terry fished in the glove compartment, found what he was looking for, and slipped it into his pocket. Taking a deep breath, he climbed out of the car to face them.

Lee, Pat, and Mark were out of the SUV in seconds, automatic pistols popping up from the low-ready to head shots—he could see squarely into each of the three barrels. They were spread out, bracketing him professionally. No human motion could be fast or skilled enough to survive the potential fusillade. Good old-fashioned overlapping fields of fire. Nothing better. "Well, Terry," Mark said. "I told you we'd see you again."

"You're making a mistake," Terry said. "I'm no danger to you."

Pat's narrow face sharpened in a sneer. "Not in a minute, no."

"Why, damn it?" Mark said. "Why did you turn against us?"

Terry felt no fear. But along with the cool wind whistling through his bones, he did feel a measure of sorrow. "You wouldn't understand. But it wasn't turning against you."

Mark's eyes flickered to the groceries in the backseat. "That's a lot of food. Planning a party?"

"There's a family," he said.

"Olympia?" Mark asked. "The kid?" His expression was unreadable, but not quite as flinty as it had been just a moment before.

He nodded. "They're in trouble."

Mark's eyes narrowed. "Is that what this is about? The woman?" Terry knew that expression. *Please. Help me understand.*

"In a way."

Lee shifted uncomfortably, keeping his weapon aimed at Terry's face. "Let's end this."

Father Geek slapped the side of the SUV. "Wait a minute. Wait just a minute, all of you. Death lasts a long time. It doesn't answer questions."

Pat sneered. "Maybe not, but it does solve problems."

Mark seemed to swell, as if he had swallowed his own shadow. He lowered his pistol, still at the ready but no longer lining up on Terry's skull. "Pat, stand down, soldier. Terry, it's not too late. We can do this together."

"Yeah," Lee said, "it's too late." His eyes said this was the worst kind of lie: one that half of him wanted to believe.

"Stand down!" Mark snarled. They glared at each other.

Mark sighed wearily, and looked as if he wanted to sit down. Fatigue radiated from him like a low squealing sound, only something felt rather than heard. "Terry. Do me a favor. It's Christmas. Probably my last one. Give me a reason not to kill my friend."

Terry shrugged. "Ask the cops pulling up behind you."

The Pirates looked back over their shoulders. A police car had slowed at the mouth of the alley, and Terry waved merrily at them. The black-and-white backed up and then crept toward them. The Pirates slipped their guns back under their coats and assumed more casual stances, exchanging wary expressions.

"What's going on here?" the first officer asked after the car rolled to a halt. None of them seemed to have seen the handguns or noted the aggressive body language. The two vehicles were facing each other at an angle, as if there had been a fender bender.

"This guy cut us off on the road," Mark said, the very soul of reason. "We were just having a little conversation."

They glanced at Terry. It was clear: the choice was his. Would these men live or die?

"Well," the cop said. "I guess you did us a favor. We need him in connection with a theft at the Salvation Sanctuary."

Lee smiled tightly. "Seems like a shady character to us, Officer."

"Well, do you want to press charges?"

"No," Mark said. "I think we can leave this to you, sir."

A third vehicle pulled in behind the cop car. It was dark and sleek, with no official trappings.

"This is fucking ridiculous," Lee muttered.

A tall, lean man exited the car. Terry noted that the others seemed to defer to him. "Thank you, Officer." A Southern drawl. "I believe we can take it from here."

"Are you sure you don't need anything?" the cop asked.

"Get in touch with your captain."

The other cop in the car was looking at his dashboard computer. "Sir? He's right."

Mark cleared his throat, and the Pirates relaxed, or pretended to. "Sir, happy to be of service. Merry Christmas . . ."

"Merry Christmas," the cop replied.

Mark made careful note of the tall man's license plate on the way out. Terry approved. Mark didn't know what was going on, or what this apparent alpha wanted, or who he was . . . but you never pass up a chance to snag some intel.

They found Terry's gun when they searched him, which caused a little excitement. Terry kept his cool, and continued to comply with the officers. They handcuffed his hands behind his back, guns at the ready. He was anchored into the car, still under threat from multiple weapons, no chance to respond. "My name is Tony Killinger," the tall man said. "Security chief of the Salvation Sanctuary."

"Congratulations."

"Where are they?" Tony asked.

"I don't know what you're talking about."

"This isn't the car he was driving yesterday," the other security man said.

"Well now, I'm bettin' we can check the license plate," Tony replied, and smiled at him.

Suddenly, and with crystalline clarity, Terry realized taking the Cherokee had been a terrible mistake.

One of the cops looked up in excitement. "Sir! We have a hit from Homeland Security. This man is wanted in connection with the threats made against the president."

Tony's smile was tight and hard. "Check with your commander. We'll take it from here."

"But . . ."

Without reaching for a weapon, somehow the security man had totally dominated the situation. "Stand . . . down."

♦ ♦ ♦

A half-mile away, Father Geek had pulled the SUV over to the side. The motor pulsed through the wheel, warming his hands.

"What now, genius?" Lee asked.

"Well . . ." Geek scratched his head, frowning. "I thought cops might get a fix on him, and give us a chance to get to him first. If they caught him, at least we'd know it, and could change our plans. Better than being caught flat-footed."

"Maybe we should have left well enough alone," Mark said.

"Not too terribly likely," Pat said.

Father Geek rolled down his window and spit out into the cold. This was a clusterfuck, but one he'd half-expected. "What the hell do we do now?"

"They'll run the I.D. Find out who he is . . ."

"So he tells them who we are and what we're doing, and we're screwed," Lee said.

"We fall back to the secondary plan," Mark said. "We have two chances to get our goods. One is in Georgia. The other is in North Carolina. These are state guys. If they check Homeland, they'll grill him until they find out the flag is bogus, and then grill him even harder. They won't have anything to charge him with, but if he gives us up, we'd better be lost, and fast. There's nothing to connect us, but it could get unpleasant if they lay hands on us. If nothing happens in Georgia . . . but something happens in North Carolina, we'll be out of the country before they can coordinate. We go dark. So far, we've not accepted any stolen equipment, I've destroyed the plans, and Terry doesn't know the name of our supply contact. We might squeak through this. Compartmentalization is a wonderful thing. So there's no evidence. No crime."

Father Geek's phone rang. He glanced at it, and didn't recognize the number. "Don't know who the . . ." He answered it. "Hello? Hello . . . ?"

Then . . . his eyes widened. "Uh . . . guys . . . it's Terry."

"Odd time for a chat. What is it?" Mark asked.

In answer, Geek put the phone on speaker. They could hear every word in the security car. "*Why do you want the woman? The boy?*" Terry's voice.

What was this? Who was he talking to? And . . . Geek couldn't avoid the suspicion that this had not been a butt-dial. For some reason Terry wanted them to hear this conversation. But why?

"*Big things happening, champ. Big things. And the queen figured it all out.*"

"*Madame Gupta?*"

"*That's the one. That kid . . . he's pretty special. He's the only one we ever did find who can do the trick and keep breathin'.*" A pause. "*At least we think he can live.*"

"*What trick?*"

"*Now, what kind of citizen are you? Haven't you been watching the news?*"

Another voice. "*We have the address. Let's motor!*"

"Hannibal is connected to all these killings? To Gupta? What's going on here?"

"I suspect you'll find out. And you probably won't enjoy what ah believe they call 'the process of discovery.' "

Then the sound of a car pulling out. Geek felt as if the bottom had dropped out of his stomach. The implications of this call were . . . impossible.

And unavoidable. He placed the phone on mute.

"What was that?" Lee asked.

"I'm not sure what we just heard," Mark said. "It wasn't his phone?"

"No," Geek answered. "Different number. Might have been a burner."

Mark drummed his fingers on the dashboard. "I don't know about you guys. But as far as I'm concerned, this changes a few things."

"Like what?" Lee asked.

"Someone is killing people in a way no one can figure out. And Terry's squeeze is some part of it. Maybe a big part of it."

Lee shrugged. "Maybe behind the whole thing. But so what?"

"Whoever is doing this is planning to kill the president. Today."

Pat shrugged again. "I voted for the guy with the magic underwear."

"That's not the point. So the kid, and the woman, and Terry are a part of it somehow. If it's true, she's done a lot of damage."

"I believe the technical term is a 'shitload,' " Geek said. "I remember taking an oath, once upon a time. Same one you guys took. Something about enemies foreign and domestic. I wasn't born in this country, but I bled for it and it's mine now. If anyone living has a beef with Colonel Shitbird and his pogue-ass Sergeant Major Douchebag, it's me and I'm saying we reevaluate our targets. It has really bugged me that Terry broke with us— he's our bro. He was there. It had to be something big. How can it get bigger?"

"I say we reevaluate," Mark said. "What do you say?"

Pat sighed. "I say . . . we stick around. I didn't vote for the bitch, but she's still my fucking president." He sighed. "And let's not go all hero and shit. We still owe O'Shay, damn it."

CHAPTER 49

The house was bursting with the rich aroma of baking biscuits and hot cocoa. Nicki was outside gamboling through the snow with Pax, who was as bouncy as a kitten. "Fetch, Pax!"

Pax ran happily off. She fetched the ball . . . and then saw a rabbit. Pax ran off after the terrified bunny, who scampered away through the snow.

"Paxie!" Nicki called.

"Don't worry," Olympia said. "She'll come back, hon. She's just having fun."

"Won't be fun for the rabbit."

"Hot cocoa," Hannibal said in delight.

"Hot cocoa," Nicki said approvingly. "You know, you're just a little chatterbox, Mini-me."

"Strange, isn't it?" Olympia said. "Something about this whole thing seems to actually be good for him."

"Maybe good for all of us," Nicki said.

Olympia and Nicki went inside and sat at the table, sipping cocoa. The buttermilk biscuits, found stacked in plastic ziplocks in the garage freezer, would be ready in minutes. "What do you think is happening, Mom?"

That stopped her flat. One of those questions that demanded her whole mind. "Big question. Which part of 'happening' are you referring to? In the world? At the Salvation Sanctuary? To our family?"

"Maybe to us. Right now I don't care about much else, I'm just happy for the little miracle that we're together."

Olympia sighed. "It is, isn't it?"

"Is what?"

"A small miracle."

"Isn't that what I just said?" They laughed together, the blended sound sweeter than any Christmas song. It had been too long between laughs in their lives.

"Come on," Olympia said. "Help me with the dishes."

♦ ♦ ♦

Snow exploded with each puffy footstep as Pax chased after the rabbit. Hannibal loved watching Pax running happy and free, like a dog should. She was a city dog, who had probably never seen anything so . . . so . . . well, *Christmassy.*

Hannibal was building a snowman in the front yard, freezing his fingers even through the too-big gloves Mommy had found for him. In a little while he'd go and drag Nicki back out into the yard. She and Mommy were washing dishes, but there was all day to work. It was time to play!

He heard a car heading toward them, a dim growl growing louder by the moment. Daddy Terry coming back?

Hani hoped so. Mommy was baking biscuits: the warm sweet scent tickled his nose even out in the yard. His mouth watered at the thought, and a big smile split his face at the notion of sharing one with his more-than-friend, Terry.

Hannibal turned, waving, and then saw that the driver was not Terry. And a moment later, he realized what that meant.

"Hannibal!" He turned in time to see Nicki run out of the house, huffing as she scooped him up and tried to run. Two men grabbed from either side and they spilled on the ground, and he couldn't breathe, couldn't breathe, couldn't breathe at all.

He howled with pain and fear as his mother tried to reach him. She was tackled to the ground and her hands tied.

The next car pulled up. Terry sat in the back, his face clouded with fear and rage. *Terry! Help me! Help us, Terry!*

But he didn't, and couldn't, and Hannibal's eyes washed with tears. It wasn't fair! They'd won! They'd gotten away from the bad people. This was cheating!

The tall man with the scarred eye smiled at him.

"We missed you," Tony said to Hannibal. "Yes, we did."

"No no no no no," Hannibal screamed. " 'Erry!"

Hannibal sobbed and screamed as they hauled the family into the cars. The cars pulled out of the drive and sped away. He tried to take refuge in his Game, and failed. His inner kingdom was breached, swarmed with alien trees and vines, the halls violated and humid.

♦ ♦ ♦

The security men left one car behind. "Marty," Tony said to the largest of them, a man who Nicki had thought looked much like the Avenger, Thor, but with shorter hair. "Sweep the cabin. Take everything that identifies them."

"Will do, Chief," Marty answered.

Marty waited until the cars had pulled out, and then entered the cabin. He pulled a trash bag from under the sink. Went from room to room, sweeping up trash and gifts and wrappings. Headed back out, then turned, and there in the open doorway stood a very intense and angry dalmatian-spotted Great Dane.

Pax.

"Oh, shit!"

He went for his gun, but not half fast enough, and Pax was on him. Marty tried to get his arm under the dog's jaw, levering the head up, but his heels lost traction against the ground and they fell backwards together. Straining, he managed to twist Pax's massive head to the side, and once he did, if he could wedge his left elbow under the jaw he could reach his belt knife with his left and slam it into the side of the beast's neck, could—

And at that moment his head slammed into the coffee table, stunning him so that all thoughts, all plans, were obscured in a flash of pain. And then . . .

Pax's jaws closed on his throat.

◆ ◆ ◆

Nicki gritted her teeth as their car jostled down the roads, traveling back to the Sanctuary. The one positive thing about this hideous situation was that she had discovered that anger was a terrific antidote for fear. That was a good thing, a very, very good thing. And if she survived, she'd never forget it, she was certain.

"Where are you taking us?" she asked. They had chained her hands to a loop on the backseat.

"You'll like it." His tone did not invite challenge.

Terry was slumped, unconscious. He had tried to wrest free of his cuffs, and the bastards had Tased and beaten him until he could no longer resist.

He had tried. As their real father had not. And now they were going to die. Terry was going to die. Because he had tried.

And that was when anger failed, when all the fear and grief and guilt descended on her with crushing force, and she collapsed against him, sobbing.

◆ ◆ ◆

The Pirates muttered and slumped in their SUV, morose and somehow inert. "Let's hear that again." Geek replayed the sound of the struggle. Christ, it was awful. And the sound of the family sobbing was even worse.

"What in the hell is going on?" Geek said.

"The kid?" Even Pat seemed disturbed, like a man who has peered around the corner and glimpsed something unspeakable.

"The kid has something to do with this, that's for sure," Geek said.

"But what?" Mark said.

"Hell if I know. I'm betting that the mom works for CNS, right? She has a source that knows something about the killings, something that connects these people, and they're using her family to force her to talk."

Mark grunted. "That really makes sense to you?"

"No," Geek said, "but it's all I've got."

"What do we do?"

Mark cursed under his breath. "Let's check out this Salvation Sanctuary place."

"Already have." He spun around his laptop. "It was originally the Baskins gold mine. Approximately a hundred thousand kilos of gold were removed from the ground before it petered out in about 1908. Afterward, it was owned by a succession of rich kooks, purchased in 1999 by the current group."

"And who are they?" Mark asked.

"The 'Salvation Sanctuary' is a bunch of New Agey types. Meditation, yoga, martial arts, Eastern philosophical stuff. And they follow a woman named Madame Gupta, who is supposed to be a very unusual person, physically. Same person we heard Terry talk about, and she doesn't sound very friendly. The vehicle we thought was a plainclothes cop or DHS—it was registered to the Sanctuary and the cops just gave up an armed suspect to them. That was weird, but not as weird as Gupta."

"Gupta is weird how?" Mark asked.

Geek could hardly believe he was about to say this. "They say she can lift over five thousand pounds. With one arm."

Mark drew back. "What the fuck?"

"Special rig, so we're talking overhead bone support. But still, the implication is rather frightening. She's a freak."

"How is this our business?"

Geek smiled for the first time all day. "And they also say that the center houses the most expensive esoteric book collection in the world."

That caught Lee's attention. "How rare?"

"Valued at . . . fifty million dollars."

"Fifty . . . ?" Mark said, and for the first time, he smiled, too. "Well, hey, now!"

"Let's take a look."

They pulled out.

♦ ♦ ♦

In a perfectly spaced chain, the convoy pulled through the gates of the Salvation Sanctuary. Save for the core security detail, the entire encampment was deserted now, and in desertion possessed a flavor vaguely reminiscent of a prison camp.

"Where's Marty?" the gate guard asked Tony Killinger.

He'd wondered that himself. Why hadn't Marty called? "Back at the house, cleaning up. Why?" He knew why. They needed to know if they'd left anything that could identify them. Could bitch-slap them before their plans were complete. The wrong interference could make things a little chancy.

"Give him a call," Tony said.

The cars pulled through, and the gate closed behind them.

The guard picked up his phone. Dialed it. "Come on, bro."

♦ ♦ ♦

The ringing phone echoed around a cabin that no longer held a living human being. Marty was sprawled on his back, eyes frozen open. The blood oozed now, no longer pumping from his torn throat. The pump, the beating heart, was stilled. Pax paced the floor in ovals, limping a bit. Whining. The roar in her head was gone, the big red-black thing that had swept her away when she saw the man who had hurt her was gone. But . . .

She had done a bad thing, a very bad thing. Would the girl still love her? Still feed her? She hoped so. Pax had bitten a man before, when he had been trying to hurt the girl, and the girl had still loved Pax. She had to find the girl and see if she was angry. See if Pax was still a good dog.

Where was the girl? She couldn't find her.

She trotted out the front door, into the snow. Pax barked. Nothing. Traveled in larger circles, following footprints. Nothing. The fire in her blood, roused by the kill, only slowly began to recede.

Then . . . she picked up a familiar scent. Pax had cut across the original path of footprints Olympia and Hannibal had left fleeing from the Salvation Sanctuary.

Not the girl, but the boy! And . . . the woman! This was almost as good. Almost. Heartened, Pax backtracked along the trail, seeking its origin. Following it backward, yes. But following nonetheless.

◆ ◆ ◆

Numbed to silence, Olympia observed their return to Salvation Sanctuary as through a sheet of ice.

The world was dead. Library, amphitheater, dorms, maze. . . . all deserted.

"Yes, deserted," Tony said. "You have it all to yourself now. Feel honored?"

The security car pulled up to the main admin building, three o'clock on the nose. Terry had roused himself to wakefulness, somehow emerging from sleep to waking without any apparent trace of grogginess . . .

◆ ◆ ◆

For an odd instant she wondered if he had ever been unconscious at all. Tony pulled his stun gun and held it to Nicki's head. "Now . . . this stun dart is designed to send fifty thousand volts at low amperage, sufficient to disable a grown man when directed into the center of his body. They promise that it will cause no permanent harm. If you want to find out if that holds true for a thirteen-year-old girl when she's shot in the head at close range, just make a move."

"I won't cause any trouble," Terry swore.

"No, you won't. I heard you have clever feet. Is that right?"

"I'm trained," Terry said. Indeed he was, Olympia thought. And he was . . . special now. She could sense it. Feel it. Something deep and pervasive had shifted within Terry. And with that growing realization came a spark of hope. If these monsters made one mistake, just one . . .

They had a chance. Terry would find a way, she knew it.

"Well, isn't that special?" Killinger said. "You're going to let my man put the shackles on your ankles. And remember the little girl pays for it if you make a mistake."

"I won't," Terry said.

"That's good. Keep it that way." Maureen Skotak attached the chains to Terry's ankles.

"Good," Tony said. "Now move."

The family left the car. They walked to the administration building, and there waited . . . Madame Gupta. This time, the first thing that Olympia noticed were the gloves she wore half-way down her forearms.

"Greetings," she said. "Welcome back."

"So it's true," Terry said, his face a mask of pain and betrayal. But not merely those negative emotions. Something else smoldered in there as well.

Fury. Barely leashed.

"What is true? That I seek to free the world from an illusion? To awaken it from a dream?"

"You're just another monster." His words contained more pain than venom.

"The world itself is monstrous. No great thing has ever been accomplished without monstrosity."

"That's pretty fucked-up."

She approached closer, smiled. "Even as we speak, rabbits are being torn apart in the woods by wolves . . . and all is well. I did not make this world, God did. But I will live in it."

She came to Hannibal, who would not look at her. "Little one. I know you can hear me. See me. As none of these others can."

"Leave my boy alone," Olympia said.

Gupta brought her gaze upon Olympia, and the impact was like a punch between the eyes. Olympia felt her knees buckle, but fought her way upright again. "Do not think me merely the frail flesh standing before you. Do not think that because we once honored your relationship with Hannibal, you will receive the same treatment now. Our research suggests that he loves this man. And that he is closer to your daughter than he is to you. Do you understand the implications?"

Olympia grew very still. "What?"

Gupta came closer, and whispered. "It means that I can destroy one of you. Even two. Merely to prove that I am serious. And that, then, I believe that Hannibal will know I am serious, and do as I ask to save the one who remains."

Hannibal's head lolled like a rag doll's. He seemed barely aware of anything around him.

"He doesn't know what you want!" Olympia begged. "Don't you see him?"

"As you do not. When you listen to the radio, do you mistake the static for the signal?"

"She listens to FM," Nicki said.

"Charming." Madame Gupta smiled. And lowered her voice. "Hannibal is in there, make no mistake. The difficulty is in reaching him, or in drawing his communications to the surface. You have failed him. I have not. I will not. Do not force me to replace his mother. Or his sister."

Olympia trembled, clamped her teeth down to prevent them from chattering. Gupta had them all now. Heaven only knew what plans she might have, how far she was willing to go. "What is all this about?" she asked. *Please. Information. Please.*

"You need not know," Gupta said. "Know only that my purpose will not be denied. I have waited all my life for this moment. My mother and father died before they could see it. And you, and your family, can die here, now, and my purpose will go forward. It is up to you."

"You're insane."

"I understand your perspective. Will you yield?"

Olympia looked at Hannibal. He was muttering to himself, eyes staring, but what he saw, or imagined he saw, she could not imagine. Terry. Nicki. Olivia dropped her eyes in defeat.

"Good. Good," Gupta said. "You have saved your family a great deal of pain." A moment's consideration and then: "Take the family to confinement," she said. "Keep them under constant observation."

For once, the lanky head of security seemed uncertain. "Yes, ma'am."

"Free his hands," she said, indicating Terry.

Tony looked dubious. "I . . . mean no disrespect, ma'am. Ah mean, ah know what you're capable of . . ."

"No," she said. "You don't."

He nodded. "That might be true. But this man is extremely dangerous. Based on police reports I recommend that the chains be kept on." An odd mixture of emotions warred in his eyes. "Unless you think that might get in the way."

Gupta smiled thinly. "Take them off. If there is misbehavior, the family will suffer for it."

"Where are you taking him?" Terry asked.

"It is safer if you don't know." Gupta again motioned for her men to release Terry to her.

She led him clockwise around the garden, all the way to the castle. There, she invited him to step into the elevator.

They rode up to the top level, and exited through a narrow hallway. Gupta punched a four-digit code into a diamond-shaped key pad and the door slid open. The apartment within was like a wealthy gloater's private museum. Or an artist's private studio, hung with the fruits of an untrammeled imagination she dared share with no one, ever. Anywhere. He wondered how many people . . . how many *men* had ever been here.

"Why am I here?"

She ignored the question. "Do you take wine?" Without awaiting an answer she pulled two stainless steel wine glasses from a cooler and poured from a carafe. Something about her mood and aspect had changed. She seemed so small, the top of her head barely reaching his chin. Softer. More feminine. Almost as if she were presenting him with different angles on her psyche.

He took an offered glass, but waited until she sipped to join her. "I spend much time alone," she said. "Having followers is intoxicating. It is also isolating."

"I can understand that," Terry said. He drank.

"When this is all over, I will be one of the wealthiest women in the world."

"When what is over? What exactly are you doing?"

She smiled. "Beauty is mysterious as well as terrible," she said. "A lady must have her secrets."

"The full quote is: 'Beauty is mysterious as well as terrible. God and devil are fighting there, and the battlefield is the heart of man.' That's from *The Brothers Karamazov.* Read it."

"I myself have not," she said, pleased. "You have things to teach me. That is wonderful."

"Peachy," he said. Damn it, he'd pulled that quote out of a college lit class, and had hoped to . . . he didn't know. Impress her? Get a rise? She'd just rolled with it.

"But know," she continued, "that this is the beginning of an era. A great teacher must have flair, a touch of the dramatist's art."

"And you are a great teacher?"

"The greatest since Gandhi," she said, as if reciting an article of faith. "When this act is over, there will be a pause, a chance for the audience to take a breath. And then the next sequence will begin, and it will be . . . magnificent. I will change the world."

She came closer. "I will take the greatest dreams of conquerors, and shame them."

"How?"

Another smile. "Think of it. Wave after wave of deaths, and much of the world now believing that the end is coming. What will result in the financial markets?"

"Devastation," Terry said.

"Yes. And what do you think a person who anticipated this, and knew that the world was *not* ending, and that those markets would recover fully once the pattern of deaths ended . . . what do you imagine such a person could do with, say, fifty million dollars to invest in various stock futures?

I can tell you: reap over twelve billion dollars. And that is a conservative estimation."

He blinked. "You mean . . . all of this, and you're just another scam artist?"

"Hardly 'just another.'" She smiled. "I would think you'd agree that there is an impressive elegance to it all. I will emerge fabulously wealthy. Were I to do the same thing again . . . and I assure you I could . . . I could be the wealthiest human being who has ever lived. And after I have rocked the world until it cowers in the shadows of their antediluvian belief systems, mumbling prayers to their fathers in the sky, seeking salvation . . . I will sally forth, a golden creature representing every value human beings treasure, be they spiritual, physical, or financial."

Or sensual, he thought. Everything about her stimulated him, on almost every level. Fear, rage, desire, all in a toxic tangle. *God damn, this woman is amazing.*

"There has never been a teacher like me, Terry. Can you deny it?" The impact of her will was like a velvet hammer. She paused, as if she herself was overwhelmed by the strength of her vision. "The West will suffer for rejecting the East. India will suffer for what it did to my people."

A pause, then she leaned closer. "You love this country. This 'America' of yours. And . . . it has been good to me, as well. But can you tell me there is no part of you that wishes vengeance for what it did to your people? *Our* people."

Terry chose his words carefully. "You mean, if there was a button, and I could push it, would I reverse the history? Sure I would. In a heartbeat. Be fun to watch the squawking, especially from the assholes who think white people would have done better. But do you mean do I want to hurt millions of people I swore to defend? Hell, no."

"But why did you feel compelled to defend people who deny you your humanity?"

Terry felt his neck getting warm, but calmed himself. "Life is shitty, princess. But anger is poison if you can't use it as fuel. And it's just fear, wearing a mask. My daddy taught me that. And taught me to surround myself with people who didn't give as much of a shit about my skin as they do about theirs, and the fact that I can save it. That's something fairly rare in human history, and I think it's worth protecting." He paused. "Let me put it another way. There's a line from an old John Wayne movie: 'I won't be wronged, I won't be insulted, I won't be laid a hand on. I don't do these things to other men, and I require the same of them.'" A wan smile. "That's me. My daddy said that if everyone took care of his family and the families to either side, the whole world would work. Well, I found a little world where we trust each other to do just that. There are still problems, but it's with the people. The machine cares more about how strong a cog is, and if it can handle the job, than what color it is. I can deal with that."

She shook her head in wonderment. "I never had eyes to see America as you have. Perhaps I see its failings more clearly than its strengths. But with your eyes, your voice . . . I might understand more. I wonder . . . do you love this country enough to help it? What is a warrior? What a shame if it is someone who must continually search for war."

"What do you want from me?" he asked. He was solid in his beliefs. He had thought through every link in his argument. But although she could not rebut him, he felt as if he was falling through a fog.

She was very, very close now. "All I have ever dreamed will come to me. Power. Money. Fame. The worshipping crowd. And they will swallow me whole, unless I have one thing."

"What is that?"

Her hand was a smooth warmth along the inside of his thigh. "Something to keep me human. I will be an empress. I will need . . . an emperor."

Her eyes locked with his as she backed away, and stood beside a golden statue of the gods Shiva and Shakti, their limbs intertwined. Her robe shimmered in the light. Her body within it was perfection. She was . . . had to be . . . at least fifty years old . . . perhaps sixty. Impossible. Wasn't it?

"And such a man would need not fear for the family he already loves. And would help me to create a new family." He felt intoxicated, barely able to stand . . . except for one part of his anatomy, which was experiencing its own very localized epiphany. He felt some force or power radiating from her he could not name: not a scent, not a sensation, not a sound. Something that communicated with him on a different, more primal level. Something against which he had no defense.

She caressed the statue. "Are you familiar with the story of Shiva and Shakti?"

"A little." Actually, no, he hadn't the slightest idea.

She nodded as if she'd expected that answer. "The Tantrikas believe that the universe was created and nurtured by two fundamental forces, which are permanently in a perfect, indestructible union."

"I've heard that, I think."

"The tradition has assigned to these principles the forms of masculine and feminine deities. Accordingly, Shiva represents the basic building blocks of the universe, while Shakti is the dynamic potency, which makes these elements spring to life and action."

"What kind of actions?" He was compelled to shake his head. She was entrancing him, deliberately he was sure. It felt as if someone was injecting Freon into his brain, shutting down one cranial fold at a time.

Her voice had become a metronomic pulse, a rhythm with what Father Geek might have described as a "fork": dry information on one level, and a seductive call on another. His mind could focus on one or the other, but not both. Wherever he directed his attention, the other tine lanced home. ". . . from a metaphysical point of view, the divine couple corresponds to two essential aspects of the One: the masculine principle, which represents the abiding aspect of God, and the feminine principle, which represents its energy, the force that acts in the manifested world, life itself considered at a cosmic level."

"So it isn't just an energy. It is also a position," he mumbled. His lips felt thick, unresponsive.

"Yes," Gupta said, eyes vast. "From this point of view, Shakti represents active participation in the act of creation. Maybe exactly this Tantric view of the feminine in creation contributed to the orientation of the human being toward the active principles of the universe, rather than toward those of pure transcendence."

He shook his head sharply, trying to clear it. "What does this have to do with me?"

She held up her flat palm. *Silence.* "Therefore, Shiva defines the traits specific to pure transcendence and is normally associated, from this point of view, to a manifestation of Shakti, who is terrible indeed. Kali and Yama are the worldly aspects of Shakti and Shiva. They seem to be death, but are actually life itself."

He heard himself say it again: "What do you want with me?"

She was closer now. And then closer still.

He felt his conscious mind shutting down, a tunnel swirling with darkness at the edges, the only light that which danced in her eyes.

Those eyes consumed him. And then the eight hands of Kali were upon him, everywhere at once.

◆ ◆ ◆

Entering the dance of flesh and spirit was the single most glorious moment of his existence, driving away all other thought, all history, all ego, all identity. He saw his future, his reality, his hopes and dreams as nothing compared to the energy that had created and birthed him, let alone his glorious potential.

Her body might have been made for this, every touch, taste, warmth, and wetness, every motion intertwining their hearts and ganglia so that they were one striving creature, and without speaking she seemed always to be whispering to him *thou art a god* until, when the paroxysm rocked him, there was nothing within him strong enough to deny.

And in that fevered moment was lost, and found.

And where normally he would slide down into satiation and the desire for rest, through some wizardry beyond his ken she caught him and guided him back up again, into another dizzying loop, and then another . . .

Until he could not remember his name, or who he had been, or anything except the universe of exploding stars he held so tightly in his arms . . .

And Indra was the sun.

◆ ◆ ◆

Afterward, they lay together quietly, her arm draped across his chest. An utterly asinine phrase danced through his mind, something concerning a child's toy. *Some assembly required.* That was him, right now.

"Feel that," Gupta said, running her fingers over the ridges of his abdomen. "Feel the connection. It goes back to the beginning of life. Forward to the end of the universe. We are made of the same stuff as the stars."

"I don't know who I am," he said finally. It was a calm statement, but the truth was that at that instant he could not even remember his name, or any of his history. He was merely content to . . . be.

Yes. Just be.

"I do," Gupta said. "Come with me. Be my consort. Grow to be my emperor, my king. I offer what no one else in the world can give you. I will set you free."

He felt the pull of her words, heard their truth. There *were* no rules. No limits. No ultimate reality. Only a search for meaning, a search to answer twin questions:

Who am I?

And: *what is true?*

And in that moment, he knew that the answer was that he was the man who would, in this moment, say yes.

◆ ◆ ◆

Terry walked at Indra Gupta's side as if he had been there, her sacred warrior, since before the wheel of time commenced its spinning. Together they walked the deserted pathways of the Sanctuary, north to the concrete-tiered crescent of the amphitheater, deserted now save for the Dorseys, bracketed by a half-dozen guards. Yes. He remembered them, the family who lived across the street. The boy and girl, and the woman with whom he had dallied. Now, they needed to yield to Her will, and all would be well.

The girl spoke first. She was a pretty thing, heart-shaped face framed with soft dark ringlets of hair, her pouting lips turned down in a frown.

There was no need for frowns. All was well.

"What's going on?" the girl asked. *Nicki.* That was her name, Nicki. It didn't matter, but it was nice to remember it.

"I don't know, baby," the woman said. Olympia said. Yes, that was her name. Olympia. A good name. She was a good woman. He hoped that she would be sensible. The time for resistance had passed.

Olympia was terrified, that much was clear in her voice, her eyes, her posture. *All is well,* he wanted to say to her. *If you cooperate, you and your family live. If not, your life will end and we will convince the boy to act by other means. But no matter what may happen . . . all is well.*

"Stop here," his love told him, and he did.

Olympia stood so rigidly that her bones might have fused together without joints.

"Oh, shit," Nicki whispered.

"Tell them." Again, his love's honeyed voice.

Terry smiled at them as if he was looking down from some height so vast that they had no individual existence, as if they were a part of a vast crowd, not three people he loved, and knew, and had held. "I have made a choice, and it is the only one for all of us."

"Terry," Olympia whispered. Her mouth had barely moved.

"I'm not what you think I am."

"No one ever is," she said, her face streaked with tears.

"But it is the best, for all." He saw now that she could not understand, and for that, he felt regret. Death comes to all, but she would experience great fear as that moment approached. A pity.

"Take the woman away," his love commanded.

The early evening wind whistled around them. Christmas night. A time of miracles. *Yes,* he thought. *This is all miraculous.*

"Terry," Olympia begged. "Don't let them do that. Don't let them use Hani for whatever they are doing. They'll kill me."

"You don't understand," he said. "You've never understood. But you will. Everything will be fine."

He balanced on some strange edge. What was a life? How could a single human life be important, more important than an ant or a star? The woman had twice rejected him, hadn't she? She had made her choice, and chosen to be nothing to him. He had the right to his own happiness in the brief moments on earth that were allowed to human beings, and—

And then, tears streaming down his rounded cheeks, Hannibal spoke. "Daddy. No."

Whispered words. Soft words. Their eyes locked. Hannibal reached his hand out. Small hand. He had done this before. When had that been? He could not remember. But as in that previous time Terry took Hannibal's right hand. Soft hand.

Teetering between worlds. All the worlds that might ever be on the one side, the boy's small warm hand on the other.

How could any man have walked away from this child? he thought. And with that thought, memories returned to him. *I promised him I would not leave. Not because it is important. Just because.*

Terry sighed. And realized in that moment that somehow Gupta had led him perilously close to a pale, empty place where there was no meaning except her own radiance.

The narrowest escape of his life. And what was strangest, and most terrible . . . was that even now, knowing the artifice, he yearned for her embrace.

"I can't," he said to Gupta, voice leaden with grief. He was speaking his own death sentence.

"I know," she said, resigned. "I knew. But I had to try."

There was not even resentment in her gaze. The expression was more . . . a sadness. They laughed together, the music twined together with such genuine intimacy that both stopped for a moment, both by surprise.

What a beautiful night, Terry thought. *What a lovely, lovely night.*

She doffed her cloak. Beneath it she wore a clinging white pantsuit, something of ritual purity.

"No man can kill a baboon his own size," she declared, as if reciting a manifesto. "Even if you filed down the nails and blunted its teeth. The full capacity of the human body for strength and speed is limited by our civilized rules. Long ago, in another land and time, a way was discovered to unleash this full potential. Every martial art, no matter how fierce, is only a pale shadow of this truth. The approach to the animal is perilous. Morality exists to blind us to our true natures."

"Murderers always justify their actions," Terry said. "Whatever war you've been fighting, these are innocent noncombatants. You're over the line. And I swore to protect people just like these. I forgot that for a while. Thanks for helping me remember, Indra."

She shook her head in disbelief.

Hannibal's eyes wandered.

Nicki was trembling, but managed to steady her voice. When she spoke, her voice dripped with caustic scorn, and a trace of the old Elizabethan accent. "I can't believe this dissembling harlot is wasting perfectly good air."

Gupta's answering smile was deadly cold. "You have spirit, girl, and if you are not cautious, that is all of you that will remain."

She turned back to Terry. "The only thing you have left me to do is to reveal unto Hannibal his true nature. And the only way I can do that is to render the man he respects most in all the world into meat. Animal draws animal. The sight will break him, and from that broken form I can rebuild. He will yield."

"Burn in hell," Olympia said.

Part of Terry wanted to warn her to silence. But most of him knew it was hopeless. They were all going to die.

"Yes, as will we all," Gupta replied, turning to her security men. "See!" Gupta screamed. "Witness what happens here."

Terry regarded her carefully. "Can I have a moment?"

Gupta bowed, gracious to the last. If one hunger was not to be filled, there would be another. "Yes. Of course."

He approached Olympia. Her lips trembled as she spoke.

"I've seen how you've changed," she said. "Nicki told me what you can do. Maybe . . ."

He shook his head. "Let's not kid ourselves. If she had any doubt at all, she'd never give me the slightest chance."

She sagged, then pulled herself up again. "Oh, God. What do we do?"

"Die well."

They kissed. There was a last time for everything. He went to Nicki. She peered up at him through her limp and ragged hair, tears streaking her face.

"Damn it," she muttered. "This isn't fair. It isn't fair."

"If something happens to me," Terry said. "If I don't make it through this, and somehow you do . . ."

The tears were streaming freely now, her face puffy and swollen.

"Terry . . ."

"Listen to me. I know what happened. That your father ran away from you, and Hannibal."

Her eyes widened. "You know?"

"I know. He was a weakling and a fool. If you make it out of here, no matter what happens to me, don't let it stop you from loving someone else."

Tears dripped down her cheeks, silvered her face. "It hurts too much."

"That's like saying we won't eat tonight because we'll only be hungry again tomorrow. Love is all that holds us together. You're the strongest one in your family. Your mother and brother will need you."

"It's not fair."

"It's not fair," he said. "Or unfair. It just is."

She glared. " 'Take her away; for she hath lived too long.' "

He had to smile a bit. Everyone finds their own defensive mechanisms in the face of oblivion, in the grip of fear. He had to admit that Nicki's were better than most. "What?"

"Kick that bitch's ass," she said.

He nodded. "I'll do my level best."

And finally, he went to Hannibal.

" 'Erry." The man knelt before the boy.

"I tried to protect you, little guy." Terry's eyes were misting, damn it. "I'm so sorry. I blew it. I don't know why these people want you. What they think you can do for them. But . . . try to do it. Please. It's going to be very, very bad if you don't."

"Love you, 'Erry," Hannibal said, and slipped something into Terry's hand. Their eyes locked, some communication beyond or beneath words alive in that clandestine gesture.

"Draw her a story," Hannibal whispered. "Good story."

For just a moment, there was something else in his eyes, a darkness blooming in the light like a rogue shadow. Then gone again.

He kissed Hannibal's forehead. "I love you, too."

Then Terry stood, and in so standing, prepared to die.

CHAPTER 50

"Oh Yama," asked Kali, "what are the limits placed on liberation?"

Yama replied: "My dark-skinned one: there is no limit placed on liberation. If one understands this, then even one with great karmic burden, if they are willing to let the fruits of ego die, may achieve muksha (liberation from the wheel of reincarnation) with the last breath."

—*The Yama Sutra*

Not an hour earlier, Pax had gone out into the snow. Where was the family? The girl? Pax liked the girl. Girl gave her treats, petted her, took care of her when the humans she lived with were gone. Played fetch with her even when the humans were there, but ignored Pax. Pax liked the girl better than she liked the humans whose house she usually slept in.

She barked. Nothing. Traveled in larger circles, following footprints. Nothing.

Then . . . she had cut across the original path of footprints Olympia and Hannibal had left fleeing from the Salvation Sanctuary. Smelled them both.

The woman! The boy! Pax bounded up and down and up and down, barking happily.

And she started following it. She was following the trail backward, because several men had cut across the trail in the other direction, obliterating it, and she was not a trained tracker. But she knew what she smelled, and what she smelled was the woman and the boy who lived with the girl. And that was good enough for Pax.

♦　♦　♦

The Geekmobile had pulled up on the hillside north of the main road, from where they were able to look down upon the compound. Geek had reconned the area using Google Earth, letting them pick out this location. They were peering down on the amphitheater in the northernmost edge of the Salvation Sanctuary. "What's going on down there?" Mark asked.

Lee peered through his binoculars. "It looks like Terry is about to fight somebody."

Mark grunted. "That . . . should be entertaining."

"It's a woman."

Pat's left eyebrow shot up. "That should be brief."

Geek chuckled. "A sexist bastard on top of everything else. Impressive."

"Just keeping it real."

"What do we do?" Lee asked.

"It seems designed to be a spectacle of some kind," Geek said, adjusting his binoculars. "Conveniently drawing all attention, one might say."

It was true: the guard staff was watching.

"What's our play?" Lee asked, and a bit of the old respect had returned to his voice.

"If we're going to do something," Mark said, "it should be now. It might be time to infiltrate and see about liberating those books. Geek, do your magic."

Then a familiar shape down near the fence caught his attention. "What in the hell?" Mark said. "I do believe I have seen that mutt before."

"What dog?" Pat asked, snatching the binoculars and peering.

"Big white spots . . ." Mark's eyes widened. "Shit, that's Pax!"

"You know that big bastard?"

"Big bitch, actually. Yeah, I'd know her anywhere. Don't you remember her from the party? What in the hell . . ."

"She belongs to the kid?" Geek asked.

"Might as well. Belongs to their neighbors. Kids ended up taking care of her half the time. Loves those kids, especially the little girl."

"So . . . what's she doing?"

"Looking for a way in. I think she's doing the same damned thing we're doing."

At last, after many false starts, Pax came to the place where a heavy tree branch jutted over the wall. She ran back and forth, sniffed the ground, and pawed in frustration.

"Why is the pooch stopping there?" Lee asked.

"Because . . . there's a tree near the fence. A branch. I can see it. I'm betting that's where Olympia . . ." Mark said.

"I think that's where she got out," Geek said. "Jumped down. And that means . . . that's where we can get in."

"Gentlemen," Mark said, "time to get hot. Geek, you stay up here with eyes on and stay on comms. Cover our egress. See if you can find us a different route out. Everyone, gear up and commo check. Roll in five."

"What's the plan?" Geek asked.

Mark grinned. "Plan A: we stealth in, cap the bad guys, snatch the good guys, liberate expensive books, be big damn heroes, and waste away in Margaritaville. Plan B: I think there's some hell to raise."

"Straight stealth sounds good to me. Raising hell might not be profitable," Lee said.

Pat Ronnell smiled merrily. He opened a black nylon bag and pulled out a 30-06 scoped deer rifle. "In my life, hell has always been its own reward."

◆　◆　◆

Terry circled Madame Gupta. She stood calm, balanced, not even bothering to turn to face him. Attack her back? Somehow he couldn't bring himself to do it.

But when he faced her again he slid closer and closer, her calm, unmoving form as still as the pause between two heartbeats. She closed her eyes.

"Begin," she said.

So he did. Without sound, without telegraphing, Terry threw the fastest punch of his entire life at her throat, such a blur that he barely saw it himself.

And in the next moment, Terry lay sprawled on the ground, nose broken, head ringing. He inhaled and coughed blood. Madame Gupta stood over him, peaceful as a nun at prayer.

"This can only end one way," she said. "You will tell the boy to do as I wish, stand together with me to help him, or you will die. I will not let your selfishness interfere with his destiny."

Pain was an old friend of Terry's, but the shock was newer. Even with his enhanced skills, he had no idea what had just happened. Fear washed through him, but he did not judge or resist it, and it receded. He spit blood again. "You don't give a shit about his destiny. You have another play in mind."

"And what is that?" she asked.

"You're killing people. Somehow. The boy is a part of it. Somehow."

She smiled. "Do you know how insane that sounds?"

"Do you know that isn't a denial?"

"Stand up," she said. "The lesson has just begun."

Grappling range. Striking didn't work. But if he could close with her, his superior strength could . . .

It was like trying to squeeze a handful of Jell-O. The pressure and speed and strength just seemed to pass through her, and she simply could not be thrown, or locked, or swept, or choked. Whatever he did he ended up slamming into the ground until it felt as if his entire body was a single enormous bruise.

She was killing him by stages. With effortless precision she attacked joints, then muscles, and then nerves. Shocking and shaking him, driving him to his knees and then throwing him to his back, numb and then scaling the heights of agony, blind and then opening doors of perception so that he could see more clearly just how hopeless it all was.

Taking him apart . . .

Some assembly required.

"This is tragic," she said. "You are by far the best student I've ever had. You see, don't you?"

She leaned closer, peering into his bloody eyes.

The snow was falling again, diffusing the light. The air around her seemed almost to glow.

"Get up. Get up. I would have more."

There was a hunger beyond fleshly passion in her eyes. And he saw something that no one else had ever seen in this bitter, terrifying harpy— she was alone. Terribly alone. No one touched her. There was a sensual quality to her motion, her cant of eyes and lips, but in combative motion she was so terribly precise as to be almost insectile.

And simultaneously yearning.

In another world . . . it seemed to say. A desire, a burning need to have an equal, a mate. Even for a moment.

He pushed himself to standing again. Summoned his strength yet again.

She nodded approval. "Good. You have much strength. Many skills."

"Because of you." He forced formality into his voice. "Because of my beliefs, my honor, I cannot yield."

She shook her head. "You foolish man. Did you read tales of knights and maidens as a boy? I see that in you. Protecting the weak." Her expression softened. "If only there had been more men like you, there would be fewer women like me."

Terry smiled. "There are no women like you."

Something sparkled in the corner of her eye. What was that? A tear?

"I see you," she whispered. "No lies. No games. I set you free, would have made you a king. A god. And you choose to be a man. This boy's father. This woman's man. I see it."

Was she crying?

"No one ever wanted me," she said. "Protected me. I had to protect myself, can you understand?"

"I understand," he said, spitting blood again. "Neither of us can help being who we are."

"I'll make you another offer." It was a plea. "Be with me, and the family lives. Can't you find it in your heart?"

There it was, her eyes as hot and wide as if she were an open furnace, an unshielded reactor. In that moment, if he had spoken, all might have changed. But he waited too long, and the door slammed shut.

"No," she said and pulled back. "I beg no man. You have made your choice." Her voice echoed through the lightly falling snow. "He has made his choice!" she screamed.

"If I have to die," he said fervently, pushing himself back up. "Let it be like this. Please. Show me the dance."

Hannibal stood, staring, small hands fisted at his sides, breathing like a steam engine.

"Hani?" Nicki asked.

He ignored her, eyes wide.

♦ ♦ ♦

Tony Killinger watched, astonished, excited . . . and a bit jealous. The erotic connection between these two was glaringly obvious, and forced him back to memories of his own private encounters with Indra. She had shunned him, and in his heart he now understood why.

He had not been worthy. A lioness needs a lion, and even if not at her level . . . this man was that.

Tony hated him, and envied him, at the same moment.

Gupta and the soldier seemed to have moved to another phase. And if he was not worthy, was not equal, still he was closer to her level than any man had ever been. She had absolute timing, baffling speed, and perfect technique, with a feminine flow that made ballet dancers resemble concrete blocks thumping down a hill. Killinger had seen her move many times . . . but never anything like this. It was so embarrassingly intimate he felt like he was watching homemade porn.

Just die, why don't you, you bastard. Just die.

♦ ♦ ♦

Blinded by pain and blood, Terry fell again. Struggled to rise, and could not. She approached. Bent close, so that others could not hear. And when she spoke, there was in her voice something that in another woman might have seemed like desperation.

"I say to you what I have never said to another man, and may never say again. Stop this. Be with me. The woman could be allowed to live. The family you love could survive."

An ache in her voice. *You love them. You do not love me. But you could be with me, and in time, love might grow. It might.*

However small a chance that might be . . . it is worth seeking.

He ignored her request. "What was that move? Never seen anything like that."

"It was not a 'move,'" she said, exasperated. "I simply flow with the energy. *You* create my technique."

"Can you do it again?"

"I do it every time," she said, irritation growing. "It does not seem the same, because the moment is never the same. Because you cannot repeat what you did. How could you know what you did? You don't even know who you are."

Do you know what you are, Indra Gupta? he wondered. *Do you? Or has clarity become its own trap?*

"No." And he knew in his heart that it was true. "Please," he said. "Once more."

"You are magnificent," Gupta said.

Hannibal's eyes gleamed. Nicki looked at him, and at Terry. And back again.

Terry was limping now, and the expression on Gupta's face was one of sympathy. His courage had won her heart. He stood. Breathed deeply. And slid his right side, his strong side, forward.

Madame Gupta shook her head, just a little. If one hadn't been watching closely, had not been in the tunnel of focus that connected the two, it would have been easy to miss.

Regret, a bit of genuine human emotion.

And he came at her, in a move that was glorious and balletic, a spinning kick.

And she leaned back as if she had all the time in the world, so that he missed her by a millimeter. Then, as he suspected would happen, she demonstrated her own mastery of kicking arts. Her own leg flashed up. He raised a hand in weak defense—

It was the hand holding Hannibal's Christmas gift, the silver Uni multi-color pen. A special edition, crafted in steel. And her own force drove its point into her thigh. He wrenched it out, and stabbed her twice more, a blur faster than a sewing machine needle at full speed.

Thank you, Father Geek. The South African killing art: Piper. Blur-fast, like running her leg under a pneumatic drill.

Stab stab stab, three blows in a half-second.

Pain, shock, and for the first time, fear entered her eyes. Gupta took a step back, and Terry leaped in. She raised her hands defensively, technique and delicate psychic balances confused.

Terry saw every defensive motion, and instead of trying to pierce her defenses, he *attacked* them, stabbing her again and again. He was, in that moment, not the man he had been, or that he wished ultimately to be.

He was merely . . . appropriate. What was needed in that moment.

◆ ◆ ◆

Tony stood with his mouth hanging open, utterly shocked by what he was seeing. Maureen Skotak swung her rifle up, aiming at the two of them, but was unable to fire. The two combatants were a vortex of motion, moving far too fast to shoot one without risk to the other.

And before Skotak could find a point of aim, her chest exploded with blood and she dropped to her knees, an almost comical expression of surprise on her face.

Tony stared for a moment but then his paralysis broke and he dove for cover, yelling into the radio clipped to his collar.

Madame Gupta screamed, hands clasped to her wounds, blood oozing from between clinched fingers. "Help me!"

Roger Shilling, one of the two men who had tried to kidnap Nicki, raised his sidearm and drew a bead on Terry—

Then his head snapped sideways, so rapidly it was as if he'd been hit in the temple with a golf club. Red mist sprayed back, marking the bullet's exit path. The sound of the rifle shot came a moment later as two more guards flanking Olympia dropped, twin muzzle flashes sparking near the wall.

◆ ◆ ◆

Two men ran from the northwest section of wall, near the woods, assault rifles shouldered and pivoting as they approached. Three more shots rang out, dropping a guard on the far side of the amphitheater. Tony crouched, confused and momentarily frozen with shock. For the first time in a very long time, he felt an unaccustomed emotion: real fear.

◆ ◆ ◆

Hannibal was starting to see what Terry saw. Gupta had thought to teach him . . . and oh boy, was it working! When Hannibal briefly closed his eyes, the darkness swirled with light and heat. Like a bear stirring after a winter's hibernation, something massive and primal was awakening within him.

A cloud of different specks of light, like stars in a nebula, fractured into a thousand pieces.

Nerves damaged, or transmitting imperfectly. Emotional turmoil, turning his light inward.

All the darkness and dysfunction . . . but light flowing between them.

Coalescing into a figure . . . of himself. Speaking to him.

Wake up.

Hannibal blinked.

◆ ◆ ◆

Terry had lost his advantage. Splashed with her own blood, Madame Gupta was damaged, but had regained enough of her poise that even the blend of all Terry's martial arts skills and the improvised Piper knife attack could not pierce her defenses . . .

In one incredible moment, he attacked a dozen times in two seconds. He never saw the defensive movements and yet somehow she deflected or avoided every one.

Then slowly, dreadfully slowly, she moved. As if, with her energies gathered, she had all the time in the world—

Crack!

They all heard the sound of the shattering humerus, and Terry dropped to the ground, engulfed in a world of pain. When Gupta spoke, it was not a woman's voice. Or a man's voice. It was something else, beyond each, channeling its way through her. Echoed from the walls and mountainsides, a primal shriek.

"Fool!" she shrieked. "You could have had everything. Everything! Instead, I will give you a kingdom of pain."

◆ ◆ ◆

"*Razor, set.*"

"*Cowboy, set.*"

"*Nomad, set.*"

"*Geek, no change from up here. Six armed tangos. Friendlies in sight.*"

◆ ◆ ◆

Mark listened to the headset's whispers, then returned attention to the tableau at hand. He had quickly realized there was no easy way into the compound. The instant he'd seen Terry getting his ass kicked he'd made the call for plan B. Targets had been assigned. Mark and Lee had been moving as a buddy team and were within fifty meters of the wall, taking advantage of the long shadows as floodlights from atop the main building reflected and diffracted from the broken glass set in the top of the wall.

They were kneeling by trees and each had a guard in the sights of their AR-15s. Pat was farther back, lying beneath bushes. He had watch of the area, including an armed woman who looked like she was in charge of something. She was already in his scope, the 30-06 round chambered in the expensive hunting rifle.

"Nomad, this is Razor. We go on you."

"Roger. Shooting in three, two . . ."

Pat hit his first target, dropping the woman clean. As he racked the bolt he saw Mark's and Lee's targets drop, controlled pairs aimed center mass. Now they were up and moving in.

Pat picked up his next target inside the amphitheater. The last two were outside the amphitheater, pistols up and aimed at Mark and Lee as they tried to come to save their boss. They died never realizing Pat had already planned their deaths before he fired the first shot. Pulling the trigger was just the confirmation, a smooth, intimate gesture during which Pat had his entire being focused on the person in his sight picture. And then ended him.

His comrades were moving forward as he watched the old woman make a weird shuffle kick at Terry. Pat didn't worry about that. Mark and Lee would take care of the situation down there. There was one last guy, a tall black man who looked like he might have been armed, who had dove down between stone seats. Pat scanned for him.

Calm, he felt that sense of power as he controlled the life and death of all in his view. He had righteous targets and his brothers were trusting him to do whatever he decided. All was good and proper in his world.

He died as 5.56mm rounds ripped into his body, puncturing like ice picks on the way in and blowing baby fist–sized hunks of meat on the way out.

♦　♦　♦

Mark's team didn't know two things. One, Tony had outfitted his reaction squad in Level III body armor and helmets under their winter coats ever since the local area went into emergency conditions. Even if the authorities didn't twig on them, they knew they would be a target for looters or people seeking sanctuary, and Georgia residents tended to be armed. Unlike the regular group that Tony used for protecting Madame Gupta and maintained a lower profile, these guards were intended to provide overwhelming response when needed.

The other was they had modern military optics cantilevered from their forehead mounts on the helmets. As the setting sun cloaked the small valley, it also let the guards use infrared to sight in on Pat from several hundred meters away. The guards had come over the opposite side of the amphitheater. Pat had been focused on Tony and never saw the reinforcements.

The other half of the react squad arrived from the direction of the admin building. Lee was the first to respond, firing center mass. The trauma plates stopped the rounds even as they returned fire. Lee was struck multiple times even as Mark dove to the ground, seeking some sort of cover. The next fusillade hit his right arm halfway between elbow and shoulder. His rifle dropped with a clatter. He tried to reach across his waist with his left arm for his pistol as the three guards duckwalked toward him.

"Stop!" Gupta called, blood dripping down her face. "Halt this. Capture them. We may need more meat."

She stood over Hannibal, heaving for breath. Turned to Olympia. "I think we are ready to begin. Don't you? Take this garbage."

♦ ♦ ♦

"Shit," Mark said. When the three guards facing him kept breathing, he knew Pat wasn't. A glance told him Lee was gone. Mark rolled onto his back and stuck his hands in the air, the right one sagging at an angle as blood drenched his shirt. It was a through-and-through and had missed the bone, but it had stopped him long enough to lose the fight. He just hoped he hadn't lost the war for himself and Terry.

The tall security alpha was on his feet and giving orders. Mark was disarmed and driven to his knees, hands behind his head as blood continued to stain his shirt. As the other three combat-loaded guards came into the amphitheater, one of the first three pulled open a small trauma kit and tied off Mark's bicep using an Israeli pressure bandage. His hand was numb with sharp needle sensations in his fingertips. Probably nerve damage, he guessed. Mark recalculated the odds. He carefully complied with Tony's orders, knowing he had no options at this point.

Mark saw Terry and nodded, hands behind his head. "I'm here to rescue you."

"Aren't you a little short for a storm trooper?" Terry said.

"Shut up, Carl." Both men grinned. Inside joke, not for civilians. *Another fine mess.*

"Fancy seeing you here," Terry said.

"You look like shit."

"You should feel it from my side."

Ho, ho, ho. Sometimes, macho bullshit was all that kept the screams at bay.

They were prodded along, Terry leaning heavily against Mark.

"Who *is* this bitch?"

Tony Killinger stomped on the side of Mark's leg. The crunch of breaking bone was horrific. Mark crumpled to the ground, clutching his knee.

"Y'all be mindful now," Tony said. "No way to talk about a lady."

◆ ◆ ◆

Pain such as she had not known since the horrible days in London coursed through her body as they descended into the mine, toward the laboratory within. Although she was strong on the outside, within her, Indra Gupta was not the goddess Shakti, or Kali, or even their human equivalents . . . but merely the girl again.

Where was Daddy? Where was Mommy? Where was someone to take her hand . . . ?

That voice was another, younger woman's. A voice from another life, and she banished it.

The man was hurt. She had broken his weapon, his right arm, damaged his right leg. He was done. But his woman and her children comforted and supported him, helped him below. And his companion, the large man, had clearly risked his life for friendship.

What of her own family?

The ones she had recruited from the prison. They guarded their captives, as they had been directed. But something had changed. Their belief in her invulnerability had been shaken. They watched her with caution, whispering among themselves.

Not one of them offered her help, an arm. A smile.

"You all right?" Killinger asked as the elevator reached the lower level. Meaning: *how's my meal ticket?*

That was the expression, wasn't it? She frightened them. She promised and provided rewards. They followed her. But if she was weak, even for a moment, like any school of sharks they would turn on her when they smelled blood in the water. Kill them all, and take the books in the library, and burn everything she had built to the ground.

She had sent away the fools who had honestly believed in her. And kept the animals who knew what she was, and who she had been fool enough to mistake for family.

What the Dorsey woman had was family. What Terry had chosen was family.

She, Indra Gupta, had created nothing but a pack.

She was torn. Wished that she could have time to think about what was happening, consider it.

Was it possible . . . just possible that she had been wrong?

It was too late now. She wanted to ask this woman, for whom the man would die:

Is this love?

♦   ♦   ♦

Exhaustion and fear had no limits, knew no depths.

Bleeding, broken, and under guard, Olympia and her shattered clan descended into the mine. When darkness yielded to incandescent light and a half-deserted laboratory, she was too tired to be surprised. "Adam Ludlum's original notes were quite thorough," Madame Gupta's voice echoed against the stone. "He first revealed his abilities in a Faraday cage, isolated from electromagnetic radiation. It was theorized that such radiation somehow blocks the ability. That this is why we no longer live in the time of miracles. Down here, three hundred feet beneath the surface, it is even easier to isolate and express the capacity."

Who was this Adam Ludlum? How did he relate to the rest of this? Her mind was so fuzzy with pain that she couldn't make sense of it all.

There were only three technicians to augment the four surviving guards. Gloved, Gupta's minions began to hook Hannibal up to the machines. His eyes were wide and staring.

They locked with Olympia's in a way she had never seen, pleading with her. "What are we doing here?" Olympia asked. She noticed that the blood had already crusted on Gupta's wounds. Oh, God. This woman wasn't even human. She couldn't be hurt. Couldn't be stopped.

They were doomed. Terry had fought a long, hard, impossible battle to win a single moment's advantage, and had failed. All was lost.

Gupta took her arm, and guided Olympia to a side room, an office with a desk, a sink with a sharps disposal unit, a leather chair, and a table suitable for medical evaluations. Gupta switched on an overhead fluorescent light. With three fingers like spikes she pushed Olympia up against the wall.

"You have one chance," Gupta said, as if reading her mind. "One chance to save your family. You will convince your boy to do as I ask."

"I can't," Olympia said. "He can't hear me the way other children do.

He won't just follow orders . . ." Not quite truth, not quite a lie. She prayed Gupta wouldn't know the difference.

"You are his mother, the woman the man I had chosen chose, and placed above me. You are a family. You have this thing called 'love.' Show me that you are worthy of his choice, their love." Blink-quick Gupta slapped her face, and Olympia staggered back. The slap was not hard, but it was shocking, more an electrical jolt than a blow. Numbing. Disorienting at a time when she desperately needed her every sense.

"Do not tell me what doctors say. We are not mere minds and bodies. If we are, then he is useless to me, and you will all die. Him last, watching you and your daughter die first."

Olympia's eyes burned with tears.

Gupta came closer. "Pray that the real Hannibal is in there. Somewhere. That what we see and hear of him is like a voice from the bottom of a well, distorted by echoes. Speak to him. Do this, do your best, and you may survive this. But do not attempt to thwart me."

Sobs bubbled up in her throat until she lost control and babbled out her terror. "What is it you want me to do? What is it you really want him to do? Tell me the truth, or I can't help you."

Gupta was regaining her poise. Regaining the false *good mother* air. "Fair enough. Fair enough. You are an intelligent woman. A reporter."

"Yes."

"You stand at the heart of the most important story in the history of mankind. We are changing the world."

"You?"

The corners of Gupta's mouth curled up into a death-head smile beneath the bloodied skin. "Haven't you been reading the papers?"

A worm of horrible suspicion was working its way to the surface. "You? How? It's poison . . . or microwaves . . ."

Her mind swirled. And yet, on some level she had known. Had known since Maria's death. And she'd known that she knew, and that she was keeping the knowledge from percolating fully into her conscious mind. It was just too big, too frightening, too impossible.

"There is a truth beyond truths," Gupta said. "A reality beyond realities. And one is the perception of separateness. The mystic Savagi, here in the most sacred, the most valuable book in the world, wrote of this in his divine *Transformations*."

"I don't understand." *We know of no mechanism precise and powerful enough to accomplish this.*

"You needn't. All you need to know is that the world is not ending. Only the lives of a few of its billions. And from the death of those few, comes a new life for me and mine."

"What?" Olympia blinked. Something was lurking within Gupta's words, just out of conscious perception, a shape in the fog.

"Those few control the financial heart of a world. Money is the blood of the modern world, and I will in one stroke undo centuries of pain."

"How can you do that? What would give you that power?"

"All you need to know is that after today the deaths stop. There is no apocalypse, except that which yawns for you and yours. And that if you help me take this last step, your family will be richly rewarded. With far more than just your lives."

"What do you want him to do?"

The skull shape disappeared, replaced by the kindly mother. "Look at a computer screen. Drink a chocolate milk."

"Chocolate milk. What's in it?" Olympia asked. "Don't lie to me, please."

Gupta examined her shrewdly. "Yes. All right. Mixed into the cocoa is a mild hypnotic, something to help him relax. More harmless than the medications given to children with ADD . . . but it will help him focus. Allow him to do what he must do. Your next decision will lift your family to heights of power or sink them to depths of pain. We see in this moment. We will speak to each other as two women. Two mothers."

◆　◆　◆

Indra Gupta was lying. Olympia could feel it. What had the man said? A possible way to kill at a distance? That the ultimate weapon might well be the human mind itself, rather than artificial devices it could create. The mind. "Entanglement." And . . . DNA. How hard would it be to get DNA samples from twenty or thirty powerful men? Blood. Hair. Skin. Saliva. Semen. And if you couldn't get the sample, you just kept them off the list.

Easy peasy.

Her mind was racing, trying to understand. Running out of time. "You are a mother?"

"The mother to a new world. And in that new world a child like Hannibal will be elevated above all. And as he is your son, you, Olympia Dorsey, will stand with him."

"And you want him to . . . make contact with these men and women. And then?"

Gupta looked at her almost pityingly. "Awaken them from the dream of life."

A stone rolled onto her chest. Gupta wanted to use Hannibal to kill people? But how? Her mind offered no answer. Yet, Olympia believed the woman with all her soul. The air near Gupta vibrated with the truth of her words.

"Oh, my God."

"Yes. Now. Parents must awaken, if their children would be safe. Within the dream is morality. The universe does not care. If you would have him slumber a little longer, you must act. He could be a great man. A *whole* man. I will teach him secrets undreamed. You would be mother to a young god. Or you can watch these men who sought to save you die, and your daughter die, screaming your name. And then you will die, in front of your son. The choice is yours."

She leaned close. Her eyes were as bright as coals. "I will drag Hannibal out of his cocoon and splinter your bones in front of him. Do not test me."

A contest of wills. Olympia was the first to look away. If she said yes . . . they might live. But at what cost? Could Hannibal survive such horror? Could his soul? The world spun. She heard herself say: "Take me to my son."

She was escorted back out. Examining each face she passed in turn. Seeking a way out of the trap. Seeing nothing except the overhead light tubes, the abandoned computer stations, the rock walls that had once seemed so exciting and mysterious, and now seemed to be the very gates of hell.

Terry and his friend Mark slumped against the wall, battered and broken and heavily guarded. No help there.

"Mom," Nicki said. "Did she hurt you?"

"No," she said.

"Whose blood is on your cheek?"

Olympia stopped, breathing slowly. Gears turning behind closed eyes. *My cheek? The slap? Blood on Gupta's hand . . .*

Her own blood.

And . . . a door opened.

Bless you, Sloan. Bless you, darling Nicki. Bless that bearded geek at the White House briefing.

She kissed her daughter. Went to Hannibal. He stood in his dirty, torn jeans, and his soiled denim jacket, with his eyes rolled up, stemming from side to side, as if desperately seeking shelter in some internal hidey-hole.

"Hani," she whispered to her son. "If you've ever heard me, hear me now. Do what they tell you to do."

"Do it?" Something touched his eyes. Fear? Hunger?

"But first," she said, "give Mommy a kiss."

Hannibal's lips touched her bloody cheek.

♦ ♦ ♦

The bad man named Tony guided Hannibal to a seat in front of the computer. The computer where, not too long before, he had watched Serge hiding among the soccer balls. Back when he had thought these were nice people. Madame Gupta was pretending to be his friend again. "You are the most powerful boy I've ever met. Perhaps that anyone has ever met. I know what you want, and what you need."

Liar, liar, pants on fire.

She stroked his brow with the back of a brown hand. He wanted to bite it.

No. Wait. Soon.

"Give me what is mine, and I will reciprocate. No harm will come to those you love, and whose only sin is loving you. And all I want you to do is follow the threads. Connect with each of them. That is all you have to do."

One of the technicians gave her a glass of chocolate milk. She, in turn, handed it to Hannibal.

He turned, looked at his mother, whose eyes were wide with horror.

She shook her head. *No.*

It's all right, Mommy, he said in silence.

Hani can do this.

Hannibal's eyes were wide. His mind was wide. The world within his mind a nest of broken links. Tangled wiring. Messages using redundant pathways to communicate meaning.

He knew he had whispered something to his monkey friend, Serge. Knew what had been whispered to him, just below the threshold of consciousness.

Die for me. That was what he had whispered. Serge had heard. And then . . . Serge had not been there. He had not realized that, the memory hidden even from himself.

But now he knew. Somehow, they had made him hurt Serge.

He saw a universe of energy, infinite fluxing fields and in the midst of those fields, a dozen threads. Running through a profusion of living beings, billions of tiny faces, connecting to twelve very special men and women.

Hannibal licked his lips. Followed the blood and the coded information as it entered his body. Broken down by juices in the mouth? Crossed the blood-brain barrier where? Another thread, joining the twelve . . .

Gupta herself.

And he veered away from the twelve, gained fire, and headed straight toward her.

Die for me.

♦　♦　♦

Gupta's smile wavered. And then . . . the muscles in her face cramped, hard.

"What?" She moaned, holding her head in her hands.

Hannibal turned and looked directly at her. "You shouldn't have hurt my mommy."

Gupta's gaze went from Hannibal's eyes to a fleck of blood on his lips. To Olympia's cheek. To the blood on her own hands. Her blood.

For all her planning, all her care . . . blinded by pain and rage, she had made a single, horrible mistake.

"Stop! Stop!" she screamed and then pain overwhelmed thought and her hands slapped the sides of her head. The security men were staring at her, not at Hannibal.

And then—the lights went out, leaving the mine in total, terrifying darkness.

Gupta shrieked and fell to the ground, rolling and shrieking inarticulately, vomiting out a flow of meaningless syllables, agonized glossolalia.

She could think, barely. But could no longer form words.

♦　♦　♦

Once Hannibal started killing, he could not stop. The breath exhaled by the security team and by the technicians contained cells from the linings of their lungs, millions of expelled motes of flesh. Something Gupta had not considered.

No one could think of everything. And no one could have known just how deep Hannibal's well of capacity might be once awakened.

Hannibal had inhaled those cells with every breath, and they were the key to the DNA of every human being in that underground bunker. In his mind they were like strands of an infinite spider web connecting all the world. He followed the strands through his personal night, found them, gripped them, and twisted them.

All around him the dark swarmed with screams of horror and pain.

The lights flickered back to life. The boy stood, smiling like some kind of blood-maddened animal, hands outstretched, fingers outstretched as if playing a harp, as the guards and technicians writhed in agony, dying.

Olympia shook him. "Hannibal!" she screamed. "Stop it! Stop it now."

"All die, Mommy," he said placidly. "All have to die."

Terry and Nicki and Olympia surrounded Hannibal, hugging and kissing him, whispering, doing all they could to drag him back from the abyss. "Come back, Hani," Nicki said. "You have to come back to us."

"All die. All die. All die . . ."

"Hannibal," Terry said, his voice soothing. "There are lines you can't get back across. Trips you don't want to take. Don't do this."

Hannibal's eyes rolled down, focused on Terry's face. His narrow chest fluttered like hummingbird wings beneath his soiled shirt.

"Listen to me," Terry said. He paused. "Listen to your father."

"Daddy?" Hannibal said.

"For as long as you want me."

His eyes were rolled up, exposing the sclera. Just white. Olympia kissed his ear and whispered to him. "Your house, remember, Hannibal? You've made that house over and over, again and again. It has everything you've ever seen or thought in it, and everything you love. We're there, too. We can all be there, together." She glanced at Terry. He nodded.

Hannibal's lips quivered, and then tears broke from his eyes in a vast fountain. "Mommy. I love you. Daddy. I missed you so much. Nicki. My Nicki."

They held each other.

Then . . .

◆　◆　◆

The emergency lights cycled with red and white glare, revolving and flashing in the darkness.

Mark knelt over Tony, who drooled blood from ears and mouth, mewling like half-crushed roadkill. Tony laughed, a single pain-filled barking sound. "Now . . . ain't this a pickle?" he said.

"For Lee, you bastard," Mark replied, and hit him once more, in the throat. Tony made ugly sounds, his heels drumming against the ground, and then was still.

"Lee?" Terry asked.

"Bought it."

"What about Pat?"

"He bought it, too." Mark grunted. "But I didn't like him." He looked up at the lights. "I think Geek cut those lights."

"Little bastard is good."

Madame Gupta lay half-curled into a fetal ball. She looked small, and weak, and shattered. And for the first time . . . old.

"I see now . . ." she whispered. And she was crying, the tears welling into a river. "Shiva. Shakti. I see." She looked at him, eyes already dimming, life draining away with the blood that seeped from every orifice. She looked up at him, and her lips, wet with blood, curled into the beginnings of a smile.

"Love the boy. Love the woman. There is only . . ."

"There is only Shiva," he whispered. "And Shakti. In all their forms. You freed me."

From some inner well of strength, she managed a smile. "Love me . . . just a little?"

He cradled her head in his arms, smoothed her brown skin with his fingertips. Their skin, so much alike. Such different paths to the same place. Awareness. It was never, ever too late.

"I always have." He traced her hair with his fingertips. "Through all time. I've loved you all my life."

He kissed her forehead softly as she exhaled one final time.

Terry sighed, and set her head down. He rose, and limped over to Olympia.

"Are you all right?"

"Now. I think. Your friends . . . they did this? They saved us?"

"Wasn't the plan," Mark said, and he glared at Terry. "But . . . I was just being neighborly."

She threw her arms around Mark's thick neck and kissed him gently. "Thank you. So very much."

"Pleasure was mine," he said.

Olympia peeled herself away, and her family snared her in a group hug. "Nicki. Hani. What happened? Do I even want to know?" She didn't wait for an answer, but grabbed Hannibal tightly. "Don't ever scare me like that again!"

The group hug broke.

"What do we do now?" Terry asked.

"I thought maybe a trip to the library," Mark said.

And despite his pain, and the carnage that surrounded them all, Terry managed to laugh.

♦   ♦   ♦

Later that night, there was a terrible fire in the Salvation Sanctuary. And by the time the engines and firemen arrived, the entire facility was deserted, but for the charred and broken bodies of the dead.

CHAPTER 51

In the final analysis, the most pressing questions would probably never be answered. Burned bodies were recovered from the smoking wreckage and autopsied, conjectures had been made, and theories proposed.

The deaths of seventy-two famous and infamous men and women around the world had been attributed to a variety of causes. There were still questions about whether the thousands promised had actually perished. There were rumors, and assumptions, but in the end no one actually knew.

Why the bizarre string of deaths had ended no one could say. Both intelligence agencies and megachurches claimed responsibility, but whether prayer or spy craft had brought the world back from the edge of disaster was a matter that might never be resolved.

The answer whispered most frequently among those who knew of the events at the Salvation Sanctuary? The Israelis, who had lost their minister of defense. The destruction had been too clean, too complete, too ruthless for anyone else.

Don't mess with Mossad, it was said, although Tel Aviv disavowed all knowledge of any deadly actions in the Georgia mountains. *Right,* the world winked. And they don't have nukes, either.

Slowly, the world's financial markets tiptoed back from the abyss. Fortunes had been made and lost, and the existence of odd sell or buy orders, however many tens of millions of dollars they represented, or how slender the margins on which they had been purchased, were simply additional mysteries, topics of backroom conversations on Wall Street and little more. Forensic accounting would be unwinding the threads for years. It was possible that conclusions would never be reached at all.

Life went on.

CHAPTER 52

NEW YEAR'S DAY

♦

Dobbins Air Reserve Base was located north of Atlanta off U.S. 41, acres of low buildings and concrete landing strips surrounded by commercial and residential districts.

The front gate slid open, and a three-vehicle convoy exited. A Humvee, a three-ton truck, and a bulky green jeep. They merged onto Route 41, picked up speed, and disappeared into the flow. Then . . . police cars closed in from multiple sides, lights flashing, halting traffic. Blue windbreakers emblazoned with various white letters swooped in behind the body-armored police. Hands were in the air, then on the hoods and sides of the vehicles.

Two men were watching the convoy from a rooftop a half-mile away as all within were arrested. One man had been at the wheel of a specially configured, wheelchair-accessible SUV, and the other beside him had plastic casts on his left arm and leg and walked with crutches

Father Geek sighed, lowering his binoculars. "It would have worked," he said.

Mark nodded, and lit a thin black Cuban cigar. It had gone out again. Damn it, the things just wouldn't stay lit.

"Yep," he said. "Sure would. Pity someone dropped a dime."

"Who would do such a thing?" Geek asked. They maintained straight faces for a moment, and then dissolved in deep laughter. Geek had made sure plenty of information, much of it classified, ended up at a half-dozen different agencies. O'Shay hadn't stopped being a shitbird after Fallujah. All it took was someone to put it together and wrap it up with a big anonymous bow.

"So . . . what do we do now?"

"I hear Mexico's nice this time of year."

CHAPTER 53

On New Year's Day President Correll addressed a joint session of Congress, her first since sequestering herself. She seemed gaunt but determined, optimistic and simultaneously cautious, asking that the world pull together, as it had through so many previous emergencies, and asking that political rivals across the aisle work together for the common good. Her words were greeted by thunderous applause. The scene dissolved into hand-shaking and back-slapping, and there wasn't a dry eye in the house.

Both MSNBC and Fox promised to strive to be more fair and balanced in the coming year, and that behavior lasted almost exactly a month, when new tax proposals hit the Senate floor, and Rachel Maddow and Sean Hannity sharpened their knives.

Human beings are resilient, if nothing else.

CHAPTER 54

The surf had been warm in Santa Tia, and the children who lived in this village nestled between the warm ocean and the foothills of the Sierra Madre Oriental spent their days helping their fathers with the fishing boats, or the farming, or the gathering, or their mothers with the thousand small tasks of mending, sorting, cleaning, and gathering that comprised life in Santa Tia.

There was electricity in Santa Tia between the hours of one and ten in the evening, but no cellular or phone service. No paved roads within fifty miles.

But it was known for its unspoiled beauty, and the fishing, of course! The bountiful catches of dorado, Spanish mackerel, roosterfish, red snapper, and Crevalle jacks were known all along the coast. Sometimes, but not often, tourists braved the rutted roads, or came in motorboats to fish here, and the people were polite, and friendly, happy to take their money, but happier still to see the *norteamericano* tourists return to their own homes.

The village was some miles south of the place rumored to be built around the grave of the first Spanish soldiers to have been killed by Aztecs. There was an old and honored tradition of repelling outsiders here, and although the fires no longer burned so brightly, the ashes were not yet cool.

Whatever storms of change had engulfed the surrounding world had not touched Santa Tia. In fact the inhabitants had been unaware that any such chaos had ever existed at all, no aspect of it influencing the life that had been very much the same as their ancestors had faced, until a jeep containing a man, a woman, two children, and a large spotted dog had pushed through the jungle almost a year before.

They had asked few questions about the newcomers, one of whom had

been known to them almost six years earlier, during an action where guerrillas loyal to a local warlord had been overcome by gringo soldiers, one
of whom had sullied the dignity of the daughter of the head of a neighbor-
ing village. It was whispered that the *norteamericano* had been a man of
honor, and had delivered the transgressor to the villagers for justice. The
people of Santa Tia remembered that story, and appreciated what it meant
about the character of the man who now came to them for shelter.

Whether that concerned the tall, cool-eyed black man who was welcomed into the village, none of the children could say. They could say that
the daughter, Nee-kee, was good at games and with the enormous dog they
called Pax, and that the boy, Hhan-ee-bhal, spoke little but ran and swam
and jumped with a joy and facility they had rarely seen. They called him
"Little Sunshine" for his smile, a name that seemed to thrill him.

The woman called "Oh" became a schoolteacher in the village, and was
excellent, and kind, and became a favorite of the other women, who in
time wove for her a marriage dress, and celebrated and sang all night the
evening she and the man exchanged vows at the water's edge.

The man had many skills related to hunting and fishing, and joined in
the affairs of the village with great enthusiasm. The days were for adult
work and children's play, the nights for children's rest and adult conversation . . . and love.

The man was strong, stronger than any man any of them had ever seen.
He worked with the other men in the fields, and sometimes went out on the
fishing boats, where he pulled nets or rigged sail tirelessly. He mentored the
village boys, teaching them wrestling and stick-fighting, and could beat any
three of the village men without harming them, such that all laughed when
the scrambling and tumbling and thumping was concluded.

In time, the village elders brought him into their circle, into the huts
where there was talking until late, to the smell of tobacco and other smoke,
and he told them of wars and death and absent friends, and sometimes
wept, but more often smiled, as if in the midst of a great cleansing.

The family smiled much, and seemed to love each other even more, and
for the people of Santa Tia, that was all they needed to know.

◆ ◆ ◆

In October an eighty-foot sailboat pulled up next to the dock built below
the house, crewed by four and containing three passengers: two white
men, one in a wheelchair, and the other upon crutches, and a round brown
woman with warm eyes who pushed the man in the wheelchair and

touched him constantly. They were friendly, and gave candy to children, and were welcomed by the family.

◆ ◆ ◆

They stood together on the deck of the yacht, which had been rather cheekily renamed the Sanctuary.

Terry had never thought to see his friends again. It seemed that life had not yielded up its complete supply of delights. "Why aren't you dead?" he said. "You've been dying for four years. I'd have thought you'd do the decent thing and croak."

"I'm trying my best, asshole," Mark said. "The doctors keep telling me to say good-bye. I'm getting tired of taking bows. If I'm immortal, I'm asking for my money back."

"Shut the fuck up, Carl," Terry said, and they laughed and laughed, as if they had been saving that mirth for years.

And then finally they quieted, and watched the surf together. "So you found me," Terry said, taking a deep, slow toke on a slender, pungent black cigar before flipping it out into the ocean.

"You ain't all that clever," Mark said. "The main reason you haven't been found is that no one is looking for your dumb ass." He flicked his cigar over the rail. Terry watched it spiral down into the deep.

Father Geek was on the beach, surrounded by a raft of children, doing magic tricks. He was good. Better than good, as if some spot of light had emerged from him, sparking a level of theatrical pizzazz he'd never had before. In a different world, he might have performed at Hollywood's Magic Castle.

In this world, he couldn't. On the other hand, Terry reflected, in this world, he could *buy* the Magic Castle.

"Eight point six million dollars?"

"That's your cut," Mark said. "After we sold the books, it came to forty-three million dollars. Five ways."

"What about Lee and Pat?"

Mark sighed. "Next of kin. But we have to figure out the right way to do it. There are officials who would look askance at that kind of money popping up, no matter how it happens. Softly, softly catchee monkey."

Almost nine million dollars? What in the hell would he even do with it down here that wouldn't put him on the wrong radar? "I don't really want the money," Terry said. "I just want to raise my family."

"Well, it's in the traditional numbered Bahamian account, gathering interest until the day you regain your sanity." Mark laughed and shook his head. "Your family." Mark laughed again. "Sure never saw this coming."

"Who could have?" Terry asked.

◆ ◆ ◆

Olympia and Terry walked barefoot along the edge of the sand, holding hands. The warm water lapped at their toes, and overhead, gulls swooped and glided, screeching their ancient mating calls.

Hannibal floated in the surf, playing with three other boys his age, and they felt no worry. The water here was shallow for almost an eighth of a mile out, then dropped off slowly, and Hannibal was a dolphin in the water. Their son waved to them, then splashed his friends.

His friends.

Hannibal had friends.

It was what photographers called the "magic hour," Olympia thought, and it was the perfect term.

"What are you thinking?" Terry asked, perhaps noticing that she had been quiet a long time.

The breeze shifted, bringing with it the smell of roasting fish, and the sound of laughter from the village. Mark and Geek were, not surprisingly, making friends quickly. She rather hoped they would decide to stay.

It was a good life here, and there was a loneliness about those men, a yearning for a real home.

That could be Santa Tia. For all of the lost *norteamericanos*.

Olympia's mouth watered as she suddenly realized she was ravenously hungry. There had been a lot of that lately. She had rediscovered many appetites. "About Madame Gupta," she said. "Do you ever think about her?"

He nodded, and squeezed her hand.

"Me, too. I was thinking about something she said at the end."

"What was that?"

"She said, '*You are his mother, the woman the man I had chosen chose, and placed above me. You are a family. You have this thing called 'love.' Show me that you are worthy of his choice, their love.*' And then she slapped me. She told me everything I needed to figure out what was going on, and then she gave me her blood."

"With a slap."

Olympia turned to face him. "You knew her. I think that at the end you knew her better than anyone."

"That's possible. And very sad."

"Then tell me," she asked, searching for the right way to phrase her question. "Was there good left inside her? She gave you a chance to survive. Did she give me one? Was there a part of her that knew she was wrong?"

Could that strange, twisted woman have seen something, learned something at the end? Olympia had learned, changed, grown. Remade her entire life into something close to a paradise she had never dared dream of, filled with love and adventure and a family healthier than any she had known. All it had taken was the courage to accept the destruction of all that had come before.

And willingness to adopt a dog named Pax.

And to admit that she was totally in love with a man who needed her heart like roses need rain.

Terry had been considering. "I remember a DVD she gave me. This man Savagi told a story about *exactly* what she was doing. I think she was dying for someone to know her, to see her."

"And join her?"

"Or stop her. Or both. I think there was a part of her that wanted to be loved so much it drove her insane. I think that as much as she was capable, she . . . loved me. And when people love . . . anything is possible. I don't know. What do you think?"

"I like to think that everyone deserves a little hope." She kissed him. "Me, I'm hoping you're in a frisky mood tonight."

"You have strange and mysterious powers of perception," he said, and kissed her back. Thoroughly.

CHAPTER 55

Water warm. Sky dark. Life good.

Hannibal floated on a wave that rolled up beneath him, embracing, tied to every other ocean in the world. The oceans warmed by a distant sun, the sun created by the cloud that birthed the universe.

This moment, this eddy, tied to every other part of the universe, as it should be.

All was well. His loving Nicki was well, and already sparking with a tall brown boy named Boruca. Boruca's smile was beautiful, and he made Nicki laugh and glow, and that was all Hannibal needed to know, that his wonderful Nicki was happy.

Mommy was happier than he had ever seen her, and it was Daddy Terry, and the new life, that made her smile. She deserved this, and much more. Terry was all Hannibal had known him to be, from the first moment. A good man, a strong man, the only one he wanted as a father. He knew this even before Madame Gupta had opened his eyes.

Even at the beginning, he knew these two needed to be together, and he hoped he could be forgiven for arranging a few things. Their meeting at the swimming pool, when he had bounced off Terry's leg. He'd just *known* Terry was fast enough to snatch him out of the air. And that that would force Mommy to stop pretending she didn't notice him. And that maybe, just maybe, she'd be able to stop pretending his other daddy, the weak one, was dead.

Pax ran through the surf, jumping up and snatching the stick from the air when Hannibal threw it. He liked that, and liked the fact that Pax had woods to run in, and rabbits to chase. And sometimes catch!

Hannibal liked playing and being safe so that everyone didn't have to worry about him all the time. That they knew he didn't need to be watched at every minute. He was trying to speak more, and said *"Buen perro!"*: *Good dog* when Pax returned the stick to him. Speaking was good, at times. His friends liked him to talk, and were teaching him Spanish.

Somehow, speaking in the new language was more fun than talking in English, and fun was good.

Pax didn't speak, and everyone loved her. Why was it that if he, Hannibal, didn't speak they got so worried?

It wasn't fair. The inside of his head was so much more interesting than the outside world. So he just brought the threads together and let them play out, and all had concluded as he wished.

Life was good.

He did not know what would become of him. He was losing his memory of what had happened with Madame Gupta. What he had done to the others who had hurt his family. But she was the one who'd opened the door of the cage. And on the other side, well . . .

The breath of all the people in the world, all who had ever lived, mingled in the air of Santa Tia. From time to time, just for fun, he followed a thread all the way to the lungs that had expelled the cells, and touched the beating heart.

He hadn't hurt them, of course. That would be wrong.

Of course.

The little girl was still in his inner house. He could not see her, but she played with his toys. He saw her footprints. Sometimes he thought he caught a glimpse of her . . .

And once there was a name smudged on the wall.

Shakti

But he still liked it there.

He saw and remembered more now. Slowly, he was coming out of his shell. He was safe. His family was safe, and happy.

But if anything ever happened to them . . . anything ever made Mommy or Nicki cry, or Terry bleed . . .

How odd.

Even to think that made something within him bare its teeth. Yes. Shakti bared her teeth.

Family was a wonderful thing.

ACKNOWLEDGMENTS

In 1986, a thirty-four-year-old writer named Steven Barnes published his fourth novel, *The Kundalini Equation*. It was an attempt to present, in fictional form, what he understood about the path of metaphysical development lurking within the martial arts. The book achieved a certain notoriety, and years later the older and more experienced version of that young writer decided to revisit that world, and ask the next question.

Twelve Days is the answer to that question.

To the teachers who have shaped me in the specific ways discussed in this book: Scott Sonnon, Harley "SwiftDeer" Reagan, Sri Chinmoy, and all of the other gurus of disciplines physical, mental, and spiritual. I would not be who I am without you. And to Cliff Stewart, who promised to guide me on the warrior path, and kept that promise. And Sijo Steve Muhammad and Larry Niven, who together are the men most responsible for the human being I am today.

Much thanks to LTC Bart Kemper, who once was a respectable paratrooper sergeant before going to the Dark Side, and Krista Krcmarik Kemper, who would have lost her membership in the E4 Mafia for marrying a field grade if he wasn't a mustang. Both have multiple combat tours and other experiences that helped them pick up the pack when The Old Soldier could carry it no further. Without these two, this book could not be what it is, and I owe them both, big-time.

Jonathan Vos Post, Marty Brastow, Toni Young, Dan Moran, Rory Miller, Beth Meacham, and Betsy Mitchell for so many things, but in the specific context of *Twelve Days*, for offering support of so many kinds over the years: emotional, intellectual, and career. No one makes it on their own.

And to Marco Palmieri, my editor, who gave me the opportunity to tell this tale.

Jason Kai Due-Barnes, my son. And my radiant daughter Lauren Nicole, who let me borrow her name. How wonderful it is to love, just because we choose to do so. And to my wife, the rather astonishing Tananarive Due.

I would love you again in a thousand incarnations, if Shiva was merciful enough to allow such bliss.

For Joyce Higa, my long-suffering sister: thank you for teaching me to read *The Five Chinese Brothers,* my very first book.

To Dr. Germone "Mama G" Miller, my glimpse of Shakti, who helped me to understand a path I've never walked. Jennifer Gray, who began a circle with me twenty years ago, and then helped me draw it to completion.

Mushtaq Ali Al Ansari, one of the great friends and companions of my life, and his lovely lady, Janet.

The *Shiva Sutras,* the *Vigyan Bhairav Tantra,* and the *Spanda Karika* are all real sacred texts.

The *Yama Sutra,* on the other hand, is an invention of Mushtaq's. He also, for decades, encouraged me to continue the tale begun in *The Kundalini Equation.* Blame him!

Savagi's texts *Transformations* and *The Myth of Love* are my own invention. Thank goodness.

Autism and ADD are serious and highly charged subjects and I wish to thank the people who have discussed them with me from academic or medical study, or personal experience. There are a variety of theories on the subject, including Thom Hartmann's "Hunter/Farmer" (in *The Edison Gene*) and Simon Baron-Cohen's "Extreme Male Brain" concept. The theory used most fully in *Twelve Days* is Kamila Markram and Henry Markram's "Intense World" hypothesis. Special thanks to John Ordover and Dr. Howard S. Schub of the Atlanta Southeast Center for Epilepsy and Neurodevelopment. These fine people know this subject intimately and through extensive research and study. Any errors in conception or execution are mine alone, and can hopefully be excused in the name of dramatic license.

Thank you all for advice and support over the years, and in some cases very specific assistance on this manuscript. Every book is the most difficult, the most important, the most painful and glorious.

Twelve Days was the longest Dark Night of the Soul I've ever traveled.

The only thing that gets you through that night is faith. Bless you all for having such faith in a guy who just wanted to try to get it right.

Steven Barnes
November 8, 2016
Glendora, California
www.diamondhour.com